Andrew Masseurs is a creatively restless spirit. While spending over twenty years creating music, four albums and an ep, he found himself inexplicably focused on writing one day on holiday. The result, his first exciting novella, *A Day in the Life: Book One*. Relishing the experience Andrew has now released the second book in the A Day in the Life series, *The Day After* and is currently writing the third book in the series.

Andrew is a loving husband and father to four kids living in the beautiful country that is New Zealand.

For the kids. My greatest creations.

The Day After

A Day in the Life Series, Book Two
Andrew Masseurs

ISBN 978-969-44-9299-5 (Paperback)

ISBN 978-969-45-9200-8 (Hardcover)

ISBN 978-969-44-9298-8 (ePub e-book)

Book Cover by Chris Era

First Published 2024

Andrew Masseurs®

www.andrewmasseurs.com

Thank you to my wife and family for your constant inspiration and support as I create. To my mum and dad who made me who I am (thank you and miss you) To the A Day in the Life book series A-Team: Chris Era, for your amazing cover artwork and Jessica Hay for your diligent editing. You are all the window into this world and I can't thank you enough.

Prologue
Shelby

"ME, WE." MUHAMMAD ALI.

S HELBY LAY UNDER HER covers. It was her favourite duvet cover. On the front of it was a large picture of Jack Skeleton from *The Nightmare before Christmas* movie. There was something about the duvet cover that made her feel at home. It was a memory from a distant past, when she and her mother spent cherished time together. She could smell the evening, popcorn freshly popped. Her favourite treats were separated into a large bowl. Her mum smiling next to her, their legs settled snuggly under a large warm blanket. The lights would be dimmed and jokes would be littered throughout the conversation. Back then, her mum was the perfect example of how to bring up a happy daughter, and she was happy. Even if it was dark and cold outside. Even if it was just the two of them in Newtown, in Wellington, in New Zealand, in the

World, in the Universe. They were spending valuable time together and how Shelby appreciated it.

The duvet cover was bought by her mum many years ago and Shelby wrapped it up over her face. Her hands scrunching up the cover to her smiling cheeks. She tried to smell the evening. Remembering how happy they were. She looked out the window. It was raining outside. The drips from the rain were slipping down the glass, mixing with the lights from the street outside, causing a kaleidoscope of rainbows.

It was late in the evening, around nine o'clock. Shelby wore her large, pale, green headphones over her ears. The curled wire snaked from the headphones winding their way to the old analogue system her mum had given her years ago. Mum probably got it from her mum, it was so ancient. She loved how the headphones encompassed her ears. Drowning out the world and all its problems. Her small earbuds were charging to the side, while she sat in this old stereo world. She hardly acknowledged her phone or any modern technology. Not while she listened to the old stereo with its old tubes and lights working to create a sound that came from a needle and vinyl. Her shoulders started to sway as her eyes closed. She did not know it, but she was the mirror of her mother. Her mum did the same when she had a rare day off. The room was dark apart from her mum's lava lamp which she had stolen and had sat beside her bed. Its bubbles coagulating slowly up and down. She loved to have it working while she sat doing homework or listening to music.

Her eyes were closed and enjoying the smooth tones of Bic Runga, singing the track *Drive*. The ambience of the soft rain hitting the third story window mixed with the pop tune made her feel warm and happy. She started to feel sleepy. It had been a long day for a twelve year old. She was not like any twelve year old. Not any we know. Each day was comprehensively filled to capacity.

Shelby's mum worked two jobs. The morning shift started at six. Her mum would wake at five. If she slept through the alarm, Shelby would wake her up. It happened often as her mum's second shift finished at 1 am, she barely had time to sleep. Shelby had grown up quickly, feeling more like a twenty one year old with responsibilities far beyond her age. She cooked her and her mum breakfast. Most days, it was the same. Boiled eggs with a slice of toast and strong coffee. Some days, when the fridge was out of eggs, which was becoming more and more frequent, she would make her mum a breakfast of whatever cereal was in the pantry. This morning her mum was spoiled and she got a boiled egg. She remembered they had argued. Money was becoming tight and it had gotten to the stage that if Shelby asked for anything, she would be thrown guilt trips on how her mum was working two jobs. How she could barely afford the roof over their heads. How she was doing it for Shelby, working her life away for her. Shelby no longer asked for anything these days. She just did her best to make her mom's day a little better. A little brighter. But, they had argued.

Mum's choice of boyfriends had steadily been getting worse. Shelby knew her mum was lonely. She also knew her choices were not only looking for love but were also hoping for a fast ticket out of this hell hole, for her and especially Shelby. Shelby felt her mum's choices now were causing them harm. Shelby was not silly, far from it. Shelby could pick out a lie, dissect it and throw it back at you wrapped in a big bow of honesty. She was way too smart for falseness and her mum knew it. Her latest pick was the worst in a long line of bad choices. Yes, he had money. Yes, he was handsome. In a rugged, blue eyed, blond with tattoos sort of way. But, he also had an attitude. Way too much attitude for Shelby's liking. He ordered her mum around and Shelby didn't like it. He treated the house like it was his. He expected to be served, but he did nothing in return. He was also staying over more. Which Shelby did not appreciate, plus he treated Shelby like she didn't exist. She could tell he was just using her mum. He also drank too much. He was taking her mum down a horrible dark hole. One filled with alcohol and drugs. Something she had only seen her mum do on occasion, but now, she was becoming an authoritative expert on the matter.

Her mum was so desperate she would do anything to keep their heads' above water. Maybe it was the cost of living. Maybe it was a realisation that she couldn't afford anything anymore. The worst choice was better than not being able to survive, or being left out on the street. Shelby told her this. That her choice was wrong. That she didn't like him. That he was wrong for her. Shelby's mum didn't like this. She did not appreciate the reality that her child was offering her.

"I'm doing this for you," her mum said. "Can't you see that?"

Shelby's mum was over tired. Was overworked and had two weeks unpaid rent and an empty fridge. "You don't know what you're talking about." Was a favourite phrase and, "everything would be fine." But it wasn't and Shelby knew better than to push it. She knew when her mum was on the edge. Better to agree than to drive her into another scathing rant. Especially when her mum was already under so much pressure. Shelby was trying to lighten the load, not increase it. Instead Shelby dropped the conversation and did the dishes. Her mum left without saying goodbye or thank you. It was not unusual. Shelby then made her lunch, picked up her mum's clothes, put the washing on and made her and her mum's bed, all before 6:30 am. Lastly, she did some reading before leaving for school just before 7:30 am.

Shelby was pretty much a loner at school. She didn't talk much and generally wouldn't suffer fools. She was not your typical twelve year old. She felt that if you couldn't keep up with the conversation then it wasn't worth making the effort. Most of the kids were wrapped up in their own insecurities. She could read them a mile away. She was a loner not by force but by choice. Her days were spent listening to music and reading in the library. If the sun was shining, she would be forced to go outside. Annoyed, she would do as she was told. Usually, with a swear word or two in muffled protest. She still hadn't found her full confidence yet. That would come. She would sit out in the sun and read. It was her escape. Her escape from the problems of home. Her escape from the pressures of not wanting to fit in. Of not caring. She knew she was too mature for her age group and hated wasting her time. She would leave at the end of the school day with all her work done and up to date. It would be better than anyone else's. She would catch the bus and have some idiot kid make fun of her. She would give them the finger and tell them to *fuck off*. Sometimes it would result in a fight. Mostly not. Other kids couldn't comprehend her or her confidence.

Shelby would get home normally at 4 pm. She would cook dinner with whatever was left in the fridge and freezer. She was used to being creative with minimal ingredients. She hardly ever saw her mum during the day. Shelby's mum would be moving between two shifts and wouldn't have the time to come home. It was just in the evenings, that she would arrive for dinner before taking off for her late night shift. Shelby finished cooking their dinner. Laid the table and sat in her favourite spot. The soft corner part of the three seater couch. She didn't watch much TV. Instead, she preferred to carry on the latest novel and drift into that far off world. Where she could escape and pretend to be someone else for an hour or so.

Tonight, mum was late getting home. It was after nine. Shelby had left her dinner, consisting of canned tuna on rice, covered on the bench. Finishing the Bic Runga album, she wondered if she should read some more, just try a different album or maybe, even write. She opened her drawer to the right and pulled out her little book of notes. In it were the musings of a twelve year old. Her class teacher, Ms Reid, inspired her to try poetry. Something she found she had a knack for. Something that helped her escape. It also helped her to cope with her inner thoughts.

"Mothers Ghost."

To say that a girl,
whose young and lost,
Must lose herself in writing posts.

To wish and hope,
That things may change,
Enter sweet courage,
Enter brutal rage.

I'm more a tree,
Than a withered seed,

That swings and sways,
When she needs me most.

I'll make her solid,
I'll heal her pain,
This girl's true sorrow,
Her Mothers ghost.

Another poem to add to the heartache of my life, thought Shelby. Outside, the rain was getting stronger. The front door opened with a bang. It startled Shelby. She sat upright looking at her closed bedroom door. The light was still off. The lava lamp drifts shapes onto the ceiling. Behind the closed bedroom door, she could hear voices. Her mum was laughing loudly. Followed by her mum's boyfriend and friends. It was going to be one of those nights. Mum obviously had the night off. She would spend it partying. Shelby felt annoyed. They hadn't spent a night together in what felt like months. The boyfriend seemed to get all her time. She felt like storming out into the kitchen and telling mum her dinner was made for her out of pretty much nothing. Oh, and also she had done the washing, folded it, put everything away and emptied the dishwasher. She stood as the Jack Skellington duvet she loved so much tore on the side bed bannister. "Fuck," she swore to herself quietly. She heard the voices rising in cadence from behind the door.

Her mum could be heard saying, "Shhh, Shelby's asleep."

When the boyfriend answered, "oh, come on, it's *Friday* night. Time to *party!*"

She heard laughter and the clinking of bottles. Frustrated, Shelby walked over to her door and listened. She hated the fact her doorway was one stop before the bathroom. It was not unusual for a new boyfriend or party invite to storm into Shelby's room, thinking it was the bathroom. She had no way of locking it. Shelby knew it would happen again tonight so she pulled her bookshelf across the pathway of the door. It took quite a bit of her might. The carpet was thick and heavy. The bookshelf was full of Shelby's favourite hardcover, second hand novels. It would not stop the door from being pushed fully open if someone was strong enough, but it would make someone think twice and hopefully, they'd ask Mum which door was the toilet. While partying, Mum would forget to warn the guests. The bookshelf now stood flush against the doorway and Shelby walked back to her bed. Next door the boombox was turned up and what sounded like Bon Jovi was sneaking under the door.

She quickly got under her covers as she heard screaming and laughter blending together, which sounded like witches at a carnival. She placed the warm comfort of the old headphones over her ears. The muffled silence sounded like a large conch shell being placed by her ears at the beach. It comforted her. Searching through the old CDs that were all her mum's, she found *Nevermind* by Nirvana. She opened the old CD player, wiped the CD on her Rolling Stones t-shirt and placed it in. The loud intro of *Smells Like Teen Spirit,* carried her away. The violent pounding of the snare intro matched the beat of her heart. She lay back angry. Happy though, that she could no longer hear her mum pretending to be someone she was not. She hated these nights. Hated them. She was scared and annoyed. Scared of what the night might become. Annoyed that her mum did not know better. Shelby closed her eyes and drifted. She was asleep by track two. Shelby was dreaming of floating babies. Floating babies being kicked into floating football goals when she woke and heard the second to last track, *Something In The Way*, being played. She thought what an absurd dream, when she lay back even further into her pillow. She stared at the ceiling, as the song helped her feel tired again and her eyelids grew heavy. She fell into a deep sleep, not hearing the front door slam as visitors left quickly.

As the next and final track played on the album, she didn't hear the argument that ensued between Mum and her boyfriend. Both of them were drunk and drug fueled out of their brains. The jealous rage that came from her mum as she accused her boyfriend of being attracted to the lady who had just left. The angry retaliation by the boyfriend. The slap from mum. The shouting and screaming by the end of the song and finally, the punches. Shelby missed it all as she dreamt this time of babies making purchases at the local dairy. Buying everything that the dairy had to offer. She was laughing in her sleep as the album finished and there was silence in both her room and also the room next door. The silence was enough to wake Shelby. She opened her tired eyes and stared at the ceiling. The shapes of the lava lamp caused different coloured circles to entwine. Her eyelids started to feel weighted as they sluggishly blinked for a second before closing.

"Shelby...?" Whispered a male voice from the other side of her door. "...Shelby, are you *awake*?" Shelby's eyes fully opened. She had never heard anyone talk to her this late at night apart from her mum. "Shelby?" Whispered the voice again. She heard something push against the door. Like the slight brush of a shoulder.

She quickly pushed the headphones off her head. They became entangled in her hair as she tried to take them off quietly. "Shelby?" Said the male voice again.

She could hear more force being pushed against the door. The bookshelf started to angle backwards. A few books at the top looked like they were about to fall out. She read the label on one. *The Stand* by Stephen King. It was a large book and would make a loud sound. She finally got the headphones off her head and backed off to the side of her bed. She moved quickly, her head darting both ways looking for something in the room that she could use as a weapon.

"Shelby, I'm coming in." Announced her mother's boyfriend. His voice, more certain. She panicked and was now standing with the wall behind her. Her heart was beating frantically. She was tough but still learning. This had never happened before. Someone was trying to get into her room and she was frozen. Frozen in panic. Frozen in fear.

The door was shoved roughly forward. It moved an inch as the Stephen King book fell and hit the ground. The noise was deafening in the silence and then stopped in an instant. Shelby thought he must be checking to see if it woke Mum. *Where the hell is Mum?* thought Shelby. Probably asleep, drunk. She hated her mum right now. She hated her with a passion. Nothing happened for a minute as Shelby stood shaking, unable to move.

"Shelby, are you okay? Are you asleep, *darling*?" asked the boyfriend in a hushed tone. She hated when he called her mum, darling. *Why the fuck is he calling me darling?* He pushed against the door. The bookshelf angled even more. Out fell more books. The children's book, *Where The Wild Things Are.* A hardcover novel of *Treasure Island. Come on Shelby, move!* she thought to herself.

But she could not. She had never been so terrified in her life. The door started rattling. It was being pushed frenziedly back and forth, ramming against the bookshelf which finally gave in. Falling over onto its back. The door was forced again, but wouldn't budge. It was now barred between the fallen bookcase, bed and doorway. A foot and hand now appeared. Shelby let out a small shriek. She started to cry. Suddenly thoughts that a twelve year old shouldn't have were flooding her brain. Her mature head filled with images and she started to tremble and shake even more.

"Shelby. I can hear you darling," he said in his creepy, whispering voice. She saw him try to squeeze his forehead through the door, but the door wasn't far enough ajar. She scanned the room and saw a plate and knife in the corner. She had left it there from her dinner earlier. *The knife?* She willed herself to move and get it. Her legs wouldn't move. The door shook. The bed started to inch toward her. The doorway opened a little further. She saw his horrible mouth. "Shelby? *Honey?*"

She felt like vomiting. *I can't move.* She thought to herself. *I can't fucking move.* She saw the knife. It stared back at her like an alluring piece of chocolate. Her favourite, a chocolate Pineapple Lump. *Come on legs, move!* Nothing happened. The door shook again and the bed was now squeezing against her trembling knees.

"Shelby, are you *cold*, honey?" Asked the boyfriend.

She started crying. She prayed. She didn't believe in God. She and her mum had never been to church. But she had read about God. In so many of her novels the fight was always between good and evil. She prayed like someone who was lying on their final deathbed. She prayed like God was her best friend and he was always listening. She prayed that the boyfriend would vanish. That he would just disappear. What else could she ask for? What else could she pray for? The door pushed against the bookshelf and she felt the pain in her knees. The door now was far enough ajar for the boyfriend to get through. She closed her eyes as she heard him rush through the open doorway. Tears were now streaming down her cheeks. Her body was uncontrollably shaking but still frozen. Her breathing was frantic. She felt like she was going to faint. She tried to take her mind somewhere else. She tried to join the babies in the dairy, buying all the food they could.

She waited for the horrible touch of the drunk boyfriend. She waited for it to happen. She pressed herself hard, backwards against the back wall, hoping to somehow fall through it. She felt a breath. Hot on her neck. She turned her face away from it. It disgusted her. She felt warm, sweaty hands start to touch her waist. She screamed and acted, her hands flailing and pushing the boyfriend away. But, her hands only felt air as she fell forward onto the bed.

The space was completely noiseless. Her eyes opened. Her breathing was still heavy. She was still hyperventilating. The room was deserted. The boyfriend, gone. *Has my prayer been answered?* She thought. *Has God answered the prayer of a scared, helpless twelve year old?*

She stood motionless for a good five minutes. Not believing that the prayer had worked. Finally, she could move her foot. Finally, she walked slowly towards the knife. She moved like her feet had the weight of solid concrete. Silently and slowly just in case the boyfriend was hiding and waiting to jump on her. She slowly picked up the knife then swiftly turned expecting to be attacked.

The knife defending her womanhood. But no attack took place. There was no evil boyfriend jumping at her.

She walked quietly towards the door. Stepping over the books and bookcase, she squeezed between the door jam. Holding the knife out in front of her she walked into the kitchen and lounge. There were beer cans and bottles everywhere. A large empty bottle of vodka was toppled over on the main table. On the oven, she noticed a saucepan with a knife on it. A huge party had taken place but there seemed to be no survivors. She walked into the lounge expecting to see her mum splayed out on the couch, drunk. She was not there. Outside, she heard a car crash into another. An alarm rang out. She ran to the window and looked out. A car had crashed into a traffic light. The traffic light was blinking orange, then red, then green. The car door was open but no one is sitting in the driver's seat. Shelby immediately turned again, with her knife still leading the way. Still not believing that the boyfriend just, up and left. She checked her room again. Nothing. She then checked the bathroom, her mum's room and the lounge once more. They were all empty of souls.

Outside the car alarm was ringing loudly. A burst water main from further down the street joined in the racket. Shelby was still shaking. She ran to the main door and opened it. Looking down the dimly lit, narrow corridor that always smelled of urine, she saw no one and heard nothing. She closed the door and locked it. Walking back into the lounge she found her mom's phone.

Why would Mum leave without her phone? Where had they gone? Did Mum wake and take the boyfriend away? Could she do that? Was she strong enough?

Shelby sat with the knife still stuck in her trembling right hand. *What the fuck is going on?* She sat in the same position for most of the night. Waiting for her mum to call. Waiting for the door to open. Waiting for a police car to meet the alarm of the car outside. Waiting for the water to stop from the burst water main outside. She waited for something to happen, anything.

Nothing did.

CHAPTER ONE

The Night of Fire

"HELL IS EMPTY AND ALL THE DEVILS ARE HERE."
WILLIAM SHAKESPEARE.

M ICHAEL DROVE THE CAR slowly through the narrow streets. The roads in places were cracked and overgrown with long grass. It was not unusual to come across a car left in the middle of the road. He drove with his tired eyes straining to see what was in front. It was the middle of the night. The moon had been covered by clouds. Every now and then he would turn on the headlights to give him an idea of what was ahead. He wouldn't leave the lights on for long though, for fear of attracting a night creature that would surely bring their doom. He had his headphones on. The sound of OK Go's track, *Here It Goes Again*, playing on his Walkman was thrashing into his eardrums. He was trying to keep himself awake while not disturbing the girls. Teresa,

Michael's wife, tapped him on the shoulder. Michael pulled his left ear cushion down. The song came booming out into the car from his left ear pad.

"Just when you think you're in control,
Just when you think you've got a hold,
Just when you get on a roll,

Oh, here it goes, here it goes, here it goes again,
Oh, here it goes again."

"We can all hear that, honey." Said Teresa, with a straight face.

"It's good, innit?" Shouted Michael, smiling, one ear still hearing the ear-splitting music. "Want me to turn it up?" He asked, knowing the answer. He turned it off. She kissed his cheek as a thank you. He smiled at her, loving having his beautiful wife back beside him.

"If you need a rest, I can take over," offered Teresa.

"It's okay, I've got it."

"*Where* are you taking us?" asked Teresa. Her body curled up uncomfortably in her small seat.

"I'm not sure. I'm thinking, maybe, the houses up on the hill. You see up ahead? It would be safer up there."

"What about *home*?" asked Teresa as she yawned and placed her hand on Michael's lap. He smiled at her and flicked on the lights again, showing a curved road coming up.

"Home is long gone, Mum," remarked Lucy, from the back seat. Michael looked up at the mirror catching Lucy's eyes. Her arms were raised stretching. She yawned also.

"Hello sleepy head." Michael smiled as his eyes went back onto the turning street. He placed his hand on Teresa's, turning off the lights once the car had finished winding up the long bend.

"The house is gone?" asked Teresa.

"Long gone," answered Michael. He turned her way. "Everyone *vanished,* Teresa. A year ago or more. Everyone, just disappeared."

"Gone," said Lucy.

"Poof!" Shelby joined in, sitting in the backseat by Lucy. She was patting Pup's head. Pup's tails were flickering slightly.

"I... I vanished?"

"You, and I thought Lucy as well, were gone. Just... *disappeared.*"

"I turned up later Mum." Said Lucy as she looked out the window, trying to make out shadowy shapes.

"...And those, those creatures, those... *monsters* that we saw back at the house."

"I had a guy once say to me: The earth has been *cleansed* and we have been chosen." Lucy said, turning her head from the window towards Michael.

"It was cleansed alright, *cleansed* of all the shit." Said Shelby, matter-of-factly. Teresa looked at Michael worriedly.

"That being we saw... it said, we... we wouldn't survive."

"We're not supposed to survive, Teresa... *Look*, as crazy as it sounds, I don't think we should say anything. To *anybody* about what happened." Michael looked between the mirror at the girls and Teresa. "No one's going to believe that we were visited by an engineer or architect who brought you all back to life and gave us a second chance..."

"...A fucking, *blue angel*," interrupted Shelby, smiling.

"Thank you, Shelby. A... blue angel." Repeated Michael.

"Blue angel?" Asked Lucy, quietly, looking over at Shelby.

"Pinocchio." Answered Shelby, fluttering her hands on either side of her shoulders.

Michael carried on, "...No one's going to believe a blue angel visited us and made us into real boys..."

"...Girls!" Corrected Shelby.

"Exactly," agreed Michael, smiling at Shelby. "We don't say anything about the blue angel unless someone brings up the blue angel first, *get it*?"

"Got it," answered Shelby. Teresa and Lucy remained quiet with serious faces. The car went soundless as Michael turned on the lights again. He swerved past a Mini Cooper sitting on the left side of the road. The car made a swooshing sound as it flew past it. He turned the lights off again.

"Did they vanish all the animals as well?" asked Teresa.

"Yep," answered Lucy.

"...And they created these new creatures?"

"Yep," said Lucy, again.

"...So, we were like a virus that needed to be *eradicated*?"

"Fuckin A," Shelby shot back.

"How come you survived, Michael? And the girls?"

"I imagine they're not perfect. A small percentage of people survived." Michael replied as he flicked on the lights just in time to see a large truck in the middle of the road. He drove to the left of it and turned off the lights.

"...And I suppose the creatures are meant to *kill* us?" asked Teresa.

"I think they're just the new breed. Some are pretty vicious, some like Pup here, are *cute* as pie." Smiled Michael. Pup's tails started to flicker when he heard his name. His butt started to lift and Shelby pushed it back down. "But, you're right, Teresa. This world is meant to kill us and should not be taken lightly. This world will *change* us, in fact, I think we need to change, or we won't *survive* and that being said, we won't get a second chance."

Teresa looked out the window. Lucy was staring at Michael with almost fear on her face. Shelby was nodding in agreement.

"I have a question for you and the girls," added Michael.

"Hit me," replied Teresa, her leg shifting trying to get comfortable.

"Can you remember anything, after you vanished? or in the girls' case, were *killed*?" Michael looked up in the mirror at the girls.

"I remember the pain," answered Shelby. "*Thankfully*, it was quick. The way I went. But, I remember the *horrible* pain."

"Lucy?" asked Michael.

"Same, Dad, it *hurt*. I remember not being able to breathe. I remember your face." Lucy's face started to change.

"That's *unlucky*." Remarked Shelby, she smirked, but no one smirked back.

"You were so *sad*, Dad. I remember that, then nothing."

"Nothing for me either." Confirmed Shelby.

"...And me." Added Teresa. Michael flicked on the lights. There was nothing in front. He turned them off again.

"So, it seems there is no life after death." He said, lost in thought.

The car went silent. The car drove for a while in a straight line. Michael noticed a dark shape ahead and flicked on the lights thinking it was another car. The lights came on to reveal a large monstrosity staring straight at the car. It looked almost asleep but once the lights came on, it bared its sharp teeth and let out a screaming roar. Pup came to life in the back seat and started barking. Teresa placed her hand on the dashboard, bracing herself. Her mouth was wide open. Michael screamed with the monster and tried to push his foot hard on the brake. His foot slipped off the side and accidently pushed into the accelerator, speeding the car hard into the creature's front. The monster flinched a little but did not move. It's tough hide easily stopping the car. It raised its front paw in response and smashed it into the bonnet.

Teresa screamed. "Michael! Michael!"

"I'm here!" shouted Michael, trying to push down the airbag that had gone off. Teresa's airbag did not release. The massive paw pushed further into the bonnet pushing the car down and backward. "Kids?" yelled Michael.

"I'm *no* kid!" shouted Shelby, opening the back door as Pup rushed out of the car beside her. "Wait! Pup?" shouted Shelby, not realising how fast Pup was.

"Lucy!?" shouted Michael. There was no response. The car suddenly raised a little as the creature tried to release its paw. Its large claw was stuck in the bonnet. Michael felt heat from his side of the car. Pup was doing his little trick. Something only Michael had discovered for the first time a few hours ago when Pup saved Michael's life. Pup was releasing a burning, shooting flame from his mouth. Michael could just see the orange flame blurred by the shattered window. The monster roared outside.

"Michael, what do we do?" shouted Teresa, panicking.

"*Get out!* Teresa! Get out before more come!"

"Michael, my door?!" Teresa screamed. She had both hands on the handle. It was stuck. The car again shook. The creature was trying to release itself. The car rose and fell, rose and fell. It felt like a rollercoaster attraction ride. The car finally fell to the ground and remained still. Outside, heavy footsteps and movement could be felt. The creature was free. Flames were rushing through the night air in streams. Teresa's door suddenly flew open.

"Come on, girl!" shouted Shelby as she released and opened Teresa's door.

"My seatbelt!" shouted Teresa.

"Oh, Jesus!" Shelby reached over behind Teresa and released the belt. Grabbing Teresa, she threw her out of the car. Michael's face showed a little surprise at how strong and efficient Shelby was for a little thirteen year old. Michael finally pushed the airbag to the side and opened his door, falling out on all fours onto the warm asphalt. He looked up and couldn't believe what he saw in front of him. Pup was running from side to side. His back legs raised. Flame was gushing out of his mouth like a fireman with his hose. The creature in front of him was towering. Like something out of a dinosaur movie, it moved violently. Swaying its huge head left and right. It was enormous, heavy and strong. It felt the tremendous heat from Pup. Its reptilian skin was lit up by the flames. It screamed in pain. Michael knew he didn't have much time. The flames would bring more creatures to them. More hunters. They would be swarming around them, just like they did when he raised fireworks to the heavens.

"Shelby!" Michael screamed. Shelby was helping Teresa get up. "...Lucy!" he shouted. Shelby instantly knew what Michael meant as she ran to the back of the car and pulled the rear door open. Lucy was unconscious. Releasing her seatbelt, Shelby dragged Lucy out of the car. Michael rushed round to help when he noticed shadows coming out from the sides of the streets.

"Shelby!" he screamed. "Teresa! *Run!*" Teresa could see the movement. She recognised the danger.

"Which way?!" she shouted.

"Away from here!" Michael shouted back.

Shelby pointed out a way for Teresa to run. An alleyway between two large houses.

"Are you...?" asked Teresa.

"I'm okay, I've got her." Answered Shelby. Teresa turned and ran. Michael flew around the rear of the car, kneeling beside the girls.

"I've got Lucy, Shelby! Run for your life. *Get out of here!*"

The shadows behind Michael were coming into focus. Some of the same creatures Shelby had seen earlier in the night. Others are new and scarier. They were attracted like moths to a flame. Attracted to Pup's light show. Michael picked up the unconscious Lucy. Shelby watched as he ran back around the car running to get Pup. "Shelby!" Michael shouted again. "*Fucking* run!"

Shelby was shaken by the power of his swear word. She turned and ran to the alleyway where Teresa had just disappeared. Turning back around, she saw Pup. Brave Pup, darting back and forth. Blowing his huge flame at the large monster. Michael was shouting at Pup. He was holding Lucy over his shoulder. She couldn't make out what he was saying because of the noise. The noise that was growing steadily louder. The noise she recognised from before. The *symphony* of creatures. They were surrounding the car. She thought Michael, Pup and Lucy wouldn't stand a chance. *There's too many!* She ran a few steps towards them when she heard something click beside her. A low sound. She instantly darted to the right and felt something pass in front of her. She felt a breath of air swish past her face. She turned to the left and saw the end of a tail. It was at the end of its flight circle and the sting had been released. Thankfully, it narrowly missed her face. A snarl came from the darkness and quick movement.

"Oh, *fuck* this," she said as she turned and ran for the alleyway. Suddenly, a noise came from the darkness ahead. Something large was moving towards her. "Oh, shit!" she yelped as she turned to the left and ran along the bank. Quickly looking for a break to her right where she could disappear, she heard a distant scream.

"Pup! *No!*" recognising it as Michael when she heard something breathing loudly behind her. "Oh, shit! *No!*" she said aloud as she sprinted between fence lines. Her breathing was getting louder. Something flew past her cheek, again missing her. "No *fucking* way!" she screamed as she darted between another fence line and ran out onto a back street. She had never run so fast. She didn't know if the creature or creatures were still behind her. She didn't slow down to find out. She just kept running and running. She ran down another side street. Down two more alleyways before jumping a fence and running towards the back entrance of a two story house. She tried the handle. The door opened. She ran in and closed it. She searched for a lock. Nothing.

Outside she heard a noise. Like a dog running into a rubbish bin. She backed away from the door disappearing into the shadows. The house was quiet. Dark. It reminded her of the nights she and Michael spent alone together, lost in shadows. With the lights turned out. Reading by candlelight. She thought of Michael, of

Pup. "Oh shit," she whispered, poor Lucy. Unconscious and Teresa. *My God, Teresa.* It happened so quickly. One minute they were together. The next, total chaos. She threaded her hands through her hair. She'd felt like this before, long ago. Her hands trembled. Her body was shaking. The adrenaline was running through her. She heard something move, like a flap being opened. *A cat door?* she thought. "Jesus," she whispered to herself. "Is there no end to this?"

She backed away from the noise, seeing a flight of stairs to the next level. Something scampered across the kitchen's vinyl floor. She stood still. Not wanting to move. Not wanting to give away to whatever it was, her whereabouts. She waited. She heard nothing. She took a step. Something moved. She stopped. Her eyes closed hard while she listened intently. She tried to hold her breath. Tried to be quiet. She waited again. No sound. She took another step backwards. Nothing. She took a step up the staircase. She felt like she was being watched. A second step, the stairs made a large creaking sound. Something breathed beside her.

"Ahh!" screamed Shelby as she turned and sprinted up the steps. She could hear it following. It was fast. Its noises, strange and unearthly. She got to the top. Her arms raised in panic. It was so dark she couldn't make out the doors. There was a light break at the end. It shone on a door that must be the bathroom. Or the master bedroom. She ran for it. Fast!

Whatever it was behind her shot out from the stairwell and smashed into the wall. She screamed. "Fuck you!" she shouted as she sprinted for the door. Opening the door, she ran into the bathroom and slammed the door behind her. There was a lock. "Thank God," she whispered, as she locked the door. It hit the door low. Small claws could be heard scratching and clawing the floor under the door.

Again, Shelby backed away from the door. She tried to be as quiet as she could possibly be. Her legs were moving slowly. The claws scratching the floor. Searching for her. *I'd rather be dead,* she thought. Her legs felt the edge of the toilet as she collapsed on the fur-covered seat. Somehow it felt comforting. She sat watching the claws moving. Beside her, she noticed a shower curtain. She grabbed it tightly. Trying to stop the trembling in her hands. Her breathing was slowing. She took in a large breath and filled her lungs. She slowly released the breath. It calmed her. She sat watching the claws, scratching the floor for over an hour.

CHAPTER TWO

The Wild Land

"YOU WON'T KNOW UNTIL YOU GO THERE, GO TO THE ONE PLACE ON EARTH WHERE, WHERE THE TRULY WILD THINGS ARE." RACHEL BREWER.

O^{NE} Shelby felt the warm sun streaming through the bathroom window. She raised her hand and let it bathe in its warmth. It felt good. She had survived the night. The scratching under the door stopped at around 1 am. She heard the creature scuttering down the stairs shortly after. Later, she heard what she thought was the cat door flip and flop as the creature disappeared outside. She hated this world. But, she was alive. She worried about her adopted family. Michael, Teresa, Lucy and brave Pup. Shelby hadn't slept. She'd sat patiently waiting for the sun to rise. Her fingers curling on the furry toilet seat. She knew with the sun came warmth, warmth and safety. When she lived with Michael most of the action occurred at night. Whether it be outside noises or just animal activity. Either the animals hated the sun or they were nocturnal.

It was early morning. Around 5:30 am. She had time to search the house for food, re-energise and then try to find her way back to the car and hopefully, back to where everyone would be waiting. *You can only hope.* Shelby unlocked the toilet door and made her way down the stairs. This was part of the new world she loved. She was always a loner. Even before the old world had exorcised its demons. She enjoyed searching empty houses. Looking around at old photos. Finding out what the owners were into. Learning. You could learn a lot from the secrets a house would give away.

For instance, in this house they had a special love for rabbits. A small makeshift fence had been made in the living room. There was still straw on the floor and upside down water bottles. The house had a certain musty, animal smell. Even after all this time, you could also tell that the family loved to hunt. There were awards on the cabinets for heaviest kill. Shelby's first thought after seeing these awards was, *gun.* She searched a few of the cabinets but found nothing. A locked cupboard held what she was after though. Breaking the lock, she found a box that read, 'Glock 42' the mighty mini and a few boxes of rounds. *Yes please,* she thought as she smiled and even started whistling.

Walking over to the kitchen, she opened the pantry door. A smell of something rotten filled her nose. Her stomach was rumbling, but everything here was tainted. She would have to miss breakfast. She turned the tap as water spat and spluttered before coming out in a steady stream. She placed her hand under the tap, making a funnel and drank deeply. "Fuck yeah!" She said, happily as her stomach felt replenished. She didn't realise how dehydrated she was. All that running last night had drained her. Walking to the door she noticed a satchel hanging on a hook. It was a leather bag with straps.

"Thank you very much," said Shelby as she filled it with her gun and bullets. Walking out into the bright sunlight, she felt reasonably positive. Things seemed to be going her way.

Walking out onto the street, things weren't so easy. "Shit, which way did you come from?" She asked herself out loud. She remembered jumping a fence. But, it was all a bit of a haze. Everything had happened so quickly. *Maybe, if I pop into another house and grab some food, it might come back to me.* She laughed as she opened another door to an empty house and walked in. "Hello! Shelby here! Just after some food and I'll be on my way."

She walked in happily whistling. This house was well-kept. It looked extremely modern. She went straight to the kitchen and opened the pantry doors. She found a few cans of baked beans and one of chilli beans. "Bingo!" she said, smiling broadly. Eating one can, she placed the other two in her satchel for later. Walking back out into the sun, she remembered which way to go. "*See*, I told you, Shelby. Food feeds the brain."

Two

She walked quickly in the direction of the car. Shelby finally came to the alleyway, where she remembered sending Teresa down. She called out her name. "Teresa, Teresa, It's me, Shelby." The calls were half-hearted. She was still worried about alerting the wrong sort of animal. She walked between the buildings, remembering how different everything was last night. *Where the hell do all these creatures go during the day?* She thought as she walked out onto the road. Her nose could instantly smell the afterburn of Pup's flame-breathing prowess. It smelt like a house had just been burnt down.

She saw the car sitting in the middle of the road. Its bonnet pushed down and smashed in. All the windows around the car were shattered. She slowly walked to the vehicle, keeping an eye out for any movement. Hoping that Michael, Teresa or Lucy might be waiting for her. She stood by the car and searched the area by sight. There were black scorch marks on the road. Pup had put up a mighty battle. But, no sign of Pup.

She noticed further up the road was a small pile of black mess. She walked closer to it but couldn't make head or tails of it. It just looked like melted rubbish. It had a smell of freshly burnt plastic. She heard an engine in the distance. Running back to the car, she knelt down beside it and looked in the direction of the arriving car. She could make out two people in the front. One looked like Lucy. The car looked like a large ute. *Could it be Michael?*

"Fuck it, it must be," she said out loud. She hopped out from behind the car and started waving the car down. Immediately, she could see Lucy waving back at her excitedly. Shelby's waving started to slow and stop as she came to realise the guy driving was not Michael. The car pulled up beside her and the window wound down.

"Shelby!" Lucy shouted, excitedly. "I'm so *happy* to see you!"

"Yeah, Lucy, me too, who's this?" asked Shelby, getting straight down to business. Her hands rested on the open window as she glared at the driver, her freckles flushing. He was smiling back at her. He wore aviators and had slick, pulled back blond hair. He had a small moustache that was manicured to perfection. Shelby thought he resembled Robin Hood.

"Howdy, Shelby, my name's Steven. Pleased to meet you."

"And you, Steven. What are you doing with my Lucy?" asked Shelby.

Steven smiled. "Helping her. She was by herself a ways back. I just picked her up."

"It's okay, Shelby. Steven's friendly..." Insisted Lucy.

Shelby interrupted, whispering, "...*Lucy*, what happened? *Where's* Michael? Teresa, Pup? Have you seen them?"

"No," Lucy whispered back, leaning towards Shelby. "I haven't seen anyone. I just woke up. I was down the other side of the bank. Down the hill under a bridge. I have no idea what happened." Lucy looked worried. "The last thing I remember was us talking about... *you know what.*"

Steven's eyebrow lifted as he started rolling up a smoke.

"Second hand smoke will kill you, I'll thank you not to smoke in front of Lucy," asserted Shelby.

"Sure, sure, sorry Shelby." Steven put the packet down, his smile narrowed somewhat. "Look, I'm going back to town. Just up the road really. It's just me and a few friends. We've come down from Rotorua and have been steadily picking people up. You know, strength in numbers and all. We'd be glad to take you both in." Shelby started tapping her fingers on the door.

"What choice do we have?" asked Lucy, searching Shelby's face.

"Thanks anyway, Stevo, but we've got some people we're meeting here. If it's alright with you, Lucy will be *staying* with me."

"It's not *safe* out here... by yourselves." Advised Steve. His head angled, looking like a pinup model.

"Shelby, what are you doing? We've got nowhere to stay?"

"I've got a place. It's okay. We'll be fine," answered Shelby.

"Are you sure?" asked Lucy.

"I'm *sure*, Lucy." Shelby opened the door and Lucy reluctantly got out.

"Hey, Shelby?" shouted Steve, trying to catch them one last time before they left. "I come back this way often. If you want a lift. I'm here to help." Steven winked and turned on the motor.

"Thanks Stevo, we'll catch you down the road."

"Yes you will." Replied Steven as he saluted them both and drove slowly away.

"Shelby, what are you doing? That was our lift?"

"I know, Lucy." Answered Shelby, "but, what if your Dad comes back here? Your mum? Pup? We've got to leave a sign, *something*, before we leave. We can't just go. They're still out here, *somewhere*."

"Sure, Shelby. You're right. Sorry, I... I wasn't thinking. My head really hurts."

"It's okay, Lucy. We've just got to be careful with who we trust. There's no *law* out here to save us."

"He was pretty *handsome* though," winked Lucy, smiling.

Shelby ignored Lucy's remark and looked at the houses sandwiching the alley. "Let's see if we can find something we can write with." Shelby and Lucy searched the garages from the neighbouring houses and found some white spray paint. Within a few minutes, Shelby had written on the road in huge letters. *Lucy and Shelby nearby. Honk the car horn!* "That'll get their attention. You never know. They might turn up when we're sleeping." Said Shelby.

Lucy smiled. "Good thinking."

"Thanks Lucy. How's the head?"

"Sore."

"Hungry, Lucy?"

"Definitely."

"I've got some cans of food. Let's pick a house nearby and I'll tell you what happened last night."

"Okay," replied Lucy as they walked towards the houses. Shelby chose a three story apartment. It looked over the street but was a house back from the road. She felt it would be safer than picking the obvious house right next to the accident. Just in case. The house was extremely comfy. All the mod cons. Not that they could use them without power. They mixed up the can of beans and chilli beans and ate their lunch. Once full, they both walked to the third story and sat by the window. The room was the master bedroom with an ensuite. It had a high ceiling, but being the third story was extremely warm. They both stared at the car. "Hard to believe a large *dinosaur* stood on our car." Lucy said, smiling. Shelby started laughing. Lucy started laughing with her.

"Yeah, and it was fighting our flying dog, which *breathed fire*." Added Shelby, Lucy started laughing even harder.

"Wait, stop!" wailed Lucy, sounding panicked. "I just ate *chilli beans*!" Shelby burst out laughing. "I can't breathe, I can't breathe." Yelled Lucy as she ran for the toilet.

"Go downstairs, ours might not *flush*!" shouted Shelby, still laughing hard.

"I'm not going to make it. I'm not going to make it." Replied Lucy, half laughing, as she ran down the stairs, her hands clenching her butt cheeks.

Shelby's laughing started to subside. She liked Lucy. She had Michael's sense of humour. She was a little naïve but as Michael had stated, they'd better change in this world or get eaten by it. Lucy would learn quickly, Shelby hoped. Her eyes went back to the car. There was no movement. Nothing was happening. Just the back and forth swinging of the long grass in the slight breeze. She looked at her watch. It was twelve past three. When Lucy got back she thought it would be time to lock the house down, close everything up and shut themselves up on the third floor. If Michael was alive, he would know better than to come out this late in the afternoon. Teresa might still try it. But, they'd hear the car horn. She smiled when she thought of it. *Not a bad idea*. She got up, stretched, farted. *Those chilli beans are dangerous,* and walked down the stairs.

Three

It was 5 pm and the sun was going down quickly. Lucy was closing the curtains and Shelby had just closed and locked the front door. There was no way anything was going to get inside. The house had been unlocked for over a year and it didn't look like anyone or anything had been in there anyway. The house was immaculate. Searching the pantry, Shelby had found a packet of still-sealed crackers and plenty of flavoured chips. Enough to fill their bellies for a week. They were the spicy variety so the down-stairs toilet was the safest place to go. Walking up to the master bedroom, Shelby had picked a novel to start from the bookcase. Lucy had chosen one too. They only had an hour left of natural light before they'd be forced to go to sleep. Turning on a torch

or burning a candle was only asking for trouble. She'd learnt that
from previous nights with Michael. As the night got closer and it
became harder to read, Shelby started to chat with Lucy. "Lucy,
how long were you by yourself for, when *everybody disappeared?*"

"I don't know, Shelby, maybe two months? Three at the most."

"Were you afraid, being by yourself?"

"I wasn't by myself, I was *kidnapped.*"

"Fuck off," said Shelby, unbelieving.

"True fact." Lucy replied, nonchalantly, as she turned the page
of her book. Shelby shook her head.

"No one left in the world and you get yourself kidnapped."

"I know, I know, I'm *lucky* that way." Professed Lucy, looking
Shelby's way but still with her nose in her book. Shelby laughed.
"I wrote it in my diary," said Lucy.

"Really?"

"Really... want me to tell you about it?"

"Nah, *I'll buy the book...* thanks though." Replied Shelby. Lucy
laughed. "It's getting dark." Observed Shelby as she dropped her
book and walked over to the two seats they placed by the large
window. Lucy said nothing. "No sign of Michael and Teresa."
Lucy put her book down. Shelby noticed. "I'm sure there out
there, somewhere, Lucy." Lucy came over and sat by Shelby. "We'll
find them."

Lucy rested her head on Shelby's shoulder as they looked at the
broken car in the middle of the road. The shadows of the late sun
had disappeared, swapped now by mid-grey tones. Shelby put her
hand softly on Lucy's head as she fell asleep.

Four

Shelby woke up startled to a voice shouting.

"I'm not dead. I'm alive! I'm *fucking* alive!" Shelby stumbled out of her chair and stood upright like a karate junior ready for a lesson. "I'm alive, see Dad?... Dad?" Lucy mumbled, her voice trailed off as she fell back to sleep.

"Jesus," whispered Shelby. Lucy was not sitting by Shelby anymore. She had made her way to the double bed and was tucked up snuggly under the blankets. Her outburst and resulting movement had pushed some of the cover off of Lucy. Shelby quietly walked over and placed the cover back on Lucy. She whispered, "swearing," at Lucy and smiled.

Suddenly, something was knocked over outside. It sounded like a rubbish bin being pushed over and the lid rolling after it. Shelby stood paralyzed by the bed, her hand holding the cover. She listened. The loud noise was traded to a soft breeze and the sound of wind escaping through a window that wouldn't quite close. "Fuck." Breathed out Shelby as she let go of the covers and quietly walked back to the window. She peered out and searched the moonlit familiar area. Nothing seemed different. The broken car still looked vanquished and lonely.

Her stomach grumbled. She knew what it meant. She needed to go to the toilet. *Maybe I can hold it.* The idea of going downstairs in the dark was not an attractive one. It grumbled again but this time noisy liquid forced its way down her middle. "Oh, Jesus," she whispered. "Fucking, chilli beans." She turned and looked at the door. The key sat in the hole. The door was safely locked. She looked at the ensuite bathroom. *Would Lucy mind? She probably would and I don't want to wake her.*

Shelby walked towards the door and quietly turned the key. The door made a clicking sound and Shelby opened it, revealing darkness. She stood waiting for her eyes to adjust. A cold breeze came up from downstairs and instantly Shelby had visions of burst windows and opened doors. She took a backward step. Her stomach minced in protest. "Okay, okay," she conceded.

Finally her eyes adjusted and she could make out the hallway that led downstairs. She remembered the thing shooting out from the stairwell yesterday and waited just a little longer before taking her first step. The floor creaked under her. She stood still and listened. She could hear nothing from downstairs. The only sound was what her imagination could come up with. She took another step, and another, and another and stopped. She was now further away from the bedroom then it was to go downstairs. She felt lost in *limbo*. Something banged outside and instantly her hands sprung up on either side. "Fuck me," she groaned. She could not move. "I just want to go to the *toilet*." A bead of sweat dripped down her forehead.

Something fell over downstairs. It was inside. She panicked. She listened for more noise. Six low, familiar, gruesome clicks sounded from downstairs or was it outside? She couldn't tell and her mind was playing games. Her body was ready to run.

"Shelby!" barked Lucy. Shelby instantly jumped to attention, like a cat being shocked. Lucy sleepily stood at the doorway looking at Shelby. Lucy yawned. "What are you doing, Shelby?" she asked, rubbing her half closed eyes. Shelby ran. As fast as she could. She ran back to the bedroom, shoving Lucy, who went tumbling backwards onto the double bed and then disappeared comically over the side, out of sight. Shelby slammed the door behind her and locked it. She then ran into the ensuite bathroom, shutting the door behind her, shouting,

"I'm using the *fucking* bathroom and I don't *fucking* care!"

Lucy sat up still half asleep. "You just had to ask," she said, calmly as she tried to smooth her wild hair down.

Five

Shelby lay beside Lucy for most of the night. Her eyes open looking at the door. For the second night in a row, she could not sleep. Visions of creatures and monsters invaded her thoughts. Creepy creatures that were distorted and full of gunk. She could feel the veins in her eyes straining. The corners of her eyes were heavy. But alas, sleep would not come. Not until the sun started to rise and finally, her eyes closed and she fell into a deep sleep. Lucy woke and yawned and stretched her arms. Creatures that sounded like birds were making noises outside and the dawning sun was up.

"Morning Shelby!" said Lucy, cheerily.

"No." Answered Shelby in protest.

"What's that, Shelby?"

"Nothing." Shelby rose and sat on the side of the bed, her shoulders hunched forward, her eyes staring sideways into an empty void.

"Good sleep?" asked Lucy, a spring in her voice.

"The *best*." Answered Shelby, dryly as she got up and went straight into the bathroom closing the door behind her.

"Mine was good too," added Lucy, cheerfully.

Shelby finished washing her face and decided it was a waste of time trying to sleep while the sun was up. She knew she couldn't do it and her body would just rebel. She would sleep when she was ready. She opened the bathroom door and saw that Lucy had already unlocked the bedroom door and was downstairs making noises. Rushing out into the hallway, Shelby ran downstairs into the kitchen.

"Found some peaches!" Said Lucy, opening a can. "And *look*, spaghetti!" Shelby smiled as she turned and looked around the lounge area. Everything looked fine. The windows and doors were all still intact. The noises from last night must have been her imagination or they came from outside. She sighed and collapsed on a stool behind the kitchen bench. "Tired?" Asked Lucy as she splashed the peaches into two bowls. "I feel *hopeful* today, Shell! I feel like Mum and Dad are going to *toot* that horn!"

Shelby had her head resting, wearily in her crossed arms. Her heavy eyes poked above the small hairs of her arms.

"You know, sometimes you just have that feeling, *positivity*. It radiates through you. Do you ever feel like that? Like that rainbow glow is filling up your soul!" Lucy joyfully, spun in a circle and slid Shelby's plate toward her. It hit Shelby's elbow. Shelby was fast asleep, snoring.

Shelby woke up on the kitchen stool. Saliva was running down between her arms. Her face was warm, sweaty and compressed with wrinkles on the side she had slept on. She straightened her spine and felt a pain in her lower back. She'd slept awkwardly. The peaches Lucy had prepared were still in front of her.

What time is it? She looked outside the kitchen window. It looked like dusk. The sun was setting. Shelby had slept most of the day. She ate the peaches quickly and ran up the stairs. "Lucy?" No answer. She ran into the bedroom. "Lucy!" Again, no answer and no sign of her. She ran to the window and looked out by the car. There, reading a book, sitting on top of the demoralised car, was Lucy. Shelby pushed open the window. "Lucy!" Lucy looked up. "What the *fuck* are you doing?" shouted Shelby. Lucy frowned a little and lifted her book.

"Reading!"

"It's not *safe* out there, Lucy!"

"I'm fine, I've been waiting for Mum and Dad all day, just in case!"

Shelby sighed. "That's nice, Lucy, but could you please come back inside?" Lucy's body language gave a signal of being annoyed as she reversed her legs down from the car and lazily walked back to the house, looking like a schoolkid who had just been told off. After a while, Lucy came upstairs. Shelby was still looking out the window, noticing the broken car's left wheel was punctured. Rubber was hanging off the centre hub in pizza sized pieces. It looked like some creature had been eating it. "We've got to be *careful*, Lucy." Lucy said nothing. "You remember what your Dad said, we can't be by ourselves. We've got to stick together." Lucy walked over and sat by Shelby. "You were very brave out there Lucy. *Fucking brave.*" Lucy's eyebrow pricked up and she smiled.

"I'll be careful in the future." Lucy replied, "I just don't want to *miss them.*"

"You know, your Dad let off some fireworks back in the day."

"I remember the story. Just before we rose from the dead." Lucy replied, doing her best impression of a mindless, walking zombie, her hands raised with wailing vocal renditions.

"Maybe, we get some fireworks, and light one up each night. Just in case they're lost..." Suggested Shelby, looking out at the vast landscape with worry. "...Just one, each night... just one."

Six

That night, Lucy and Shelby slept heavily. Both were snoring loudly. The night was unusually uneventful. In the morning, they ate another can of fruit each and Shelby laid out the plans to Lucy. "I reckon we grab a car and head for the closest town. There's bound to be a warehouse close by."

"Sounds good, but we can't drive, Shelby."

"I can, Lucy."

"Have you driven before?"

"No, how hard could it be?" Lucy and Shelby sat in a 2012 Dodge Journey. They found the key sitting in a drawer in the house behind the driveway.

"Okay, let's do this," said Lucy, smiling. Shelby could barely see over the steering wheel. She studied the dashboard and central console.

"Okay, *I give up*, where do I put the fucking key?"

Lucy and Shelby sat in a 2005 Toyota Corolla. Shelby held the keys in her hand and placed them in the ignition. "Easy as." She said as she turned the key and the motor spluttered and stopped. Lucy remained quiet with silent motivation. "This time my *fucking baby!*" shouted Shelby as the car turned over and roared into life. Shelby had her foot pushed down hard on the accelerator.

"Oh, yeah!" yelled Lucy, with her hands raised up in the air with excitement. Shelby looked down at the gear stick. It was a manual.

The car thankfully had been parked on the side of the road, facing south.

"I think I'll try number, fucking one." Said Shelby, referring to the numbers on the gearshift. She pushed the gearstick and the car made a crunching noise.

"Ouch!" said Lucy.

"Wait, I'll try this pedal," suggested Shelby as she luckily pushed in the clutch and this time the gear stick moved smoothly into a lower gear.

"Keep it there!" shouted Lucy. Suddenly the car moved forward. Shook and then slowed down.

"Easy baby." Shelby said to the car as it slowly gyrated up and down. "I'll try number two!" Shelby crunched the gears, put her foot in again and this time the car sped up.

"Very nice!" smiled Lucy as the car drove randomly left and right down the street. "Watch out for traffic."

"Don't worry, I'm the *fucking queen* for watching out for traffic!" shouted Shelby as she changed to third and started to go faster.

"You're really good at this, Shelby."

"I told you."

"I want some music." Lucy searched the CDs sitting under the radio. "Radiohead baby!" Said Lucy, happily.

"Oh, come on!" replied Shelby. Kid A's first track, *Everything In Its Right Place,* rang out loudly on the sunny streets, as both Lucy's and Shelby's heads started nodding. The car was not running smoothly as it jolted up and down every now and then. But, the fact that the car was moving made Lucy feel happy that they had achieved something together. She shed a little tear as she and

Shelby shared a moment of joy and laughter, mixing with the music.

"How do we stop the car?" asked Lucy, her head nodding to the song.

"I don't know? Drive into something?" suggested Shelby. Lucy and Shelby laughed as they wobbled down the street, mumbling loudly the words to a song they didn't know. Shelby felt elated that finally luck seemed to be going their way.

"Thelma and Louise, baby!" she shouted.

"Who?" asked Lucy.

Seven

They arrived back late in the afternoon. In a different car as indeed Shelby had driven into the back of another vehicle in the warehouse carpark to stop it. They found an automatic Mazda CX5 with keys still in it which Shelby was able to command and her use of the brake and accelerator made her seem almost professional. They unloaded the boot which was full of cans of food, water bottles, new clothes and a box of fireworks which were mainly sky rockets.

Night came quickly as Shelby and Lucy again took their places by the window, watching the subdued car. They both stared at the vehicle for an hour after the light gave up their reading.

"Firework, Shelby?"

"Why not." Shelby grabbed a large jar she had by the chair. Placing the rocket she had ready, she pushed the window open and looked over at Lucy. "Want to light it?"

"Yes, please." Lucy eagerly grabbed the lighter from the window sill and held it out by the rocket. "Ready?" asked Lucy, smiling.

"Fucking, A!" smiled Shelby.

"For Mum and Dad," said Lucy as she lit the wick.

Shelby had a look of sadness after Lucy's words. It quickly changed to euphoria as the sky rocket's wick sparkled. Its taper became smaller as the rocket shook and made a loud bang. It then flew high into the sky and fizzed into a bright light. Both Shelby's and Lucy's mouths were wide open as the street blew out into a brilliant, dazzling light. Darkness came back just as quickly as the light dissipated. They sat watching the street silently. Just as the last few days had been uneventful, so was this night. They waited for hours until both their eyes were tired. They talked quietly about their lives. About what life was like before everything had changed. It was uneventful outside. But inside, the girls were becoming fast friends. Close friends who needed each other.

"We'll try again tomorrow," suggested Shelby. Later, they both slept soundly, feeling safe in their warm, comfy beds. At the same time unbeknownst to them, outside, spider-like creatures the size of dogs were crawling in and out of the forgotten, desolate car.

Eight

Shelby woke to the room shaking. *It's an earthquake,* was her first thought. "Lucy!" she shouted as Shelby held the bed to keep her balance. Lucy woke up startled. She sat up straight with her arms out wide trying to keep her balance.

"What the hell?" Lucy shouted, above the noise. The room was moving from side to side. The bed was angled to thirty degrees and then shook and moved back the other way. The windows were shaking. *They are surely going to break,* thought Shelby. The bedside drawers fell to the ground as Shelby screamed with shock. "The doorway!" Lucy shouted. They both got up and tried to keep their balance as the floor moved like a conveyor belt.

"Holy shit!" Shelby shouted. They were both used to earthquakes coming from Wellington, but they'd never felt anything like this before. Lucy made it to the doorway first and unlocked the door. Shelby walked past the window. She noticed outside, the road was moving like a wave on an ocean. The car was shaking and riding it like a surfboard. The movement broke the axle from the back of the car and the two back wheels separated from the vehicle. "Holy fuck!" Shelby shouted as she swayed forward one step and then took two unbalanced steps backwards.

Lucy grabbed her hand and managed to pull Shelby under the door frame. The house shook and fell slightly. Like a sand castle losing its bottom. "Jesus!" yelled Shelby as both her and Lucy hugged under the doorframe. They both felt like they were going to die. Then, just as abruptly as it had started, everything stopped. "Oh, my God." Whispered Shelby, still holding Lucy tightly. "I think this world is now trying to *shake* us dead." Lucy smiled and nodded in agreement, still startled by what had just happened.

The earth moved again. The floor picked them both up and dropped them just as unexpectedly. They both screamed.

"Aftershock?" Lucy said, her voice loud in the silent aftermath. Something was pushed over downstairs. "Did you hear that?" Asked Lucy, her mouth open. The night was now soundless. Sober after the shock of what had just happened. They listened. A clicking noise broke the silence.

"Oh, fuck," swore Shelby, under her breath. "I fucking hate this."

"Shall we lock the door?" Lucy asked quietly. Something made a noise on the bottom step of the stairway. "It's inside," Lucy said, in a hushed tone, her face revealing fear. The noise made its way up five or so steps. Lucy looked like she was going to scream. Shelby placed her hand on Lucy's mouth. She placed her finger against her lips. She reached over to her satchel which was sitting on the floor by the doorway and pulled out the small gun. Lucy's eyes opened wider. Shelby nodded.

Shelby stood and grabbed Lucy's hand, pulling her into the room. Lucy stood behind Shelby as Shelby put her fingers on the outer door and started to pull it. The noise moved up a few more steps and clicked again. Shelby pulled back the safety on the gun. She went to close the door quietly. It wouldn't close. The door had shifted in the earthquake. It wouldn't line up.

"Fuck," whispered Shelby. "Lucy, *get back,*" she said as she tried to keep the door as closed as it would allow. She peered out into the hallway. Searching for whatever was coming. A black shadow moved. It looked like a narrow leg. It had spikes on it. She couldn't make out the body. Just a long leg like the front claw of a shell covered crustacean. Only bigger and a hundred times uglier. She readied herself. "We were due for something." She whispered.

The leg planted itself firmly as a large body wavered and then followed it. Shelby couldn't make it out. She heard the clicking noise and smelt a horrible smell of rancid flesh. The creature seemed to be steadying itself waiting to pounce. It must know food is close by. It moved. Shelby shot it. It hit the door and Shelby fell back. Lucy sprung forward pushing the door at the creature as liquid squirted into the room from behind it.

"Watch out!" Warned Lucy. Shelby could see it. She steadied herself, aimed and shot it three times in a row. The creature screamed an alien squeal as liquid again shot into the room, narrowly missing Shelby's face. It backed away from the door. Lucy and Shelby heard it scampering down the stairs, wounded.

"Fucker!" shouted Shelby as she chased after it, her gun in front of her.

"Shelby *no!*" Lucy shouted. It was too late, Shelby was chasing it down the steps. She slid on gunk a few times as she ran down the slime-covered veneer. She could see the creature trying to get out a broken window it must have made its way in from. She shot it again. It squealed.

"You weren't *fucking* invited!" Shelby proclaimed as she shot it in the middle of its squelching body and watched it fall limply outside. Something moved behind her. She turned and saw a large shadow standing outside the smashed window. "Want some?!" Shelby shouted confidently as she shot the shadow and heard something shriek in pain. Lucy made it downstairs.

"Shelby! Are you *okay*?" Shelby stood with the gun pointed at the window. Looking every inch a cowboy. Outside she could see something trying to get away over the fence. She opened the door, aimed and hit it. The silent night echoed with the gunshot. Lucy shut the door. "Shelby, *enough*!" Ordered Lucy, in her best teacher voice. Shelby was breathing heavily, lost in her own war.

"This fucking world." Shelby hissed despairingly. She was sweating heavily.

"Shelby, let's get upstairs. Lock ourselves in the bathroom. Before anything else comes. Shelby, it's not safe."

"Huh?" replied Shelby, still hoping for battle.

"Shelby, we'll *die* down here." Lucy's words seemed to shock Shelby awake.

"Okay." She replied reluctantly as they made their way back upstairs. Walking into the bedroom, it looked like a bomb had gone off. Liquid was everywhere. The room was a mess of broken items and glass from the earthquake. They grabbed pillows and blankets and made their fort in the bathroom. The door was thankfully locked. They did not sleep. This world would not let them. Shelby remembered what the being had said to Michael. It seemed like so long ago now.

"You will probably not survive, Michael Stevenson." Shelby sat next to the door, her gun pointed at it. For the first time, she felt like she knew exactly what the being had meant.

As daylight entered the bathroom skylight, Lucy tapped Shelby on the shoulder. Shelby had her head resting on her knee. The gun sitting angled on the other leg. "Shelby? Are you awake?"

Shelby lifted her head. "Yes."

"You okay, Shelby?"

"Yes."

"Quite a night,"

Shelby said nothing, instead she sat studying the door. "I think we need to move." Proposed Shelby.

"You're right, I'm sick of this place anyway." Agreed Lucy. Shelby looked up at Lucy as she did her hair looking at the mirror. "We need something better." Hinted Lucy, smiling. Shelby did not reply. She opened the door. The room stank. The liquid which seemed like acid, had melted into the furniture and bedding. They were both stunned by the damage. "Next door?" suggested Lucy.

"Why not?" answered Shelby as she picked up her satchel. Lucy grabbed their books, placing them in Shelby's bag as they went downstairs. The windows were smashed inwards. Glass was everywhere. Opening the back door, they expected to see the creature from last night lying on its back. It was gone. Shelby looked left and right. "How about that one?" asked Shelby, pointing to a far off house that was another three story townhouse.

"Love it," answered Lucy. She was holding a box full of their goodies that they had picked up yesterday. They walked over to the fence and opened the gate. Closing it behind them, they started walking together.

"It's nice having you as company, Lucy. Thanks for keeping me sane." Shelby said, not looking at Lucy.

"You're welcome," Lucy replied. Nothing more needed to be said.

The house they had claimed was not as nice as the one previous. It had a real musty smell due to the lack of light coming in. The curtains had been drawn and there were cobwebs everywhere. The house, thankfully, was solid though. It had survived the earthquake well. Lucy and Shelby ignored the mess downstairs. Upstairs they were in a kid's room. The only pieces of furniture were two single beds and a small table with smaller chairs. Up on the walls were pictures of mum, dad and two kids. One boy and one girl.

"Perfect family," said Shelby.

"Looks like it was," Lucy answered.

They brought up some chairs from downstairs and sat them in front of a smaller window. They stayed there for six nights. They locked the doors and shut the windows as soon as the sun closed its eyes. Each evening the moon woke, they lit and shot one firework into the sky. They read their books and stayed by the window. For six days in a row, there were no earthquakes, no monsters, no humans, no sign of Michael and Teresa. On the seventh night, just before they shot another rocket into the heavens Lucy said, "Do you think Dad might have gone somewhere else?"

"Like where?" asked Shelby.

"I don't know. Maybe, the *holiday house?*"

"You want to go there and check?" asked Shelby.

"Nothing's happening here."

"The holiday house is all *burnt up.*" Shelby reminded Lucy.

"Maybe he left us a message."

"Maybe." Shelby agreed as she shoved the firework out the window. Lucy lit the wick. The rocket shot up into the sky. Spraying a kaleidoscope of colours that then fell and danced haphazardly on the saddened car's hood down below. "How about a few more nights and then we go?" Shelby put forward.

"Sure," replied Lucy, smiling.

Nine

A few nights of nothing happening had passed so Shelby and Lucy packed the car with enough supplies to last them a few days. They both felt they needed to do something. The burnt out holiday home where Michael had staged his huge battle a few weeks ago seemed to be the best bet, just in case he or Teresa had made their way back there. If there was no sign of anything, they agreed, they would just come back and start searching the surrounding area.

Shelby had written on the road and surrounding fences. *Gone to holiday home. Hope you're there. S and L.* Enough information for those who needed to know. Shelby indicated to the right as she drove out onto the road. "Road rules," she said to Lucy. "Music?"

Lucy smiled while still waking up. She reached for the CDs. "What do you feel like?" asked Lucy.

"I have a feeling my choices are going to be limited."

"ABBA?"

"Why not." They drove off smoothly. Lucy placed the CD in, and the first song started to play. Shelby heard something that didn't seem to be part of the music. "Turn it off!" Shelby said, sharply. Lucy turned the music off. The car's motor running was the only noise.

"What...?"

"Shhh." Shelby interrupted. A car's horn rang out in the far distance. Lucy looked quickly at Shelby, her eyes widening. It happened again. *Honk.* Shelby smiled. *Honk, honk... honk.*

"Dad? Mum?" Lucy's hand hovering over her mouth. "Turn around!" Shouted Lucy, excitedly.

"I'm turning, I'm turning!" replied Shelby. Shelby did a twenty-one-point turn and headed back the way they had come. They were both smiling and eager to see who it was. "Fuck me!" said Shelby, eagerly. *Honk, honk.*

"Here we *go*!" shouted Lucy, her hands on the dashboard, she was almost standing looking over the coming rise. As the car moved over the hill their eagerness turned to sadness as in front of them they saw the car they instantly recognised. It was Steven. He was standing outside his car pressing his horn. He smiled and stopped honking and waved as they drove closer. He walked over and placed his hand over Shelby's door frame.

"Howdy ladies," Steven said, chewing gum. He had a cowboy hat on. "Glad to see you're still alive."

"Of course we're still alive," Shelby retorted. Lucy was smiling at Steven. Steven smiled back.

"I saw your sign and thought I'd honk."

"We heard," answered Shelby.

"Sorry if it wasn't who you were hoping for."

"Oh, no, it's *nice* to see you," said Lucy, enthusiastically.

"You're not who we wanted to see." Shelby said, purposely not looking at Steven.

"I sorta guessed that, sweetie." Shelby rolled her eyes. "Just the boys wanted to invite you girls down to the village we've set up. You know, it's safe and all." Shelby looked up at Steven with a straight face. "Just with the earthquake happening we were worried about you."

"Oh, that's so *nice,* Steven." Said Lucy.

"Well, sure, we got to look after each other." Steven winked at Lucy. Shelby's eyes winced.

"You'd like that wouldn't you *fucker!* Start your little *breeding* station. Start *re-populating* the earth. Is that it?" Steven backed up.

"*Wow,* little lady. We don't mean no harm. We just thought you might like company."

"Like *company*? I'm sure you'd like our *company*."

"I didn't mean."

"Fuck you."

"Look, I'm just trying to be a gentleman here."

"Well, you're fucking *shit* at it."

"Shelby!" interrupted Lucy.

"How many girls you got down in your village?" asked Shelby.

"One, and she's really nice." Lucy punched Shelby in the arm.

"Yeah, well, Stevo, we've got *somewhere* to be, so, maybe we'll see you down the road then."

Steven thought about saying something and instead just answered, "Yes... you will." He saluted, mostly at Lucy. Lucy waved back. Shelby looked back to reverse and went forward. She put her finger up as if to say, 'I know what I'm doing' and went forward again. Steven pushed the front brim of his hat up with his finger. "Would you like some help, little lady?" He asked.

"I'm fine," Shelby said frostily as Lucy pushed her head forward in front of Shelby so she could see Steven. She waved and had the cheesiest smile on her face. Finally, Shelby found reverse. She kept on reversing till Steven was out of sight. Lucy waved goodbye and he waved back smiling.

"He's dreamy," said Lucy in a musical tone.

"He's a *fucking killer*. It's written all over him."

"Oh, Shelby, one day we might need his help."

"I hope not," replied Shelby as she did a twenty point turn. One better than before and headed in the other direction.

"You're getting better at that," said Lucy, smiling.

"I know, right?" replied Shelby.

CHAPTER THREE

Companions

MAX MARSHALL FELT HIS feet start to hurt. They'd been walking for a good eight hours and needed to take a break. If he could feel it in his toes, he wondered, how were Charlie and Pete? He could feel the edges of his shoes and was sure blood was sandwiched between his socks and skin. It was late afternoon, around three o'clock and the road just seemed to keep going.

"Some nice houses along this way, eh, Charlie?" Charlie nodded looking at the houses as if they were a kingdom in heaven. His mouth was wide open. Charlie was holding Pete's hand. "What do you think, Pete?" asked Max.

"I like them," answered Pete, smiling up at Max. "They're *flash*."

"That they are, Pete. I think one of these would be a nice place to stay tonight. What do you think, Charlie?"

"Yes *please*."

"Can we?" Asked Pete. "I can't wait."

"Me too, my feet are *killing me*." Added Max as he walked over to a car and sat on the bonnet. "*Damn*, it's hot." He wiped the sweat from his brow with his t-shirt. Pete let go of Charlie's hand and ran over to Max. Max picked him up smiling. "Well, little fella. You've still got so much *energy*!"

"Yep!" replied Pete as he sat next to Max on the car, mimicking his actions and folding his arms. Charlie joined in as all three of them sat beside each other, admiring the houses presented, arms folded. Charlie pulled out a water bottle and gave it to Pete who drank thirstily.

"Which one, Charlie?" Asked Max, rubbing his sore foot over his shoe. Charlie did the *eeny, meeny, miny, moe,* thing and ended on a rather large house on the left. It looked like it was from the fifties. The windows were all blued out. "Good choice. That looks like a mansion." Max smiled at Pete and Charlie. "After you, my good sirs." He bowed to them.

"Why, thank you, my good man," replied Pete, in an English accent, as he hopped off the car and grabbed Charlie's hand. Max raised his eyebrows, amazed at Pete's instinctive talent for acting and accents.

"Good boy for being safe, Pete," said Max.

"Safety first, eh, Charlie?" noted Pete.

"Safety first," agreed Charlie, smiling at Pete. Charlie and Pete walked together hand in hand with Max limping behind them. Charlie pushed the large gate open as Pete waited patiently for Max.

"Thank you, Charlie." Said Max. "*Wow*, that house next door has seen better days." Noticed Max as all three of them looked at the neighbouring house. The house was burnt to a crisp. Its exoskeleton was the only thing left standing.

"Must have been a big fire," said Pete.

"The *biggest*," replied Max.

"No fire engines," Charlie added.

"You're right, Charlie. There are no fire engines." Max walked up to the main door as Charlie and Pete were still spellbound by the burnt skeleton of the house. He knocked.

"Max is *funny*, why are you knocking?" Asked Charlie, smiling.

"You never know Charlie. There might be someone home."

"That's right." Agreed Pete. "We don't want to just walk in, right Max?" Max knocked again.

"Well, it looks like there's no one home. Let's go in." Said Max, smiling at Charlie and Pete.

"Max is joking." Said Charlie, with a serious face. "There's never anyone home." They walked in and shut the door behind them. Max did a quick tour of the house. He checked all the windows and made sure all the doors were closed. He'd done this many times before.

"All safe downstairs!" He shouted as he ran up the stairs. The house was gargantuan. He found five bedrooms upstairs and three bathrooms. The main master bedroom looked out to the beach and had a deck that flowed around the outside of the second story. "Yes." He said to himself as he ran its length. The soft sea breeze was already cooling him down. On the deck was outside furniture and a tied up umbrella. He left the doors open as he checked out the ensuite next to the master bedroom. It was huge, tiled and quite beautiful. "This will do." He said, smiling to himself. Max kicked off his shoes and lay on the bed. "God *damn*." He said to himself as he experienced the softness of the mattress. Downstairs he could hear Charlie and Pete laughing. Within a minute, he was fast asleep.

Max woke up and cursed himself. "*Jesus*, what time is it?" The soft breeze from the sea had now turned into a blasting wind. The sun had disappeared behind a distant island and the stars were sparkling in front of him. He was so tired he had allowed himself to sleep, but never for this long. Not while he hadn't checked on Charlie and Pete.

He ran downstairs, hoping to find them playing in the lounge. They weren't there. "Oh, shit!" he swore to himself as he sprinted past the lounge and checked the downstairs bathroom. Empty. The house was huge and each room seemed endless. He ran to the back of the house and found the kitchen. It was lit by moonlight. "Charlie? Pete?" shouted Max. "Jesus, guys, where are you?" He stood by the bench listening for any sounds. He could only hear the sea, breaking in the distance.

He ran to the rear of the house and found the washhouse. The door to the outside was open. "Charlie... what the *fuck*?" He said to himself as he sprinted outside. In front of him was a massive lawn. To the right were kayaks and a small boat. Luckily the moon was bright and he could make out most things. "Charlie?" he whispered. He heard laughing coming from around the left side of the house. He ran. His feet still hurt but he wasn't allowing it to slow him down. A distant clicking sound could be heard. He'd heard it before. "Charlie!" he shouted not caring anymore.

"Over here." Came a voice. He saw Charlie as he got closer. He was leaning on the fence, looking at the burnt out house next door. Pete was sitting on the fence. Charlie was keeping him steady, while tip toeing on an angled, outdoor chair. "Pete, wanted to see the burnt out house." Said Charlie, smiling.

"*Not* at night, Charlie!" Shouted Max as he hit some rubbish bins sitting in the shadows and fell. The clicking noise came again but it was louder. It must have heard him shouting. He gathered himself and stood up. He saw it. In the far distance, coming from next door. Something was running. On all eights. A large shadow running toward Charlie. Running to little Pete. "Charlie! God damn it, *get him off the fence!*" Max screamed.

"What?" answered Charlie. The shadow was moving so quickly. They had no chance.

"Charlie!" A shot rang out in the night. It hit the creature. It hissed and was thrown to the right of Charlie and Pete, still on the other side of the fence, unseen. Max heard it hit the sand in a heap. He also heard it gather itself and leap again at Charlie and Pete. "Pete!" Shouted Max. Another shot rang out in the night. Max heard the creature flailing and scrambling back to its feet. Another deafening discharge and Max could not hear any noise coming from the conquered, vanquished creature. Max finally caught up to Charlie and Pete and hugged them. He pulled Pete off the fence as he heard a self-assured female voice from the other side of the fence exclaim.

"...Fuck yeah."

Max opened the door, startled to find two attractive girls smiling back at him.

"Good evening. Could we come in?" said Shelby, beaming.

"*Quickly*?" added Lucy, not appreciating the dark.

"Of course, quick, come inside," Max said, feeling surprised and nervous. He hadn't seen anyone in months. Shelby and Lucy shuffled in as Max closed the door and deadbolted it. "Thank you so much for what you did out there. You *saved* their lives." Max smiled.

"It was nothing," replied Shelby, matter-of-factly.

"Well, it was *impressive*," said Max.

"My name's Shelby, my friends call me Shell but you can call me..."

"...Shelby?" Interrupted Max. "*Beautiful* name."

"Mine's Lucy."

"Pleased to meet you, Lucy. I'm Max."

"Short for Maximillian?" Shelby asked.

"No... Just Max," answered Max.

"Well, Maximillian, do you want to show us the way? I can't see shit," said Shelby, cheekily.

"Sorry, sure Shell," said Max.

"No, call me... uh, doesn't matter." Said Shelby.

Max led the way, in the dark corridor as Shelby and Lucy walked behind. Lucy pulled Shelby's t-shirt. "Handsome," she whispered. Shelby pretended to disagree. Shelby watched Max as he walked ahead of them. The moonlit night was throwing shadows in places she couldn't make out. But she could make out his outline. He was fit and had a good V-shape to his torso. He had wavy black hair. His lips were full and she thought he must be Māori. He had one of those faces that always seemed to be smiling, and she guessed, he was of a similar age.

He led them out into the open lounge area. It was huge. Charlie and Pete sat in the corner of a massive L-shaped sofa. They looked tiny sitting in it, like naughty schoolboys. Max sat next to them and straight away Pete moved over to Max and sat on his lap, hugging him. Shelby thought that was adorable. Max turned to Charlie, who had his fingers crossed and his head down. Max was whispering. "Charlie, we don't go outside at night. Never, for whatever reason. We *never* go outside at night. *Ever*, ever, ever."

"Never," replied Charlie as he looked up at Max nervously and then looked back down again.

"Even if Pete wants to go outside at night. You *don't* go outside."

"I won't," said Charlie, now starting to rock back and forth.

"Good man." Max smiled. He put his hand on Charlie's shoulder and squeezed it.

"Sorry," said Charlie.

"I'm sorry too," added Pete, his head finding solace in Max's chest. "It's not Charlie's fault."

"It's okay, Pete," Max looked up smiling handsomely at Shelby and Lucy. Lucy was in love. Shelby was not so impressed.

"How the *fuck* have you guys survived this long?" asked Shelby, bluntly. She was trying to get comfortable in a small chair. She put her right leg up on the armrest. Deciding it was worse than before and placed her leg back down again.

"Shelby!" responded Lucy, shocked.

"Shhh, inside voice." Replied Shelby.

"Shelby." Whispered Lucy. Max put up his hand and made a stop sign signal.

"We don't *swear* in front of Pete and Charlie." He said, with a straight face.

"That's going to be a problem." Said Lucy, in a musical tone with her volume lowered. Shelby half smiled, but didn't answer.

"Hey guys, why don't you go find something to do. Maybe there's some games in the cupboards?" suggested Max.

"Yay, games!" Pete jumped to attention.

"Keep it down though, okay?" said Max, with care in his voice. Pete gave Max a kiss on the cheek then grabbed Charlie's hand as they both smiled and skipped off.

"My God, he's just a *little saint*," said Lucy as she got up to search the pantry for food. "Have you guys been here long?"

"Just got here."

"From where?" asked Shelby.

"North," answered Max.

"Wine! Grape Juice. Non-alcoholic. You want some?" asked Lucy.

"I'm so thirsty, yes please," replied Shelby, politely.

Max smiled. "I'll have some, thanks." Charlie and Pete came running back into the lounge, dancing.

"Wasgij puzzle!" said Pete, happily carrying an oversized box in his small arms.

"Oh, I *love* those. Can I join in?" requested Lucy, smiling.

"Yes please, Lucy," Pete said, eagerly. Placing full glasses of grape juice down for Max and Shelby, Lucy sat down with Charlie and Pete and the bottle of grape juice.

"Okay, let's check what the person is looking at and then we can work out what the puzzle looks like." Lucy suggested. Charlie had his mouth open, tongue out, head angled and one eye closed, trying to understand what Lucy had just said.

"Good idea," said Pete.

"He's a smart kid, yours?" asked Shelby with a raised eyebrow.

Max tilted his head sarcastically. "Of course he's not mine."

"So, how did you get him?"

"Long story."

"We've got time," She sipped her grape juice.

"I found him. On one of my trips. Out for food. He was in the back of a store. Came out like I was his Dad or something. Wouldn't let me go."

"Jesus, how long ago was that since the vanishing?"

"*The vanishing*? Is that what they call it? When every living thing disappeared, the vanishing?" Shelby shrugged her shoulders. "About a week. He was hungry, thirsty, dirty. We've been together ever since."

"...And Charlie?"

"Two weeks after." Max sipped his drink. "Pete and I went to the hospital to grab some medicine. Charlie was there. *Alone*."

"How?"

"He doesn't know. Charlie doesn't know much. But he's a good soul."

"I can tell." Agreed Shelby, smiling.

"Yeah, you can tell the *good ones*."

"*Well done*, Pete!" said Lucy, rather loudly. Pete looked up at Lucy, smiled and snuggled closer to her. Lucy took a swig out of the glass, finished it and refilled it quickly.

"You want to keep it down, Lucy," said Shelby.

"Oops, sorry." Lucy said as she smiled down at Pete. "Noise police." She said as Pete laughed.

"I found one!" Said Charlie.

"Good man," supported Pete. Max smiled.

"They're so happy."

"For how long?" posed Shelby. Max's face changed from smiling to gravely serious.

"You're right. It's been tough. Real tough. We've only just escaped dying a few times."

"Seen ghosts?"

"Ghosts?" asked Max, looking surprised at the notion of ghosts. "Is that something else we're supposed to be seeing? I've seen monsters. Creatures that spit fire and acid. Insects as big as a horse. But, would you believe it. No ghosts. Pete said he saw his mum once, eh, Pete?"

"I did," Pete looked around at everyone, his eyes were large. "She was *beautiful*."

"I bet she was, Pete." Said Max. "Is that a ghost?"

"I suppose." Replied Shelby. Lucy looked over at Shelby and shook her head both ways as if to say don't say anymore. She remembered what Michael had said, *don't mention the blue angel.* "We've had some close calls also." Shelby drank some more of her drink. "This new world wants to *kill* us all."

"That's why we came down this way. We're looking for a safe haven."

"We're looking for Lucy's, Mum and Dad."

"No way." Max responded, looking surprised. "Your whole family survived the vanishing?" Pete and Charlie turned and looked at Shelby both at the same time.

"I'm not Lucy's sister..."

"Adopted." Lucy interrupted as she drank some more. She wiped her face as drink accidently came out the sides of her mouth.

"That is non-alcoholic, right, Lucy?" asked Shelby.

"Pretty sure." Lucy answered as she tipped the bottle and noticed it was empty. "There's plenty in the cupboard, want some more?"

"Sure." Max said.

"I'm okay." Shelby responded.

"Can I have some water please, Lucy?" asked Pete.

"A little saint with manners." Lucy noted. "Of course, kind sir."

"Thank you." Said Pete as he went back to studying the puzzle pieces leaning on his knees.

"This is too hard," said Charlie, looking defeated.

"Don't give up, Charlie." Pete encouraged, trying a piece that didn't fit.

"What happened to Lucy's Mum and Dad?" asked Max.

"We ran into some of those monsters. It was at night."

"Shouldn't be on the road at night." Max advised.

"I *fucking* know that," replied Shelby, sounding annoyed. Pete looked up. Shelby felt regretful. She mouthed sorry to Max. "We didn't have a choice, okay? We were trying to get to safety and... *shit happened*. We got separated. We came down here because the house next door used to be ours."

"Which one? Surely not the burnt down house next door." Shelby nodded. "*Holy*, so, I suppose that's another exciting story?"

"Yep, Lucy's Dad... is a *brave* guy." Shelby tried to shorten the story.

"It's okay, you can tell me the story another day," said Max.

"We were hoping they might be here."

"*Holy sugar*, that's a great move Pete!" shouted Lucy.

"Shhh!" Max and Shelby said at the same time.

"You're in trouble." Charlie said, smiling cheekily.

"Sorry," whispered Lucy. "I'm so happy we met you guys!" Lucy ruffled Pete's hair. She took another drink. Both Max and Shelby frowned.

"We're going to check around tomorrow and leave a message for them. If they're not here, we'll go back to where we came from."

"Where's that?" asked Max. Shelby pointed.

"A few hours that way." She smiled. "You're welcome to come with us. Safety in numbers and all that." She couldn't believe she said that, remembering Steven saying the very same thing.

"Thank you, but no. We are pretty good together. We've lasted this long, we don't want to change anything." Shelby looked disappointed. She didn't realise she'd be happy to meet new people. Or that she'd like them. Or that she'd offer them passage with her and Lucy. It took a lot for her to ask.

"Okay." She said quietly. Max noticed the change in Shelby and felt he had let her down. He was thinking of his own responsibilities and didn't want to add to them. Charlie, Lucy and Pete didn't hear the conversation as Lucy was singing songs.

"I'm so *happy!*" sang Lucy merrily, as she drank her glass empty.

"What time is it?" asked Max.

"Just after ten," answered Shelby.

"Past our bedtime, Pete," said Max.

"Oh, do we have to?" Pete asked, in a pleading voice.

"We got to go to bed, Pete," said Charlie, catching Max's eye.

"Okay Charlie," replied Pete as he got up and stretched.

"Can we finish this in the morning, Lucy?" asked Pete. Lucy was snoring.

"I swear that was proper *fucking* wine." Said Shelby, smiling. "Oh, sorry." Shelby said, quickly. "Habit."

Pete walked over to Max. "Goodnight Max." Max leaned over and Pete kissed him on the cheek. Pete walked over to Shelby and put his arms up. Shelby looked down at him, not knowing what to do.

"He wants a hug." Max said, smiling. Shelby leaned over and hugged Pete. He kissed her on the cheek.

"Good *fucking* night Shelby," Pete said, grinning cheekily.

"Smart kid." Shelby noted, trying not to laugh. Max was shaking his head with his eyebrows raised. He was failing to hide his amusement.

"Come on, Pete." Said Charlie as he grabbed his hand.

"Master bedroom, Charlie. Right down the end, upstairs." Max directed.

"We'll wait." Charlie stopped at the bottom of the stairs, noticing how dreadfully dark it was on the second level. The night was turning pitch black as clouds covered the bright, half moon outside.

"You can pick whatever room you guys like upstairs, Shell. There's four extra and they're all doubles."

Shelby smiled. "Thank you."

As the house went quiet, the only noises were those coming from the locked master bedroom. Max was quietly breathing on the left side of the king size bed. On the right side was Charlie, snoring like a fifty year old man with a breathing problem. Next to them on the floor was a double sized mattress pulled in from the room next door. On the left, slept Shelby. Her mouth wide open, her body in the shape of an S. On the right was Lucy. Her arms sprawled out, and her left leg was out of the covers and hanging off the mattress. And lastly, sprawled lying in the middle, with his arms laid out on both girls, was little Pete. Sleeping comfortably with a huge smile on his face.

CHAPTER FOUR

Pete

P ETER SLEPT SOUNDLY IN the warmth of his racing car bed. He had warm, flannelette pyjamas on. They were white with smurfs running up and down them. The night was a hot one. His forehead was covered in sweat. He was sleeping in the lounge which served as a bedroom and a back office. Of course, Peter didn't mind at all. He felt loved and warm and he was happy. His mum and dad were next door in the shop. A 24 hour 7-Eleven.

On this particular night, Peter could hear them arguing. It soothed him. It was what he heard most nights and what he was used to. The bell rang in the shop next door and the arguing instantly stopped. There was murmuring as Peter's dad said hello to the customer. These were all sounds that Peter was accustomed to and he slept easily. The bell rang again as the customer left and within a minute or so the raised voices would start again. Peter did not understand much of what they were saying. He was only three. He heard words like, *money* and *problems* and *this is all your fault.*

Something about *spending too much*. Peter found it all whimsical and the loud rhythms helped him relax.

Suddenly, the arguing stopped and Peter was thrown out of sync. He cried. A loud, screeching cry. The sort of cry that only a mother could fix. The door opened and Peter's mother walked into the room. She came straight to his bed and picked him up. Rubbing his forehead and pulling him close to her face, she kissed him. He relaxed. She started to rock him back and forth in a rhythm that he knew well. It was the rhythm for him to go back to sleep. And he did. Almost instantly. He loved his mum and he loved how she loved him.

She placed him back in his bed. Noticing his red cheeks and wet hair, she took off his smurf pyjamas and let him lie in his bed with the covers off. It was a hot night. Outside she could hear soft rain start hitting the window pane. *Hopefully that would cool things down,* she thought. She kissed his forehead and swept his hair back. "Love you," she whispered, as she turned and walked out the door, closing it behind her. Peter felt adored and comforted, he slept soundly.

He would never see her again.

Outside the rain started to build a steady pace. Peter dreamt of car races and dogs. Images from his Dr Seuss books. He would not hear the entrance bell ring in the shop next door. But he would hear the heavy footsteps. The weighted sound of something large entering the store. A massive snort of air. A sudden movement of quickness. A crashing of objects. Peter's mind is that of a short life.

He would dream of dogs and cats and the creatures from where the wild things are. They are in his thoughts.

He sleeps even deeper as noises and crashes are what he's used to. He would not dream that the door could be smashed open. That behind it would be a demon of sorts. A creature made up of every man's worst nightmare. Its eyes burned with a fierceness. His mind could not comprehend these things. He would dream of picnics and food. Cartoons and songs. This is for the best. Maybe this is why the creature decides to turn. Decides to turn and walk away. There is no fear here to feed on. Just joy, comfort and happiness.

The shop bell jingles as the rather large, fierce customer leaves the store and Peter will wake up refreshed and happy, using up the first of his many lives. Happy until he finds out that everyone is gone.

Peter wakes up screaming. Lucy straight away grabs him and hugs him. "Pete, it's okay. Pete, it's Lucy, Pete." It takes Pete a while to realise where he is and who he's with. He hugs Lucy back. Shelby rubs his back.

"*I lost them*, Lucy. I lost Mum and Dad." Lucy hugs him tighter. She tries not to cry. Hearing the pain in his voice. "They're *gone*."

"I know, sweetheart. I know." Lucy said as she patted his hair. She kissed his forehead and he hugged her tighter.

"You're not going are you, Lucy?" Asked Pete, looking up at her with a tear in his eye. The connection had happened so quickly, Lucy was taken aback.

"No, Pete. We're not going to leave you." Pete hugged her and Shelby kept rubbing his back. Max looked over and caught Shelby's face staring back. He turned back over and laid his head down thinking.

Shelby sat at the breakfast counter eating dry cereal. She had become used to it.

"How's the cereal?" asked Max, smiling.

"Fucking *tasty*." Shelby answered. She was writing something.

"What are you writing? If I may be so bold as to ask." He sat beside Shelby.

"I used to write, Maximillian. I used to write poetry. I'm seeing if I can do it again."

"How's it going?"

"Shit."

"You've got so much to inspire you."

"I know, right? End of the world and everything, but, *zilch*."

"Just let it come," Max advised, nodding.

"Yeah, okay, Shakespeare." Replied Shelby as she shoved another spoon of dry cereal in her mouth.

"I wouldn't have taken you for a poet, Shell. You're full of surprises."

"Not much good it would do in this world. I'm better off learning how to make fire, or string a bow, or how to use a knife to *kill zombies*." Max laughed.

"Can you answer me this, Shell?"

"Sure."

"If you got zombie blood in your mouth, would you then turn into a zombie?"

Shelby's face was full of thought. "Yes."

"So, then..." Max was very expressive, his hands moving in spirals as he talked. "...Why would you go around stabbing zombies with *no mask on*?"

Shelby looked up in thought. "Don't know, don't care." She shoved another mouthful of dry cereal in her mouth. "But, that's a good question, Maximillian."

Max smiled. "Looks like we're coming with you." Shelby stood up smiling. "Pete likes you guys. I didn't want to put too much pressure on you as Pete and Charlie can be a *handful*."

"Share the load with us, Maximillian. We're good for that."

"Thanks Shelby."

"Call me Shell."

"I do." Said Max as he turned and walked away happy.

Shelby smiled into her cereal as she munched the dry Wheaties. Shelby finished her cereal and placed her dishes into the sink. One good thing about the apocalypse, especially when you move from house to house, was not doing dishes. She grabbed her piece of paper which had the title: *'Pete and Charlie, Charlie and Pete,'* and walked into the large lounge where she was met with laughter and smiles.

Pete was riding Lucy's back like a man on his horse. Charlie was pretending to be a horse and Max threatened to get on his back. "No!" Shouted Charlie in protest. "You're too heavy!" Max got on him anyway and they collapsed like a house of cards. Pete pretended to fall over too. They were laughing and smiling and Shelby could tell Lucy was happy in this element.

"You guys are *fucking crazy*." Said Shelby, smiling. "Lucy and I are thinking of going and looking around next door if you guys want to come." Asked Shelby, getting down to business.

"Can we finish the puzzle first, Lucy?" Asked Pete, lying on his back and rubbing his bare round tummy.

"We'll probably go for a walk and find a shop or something." Max said.

"There's a dairy down the road." Lucy smiled at Pete. "That's where we used to get our... *ice creams!*" She tickled Pete's stomach.

"Ice creams! *Yay!*" Laughed Pete.

"Oh, sorry Pete, the ice creams aren't any good anymore. They've gone *bad.*" Lucy said, drooping the sides of her mouth.

"I don't like you anymore," replied Pete, trying not to laugh.

"Michael and I cleaned out most of the canned goods, but there's still some boxes of stuff and from what I remember, there was food out the back that we didn't even get to." Said Shelby, taking her gun out of the satchel and loading it with bullets. Max, Charlie and Pete went quiet as she did it. "What?" Asked Shelby. "*The gun*? Don't you guys have one?"

"No," Pete answered.

"How do you defend yourself?" asked Shelby. Lucy also was looking perplexed.

"We *run.*" Answered Charlie, sounding like this was the obvious answer.

"What if... they're *big?*"

"We run *faster.*" Charlie explained. Pete started laughing.

"What if... they're *really* big?" said Lucy, with her arms spread apart, explaining size.

"Then..." Charlie looked at Max and Pete for help. "...We'll probably *die?*" Pete burst out laughing and Charlie started laughing with him not really knowing why dying was so funny.

"Should we get a gun for you?" asked Shelby, genuinely worried.

"We've been okay so far, Shell." Max noted.

"But, in this world, you're..."

"We're *okay.*" Interrupted Max, sternly as he got up. The atmosphere got extremely tense as everyone started to straighten up.

"No probs." Replied Shelby as she swung her bag over her shoulder. "I'm getting one for Lucy anyway and I'll get one extra for us. It'll always be around, *just saying.*" Max didn't answer.

Lucy awkwardly got up. "Pete, we'll finish the puzzle when we get back."

"Promise?"

"Promise." She hugged Pete, waved at Charlie who waved back, and Lucy and Shelby walked out to the front entrance.

"I *love* those guys," Lucy exclaimed.

"Great." Answered Shelby.

"*Family,* you know."

"Yup." Said Shelby as she opened the door, peering behind it to see if anything was there. They walked out onto the pathway. It was a cloudy day. A change from the good weather they'd been having.

"Nice to have company."

"Yep." They opened the gate and turned right. "He didn't want the gun." Observed Shelby, adding to the conversation.

"Mmm, probably has his reasons." Replied Lucy, looking at the ground as they walked.

"We're here." Shelby announced, smiling.

"Oh, Of *course.*" Said Lucy as they stood, hands in pockets looking at the old burnt down, holiday home. "Man, this was one *crazy* night." Said Lucy, emphasising crazy as she bobbed up and down.

"It *fucking* was." Agreed Shelby. "I don't know how he did it." Shelby said as she started walking over the debris.

"Be careful." Lucy warned, walking behind her.

"I mean, what a fucking *death wish*, lighting fireworks and bringing in all those creatures," Shelby said.

Lucy kicked a piece of burnt board. "Ooh shit."

"What?" asked Shelby.

"I've seen these before."

"Gross," said Shelby, her face looking like she was chewing glue. Under the blackened board was a mass of translucent eggs. Inside were the early stages of insectoid growth.

"I'm going to vomit." Lucy proclaimed.

"Don't..."

"I can't do it." Lucy said before vomitting. She walked in front of Shelby, rushing to the back of the house where the lawn turned from white, to black, then grey and finally, brown. "Shelby!" Lucy called as Shelby was almost spellbound looking at the insectoid parasites moving in their own juices. "Shelby *come*."

Shelby turned and jumped over a few boards before arriving next to Lucy who was sitting down and seemed to be weeping. "Shell, *look*." Shelby sat down next to Lucy. In the garden were two makeshift crosses painted white. Lucy was now crying loudly. "It's..." She couldn't say it. Shelby put her hand up to her mouth. Seeing the two crosses made the pain Michael was going through hit home. "He'd *written* on them," said Lucy.

"He did." Shelby replied, now starting to cry too. His words moved them both. One cross read:

Lucy Stevenson.
Beautiful daughter
of Michael and Teresa.
Forever in our hearts,
2012-2027.

and the other,

Shelby,
2014 – 2027.
Taken from me.
A pain in the ass,
Miss you.

Lucy put her arm around Shelby's shoulder. Shelby replied by putting hers over Lucy's. No words were said or were needed. They cried.

"*Hi* girls," Max said. Both girls immediately stopped crying. "What's going on?" he asked. Shelby was trying to wipe her face. Lucy did the same but with her t-shirt.

"*Fucking* nothing," said Shelby, getting up and walking towards Max.

"Oh, it sounded like you guys were *crying*." Shelby pushed Max and turned him to go back the other way.

"Can't two girls *grieve* for their burnt, holiday, *fucking home!*" snarled Shelby, while pushing Max.

"Of course, um, sorry, I didn't realise." Lucy was walking behind them still trying to wipe her face. She looked back at the crosses.

"Just keep walking Max. We need our time to mourn."

"Sure, sure, I'm so... *ew*, what did I just step in?" asked Max, looking down.

"Just *fucking* keep going," Shelby barked.

Lucy made a funny noise and vomited again after seeing what Max stood in.

"Weren't you supposed to be going to the dairy?"

"Yeah, uh, Pete and Charlie wanted to go to the toilet, I was just waiting."

"Okay, okay, well off you *fucking go then*, there's Pete and Charlie now. *Bye, bye now.*" Max walked over to Charlie and Pete, they all waved happily back at the girls. They started their walk towards the dairy.

Lucy caught up to Shelby wiping her mouth. "That's so *gross*, he stepped in the..."

"I know," said Shelby. "How about we do some writing on the front of the street. It'll let Michael and Teresa know we've been here."

"Sounds good, Shell."

Lucy was trying to avoid looking at the eggs that were now opened with dead carcasses of insectoids spread everywhere. About an hour later Max, Charlie and Pete came walking back up the street. They were in good spirits, each carrying a backpack full of goodies.

"Hi girls! Said your *goodbyes?*" asked Max smiling.

"Have a heart." Answered Shelby. "This is *tough* stuff."

"Of course, sorry." Max's smile quickly turned upside down, his head bowed down with respect.

"You're so *mean*," whispered Lucy. Lucy and Shelby were sitting admiring their work. Max, Charlie and Pete looked down on the road as they got close to it. Sprayed in white spray paint was the sentence. *Here, but you're not. Back to the crash scene. S and L.*

"Cryptic." Said Max, looking confused.

"I think we should spend one more night here and leave in the morning. What do you reckon?" Asked Shelby.

"As long as you've said your goodbyes and are ready," replied Max, respectfully.

"I think we have Maximillian."

"What do you reckon boys? Want to go on a *trip?*" asked Max.

"Yes!" said Pete excitedly.

"Yes!" said Charlie. "Where are we going?" asked Charlie, his head turned sideways.

"Somewhere *nice,* I hope," replied Max. Shelby and Lucy got up and wiped their butts of gravel.

Lucy went running to Pete. "What did you get us?"

"*Lucy!* We got biscuits and crackers, cans and cans of fruit and vegetables. Rice and... I can't remember anything more."

"*Soup!*" Charlie recalled.

"That's right, soup. Good on you, Charlie," said Pete, patting Charlie on the back. Charlie looked back at Pete with pride. Lucy put her arm around Shelby as they all walked up the path and back into the house, while Charlie and Pete kept trying to remember the food list.

CHAPTER FIVE

Charlie

C HARLIE COULDN'T SLEEP. HE was lying on his side staring at the wallpaper. Investigating its shapes. Staring at the lady on the wall and the decorations around her. Wondering if each repeated image was the same, as she darted off at different angles.

There was a soft pitter, patter of rain on the window that was soothing him. Soothing him as his fingers entwined and nervously played against each other. He hated being alone. It was something his parents had been trialling for a week now and it wasn't getting any easier for him. They'd decided he was too big and too old to be comforted by sharing their small double bed. His bed felt enormously vast and empty in comparison.

He had his soft toy, Bingles and he tried to imagine it was his mum but it wasn't the same. He loved his mum and dad and was worried he would lose them. Like he had done at the K-Mart store. He was looking at the Gi-Joe toys and the superheroes he so loved when he decided to grab one and help it fly. Fly through the store. How happy he was making the noises and running through the aisles. Running through the aisles till he realised he was far away. Standing where the washing machines and fridges were. He still tried to help the superhero but his mind was scared. *Where's the toys?* He'd asked himself. He was young. He remembered not having words and just crying. Breaking down and crying. He'd lost his mum and dad and they had lost him. He remembers sitting in a room and waiting. Scared he would be told off, and he was. His dad told him off for running away, and his mum hugged him.

Or the time when he ran from his mum at the pools, when she had told him to stay with her. She had gone to get a coffee and he left her side. He wanted to try the water. To feel its coolness. To have fun like the other kids and not have to swim in the shallow side. He had lost her again as he sank beneath the water. His feet searching for the bottom of the pool that never came. His eyes wide open, his hands trying to fight the water that was towing him under. He was pulled out by the lifeguard who'd told his mum off, for not looking after him. He had lost her then and he'd always remember the feeling of water engulfing him. He tried to draw in breath but only swallowed bad tasting water.

Now he is sleeping in a room by himself. He tells himself, "I'm a big boy."

His dad had told him, "big boys sleep by themselves." *By themselves,* he thought. He grew tired of looking at the lady who sometimes would look like a cat and then a tiger. He looked around the room though he knew his mind would make up things and it wasn't such a good idea. *You're a big boy.* He would imagine things were there with him. His hands moved and were placed between his knees. Trying to calm the fidgeting.

He saw his chair with clothes laid on it. The darkness made the chair into one crooked, monstrous figure. A stunted hunchback hunched over in front of him, swaying forward and back, forward and back. The two gaps at the top of the chair were its eyes staring back at him. "No," he whispered to himself as he placed his head on Bingles. "Mummy?" he said.

She would say to him. "Be brave." He looked up again.

"I'm a *big boy*," he whispered. "I'm *brave*." He opened his eyes and the chair had moved closer. *How?* He thought. "Mr Bingles, *help*." *Be brave.* He placed his head into Bingles and cried. Something touched him. He screamed.

"Charlie? Charlie, are you *okay?*"

"*Oh*, Mum... Mum." Charlie was crying.

"Come to bed," said Charlie's Mum, the back of her hand on his cheek.

"*Yes*, Mum." Almost instantly, Charlie had stopped crying. He was holding his Mum's hand tightly as she led him out of the room. He turned as he left. The chair seemingly had turned around and was looking back at him. A figure hunched with large ape-like arms hanging to the floor. A large inhuman smile flickered in the dark as it took a few awkward steps towards him. He shuffled quicker than it did, and knocked into his Mum, hugging her.

"What's *wrong*, baby?"

"Nothing Mum."

"Be brave, my little boy." His imagination was winning. But he had his Mum. For tonight, he had won the war. He would not lose his parents tonight. No, tonight he would be with them.

Charlie snuggled between Mum and Dad. It was hot and the pitter patter of the rain was now becoming steadier and heavier.

He had his left arm on his dad's face, his right leg hanging over his mum. It was so hot there was no need for a cover. Their own body heat making them sweat. His dad pushed Charlie's arm back onto his side. His mum turned to the right and Charlie for a moment was stranded by himself in the middle. He was fast asleep and snoring.

He moved his arm to the right and it fell onto nothing. His left arm he moved, swiping across the left side of the bed, like a person doing snow angels, he felt nothing again. He was awake in an instant. The night was dark. The rain now was strong behind him. He sat up. "Mum?" He looked around the room. "Dad?" There was no answer. *Be brave.* "Mum? Dad!" he called again. *You're a big boy.* He started to shake. He felt a tear fall down his cheek. "Mum? Bingles?" The only answer came from the rain hitting the window hard behind him. It was so hard when he called out for his Mum again, he could not hear his own voice. He moved his feet to the left of the bed and pushed himself off. He stood frozen by the bed. "Mum, *where* are you?" he shouted. "Mum!" he screamed, now starting to panic. There was no answer. He took a step forward and stopped. A loud creak came from behind the open door. "Dad?" A figure shuffled awkwardly into the door frame. It was the hunched back shape. Its large arms pulling it forward. A horrible smile etched on its dark face.

"No!" screamed Charlie as he hopped back on the bed and pulled the covers over his body and face. His breathing was fast. *Mum, Dad, where've you gone?* He held the sheet close to his face. Trying to cover himself, like armour. To somehow protect him. *Be brave.* "I'm *trying*," he answered. "But you're *not here*! You've *left* me again!"

You're a big boy.

"I'm not! *Not yet!*" he shouted. A noise could be heard shuffling up the room. Like a chair being shoved forward. Left, right, left, right. Charlie's eyes opened wide in reaction. "Oh, Mum, I'm so scared, *Mum!*" He screamed as he turned his body away from the noise. Curled up in his sheet. Something touched him. It felt like a hand. "Mum?" He questioned. He pulled the sheet down and slowly turned his face to see who it was. It wasn't his Mum. It was the horrible face of the shadow. Its eyes were red and black. Its elongated smile exposing rows of sharp, serrated teeth. Its forked tongue slipped in and out of its wide mouth like some horrible devil.

Charlie screamed. He fell off the left side of the bed and ran. *Be brave.* He ran for the door screaming. He did not look back. He ran down the hallway and heard the chair shuffling faster behind him. He told himself not to look. For surely it would be his death. "Mum!" He screamed as he ran down the stairs. "Dad!" He shouted as he opened the front door and ran out into the empty street. He ran up the pathway. The rain beating on his wet hair. The rain soaking into his pyjamas. His feet were heavy. His socks, drenched from running in puddles. He could hear it behind him. Chasing him. He was crying. So many tears. It was fast.

You're a big boy.

"I am Dad!" he screamed. There was no one on the streets with him. There was no one for him to hold onto. To help him. He turned and looked behind him. The shadow was now tall, tall and slender. Moving at an impossible speed. It's horrible smile, larger than before. Its teeth are more like jagged, crooked blades. Its fingers like talons, dragging on the concrete. He screamed, turning back, he slipped. He fell into a puddle. *Be brave.* "Help Mum," he whispered. He could not run anymore. He'd given up. The shadow was too fast. He cried. His body was wet, from sweat and rain. The rain falling on him like nails hitting wood. "Help, Mum, *please.*" He whispered as his gasping breathing overtook him and he fell unconscious.

Alone, in a world that was as empty now, as him.

Max hugged Charlie sensing his unease. Charlie hugged him back. "I'm *brave*, Max." The half asleep Charlie said.

"You sure are, *big guy,*" said Max as he hugged him harder.

"Love you," said Charlie.

"Love you too." Max said, warmly, as Charlie fell asleep restlessly, while Max lovingly patted his head.

CHAPTER SIX

The Trip

S HELBY SAT IN THE front of the car. She was beeping the horn incessantly. "Come on, come on," she said, impatiently. It was again a cloudy day. A strong north-westerly wind was blowing a gale outside. The weather seemed to be getting worse. Finally, Lucy came out holding Pete's hand. They were blown directly to the left and they both laughed. To beat the wind Lucy decided to run. She hopped in the rear seat with Pete.

"Sorry we took so long. Last toilet stop on a long trip."

"Good thinking," said Shelby, still tapping the wheel. Charlie came out next. He looked up at the sky, and when he came out his hat was blown off. It disappeared over the fence and flew swirling into the sky. Charlie chased it for a few steps before shouting something no one could hear.

"Charlie lost his hat," said Pete.

"He sure did." Lucy replied, smiling.

"It was the wind," added Pete.

"No *fucking* kidding," whispered back Shelby, sounding frustrated. Lucy shot Shelby an unapproving look. Pete was smiling. "*Come* on," said Shelby, again. Max came to the door carrying a heavy canvas bag. He shouted at Charlie who pointed to the sky. Max put his hands up and pointed at his bag. They both walked to the car. The wind blew Charlie to the left as Max caught him and helped him get in the car. His words carried into the car once Charlie was in.

"...It's a blue one with stars, like Captain America."

"Yeah, but that one was my *favourite*." Charlie protested as Max reached over and buckled him in.

"You'll like this one better."

"Yeah, Charlie. The Captain America one is *so cool*." Agreed Pete, helping Max's argument.

"Oh, *okay* then." Answered Charlie, still feeling a little down. Shelby was looking in the mirror. Max got in the front.

"Sorry Shelby, pays to go to the toilet otherwise we'll be stopping somewhere we don't want to be."

"Good thinking," said Shelby, looking agitated. "You want to drive?"

"No, I don't know how," Max explained.

"Oh," said Shelby as she started the car.

"It's why we walk," said Max.

"Right. I'll have to teach you one day."

"Okay," replied Max.

"It's not that hard." Shelby said as she indicated to the right and then pulled out to her left.

"Yeah, I just don't want to *crash*. If anything happened to *me*..."

"It's okay, Max, you've got us now." Shelby smiled. "Pick a song, why don't you." Shelby swerved, missing a car that was in the middle of the road, she beeped the horn at it, swore blue murder and then carried on.

"You okay?" asked Max, sensing tension.

"I'm great, how are you?" asked Shelby back, smiling a cardboard smile. "Music please."

"I'm not really a music man. I don't know, try this." Max randomly chose a CD and placed it in.

"Whatever it is, Max, I'm going to play it *fucking loud*."

Pete in the back whispered something to Charlie who laughed. A piano started playing. The feeling was upbeat. Nothing like the day outside. A tree branch flew across the road as Shelby braked.

"Nice one," said Max, bracing himself. A male voice sang the words.

"Thank you for being a friend, travelled down the road and back again."

"I like this," smiled Lucy.

"Your heart is true, you're a pal and a confidant." Pete started bobbing his head. Charlie joined in. *"I'm not ashamed to say. I hope it always will stay this way... my hat is off won't you stand up and take a bow."* The song carried on playing. Lifting up the souls of the new friends as the car drifted off into the distance.

Shelby had been driving for over an hour. Next to her, Max was trying to stay awake looking out the window. The music had stopped for a while. In the back, Lucy was sleeping with her head resting back on the leather seat. Pete was asleep, leaning his head on Lucy and Charlie was snoring. He was leaning on Pete's shoulder, his mouth wide open. "So, what's your story, Max?" Asked Shelby.

"Mmm? Oh, nothing much to tell really."

"Really? What about the vanishing? How did it happen to you? Were you with your family? A *girlfriend*?"

Max looked over at Shelby smiling. "I'm fourteen, Shelby."

"A *mature* fourteen, obviously," responded Shelby, studying the road. Max looked back to the front.

"No, no family. Just friends." Shelby gave him a look that said, tell me more. "I was at an orphanage. They were my family."

"No luck, getting into a family?"

"Never quite worked for me. Don't know why. I'm not sorry though, I had some great friends and memories."

"Yeah, *fucking memories*." Said Shelby, looking gloomy.

"Sounds like you've got a sob story also." Shelby turned to the right and missed a truck, she straightened up again.

"Sort of, it's not something I want to talk about."

"Oh, so it's okay to ask me about the vanishing but not okay for me to ask you?"

"Just... my mum disappeared and I'm not sad about it." They stopped talking for a while. Max reached over and touched her arm. Shelby felt her arm shiver like electricity had just pulsed through her left arm and resuscitated it. "Maybe, a little sad." She added.

"Stop!" Cried out Lucy from the back. She was awake and was the only one paying attention to the road. "Shelby, *stop!*"

Shelby put her foot hard on the brake bringing the car to a skidding halt. She pulled the hand brake up.

"Holy shit," whispered Max. "Stay quiet. Don't *wake...*" It was too late. The sudden stop in momentum had woken both Pete and Charlie. About fifty metres in front of them stood a large predator. It was probably twice the size of an elephant. It walked out from between two houses, smelling the air.

"Fuck me," said Shelby, quietly. It looked shaggy. Like a souped-up mammoth without the trunk, though this was no herbivore. Its fur was matted and curled. The coat couldn't hide the powerful muscles as it walked slowly out onto the road. A car lay abandoned in the right lane. The creature licked it. Tasting, to see if it was edible.

"What do we do, *what do we do?*" asked Charlie, instantly recognising danger.

"Don't panic." Shelby advised, her eyes said otherwise.

"We'll be okay, Charlie, *don't worry*. You okay, Pete?" asked Max.

"I'm good," answered Pete.

"I'm brave." Followed Charlie.

"You are Charlie. *You so are.*" Max said calmly, reaching his hand back on Charlie's lap. He turned back to see the monster roaring at the inedible car. It smelled the air again and barked a deep snarl that resonated like thunder. A deep grunt that sent vibrations through the vehicle.

"What if it comes this way? *What if it comes this way?*" asked Shelby, going against her own advice. Stress was oozing from her pulsating vocal cords. Her fingers were gripping the steering wheel, hard. They were trembling. She was searching the dashboard hoping for a button that said, *rocket*.

The creature pushed its side against the car. Trying to scratch an impossible itch. The car moved a metre or two.

"Wow," said Max. It shook itself. Something flew out from under its immense coat. "It's even got animals living inside it."

Shelby was starting to panic as the monster took a heavy step towards them. "What do I do, what do I do? *I can't drive!*" said Shelby, panicking.

"Can you *reverse?*" asked Max, trying to remain calm.

"I did it... *once.*"

"What about turning around?"

"Yeah, *nah,*" said Shelby.

"I wouldn't do that." Lucy agreed. The monster shook its head. It lowered it and raised it once more roaring into the sky.

"I'm scared," said Pete.

Lucy hugged him. "It's okay. We'll be okay."

Shelby was still searching the dashboard looking for an amen. She noticed a triangle coloured red. "What's this? *Turbo boost?*" She pushed it. A slight ticking noise could be heard.

"What's that? *What did you do?*" asked Max.

"Pushed this *danger sign,*" answered Shelby. "I don't know, maybe *it'll fucking help us!*"

"Yeah, maybe it'll call... *the danger police!*" said Max, sarcastically, matching her rising speech rhythms.

"Funny, you're funny." Outside the car, the indicators on both sides of the front of the vehicle were now blinking. It did not go unnoticed by the monster, who started to see red. It bent down low and like a rhino, started to paw the ground. Asphalt and dust started to rip from the tar seal underneath it. It snorted. "Oh, my God," said Shelby. "I fucked it."

"Get ready!" shouted Max.

"What do you mean?" screamed Shelby.

"What's happening?" yelled Pete.

"Are we *dying?*" asked Charlie.

Lucy said nothing, her mouth wide open.

"You're going to *reverse!*" Max noted in a panic.

"What? I can't even drive *forward!*" replied Shelby.

"It's either that or we *run!*" said Max. The monster started charging.

"Fuck!" Said Shelby as she floored it in reverse. There was a huge amount of smoke in front of them as they tried to speed away.

"Handbrake!" Shouted Max. Shelby released the handbrake and the car immediately accelerated more quickly. "Keep it straight!" Shouted Max. Shelby was looking behind her but she was too short to see above the rear seats.

"I can't fucking see anything!" she shrieked.

"Use the mirrors. I'll try and guide you!" shouted Max, still trying to remain calm. Shelby brought her head forward. She immediately regretted it, seeing the huge creature only twenty or so metres away and gaining. She looked in her right and left mirror and tried to keep the car in the middle. "That's it! You're doing so well. Little left, bit to the right, *no*, that's left, right! *Right!*" shouted Max. Pete was crying with fear. Charlie had his head in his hands, trying not to look.

"Faster!" yelled Lucy. Shelby moved her eyes from the left mirror back to the centre and screamed. The monster was right on them. Its head down low. It rammed the bonnet. The car jumped up as if in slow motion and fell back down again. Everyone screamed in unison. Shelby tried to keep the car straight but was struggling. "Faster!" called Lucy again.

"I'm trying, Lucy! *I'm fucking trying!*"

"She's *fucking* trying," repeated Pete, sweetly, while looking up at Lucy with big eyes. Lucy rubbed his cheek affectionately.

"I know, *I know.*" Lucy admitted. The monster lowered its head again. *Shit, this could be it.* Thought Lucy. Max saw a break in the road to the right.

"Shelby, turn right! *No*! *Other right!*"

Shelby made the correction as the car swerved and disappeared down the side street. Its tires angled dangerously. The monster couldn't course correct in time. It tried to change direction but instead tumbled over its own heavy weight, disappearing in clouds of smoke in the far distance. Shelby was straining, holding the steering wheel tight as her wrists fought the car's inertia, finally stopping it as it let out a small whine. Like a creature that had given up.

"Start it up!" shouted Max. The monster was out of sight to the left. "Shelby! *Start it up!*" shouted Max, again. Shelby turned the key but the car wouldn't have it. A paw came back into sight. The monster's left paw. "Shelby!" Max shouted.

Pete joined in. "Shelby! Start it up, *Shelby!*"

"Shelby!" Lucy was jumping up and down. Shelby turned the key. The motor fluttered and died. Charlie started impatiently hitting the back of Shelby's seat.

"This *time*, you piece of...!" Shouted Shelby as she turned on the car and heard it scream into life.

"...Fuck yeah."

Placing the gear back into reverse. She stepped hard on the accelerator as the car sped down the side street. The monster was back in full sight. Angrier and hungrier than ever. Checking her mirrors, Shelby tried to keep the car in the middle. "I'm fucking *good* at this!" She said, with no humility as she smiled at Max.

"Concentrate." He advised, smiling back. She looked in the right mirror and the street seemed empty. She looked ahead and the monster was charging. But it was still 50 metres away. Slowly gaining. She looked in the left mirror and there was a man in the middle of the road, dressed in camouflage with his hands out as if to say don't hit me.

"What the fuck?!" she said as she spun the wheel hard right to avoid him. The car swerved as the front left tyre broke loose and bounced across the road like a prisoner finally being set free. Everyone's eyes followed the wheel as it comedically bounced down the road and disappeared over a fence.

Shelby tried to correct the car but had totally lost control as it swerved past a pole and drove backwards into a Starbucks coffee shop. Managing to hit the brakes in time, the damage was only to her pride. "*Coffee* anyone?" Shelby asked, dryly.

The man in camouflage stood directly in front of them. It looked like he was running from something. He looked like he was in control. He pulled a shotgun from behind his shoulder as he shot behind him. Not towards the monster but behind him.

"He's shooting the wrong way?" said Pete, innocently. Everyone was stunned and shocked by what had just happened. The guy shot again. He then grabbed what looked like a grenade, pulled the pin and threw it, again, behind him. He looked to his left, then to his right. Then to his left. Shelby thought, *this guys a goner* when he started running towards them.

Suddenly, what looked like large insects charged past him and went full tilt towards the monster. One insect, two, three, four. They were huge, gross and fast. The man ran to the back of the car.

"Let me in!" he screamed. He tried the door, it was locked. "Let me in! I can help!"

"Charlie! Open the door!" shouted Max. Charlie lifted the lock and opened the door.

"Hello," said Charlie, politely.

"Move over, buddy!" said the man as Lucy placed Pete on her lap and Charlie moved across, making space.

Getting in the car the man slammed the door and shouted. "Move it, lady!" In front of the car, the individual insects had now become many. They were massive things. Spindly and awkward. Black goo was falling off their bodies. Shelby turned the key and the car straight away roared into life. One of the insects heard the noise and stopped, turning slowly and awkwardly towards the car as Shelby hurtled the car straight ahead and shoved the creature into the adjoining shop. A Nike store.

"Shoes," said Lucy, dreamily. Shelby turned the heavy steering wheel as sparks spun out from the missing wheel. The massive insects darted out of the car's way as in the rear view mirror she could see the insects crawling over the screaming monster. It was battling a winless battle against a foe that was too many and way too vicious. Her hand went to her open mouth in shock as she felt almost sorry for the poor creature.

"That's one horrible way to die," said the man in the back. Shelby looked in the rearview mirror. The man had black marks under his eyes. He had a full-on mullet and wore an army uniform. He was littered with weapons. Upon closer look, he didn't look so old.

"How old are you, *Rambo*?" Asked Shelby, her body bouncing up and down with the movement of the car, driving on three wheels.

"Sixteen, ma'am," answered the man.

"What's your name, soldier?" Shelby asked. Lucy laughed.

"Tim."

"Got a last name, Tim?" asked Shelby, with interest.

"Tim."

"Nice to meet you, Tim." Said Max.

"Nice to meet you, Tim." Copied Pete.

"I don't like to get attached, *I'm afraid*." Replied Tim, with a straight face, looking out the car window. Lucy gave Max a look that said, *that's a bit rude*. Max nodded, agreeing.

"Tim, so, where do you live?" asked Shelby.

"Outside of town."

"Can we give you a lift?" she asked.

"I'm already feeling sick, can you pull over and drop me off here?" asked Tim, his head bouncing up and down.

"We did just save your life," said Shelby, looking up at the rear mirror.

"You might think that ma'am, but... *I know better*." As the car came to a stop and Tim opened the door.

"Wait," shouted Lucy. "How will we find you?"

"With all due respect ma'am..." said Tim looking back at Lucy. "...I'll *find* you." He shut the door. Placed his gun in front of him and started running down the street like a soldier on war duty.

CHAPTER SEVEN

The Golden Heart

> "COURAGE IS RESISTANCE TO FEAR, MASTERY
> OF FEAR, NOT ABSENCE OF FEAR."
> MARK TWAIN.

S HELBY BROUGHT THE CAR to a stop, angled at forty five degrees outside the house she and Lucy had been staying in. The wind outside was now at storm levels. Tall trees were at dangerous angles threatening to fall over. Inside, the car was reasonably quiet apart from the sound of everyone stretching their bodies.

"The smashed car is on its side." Noticed Lucy. Something large had forced the broken car onto its left flank.

"I saw that." Replied Shelby.

"Doesn't look like anyone has left us a sign." Said Lucy, sounding a little down. Shelby didn't answer, instead meeting eyes with Lucy as they both exchanged sad looks. Lucy was hoping, also, that

Mum or Dad may have left something to suggest they were alive. It was now over seven days. Shelby was starting to lose hope.

"Now, boys, be careful out here. The wind is *really strong*," advised Max, with worry on his face.

"I'll hold Pete's hand." Lucy said.

"...And I've got you, Charlie," said Max, smiling.

"Who's got you, Shelby?" Asked Pete, with genuine care in his voice.

"Maybe *you*, Pete."

"Okay," Said Pete, smiling like he had a very important job. They were blown about as they walked quickly to the door. Lucy opened it with her right hand while holding Pete. Pete held Shelby's hand tightly, while Charlie was being held across his chest by both of Max's arms. It started to rain heavily.

"Quick, *get inside*!" Max shouted as they all tumbled inside, Pete and Charlie both laughing at the commotion. Max quickly shut the door and the house fell reasonably silent. Just the sound of the whistling wind outside.

Suddenly, there came a loud knocking at the door. They all looked at each other with amusement and surprise. Shelby quickly went to grab the handle. "Be careful." Said Max.

She pulled the chain across before opening the door and peering out. Behind the door was Tim. He still had his gun in his hands. He was looking left and right like a soldier expecting danger.

"Ma'am!" he shouted, trying to be heard over the wind. "Just checking to make sure you got back safely!"

"Were you following us?" shouted Shelby back.

"Couldn't miss the sound of the vehicle!" answered Tim.

"Well, Thank you, *Commando*, we're all safe!"

"Best stay inside. It's going to be a *wild night!*" Tim shouted, still not looking Shelby in the eye.

"We will!" yelled Shelby.

"Alright then!" Tim shot back. Shelby had the feeling Tim was looking for company.

"Did you want to come in and grab some food or something?" Shelby asked. Everyone behind her was a little shocked at Shelby's sudden discovery of kindness.

"Thanks ma'am but, no, I've got to get back to base."

Shelby smiled. "Maybe tomorrow, for lunch?"

"Lunch sounds good, ma'am." With that Tim turned and ran down the pathway, he looked left and right and shot off down the road. Shelby closed the door.

"That was nice of you," said Lucy, smiling.

"He did help us, I think. I don't know, there's something about that guy," Shelby said. Max said nothing. He looked a little wounded by Shelby's interest.

The house was feeling full. It wasn't the biggest and a few extra bodies certainly made a difference. They all decided to set themselves up upstairs. They could lock the door and there was a bathroom directly to the right. A few mattresses were added next to the two kids beds' and they were all set.

In the late afternoon, Pete and Charlie had already forgotten about the day's close call and were playing a game Lucy had found, Connect Four. Shelby and Max sat in the kitchen watching.

"That was too close today," said Shelby.

"Yeah, that was scary," replied Max.

"It's getting dangerous, even during the day." Max nodded. "You guys were only walking to the dairy yesterday, imagine if you came across those... *those creatures*."

"We wouldn't stand a chance," answered Max, who was playing with a pack of cards.

"Charlie, that's *cheating*, you can't play two counters at once." Pete said, in a raised voice. Lucy tried to help them work it out.

"This world isn't meant for kids," said Shelby, looking worried. Max nodded again. "*Especially*, two nice kids," added Shelby.

"Pete, you're *cheating!*" Charlie yelped, sounding very annoyed.

"No, I'm not, *it was my turn*," Pete shouted back.

"Not so nice at the moment," Max said smiling.

"When you've got to win, the gloves come off," said Shelby. Max nodded.

"You did well today Shelby." Max said, looking at her straight in the eyes. "I was really, *really impressed*."

Shelby smiled, "We help each other, don't we?"

Max touched her hand softly in response. "Cards?"

"Sound's good," Shelby replied, smiling back.

The night went without event. Lucy and Shelby chose not to light a firework. The wind was too strong and they were worried the rocket could come back at them or wouldn't even light. They slept soundly, tired after the day's events.

At 11:59 am there was a knocking on the door. Pete ran to it but Shelby held him back. "You never know who it could be," said Shelby. "We best be careful."

"Okay, Shelby." Answered Pete, sounding like a schoolboy talking to his teacher. She opened the door slightly.

"Morning ma'am." Tim said, his gun at the ready. His head was down.

"Morning slick. How's your morning been?"

"Good, good." Tim stood outside waiting for Shelby to say something. She was waiting for him to add to his story.

"Nice to have the sun out and the wind gone..." Started Shelby.

"...I better come inside." Tim interrupted, not one for small talk.

"Right," said Shelby as she undid the chain and let Tim pass. Tim walked in, placing his gun behind his back.

"I'm Shelby," Shelby noticed Tim had grenades running down the sides of his chest. He had again painted black marks under his eyes and looked every bit a man on a mission.

"Hi Tim," said Lucy, shaking his hand. "I'm Lucy."

Pete and Charlie followed, smiling broadly and shook Tim's hand also.

"Tim,"

"Pete."

"Tim,"

"Charlie."

Lastly, Max came up and said in a low, commanding voice, "Max." Shaking Tim's hand with the strongest grip he could possibly muster. Tim smiled without saying anything. Walking over to the dining table, Tim said nothing as he noticed the cans of food displayed. Plates, forks and knives had been set neatly.

"Take a seat," offered Shelby, trying her best to be polite.

"Nice to have you here." Added Lucy, smiling.

"It's not often we get guests." Smiled Shelby. Pete laughed at this remark. Charlie laughed too.

"Is ah, this what we're having for lunch?" Asked Tim, spying the cans of baked beans, peas, sardines and canned fruit.

"It's the best we've got." Max answered aggressively.

"Sorry, I don't mean to be rude." Said Tim, responding to Max's annoyance. "Just, I'll have to get you all around for lunch or dinner one day. I'll put a real banquet together."

"Sounds yummy," said Shelby, smiling. Pete was rubbing his hands together. His tongue licking his lips. The conversation went dead for a while. Shelby, Lucy, Pete and Charlie were all smiling. Max and Tim looked very serious. Finally, Max broke the silence.

"So, what've you been up to, Tim?" Max was tapping the table with his fork.

"Nothing much," answered Tim.

"We've been up to a lot, Tim," Shelby piped up. "Since the *fucking vanishing*." Tim lifted his head and for the first time met Shelby's eyes. Shelby noticed they were very light green. "Sorry for swearing, Tim."

"It's okay."

"I was with Lucy's parents. Mike and Teresa. We crashed out here a few days ago. We lost them and a flying dog. Answers to Pup."

"*Oh*, I want a flying dog!" said Pete, his eyes opened wide.

"*Me* too!" Charlie agreed.

"Have you seen them? Older guy." Asked Shelby.

"Hawaiian shirt," Lucy jumped in.

"look's a bit... *nutty*." Shelby added.

"Tiny jean shorts."

"Lots of hair,"

"big *bushy* beard!" Lucy finished, grabbing her cheeks, they both laughed.

"No," Tim said abruptly. Lucy and Shelby both went from smiles to straight faces.

"How about Teresa? Brown hair, quite beautiful, late forties, white blouse, blue jeans?" asked Lucy.

"No, sorry... or the dog... thing." Tim responded.

"This fucking world," said Shelby, sounding fed up.

"Yeah." Agreed Tim.

"Has it been tough for you?" asked Lucy.

"A little," answered Tim. "More so the people around me."

"How so?" asked Shelby, sounding interested. Max was still tapping his fork.

"I've met a few people. Since the... *vanishing*."

"How many?" asked Pete, bravely trying to join in the conversation.

"Well, there was Mrs Chamberlain." Tim made himself comfortable as he placed his gun on the floor. "She was the first person I came across. She was a little older. She would come out every morning and walk to check for her paper. I said to her, there's no paper coming. Everyone's gone. But, I'd find her slowly walking out every morning, without a care in the world. I'd bring her an old magazine or something for her to read."

"Aww," Lucy sighed out affectionately.

"But, it wouldn't stop her. I even started bringing her supplies. She'd ask for things like milk and cheese. I just said to her. It's all *spoiled*. It's all gone. She wouldn't have it. I warned her to stay inside, you know. Once the creatures started appearing. Especially at *night*. 'Don't come outside', I'd tell her. 'Even if you hear something scratching around in your backyard. stay inside', I'd say."

"Did she stay inside?" Asked Charlie. His eyes were wide open with what looked like terror.

"She was *eaten*, right Tim?" said Pete, with an evil little grin. "*Eaten*, while getting the paper!"

"Pete, *no!* Maybe you kids should go and play a game or something," said Lucy, sounding stressed.

"Oh, no, I want to hear more stories about monsters eating people," whined Pete.

"Me too," Charlie noted.

"*Here boys*, I'll set you up." Ignoring their pleas, Lucy grabbed some cans of fruit and set up Charlie and Pete in the lounge. They protested but gave in, sitting behind their table pretending not to listen to the conversation. Lucy came back and sat down.

"Carry on," said Shelby.

"There's not much more to say about Mrs Chamberlain. Other than that, she was nice and made an *incredible* chocolate cake."

"Sad," said Lucy.

"Then, there was Mr Lee. I *loved* Mr Lee. He was very cool. I found him on one of my rounds. He was tending to his garden, on the third floor of the Newtown apartments. He asked me to come up. Had a warm meal waiting for me. Asked me if I was part of the army, come to *save* the day." Tim looked at them all. "...I wasn't."

Tim shifted in his chair, trying to make himself more comfortable. "Do you mind if I try some of the baked beans?" asked Tim. "I skipped breakfast for this."

"Of course, got to *feed* those muscles," answered Shelby, smiling. Tim carried on,

"Yeah, I lost my whole section, platoon and battalion. *All gone*. I told Mr Lee this and he understood. Not like Mrs Chamberlain. He said he'd noticed *strange animals* walking around down below. I gave him the *warning*. Don't go outside, especially at night. Stay home and I'd bring supplies. He was a *good man*." Tim left it at that and opened his can. The beans, slopped out onto his plate. He grabbed his fork and ate hungrily.

"What happened to him?" asked Max, finally joining in. Pete and Charlie both looked over, secretly listening to the conversation.

"Well, It's a little hard, you know, it's why I don't like to get *attached*." Tim took a second and wiped his mouth with the back of his hand. "We did a few things together. He was into Tai Chi and some fighting arts which he taught me. He was *tough*, Mr Lee. I reckon he would have *bested* any of those monsters. Apart from the big ones." Tim took another mouthful. "I enjoyed visiting him. We would have our little chats about the world, about the old world. He thought this was our *damnation*. That we deserved it." Tim took another mouthful.

"Then one day, I took him up his groceries and he was talking about *ghosts*." Lucy elbowed Shelby. "About how he'd seen his wife, whom he had not seen in over twenty years. He was babbling on about how he thought it was a *vision*, a sign for him to move on." Lucy put her hands up on her mouth. "I turned up the next day. He was gone and outside on the sidewalk... *the fall* must have *killed* him. Either that or he was attacked. I couldn't tell from what was *left*."

Pete was nodding. Charlie was looking confused. Tim took a second to gather himself. His fork frozen above his plate. "He was my *closest friend*, Mr Lee. I was surprised he'd *left* me."

Lucy started to cry. She looked over at Shelby, who also had become teary. Shelby looked over at Max who was pretending to watch Charlie and Pete, his eyes definitely watering. "Anyway, I don't want to just tell you sad stories. There's also the *Doc*. He lives about two kilometres from here in a stately house. He's a good man to know in this world. If you get hurt, *he'll help you*." Tim started to eat again.

"Can you give us his address? I'd love to meet him," asked Shelby.

"Sure, but I haven't seen him for a while. I hope nothing's happened to him, but you just don't know in this world. It's like... *all our days are numbered*."

They all went quiet over Tim's sobering words. Shelby started to pass out the cans as they all started to eat. Not a word was said. Half an hour later, they'd all eaten their fill, when Shelby finally broke the silence.

"Well, Tim, it's been so nice to meet you."

"And *you*, and *you* all." A smile finally breaking on his face. "I haven't seen anyone in a while."

"No?" asked Lucy. "What about the *handsome guy*, Steven, the one with the cowboy hat that drives around here sometimes?"

"No, I haven't seen him. Maybe, one day."

"Maybe," said Shelby, "Well, as I say, it's been lovely to meet you. It seems you have a real *heart of gold*." Shelby acknowledged, smiling as she stood up.

"Thank you, ma'am. It's been nice meeting you all, and you really should come over for lunch or dinner and stay," Tim suggested with a smile. "A word of advice though."

"Yes?" said Shelby, eager for more information. Everyone leaned in closer to Tim. "*Board* up the windows." Tim looked around the lounge and kitchen. "It won't keep them out. Especially if they know you're *inside*. Or, find somewhere better to live."

Max stood up. "We'll take care of it."

"Good," Tim responded. He put his gun back on his shoulder. "I've told you a few stories, but there's plenty more. Stay safe and do nothing stupid. If you go outside, take a weapon with you. *Early morning* is *best* and *stay away* from the hills and water."

"Tim?" asked Shelby.

"Yes?"

"Did you want to come around tomorrow for dinner? Maybe you could stay and give us some more pointers."

"That would be nice. I'll be here." Tim smiled, shyly. Gave a half hearted wave to everyone. Pointed his gun in front of him, opened the door and ran down the pathway. Shelby thought she could almost hear the *hut, hut, huts,* going with him. She closed the door.

"He'll be a good man to have around," said Shelby, turning to look at the others. "Now, let's get these windows *boarded up*."

CHAPTER EIGHT

The Bells

S HELBY WALKED SILENTLY, TIP-TOEING between bodies. Max and Lucy were both sleeping as quiet as a mouse. Charlie and Pete, on the other hand, were both snoring loudly. *Funny*, she thought as they've both got the proper beds as well. The curtains were drawn, so the early morning sun wasn't quite stirring the sleepy heads. She knew, soon though, they would be awake and complaining about the freezing cold water as they had their early morning showers.

She made her way down the stairs noiselessly and entered the kitchen. The kitchen and lounge now had an eerie feeling. Following Tim's advice, they had broken boards off a neighbouring fence and nailed them across the windows. It was makeshift, but they had no idea how long they would stay in this house. The toilets only had a few good flushes and then they'd stop working. It was easier just to move to another house. You could just imagine a whole town of houses stinking from their shit and piss. *Horrible stuff*, she thought. Max had been emptying a bucket for everybody. He drew the short straw.

The lounge, though, looked like a car had driven past and shot bullet holes through the wooden, boarded up windows. Light was fighting to get through the natural holes and gaps in the wood. It looked every inch like a photo from a cabin in an apocalyptic world. The night had been quiet and thanks to Tim, they'd all felt safer walking to the toilet (using the bucket) or even coming down to the kitchen for a glass of water. What was it, Tim advised?

"If you go outside, take a weapon with you. *Early morning* is *best* and *stay away* from the hills and water." She nodded, remembering Tim's words. She opened a can of fruit. Scoffed it down and drank a glass of water. Feeling refreshed and not too full, she checked the gun in her satchel. She then threw it over her shoulder and walked out quietly, trying to close the door without noise behind her and locking it shut.

She turned and smelled the air. It was crisp and fresh. The sun was just coming up and what sounded like birds were chirping in far off trees. Checking her surroundings, she saw no signs of any animals, insects, creatures or bus-sized monsters.

She walked out briskly. Her mind was now thinking of Michael and Teresa. She was here because of Michael. He was the reason she was alive. He had put his life on the line for all of them and they were now living and breathing because of him. She owed it to him to pay it back. For too long now, she'd been distracted by other matters. Trying to survive, meeting a new family, but now, she was back on track. Now, her full attention would go to Michael.

She made her way to the road where the battle had taken place. Looking both ways because of habit rather than danger, she crossed the road. As she crossed, she noticed the sad, broken car was now back on its front. All its wheels were gone and it looked like it had been squashed by a car compactor or a massive monster. *You're having such a hard life*, she thought.

Standing on the other side of the road, a large bank of grass angled steeply. It went at least a hundred metres both ways. Down the bottom of the bank was dense forest. She cursed herself for not exploring this perimeter before. *Maybe Michael is down here, somewhere. Maybe, they were all thrown off the side by some huge creature.* She held her satchel tight by her body and walked on an angle carefully down the bank. She could see both ways, north and south were pretty clear. There were no signs of bodies. She decided to walk along the entrance of the dense forest. Either way, it was not safe to go further than what the light could illuminate. Certainly, it was a death call to go in too deep.

She made her way along the hundred metres going South. Seeing nothing but hearing a lot. Sounds were thick and fast coming from inside the forest. At one stage, she thought she saw something move. Something small and quick. But it was gone by the time she had looked its way. Walking back the other way, she started to whistle to make herself feel braver. As if to make herself feel like there was nothing to worry about. Even though her mind was telling her it was crazy. *Michael would do the same, in fact, he would go into the centre of the forest.* "No, he wouldn't," She answered herself. *He probably would,* her mind replied.

She was almost at the end of where she thought was far enough, when a lizard the size of a small dog sprung out of nowhere. "Ah, fuck," she whispered, knowing this can't be good. *I was almost finished.* The lizard moved swiftly towards her. It looked up at her. She took a step back and pulled her gun out.

"What do you want, *you fucker!*" she said, firmly. She noticed the lizard's face was eyeless, in fact, it just had patterned lines equally spaced meeting at its nose. "What the fuck?" The lizard's face blew open like a magical, hypnotic flower. It paused, while Shelby stared, spellbound at its enticing radiance. Then, from the centre of its allurement, spewed out an acidic liquid. She quickly darted to the right, "Oh, no you don't!" she said as she moved like an experienced gunfighter and shot a bullet straight into the centre of the charming, life-threatening flower. Its face exploded, leaving behind the four legs and it's behind. Or what she thought was it's behind. The four legs started to walk backwards as its bottom turned up to her, revealing its open jaw. Rows of jagged teeth were displayed as it spewed out more liquid that missed Shelby by an inch. "Fuck me!" She said as she reacted slowly and moved a second too late. She shot again but missed, hitting dirt. The lizard ran quickly off into the forest, not wanting to lose another part (she noticed a small bud was already growing from its shattered behind) it jumped into the air, *vibrated* and then disappeared into the solid ground.

Shelby sat on the soil with her mouth open. *What the fuck did I just see?* "It *swam* into the bloody ground." She said, out loud. Visions of monsters coming up through the house's floor, picking up Pete and Charlie and disappearing into the floorboards started swarming her brain. "Not going to happen." She hoped as she wiped herself clean of the dust.

She stepped over the foul liquid which was now steaming and made her way back up the bank. "I can't get a *fucking* moment to myself." She complained as she grumpily stomped across the road, annoyed at almost being killed again. She shook her head. "This fucking world,"

She looked in the far distance, seeing the bridge. It worked its way from the bank and created a travel way that met with the suburb she knew as Plimmerton. Swearing to herself, she remembered Lucy saying she had just come from the bridge when they first met. *Maybe, there might be something there. Maybe, Michael had saved her and collapsed. Maybe, little Pup carried her there and was squashed by her weight?* So many maybes.

She walked into a house that had a rather nice large pickup out front. Walking in, she made her usual announcement. "Hi, Shelby here, I'm just going to *steal* your car." It was nice that people just left their keys on the table, or by the bedside drawer, or in the top drawer in the kitchen or even better as you walked in the door, sitting in a bowl. It was almost as if they didn't expect to just...vanish.

She sat in the comfy seat. "Mmm," she enjoyed its new car smell. She turned the key. Dead as a doornail. Shelby sat in a Honda Civic. Not as nice as the last one but, it did start first time. She made her way to the bridge. While parking the car she noticed two large concrete pillars. They were both decorated with graffiti. *Dead man's graffiti.* She decided to pop down and have a look. See if there was anything that might give clues to Michael's whereabouts. The soil was damp and grimy. Searching around the edges of the water she saw nothing strange. No body that was decomposing. No dog with three tails with its tongue-lolling. No wife lying on her side, half eaten. No, there were no signs that anything had happened here.

She walked back up to the car and sat on the bonnet, looking back at the view. The hills were green. The sky was a gorgeous blue. It was now late morning. There was a gentle sea breeze. If it wasn't the end of the world it would have been mistaken for a rather perfect day. "Where the fuck are you, *Michael Fucking Stevenson?!*" She shouted to the vista. There was no reply. She crossed her legs and slumped.

"What was that?" She said to herself. Again, in the distance, a sound rang out. A soft sound carried on the breeze. It sounded like a bell. A bell ringing. "A fucking bell," Shelby said as she started to count. "Six, seven, eight, nine and ten." She looked at her watch, 10 am. "What the...?"

"Hi, Shell," Lucy interrupted. Shelby spun around following the voice. Behind her, leaning against the car doing stretches, was Lucy.

"Lucy?"

"*Yep*, just thought I'd go for a *jog*. You know, give me time to think." She was touching her toes. Shelby's face was wrapped in surprise.

"Lucy, *no*, you can't just go for a *jog*."

"Why not? looks like you've just come back from a nice walk." She grabbed the back of her foot and pulled it to her butt.

"It's too fucking *dangerous* that's why not. You've got monsters out here that will think you're a moving fucking *popsicle*!"

"Moving popsicle, *ha!* No chance."

"Lucy, seriously, do you have a gun, a weapon?"

"My *speed*." She smiled, lengthening the word speed, as she stretched out her calves.

"Get in the car!" Said Shelby curtly, as she got in. Lucy followed.

"Have you got any water?" asked Lucy. Shelby looked like a stunned mullet.

"Are you *okay?*" she asked Lucy, sounding worried. Lucy suddenly went quiet. "Lucy, are you *alright?*" asked Shelby, again.

Lucy paused as she stared at Shelby. Her face started to change as she turned and looked down at her hands. "...I just... I just want everything to go back to normal!" Her voice lowered in a long, whiny tone. Her head fell into her hands. She was bawling.

"Oh, Lucy." Answered Shelby, not knowing what to say. She put her hand on Lucy's leg. Lucy came up with long strings of snot coming out of both nostrils.

"I just, I just..."

"Let it out, Lucy," said Shelby.

"I don't know what I'm doing, Shelby!" She broke down again. She came up. Her face was a mess. Tears streamed down her cheeks. "One minute... I'm doing *Tik Toks*, I'm looking for a boyfriend, a *handsome boyfriend*, the next minute... *I'm taking shit out in a bucket!*" Lucy was now crying uncontrollably. Shelby patted her leg.

"It's okay, it's okay, Lucy, we all feel that way, believe me, *believe me!*" she said, as Lucy laughed a little.

"I just... I'm looking after Pete and Charlie. Don't get me wrong, I love Pete and Charlie. But, we go for a nice drive and *almost get eaten by a huge, fluffy Mammoth*! It's a lot to take in, you know?"

"I know, *I know*, I'm there with you."

"Yes, you are," said Lucy, putting her hand on Shelby's. "Yes, you are." Shelby wiped Lucy's face.

"It's okay to go a little crazy every now and then Lucy, I just screamed out for your Dad."

"Did you?"

"I did."

"Did he answer?"

"No."

"Didn't think he would." They both started laughing.

"You know what though, Lucy?"

"What?"

"We are *fucking* alive," Shelby exclaimed. Lucy smiled.

"We are alive." Lucy whispered back. Shelby closed her eyes and put her hands in the air praising her words.

"You know how many people weren't given a *fucking* chance?"

"How many?"

"Zillions." Shelby smiled. Lucy laughed. "...And here we are. Say it with me, Lucy. *We are fucking alive!*"

"Do I have to swear, Shell?"

"Damn right."

"We... are fucking... alive." Lucy answered a fraction of a second off and was a little timid. Her hands were in the air also.

"Liberating, isn't it? Louder now! Like you mean it, Lucy!"

"We are fucking alive!" They were both roaring with laughter. Shelby brought her hands down and started beeping the horn.

"Louder!! We are fucking alive!!" A bird flew in front of the car, miles in the distance. Shelby couldn't stop her hand as she hit the horn loud and long. The bird turned its head and looked their way. It dived, on a vicious angle, swooping down low to gain speed. "Oh, shit," Shelby said in a low voice, her face suddenly falling serious. The bird's wings were getting wider and wider as it got closer.

"I'm never going running again," said Lucy quietly. "Start the car, Shelby! Start the car!" Shelby turned the key. The car wouldn't start. "Shelby! Shelby!" shouted Lucy.

"I'm trying! I'm trying!" shouted Shelby back. The bird landed on the roof. It felt like a rhino had just landed on the ceiling. The car roof started to bulge. "It's not working," whispered Shelby.

"We should run for it," said Lucy, holding the door handle. A pecking noise came from the roof. The ceiling suddenly started to look like someone was hammering nails.

"Don't you dare," whispered Shelby.

"Together! Shelby, we run together!" A large beak poked its way through the ceiling. Like a sharpened machete scything through butter. It narrowly missed Lucy's shoulder. "Stuff that, we're running!" said Lucy as she turned the handle.

"Lucy! We won't make it!" Shelby warned. Lucy turned and looked at Shelby, deadly serious.

"...We will." She turned the handle, opened the door and ran. *No.* Thought Shelby. She watched as Lucy became smaller and smaller in the distance. *Fuck, she's going to make it.* She felt the car lift a little. Like a weight had been lifted. Something was released and she heard the loud screech of the bird. Lucy was now out of sight.

"No, Lucy..." Shelby whispered to herself. Knowing it was only a matter of time. The bird's wings moved. The loud swooshing of powerful wings. A matter of time before the bird would catch its prey and Lucy would be dead.

Bang! bang! bang! Three shots rang out into the sky. A scream followed. It was Lucy. Shelby opened the door and looked above the damaged car roof.

"Well, looks like you owe me one!" said Steven, hanging out of his car. He had his cowboy hat on and aviators. He blew the nozzle of his rifle. "No need to thank me." He bowed with his hat off, placing it back on smiling. Shelby ran out from the back of the car. In the far distance, Lucy was on her butt. Trying to crawl her way out from under a huge shadow. The bird was at least the size of a car. Nature had magnificently painted it like a colourful parrot. Gorgeous, vibrant blues, purples and greens. But, its head was different. It was vicious, shaped like a creature not of the old world. It had three bleeding holes protruding from its back.

"Gross," said Lucy.

"You're alive." Shelby reminded her.

"Thanks to me," added Steven. Shelby said nothing.

"Want a *lift*, girls?" asked Steven, as he lifted his hat off his head. His blond hair was still perfect.

"What is it with you? Do you just drive up and down this road all day?" asked Shelby, rhetorically as she went back to the car and grabbed her satchel.

"Nice to see you again, Steven." Lucy said, in a musical manner as she swayed back to him, wiping her bottom. "Thanks for saving my life."

"It was nothing, *beautiful* lady." Replied Steven as he flew back into his car like a well trained stuntman. Lucy got in first, making sure to sit close to Steven, their shoulders rubbing together. Shelby, last on the three seater.

"Where to, ladies? Somewhere safe? *Back home with me?*"

"Ew," said Shelby.

"I'd Love to see your home." Answered Lucy, smiling dreamily. Steven smiled back as he started the car.

"Now, what are you girls doing out here by yourselves?"

"We were looking for Lucy's dad, mum and dog," Shelby answered curtly.

"Right, right, right," Said Steven, a toothpick hanging out of his mouth.

"You haven't seen them yet?" asked Shelby.

"No, haven't seen anyone, apart from you *two lovely ladies.*" Lucy laughed and patted Steven's arm. She noticed lean muscle. Looking up, she fluttered her eyelids. He smiled even more.

"This is us," said Shelby.

"*Wow*, that's right, just up the road," said Steven. He kept driving.

"You've *passed* the house," Shelby noted, looking back.

"*Look*, why don't you two come over for lunch? Come and meet the boys and the girl too. They'd love to meet you."

"Oh, that sounds so nice." Lucy smiled.

"Fucker..." Shelby had her gun out, pointing at Steven. "...Stop the *fucking* car." Steven stopped the car and put his hands up.

"Take it easy, little lady, just trying to be *hospitable.*"

"My names Shelby, and when I say stop, we *fucking stop*, get it?"

"Shelby!" yelled Lucy, shocked at the gun waving in front of her face.

"It's okay, Lucy. Shelby's right. I should'a stopped. Sorry Shelby."

"Come on, Lucy." Shelby backed up and opened the door.

"Sorry, Steven."

"It's okay, Lucy."

"Thanks again for saving my life." Lucy kissed Steven on the cheek and squeezed his arm.

"You're very welcome, *sweet lady*." Steven said as they both shared a huge smile.

"See you next time," said Lucy, blushing.

"Yes you will, yes you will." Said Steven as he waved. Shelby closed the door. "Be seeing you down the road." Steven said, leaning down and smiling.

"No, you won't," replied Shelby, bluntly as she placed her hand behind Lucy and ushered her back to the house. The car stayed still for a while before slowly driving off into the distance. Lucy watched it as it disappeared over the rise.

"He saved my life."

"He's a fucking *creep*."

"Shelby."

"Lucy."

"We *owe* him."

"We owe him *nothing!*" said Shelby, angrily as she pushed the gate open. They walked down the pathway, not saying anything to one another. Sitting in front of them at the door's entrance was Max. He didn't look very happy. His hands crossed and laid out on his knees. It looked like he'd been sitting there a long time.

"I need a *gun*," he said.

CHAPTER NINE

Numbers

O^{NE}

"You can't just *leave* like that." Max said, angrily, looking annoyed. Shelby and Lucy both looked shocked. "You need to talk to me first. I've got things planned and when you just *leave...*"

"What plans?" asked Shelby. Max gave Shelby a hard look, but didn't reply. Shelby regretted talking.

"Sorry," said Lucy.

"Me too," agreed Shelby, in an apologetic tone.

"I worry."

"We know," said Shelby.

"We gotta *stick together*."

"We were just *investigating*. It's what we *do*," said Shelby.

"Well, next time, *tell me*. If anything happens, I know where you are and maybe I can *help*."

"Aw, sweet," said Lucy, smiling.

Shelby kissed Max on the cheek. "Thanks for caring," she said as they walked into the house. Max sat on the doorstep for a while. His hand resting on his warm cheek.

Two

They sat around the kitchen table. Shelby and Lucy told Max what had happened. "We really need guns." He reaffirmed.

"You're right." Shelby agreed. "The main thing is though, *no sign* of Michael, Teresa or Pup."

"It's nearing two weeks," added Lucy, looking sad. Max said nothing, not wanting to bring the mood down even further. The chances of them being alive were slim. "Maybe our search needs to go *further into town*." Lucy proposed. Max was tapping the table again. Pete and Charlie were busy eating breakfast. They both looked like they'd just had showers, their hair combed neatly to the side.

"We could get your guns and do a search at the same time," suggested Shelby.

"We should just do a *search* today. It's already getting *late*." Max advocated.

"Wise," said Lucy.

"Okay, I've got to grab another car, but that's our plan. A drive around town and see what's out there?"

"Done." Max concurred.

"We need to get *back* before *four*," Shelby reminded the group. "Tim's coming over."

Three

Piling into a large ute that Shelby had found a few blocks away, they set off. Driving through the city streets was a reminder of just how things had changed. It was dead quiet. They didn't play music and weren't talking. The shops that were normally filled with bustling customers were empty and noiseless. Once busy streets were mostly vacant of cars due to the vanishing occurring at night.

"It's so *quiet*," said Pete.

"It really is." Shelby agreed.

"Look!" shouted Charlie. "A *McDonalds!*" It was a McDonalds that was overgrown with weeds. Some of the windows were smashed inward. Something had been inside it.

"Oh, I'd *love* a hamburger!" said Pete.

"Or nuggets!" added Charlie.

"Big Mac!" shouted Max.

"I don't know, they were starting to taste like *fucking plastic*," said Shelby, smiling.

"I'd eat a Big Mac right now." Lucy thought out loud.

"Yeah, *me too*," agreed Shelby, giving in.

"I'm *hungry*," said Pete, moaning, rubbing his little round tummy.

"I need to go to the *toilet*," added Charlie.

"Well, looks like that's the *end* of our excursion." Shelby said as she turned the car around.

"Shelby, look!" shouted Lucy, excitedly. "North City Plaza! *The mall!*" Shelby started nodding. "New clothes!" said Lucy, smiling broadly.

"New shoes!" added Shelby.

"Do they have a toilet?" asked Charlie.

"We're going home, Charlie," said Lucy.

"Oh, we're *not* going to the mall?"

"No, we'll come back tomorrow, Charlie, and check it out," said Max.

"Damn right!" exclaimed Lucy. "Oh, God, Glassons!"

"Shopping!" said Shelby, returning Lucy's joy. They drove back home, all feeling a little lighter. Like, they had something special to look forward to.

Four

"Tim! *My man*," said Max, feeling more secure in himself after Shelby's kiss on the cheek. He shook Tim's hand as he opened the door.

"Sir," said Tim, feeling a little shocked by the welcome.

"Had a good day?"

"Really good, thank you."

"Oh yeah, what made it so good?" asked Max, his mouth open.

"Well, I got the Bushmaster going."

"Bushmaster?"

"Yeah, she's a *beast*. Want to come out and take a look?"

"Hell yeah," said Max as he patted Tim on the shoulder. Shelby and Lucy smiled as Tim and Max walked outside, looking like two dads showing off their latest car.

"I want to *fucking* see this!" said Shelby as she ran out after them. Lucy carried on placing cans on the table. Outside, parked further down the road was an Australian Bushmaster.

Five

Checking to make sure it was safe to be outside they stood beside it, admiring it. The Bushmaster was a massive, camouflaged army off road vehicle. Tim had spray painted the side with the words, *The Beast*. "Like her?"

"*Love* her," Max said.

"She's pretty quick, a bit noisy, but I feel safe inside her," explained Tim.

"That's what she said," Shelby quipped, smiling at both Tim and Max. Max laughed, not expecting such a remark. Tim stayed deadly serious.

"How fast does she go?" asked Max.

"Hundred," answered Tim. "But, if I run into trouble, I can *shoot* whatever it is off the face of the earth and if it's a big mother, well, I'll just sit inside till they get bored and leave. She's *blast-resistant*."

"Sounds like a plan, Stan," said Shelby, walking back to the house.

"How many can you get inside?" asked Max as they walked back to the house.

"Ten soldiers."

"I've been meaning to ask you, Tim... we need *weapons*."

"Well, sir, you're talking to the right man," replied Tim, beaming.

"You can call me, Max, you know." Max suggested, his arm hanging over Tim's shoulder.

"Thank you, sir." Tim answered.

Tim and Max had suddenly taken over the table conversation. Talking about their favourite movies, TV shows and comics. When video games were brought up it was all over and Shelby and Lucy excused themselves to the lounge playing a Harry Potter board game they'd found with Pete and Charlie.

"Tim's offered us a lift to the mall tomorrow," shouted Max, smiling. "On the way through, he'll stop off at the base and grab us some weapons!"

"Listen to those two," whispered Shelby to Lucy. "Best of *friends*."

"I know, isn't it *cool*," whispered Lucy back.

"...For a guy who doesn't want to get attached, he sure does get *attached*."

"He can't help it," said Lucy. "What you said before, *heart of gold*." Shelby nodded as the boys laughed out loud about some joke Max had said. After a few hours, the sun had disappeared and night had quickly crept in. Max offered to put the two boys to bed. They kissed and hugged everybody, including Tim, before going up the stairs. They all sat in the lounge which was now pitch black.

Six

"You know, I can turn the lights on back at base," said Tim.

"Really?" asked Lucy.

"Yeah, there's a basement, no windows. Games room. I've pretty much made it into my *man cave*."

"Wow," said Lucy.

"I've got a generator, so I've got TVs and games."

"Michael would *love* it," said Shelby, smiling. Lucy looked over, sadly.

"The boys would love it too," Lucy added.

"You guys should stay one night," Tim suggested.

"We will." Shelby replied. "Funny, I don't miss technology. Better without it, in fact."

"We *wasted* a lot of time," said Tim.

"A *lot* of time." Shelby agreed.

"Shall we light a rocket?" suggested Lucy.

"A what?" asked Tim.

"A firework. We light one every night so Michael and Teresa can see it." Lucy said.

"Michaels got an attachment with fireworks. He'd know it's us straight away." Shelby said, winking at Lucy.

"Sounds like you're lighting a candle for dinner." Tim said.

"Why?" asked Shelby.

"Well, you do remember there are creatures out there that want us for *dinner*? Sounds like you're lighting a candle and we are the *dessert*."

"It's only one," said Lucy.

"Where are you going to do it?" asked Tim.

"We usually do it upstairs, but the kids are up there now. *Outside*?" suggested Shelby.

"Yeah, okay, I've got my gun, but we just light it and shoot back inside, okay?" offered Tim.

"I'll grab the rocket and Max," said Lucy as she ran upstairs.

Seven

Shelby and Tim walked out the back. The night was bright and brilliant. There was not a cloud in the sky and the stars were twinkling. They sat on two wooden chairs, admiring the sky. "Good to see the backyard is fenced," whispered Tim.

"It's *good* to have you around, Tim," said Shelby. "We feel... *safer*."

"Thank you, ma'am, it's nice to be around people, *good people*." Shelby smiled. "It's one *spectacular* night." Tim whispered as he looked up at the bright sky. "A shooting star." Noticed Tim as he pointed at the sky. "Quick, make a *wish*."

"I wish... that it's not a *fucking meteorite* that's going to blow up the *fucking world*, cause it *probably fucking is*," whispered Shelby, smiling.

Tim smiled, "You're probably right."

"Tim, if you don't mind me asking," Tim looked over, interested, but not looking at Shelby's face. "Why, don't you look at people's faces and call us by our names? Is it because you don't want to get *attached*?"

Tim crossed his fingers over his belly, like someone deep in thought. "It's true, I've *lost* a lot of people since the vanishing."

"How many?" asked Shelby.

"Seven." Answered Tim, he sat forward in his chair. "I don't want to add more, Shelby." Shelby nodded. "But, that's not the only reason."

"Oh?" said Shelby, wanting to know more.

"Yeah, I like you ma'am. You don't mince words and you're *honest*."

"Best way to be," Shelby said, smiling.

"I see *numbers*."

"You *see* numbers?"

"Yes, since the vanishing, I don't know why. But, I see numbers above people's faces."

"Numbers? Like what? *birthdays*?"

"No, like, *days left*."

"Days left?"

"Yes." Tim started to lean towards Shelby, His right elbow resting on the chair arm. Like he had something important to say. "When I first met Mrs Chamberlain, I saw the number seven. She died seven days later. When I saw Mr Lee, he had twenty four."

"Shit," said Shelby, stunned. "That's horrible."

"It is, but I can *improve* them, or others can I've noticed. When I suggest things or help, the numbers can go *up*."

"What are my numbers?" asked Shelby.

"I'd rather not say."

"Come on," Shelby said, sounding frustrated.

"Would you really want to *know*?" asked Tim, his face wise beyond his years.

Shelby paused, thinking. "No." She answered. "But, the others, Pete, Charlie, Max... Lucy?" Shelby looked worried.

"Their numbers have been going up, yes." Tim noted, in his most positive way.

"Have you looked in the mirror?"

Tim smiled, "You're quick... no, not lately. I try not to look in the mirror. The knowledge would... probably *kill* me."

"My God."

"I know," said Tim, looking over at Shelby. "You *believe* me?"

"There's monsters roaming the earth and everyone has vanished. *Yes*, I believe you."

"That's why, I don't want to get attached. The first thing I see is your death notice." Shelby looked down in thought. When she looked up, her eyes were pooling with water.

"Tim... Charlie, Pete, Max, oh, my God, Lucy...*how long*?"

Tim looked up at the sky, thinking of his next answer. "Keep them close, keep them safe. Keep them *happy*," he said. Shelby's hand went up to her open mouth.

Lucy walked in. "Got it! And Max."

"Fireworks eh? Jesus, it's like we're back to *normal*." Said Max, walking outside and sitting by Tim. Tim smiled at Shelby, while she struggled not to cry.

"Alright, who wants to light it?" asked Lucy.

"Let Max *do* it," said Shelby, quickly trying to hide the emotion in her voice. "Have some *fun*!"

Max smiled, with a... okay then, look on his face. Tim watched on without saying a word. "Lighter please," Max requested.

Shelby whispered into Tim's ear. "They're not *fucking dying* on my watch."

Tim smiled. "Or *mine*, ma'am."

The wick lit and burst into flame as the rocket flew into the air. A sparkle of red and blue lights filled the sky, with the friends all looking up and smiling. Shelby put her arm around Max.

"Nice job, sir Max." She said as she kissed his cheek.

Eight

Upstairs, Pete was lying on his side, looking out the window. "You *awake*, Charlie?"

"No," replied Charlie.

"You *see* that, Charlie?"

"I *see* it." Charlie answered.

"It's *beautiful*."

"Sure is, Pete."

"They're lighting fireworks without us, Charlie." The sparks outside were lighting up their faces. Both of them had their mouths wide open. "I *love* fireworks, Charlie."

"Me too, Pete."

"Why wouldn't they invite us?"

"I don't know," answered Charlie, looking a little down.

"It's finished," said Pete. They both lay quietly in their beds, waiting for more. Nothing happened. They heard whispered voices downstairs and a door closing. The night went quiet.

"Goodnight Charlie."

"Goodnight Pete."

Pete was asleep within a couple of minutes. Charlie, on the other hand, was awake most of the night. Feeling sad for Pete and also re-imagining the firework in his head, over and over.

CHAPTER TEN

Birthdays

"LIVE NOT ONE'S LIFE AS THOUGH ONE HAD A THOUSAND YEARS, BUT LIVE EACH DAY AS THE LAST." MARCUS AURELIUS.

S HELBY SAT AT THE dining table working on her poem. It was early morning and the house was alive with activity. Tim had slept in the lounge, (in his uniform, with his gun on his chest) while Pete and Charlie were already downstairs trying to make breakfast. "Good morning, *Shelby*." Pete greeted.

"Morning Pete, good sleep?"

"Pretty good, thank you." Shelby smiled at Pete.

"Morning *Shelby*," said Charlie.

"Morning Charlie, good sleep?"

"No."

"Oh," answered Shelby, surprised at Charlie's individual response.

"We *missed* the fireworks." Charlie noted, looking a little unhappy.

"Oh, well, there was only *one*," Shelby said. Charlie looked away. Shelby looked at Pete. "*Just* one." Pete looked away. "Guys, *come on*." Implored Shelby, with her arms spread wide, pleading innocence.

Tim walked into the kitchen, stretching.

"Morning Tim," said Pete, as Tim passed him.

"Morning Tim." Charlie said, both boys failing to pass on their disappointment to Tim. They both got off their chairs and walked to the kitchen bench. Grabbing a box of crackers, they walked into the lounge and sat together eating.

"What the...?" said Shelby, feeling a little hurt.

"Looks like they're *working* you," said Tim, smiling.

"Little rascals."

"They must have seen the rocket." Tim mused.

"Yeah, but it's too *dangerous* for them to be around when we light it."

"Agreed." Tim nodded. "Should we do something else for them?"

"Maybe." Shelby replied, thinking.

Max walked into the room smiling. "Hey guys, how's the poem going, Shell?"

"Not bad Max, finding inspiration."

"Sounds good, when can we hear it?"

"It's not really for reading out loud." Shelby said, shyly.

"You're a poet and I didn't even know it." Said Max, smiling.

"Mmm, talent right there," replied Shelby.

"Morning boys!" said Max, noticing they were unusually quiet. The boys sat staring vacantly into space, eating their crackers. They didn't answer. Max sat down next to Shelby and Tim joined them. Lucy walked in noticing the meeting and sat down at the table also.

"Everything *okay*?" Lucy whispered, noticing something was up.

Shelby sat forward. "The boys saw the firework last night. I think they feel like they *missed out*."

"Ohhh," said Lucy and Max at the same time.

"You know..." Shelby straightened herself up like she had a great idea. "Michael once celebrated my *birthday* and it really helped *perk me up*."

"How long ago was that?" asked Max.

"About a year."

"Well, we should *celebrate it again*."

"*No*, not me silly, *the boys*," Shelby pointed towards Pete and Charlie, who looked miserable while eating their crackers. Lucy nodded, smiling. Tim nodded like he thought it was a great idea. "You know, make their days... *happy*." Shelby lost emotion as her voice cracked and Lucy wondered why.

"Hey Pete?" said Max.

"Yeah?"

"When's your *birthday*?"

"Don't know."

"Hey Charlie?"

"Yeah?"

"When's your *birthday*?"

"Don't know." Pete and Charlie started to smile.

"Ha, ha, Charlie doesn't know when his birthday is." Said Pete, laughing and pointing at Charlie.

"You don't know *either*." Said Charlie, pointing back.

"Wait, no, I was two, no, three when Mum *disappeared* so, that means I'm three now, wait, *no*, that was a year ago..."

"...So, it must be your birthday *today*!" said Max.

"Oh, is *it?! Hooray!*" Said Pete, totally forgetting he was trying to play sad.

"...And *yours* too, Charlie!" Added Max, smiling. Charlie's mouth and eyes opened wide.

"Oh, no way, same *day* as Pete!" Pete started jumping up and down.

"It's our birthday, it's our birthday, *it's our birthday!*" Charlie joined in as they did circles around the lounge.

"They look happy, do we need to do *anything else*?" asked Max. Shelby punched his shoulder.

"Any ideas?" whispered Lucy, leaning forward.

"I've got a games room back at base, TV, video games all on generator." Tim suggested in a hushed tone.

"Nice." Lucy praised, nodding slowly.

"We could stay there for a while and then head over to the mall," suggested Shelby.

"Toys!" said Lucy.

"Toys for the *boys*," Shelby replied, nodding.

"You should *write* a poem," said Max, dryly. Shelby punched him.

"You can all fit in the Bushmaster, and we'll pick up some weapons for you on the way," Tim said.

"Sounds like a plan, Stan." Shelby nodded, getting up.

"You know you're really good at this rhyming thing," Max pointed out, smiling. Shelby punched him again.

"Hey boys! Who wants to *play* video games!" shouted Shelby.

"Me!" the boys yelled back.

The house was full of excitement as the boys got themselves dressed for a day out. Max told them it was a special day so they should look their best and they did. Tim and Shelby waited downstairs at the table while Lucy got herself ready.

"It's like a *normal* day," Shelby said, smiling at Tim.

"Funny how a normal day can be so *special*. It's a nice thing you've done," Tim replied.

"Well, after our talk, I feel like we should make every day *count*." Tim nodded in agreement as his rifle rested across his legs. Large footsteps could be heard pounding down the stairs as the boys came running into the kitchen, jumping at Tim and Shelby. "Oh, so much *happiness!*" said Shelby, laughing.

"Shelby! We're going to play video games!" said Pete as he danced a jig.

Charlie joined in, "...and billiards."

"...and darts," added Pete.

"...and we're going to the mall," said Charlie.

"...and we can pick as many toys as we *want!*"

"Wow, wow, wow, maybe one or two," said Shelby, smiling, "but, you can *play* with as many as you want."

"Can *we*?" asked Pete.

"Yep."

"Oh *boy!*" said Pete, jumping for joy. Max came in and lifted Pete into the air. Tim did the same with Charlie. Lucy came running down the stairs dressed to kill. She had make-up on and huge hoop earrings. Shelby did the wolf whistle sound.

"You never know who we might *see*," Lucy said, blushing as she noticed everyone looking at her. Tim led them out as they were all shouting and cheering. At the back, Max whispered into Shelby's ear.

"*Thank you!* I've never seen them so *happy*."

Shelby patted Max's back, too emotional to say anything. She then punched him for good measure as they closed the door and skipped towards the Bushmaster army vehicle.

CHAPTER ELEVEN

Tim's Man Cave

"MUSIC, *MAESTRO*?" ASKED LUCY, sitting in the front seat next to Tim.

"Sure ma'am, I've got my old MP3 player wired up to the stereo."

"You've got all *official* when you're in your *big* army vehicle," smiled Lucy. Tim blushed a little. Behind them sat Pete and Charlie. They both looked incredibly small in the oversized seats. Both still smiling, seatbelts held loosely around their waists. Behind them, Max and Shelby were busy in conversation. The truck was pretty quiet considering it was built like a tank. "Pick us something *happy!*" said Lucy, placing her legs up on the dashboard.

Outside the sun was shining. It was still early in the morning. Tim multitasked as he swerved, missing a large bus and chose a song. *Paint it Black,* by The Rolling Stones, started playing. Tim started smiling and nodding his head up and down. "Oh *yeah!*

Tim!" said Lucy as she joined in. Little Pete and Charlie raised their arms laughing. Shelby and Max still carried on their conversation.

The music came to a stop as they drove up a long stretch of road. No houses were in sight. Outside, they noticed a rather large bird fly close to the vehicle. It's eye trying to look inside. Everyone started to feel a little unsafe. It glided next to them, almost like it was part of the truck. It couldn't see in due to the reflected glass. Giving up on its curiosity it screeched at the truck and tapped the glass. The glass stayed firm. It then flew up and away. A slight unease settled on the day trippers.

"How about *this*?" shouted Tim. *Toot toot chugga chugga, big red car,* rang out from the speakers.

"*Greg*! It's Greg, Charlie! *The yellow wiggle!*" shouted Pete, excitedly. He started to sing along. Charlie didn't recognise the name but he knew the song as he sang along too. In the back, Shelby and Max stopped their conversation and started vigorously pointing, singing along as well.

"Nice *save*," said Lucy as she started singing also.

They finally made it to the army base. Tim stopped outside a large gate. "Won't be a second." He pulled his gun out from under the seat and ran out to the side of the gate. Shelby could hear the *hut, hut, huts,* again as he ran. He unlocked a large padlock and pulled the gate open. Checking both ways, with his gun ready, he made it back to the truck. Driving in, he stopped the truck and did the same, but in reverse. "Pay's to be *secure*."

"Definitely," Lucy replied. "Ever get any *weird* creatures in here?"

"No, ma'am, not the *walking* kind." Lucy looked up in the sky, remembering her encounter with the bird previously. The sky was blue with no clouds, and no birds. Tim parked up outside a large building that looked almost like a school. He opened his door, "I'll take cover. The door is open, so make your way in *quickly*." Said Tim as he crouched outside the vehicle, his gun moving in all directions.

Pete and Charlie hopped out first. Oblivious to any danger, they were talking about video games they'd played. Lucy ushered them quickly inside. Shelby and Max next.

"All *clear*, Rambo!" shouted Shelby as she held the door open for Tim.

"Thank you, ma'am." Tim said appreciatively, as he closed the door and locked it. Pete and Charlie were running ahead. "Stay *close!*" He shouted as he moved to the front of the group. "As you can see, there are too many windows to board up. The perimeter is *safe*, but not *secure* till we get downstairs. Follow me. Lucy, if you could please *look after* the boys." Lucy grabbed the boy's hands. Tim upfront was checking behind doors and waving the team forward.

"He's *very good*." Whispered Max to Shelby. "A little *over the top*." He added.

"He probably has reason to be." Said Shelby as Tim waved them downstairs. The large hallway became darker the further they went.

"Stop!" he commanded, holding up his fist. The group all huddled together, expecting some monster to come charging from the other end. Tim turned to a box on the wall and threw up some switches. Suddenly, the hallway was bathed in light. Pete and Charlie blinked and rubbed their eyes. "Follow me," Tim said as he hut, hutted down the hallway. For some reason, the group followed him in rows of two, and were almost in sync with his footsteps.

They arrived at a large door that read, blast room. Maximum, forty people. "These blast shelters were built in the forties. Built to last. Once the door is shut, no one can get in. *Safest* place to be," explained Tim. The boys were eager to see what was on the other side. Tim punched in some numbers and the door opened releasing a blast of air. Shelby wished she'd paid notice to the sequence. "Welcome," said Tim. He flicked on the lights and the room's fluorescents came to life. He then walked around the room turning on lamps. Once the lamps were on with their soft glow, he turned off the fluorescents. "Takes off the *harsh,* cold feeling, gives it a bit of *warmth,*" he said to Lucy.

"I like it, *Mr House and Garden.*" an impressed Lucy offered. The room was massive. Like a small factory. One side was filled with brick and gave the large room an almost apartment-like feel. The rest were grey concrete blocks.

"This used to be a bunker, back in the day. Don't think it was ever used, but it was pretty bare. I had to use my *imagination* a bit."

"You've done *well*, commando." Shelby said as she eyed the huge, soft leather lounge suite in the middle of the room. The boys were already swimming in its vastness. A large furry rug lay in front of it. Max was admiring the two large flat screen TVs Tim had placed beside each other.

"Two screens, Tim?" asked Max, smiling.

"I like to multi-task. Usually, I have a movie on while I play PlayStation."

"*Oh*, you've got a PlayStation? *Which one?*" asked Pete, looking wide eyed.

"The *best* one." Tim promised, smiling. "PlayStation One. I'm afraid, without the network working it's just back to basics. Took me a long time to find a PlayStation One and games. I'm trying to build up a bit of a game station set up here."

"Nice Tim," Max praised.

"The screens are ninety inches," Tim shared proudly. "Soundbar is wireless. But *kicks ass*. Had to stick to Blu-rays for movies. No internet of course, but I've got the best, *Platoon, Full Metal Jacket, Apocalypse Now, Shrek.*"

"*Shrek?*" asked Lucy, smiling.

"Yep, nothing but the *best*." Tim reaffirmed, straight-faced.

"Michael would *love* this," Shelby said with a smile.

"He sounds like *my type of guy*," Tim said. "Come on, birthday boys, what do you want to *play* first? *Crash Bandicoot?*"

"*Yeah*, Crash..." Pete said, happily. The boys were happily playing game after pixelated game. Shouting and cheering without worry, it did feel like a normal day. Pete and Charlie were crawling over Tim and Max, they all looked like one happy family. Lucy and Shelby sat back on the huge table Tim had placed by a makeshift kitchen, consisting of a gas cooker, microwaves, fridges, plus a large, stand alone freezer.

"Help yourselves!" shouted Tim as he concentrated hard on a four player game of Toy Story. Shelby and Lucy opened the fridges.

"Oh, my God... *Coke*," said Lucy.

"He's got pies, pizzas and vegetables!" Shelby noted, astounded.

"Grow my own! Plus, the army freezer is stocked with food. Enough for decades. Just gotta keep it running, *gotcha!*" Tim called as he shot Pete's car, Woody. They opened the freezer.

"Chickens, sausages, chops, mince. You've got *everything!*" A shocked Shelby managed.

"Well, I'm happy to share, ma'am. *Best* to give back," Tim responded, still concentrating.

"Nice one, Pete!" Max hollered.

"Thanks Max, you're doing so well, Charlie." Pete said, encouragingly. Charlie didn't answer, he was leaning to the right, trying to help his car turn a sharp bend. Shelby and Lucy sat back down. Lucy with her Coke and Shelby with a can of V energy drink.

"This is too much," Shelby said.

"You notice the bunks?" asked Lucy. Tim had a huge king size bed against one of the grey walls. It was made perfectly in military style. To the side were four bunks with enough bed room for eight people. "Looks like there were more people here at some stage," said Lucy.

"More stories," replied Shelby as she grabbed out her poem.

"Inspired?" Asked Lucy.

"By *kindness*," answered Shelby as she started to write.

The day quickly left them as they enjoyed Tim's hospitality. The mall had long since been forgotten. Tim made them a huge lunch. They gave the games a miss in the afternoon and watched *Shrek*. Tim followed this with a huge dinner. They then played more games in the evening, followed by Pete and Charlie's last pick of the night, since they were the *birthday boy's* of Ratatouille. After the movie finished they all felt especially positive.

"Can we go to the mall now?" Pete asked, through half baked eyes.

Lucy laughed. "Tomorrow, birthday boy."

"But, it's our birthday *today*." Pete reminded the group, rubbing his tired eyes.

"We'll celebrate it *tomorrow* as well." Lucy explained.

"Oh, good," Charlie said before leading the charge for the boys to hop into their bed bunks. They fell asleep quickly in their clean, crisp white sheets.

"Thanks Tim," whispered Shelby as they sat around the table.

"Your welcome, ma'am." Tim replied, still not looking at her face.

"The boy's had a great day, Tim," Max followed, tapping the table.

"We *all* did," added Lucy.

"You're all welcome. It helps me as much as it helps you," Tim said. "...And you're all more than welcome to stay as long as you like."

"Aw, Tim." Lucy responded, placing her hand on his arm.

"It does get lonely in here."

"Even for a soldier?" asked Shelby.

"More so," Tim answered. "I don't know about you guys, but you start to hear things, see things, you start *talking to yourself.*"

"I do that anyway." Shelby said, smiling.

"We all do," said Max, agreeing.

"Well, the offer is there. I have security, comfort and more food than you could ask for." Tim looked down at the table, waiting for an answer. No one answered.

"Thank you Tim, that's very kind of you." Lucy responded, finally breaking the awkward silence.

"Well, big day tomorrow, Got to *spoil* these boys some more." Shelby yawned as she stretched for the ceiling.

As they slept the only sound was the sound of a small vent letting in air.

They all slept soundly, except for Shelby. Her mind was full of dreams of Michael. Wounded and making his way to the broken car. He was calling for her but she was not there.

"Where are you Shelby?" he called. "...How could you leave me?"

CHAPTER TWELVE

Days Without Incident

T IM WOKE BEFORE EVERYONE else. He made his bed, tucking in the sheets tightly and he smoothed out the creases, his hands like irons. Today was important. Today was his first day. His head felt cold. Freshly buzzed on the sides and back with a flat top making him feel like soldiers he'd seen at the movies. He'd seen them all and had them sitting proudly on his shelf at home. *Apocalypse Now, Saving Private Ryan, Platoon, Full Metal Jacket, 1917, Inglorious Bastards, The Hurt Locker, Edge of Tomorrow, The Dirty Dozen,* even *Tropic Thunder* had pride of place. You name it, he had it. Not to mention the war comics and novels he had collected. He was a walking encyclopaedia of history and information. He loved it with a passion. His dad and mum did not.

His dad, a top surgeon in the Wellington region, wanted him to be a doctor. His dad had fought hard to be a successful doctor.

Coming from Asia he had to register again to be a practising doctor in New Zealand, not to mention the difficulty he had just being recognised. Little did his dad know it was him putting on a movie one night that changed everything for young, impressionable Tim. The movie was *Dunkirk*. It moved Tim, made him feel like helping. From that day he wanted to be a soldier.

His mum was very much like his dad. Hard working and motivated. She was an accountant. She had a good job working in a good practice in Hawai'i when she met Tim's father online. Next thing she knew, they were an item and she was living in Wellington, New Zealand. She had a good job at KPMG and wished her son would pick up something that would pay good money, as she put it. But she was not as disappointed as his father when they found out he wanted to be in the army. She was just happy that he had a passion and she knew that with passion would come success. She convinced her husband to sign the forms so Tim could join the army at such a young age. Without consent from his parents, he wouldn't have been able to do it. But they signed the forms and that began his journey.

He sat on the edge of his bed. Still only clothed in his army white singlet, Y-fronts and white socks. His hands were tingling. He was nervous. He didn't want to disappoint. Not on his first day. He had trained so hard for this. Press ups and sit ups every day. The regulation 2.4 km run, every morning. Only last month he was able to finally do thirty pull ups. He was ready. He knew he wouldn't disappoint. In fact he would exceed.

He sat smoothing out his sheets. His hands pushed out the non-existent creases like sand. The room was massive. There were at least a hundred bunk beds holding two hundred recruited soldiers. The room was full of shades of grey and shadows. He brushed his forehead with the back of his hand. Nervous thoughts filled his mind. *Am I up too early?* It was 5:30 am. *Will they tell me off for making my bed before everyone else?* He didn't want to disappoint. He was so nervous he'd failed to notice the absence of bulges of bodies under blankets. Now he saw it. The many beds are unmade. Surely they would have to make their beds before they'd got up. He looked around quickly. Checking other beds, they were the same. He stood up, checking the bunk above him. Davey, the optimistic boy who gripped his hand like a vice, was gone. *Oh, shit,* he thought. *Did I miss it? Did I miss the call?* The Sergeant walking into the room and screaming at everybody to get outside and to drop and give him fifty. *Did I sleep through it?*

He walked out into the centre of the room between the two long rows of bunks. All the beds were empty, every single one. He ran outside the dorm, sprinting into the cold morning. The sun was barely over the hill. Hoping to see the team running around the army camp. There was no one. He ran into the next dorm. Everything was exactly the same. He hurried to the office. The place where he'd first met Miss Willaby. She had signed him in. The door wouldn't open. The office, empty. *What's going on?* He thought. *Where is everybody? Some parade? Some morning parade in remembrance of something?* Dates were going through his head. *Did I miss something last night?* He searched the whole compound and found no one. He felt sick. Sick in his stomach. He vomited. At no stage did he think everyone had vanished. How could you? That would be crazy. His mind was coming up with other scenarios.

He ran to the main gate. Looked up and down the street. No one. No cars. The gate was secured by a digital keypad and swipe card. There were no officers in the office directly to the left of the gate. He went back in and sat on his bed. At some stage they would be back. They must come back. He sat and patiently waited. *I'm in trouble,* he thought, *so much trouble.* By noon he was searching the compound again. By 1400 hours he was over the fence and dashing down the street. At 1600 hours he had decided everyone was gone. He didn't sleep that night. He walked and walked, searching the town. Trying to find someone, anyone. That evening, when he got back to the barracks he wrote his first of many incident reports because everything had to be done by the book.

22/1/27
Everyone is *gone*! Searched the local streets and town.
Days without incident, 0.

23/1/27
Rang mum and dad. No answer.
Grabbed a vehicle and searched in a 10 km radius.
No sight of anyone. Mum and dad's house is empty.
I think everyone has *disappeared*.
Days without incident,1.

24/1/27
Rang important numbers today. No answers.
Packed a bag. Will do a week long trip.
I haven't mentioned this, but I see a *number* on my forehead when I look in the mirror.

Days without incident, 2.

31/1/27

Arrived back. Found no one.

Drove up the North Island, as far as Whangarei.

Lots of empty cars. Shops empty.

Good things: Food is still good.

Free shopping. Plenty of everything just for me.

Bad thing, found no one. I think mum and dad are *dead*.

Days without incident, 9.

5/2/27

Searching through Wellington over the last week.

Nothing and no one. Not even animals.

Power still going.

The number on my forehead is going down.

Days without incident, 14.

14/2/27

Met Mrs Chamberlain. *First person*!

She was walking out looking for her paper.

She has no idea what's going on.

She has a number too. It was blurry.

Coming in and out of focus. I think I'm going nuts. It was the number 7.

Days without incident, 23.

16/2/27

Brought Mrs Chamberlain some groceries.

Her number still is going down the same as mine.

It says 5. I'm hearing clicks and noises at night.

Saw a massive shadow moving on the hill.

Investigated it but found nothing.

Aliens? Monsters? It didn't look human at all.

I think *I'm going crazy*.

Days without incident, 25.

18/2/27

Saw a guy in town at the local comic store.

He noticed me watching him.

He was searching through the comics.

He wore glasses, was unshaven, slightly pudgy and looked a little under the weather.

As soon as he saw me he grabbed his comics and ran down the street.

Comics were flying everywhere.

I watched him as he fell over a few times.

He picked himself up and then kept running.

Looked like he pulled his hamstring as he started limping. It was pretty funny.

He obviously didn't want to chat, so I just let him go.

Might catch up with him another time, who knows? No biggy.

Note: I checked the comics he dropped.

One was a Superman #1 (Summer 1939) I reckon that might be worth something?

Days without incident, 27.

21/2/27

Found Mrs Chamberlain *eaten*. Found her slipper with her foot in it, bitten off at the ankle.

She must have walked outside at night. Maybe she heard something.

I warned her. Hearing more strange noises.

Found a nest of eggs outside the base. Burnt them with the flamethrower.

The world is changing.

Days without incident, 0.

22/2/27

A man was screaming outside the gate.

I ran out but he was gone. I found him later, he was decomposed by some *acidic liquid*.

Just his top half remained.

Days without incident, 0.

22/3/27

Met Mr Lee today. He's on the third level of the Newtown Apartments.

Real nice guy. Made me the best soup ever.

He's very wise and he has ideas on what's happening.

His number is 14. When I said I'd come back it changed to 17?

Days without incident, 29.

23/3/27

On my way to Mr Lee was chased by some small spiders.

Creepy. About the size of cats. Little things work in packs.

Luckily I had the flame thrower. Mr Lee said this is our *reckoning*.
The bad karma we gave to the earth is balancing it out.
Brought him some groceries. He's given me a list of the best stuff
he wants. I like him.
Days without incident, 30.

25/3/27
On my way back from Mr Lee, I bumped into a lady.
She had the number 0 on her forehead.
Before I could talk to her something grabbed her from below.
It pulled her into the ground.
It happened so quickly I couldn't see what it was.
I was walking on soft soil by the water's edge. *Stay on concrete.*
Days without incident, 0.

6/4/27
Gotten Mr Lee's numbers up to 30. Definitely think that's the
number of days he has left.
The more I'm around him, the higher the number goes.
He's teaching me some self defence. He can do anything.
My number goes up around him.
Days without incident, 12.

8/4/27
Saw a guy driving around in a Suzuki Swift.
Couldn't quite make him out as he was going so fast.
Idiot, he needs to be careful as cars are everywhere on the road.
Maybe I'll start moving some of these vehicles out of the way.
With nutters like him driving around it's very dangerous.

Days without incident, 14.

12/4/27

Sick of driving around cars. Decided to start parking cars neatly
to the side.
Saves me time in the long run. Wherever I go, that's what I'll do.
No need to thank me, Suzuki Swift guy.
Days without incident, 18.

13/5/27

Mr Lee's numbers have halved. He was talking about ghosts.
About seeing his wife for the first time in years. He was crying.
He thinks it's a sign. A sign that he must go.
I don't want him to leave. He's taught me so much.
Days without incident, 49.

14/5/27

Mr Lee's numbers halved again. I can't stop them.
He went for a walk last night. He said he'd taken on some creature
that was his size.
He killed it with his bare hands, but had also seen his wife.
He sounds crazy. Said he's going to do it again tonight.
Days without incident, 50.

15/5/27

I arrived just before the sun went down. Mr Lee was still home.
I begged him to stay. He said it's his time. I went with him anyway.
We walked through the town at *night*! I was so freaking scared.
He had no shoes on and was dressed in some ceremonial garment.

He had no weapons with him. I knew he'd be safe as his number reads 3.

But, I don't know if I can keep him alive.

Days without incident, 51.

17/5/27

Mr Lee is *dead*. One day ahead of schedule.

I was ready to do anything to save him.

My number reading is not working, or he did something to speed up the process.

His door was open. When I looked over the balcony I saw remains. On closer observation it looked like human remains but was hard to tell.

Days without incident, 0.

16/6/27

No sign of Mr Lee. Have started taking care of myself.

Set myself up in the blast room. My numbers changed straight away.

Bit of work, but it's worth it.

My numbers look good, but have decided not to look in the mirror or my reflection anymore as it messes with my brain.

Days without incident, 30.

26/6/27

Met Doc today. Doctor Stanley. Indian fellow. He's *very funny*. Everything seems like a joke to him. He asked me why I have a *mullet*.

Said it made me look like a hooligan. Just saw him driving down the road.

Like nothing was going on. He said he was busy going to an appointment.

"What appointment?" I asked. "An appointment to meet you, obviously," he said.

He's a good cook. Cooks the real stuff. Tasty. Another good man to meet.

Days without incident, 40.

29/6/27

Doc is teaching me simple first aid. Good knowledge to have. Brought him back to base. He was impressed. He wants to go home though.

His numbers are the best I've seen so far.

Days without incident, 43.

30/6/27

Doc lost his whole family. Wife and two boys.

It's pretty hard for him, you wouldn't know it as he keeps joking around.

But, today I saw it. For the first time. He also reminded me of my dad.

Asked, what was I doing wasting my time trying to be a soldier.

Medicine is the way.

I told him, I like to help people in my own way.

He said, your way or my way, at least we are trying to help.

My dad would never say that.

Days without incident, 44.

13/7/27

Had one of those freaky creatures sting me last week. Made it to
Doc's.

He put me on a drip and filled me up with antibiotics.

He said, you seem to be getting better, now we just have to take
care of the insects growing in your *belly*.

He's got such a bad sense of humour.

Days without incident, 57.

20/7/27

Doc wasn't home again. Haven't seen him since he fixed me.

He gave me no warning that he was going away. Where is he?

Days without incident, 64.

26/8/27

Seen no one for a long time. Could I be *the last man on Earth?*
Starting to think so.

The creatures now outside are numerous. It's very dangerous. Especially at night.

There's a lot of activity after dark. During the day it's reasonably
safe. *Weapons are essential.*

Days without incident, 71.

29/9/27

Had a couple of beasts roaming through the streets.

Huge things. I was sitting outside the bucket fountain on Cuba
Street.

I tried to hide but they could smell me I'm sure.

Let off a few rounds into the air and that scared them off. If I didn't have my rifle I would have been lunch.

They may be big but they are also fast.

Days without incident, 105.

14/10/27

Doc's back. Went for a holiday! Can you believe it?

The worlds gone to shit and he goes for a holiday.

Man, I love the guy. He's so funny.

He went to Taupo, Rotorua, Hamilton, came back over through Tauranga, Napier and finally Hastings before coming home again.

Said he didn't want to rush. Said, why do you need to go overseas when we live in such a *beautiful country*.

He actually said, I need to see New Zealand first before going overseas.

Nutter, how the hell am I going to go overseas?

Days without incident, 120.

24/10/27

Doc's been telling me all about his trip. Each day I go over there he cooks me a different dish.

I bring him the ingredients from the base. He's very lucky. He managed to avoid being killed so many times.

He's seen a lot more creatures than me. His descriptions are so vivid.

Really scared me. He didn't see anyone. He calculated that for every 250,000 people at least 25 survived.

Going on the number of people I've seen per city.

That means if there were 8,335,977,671 people as of 22/1/27 then roughly 8,3000,000 people would be left.

I reckon that number is halving every month due to the creatures that are killing them, plus our own efforts to *destroy ourselves* which would give us a few decades before we are *extinct*.

But, don't quote us on that.

He said, we'd better eat lots of hot and spicy food then.

Days without incident, 130.

25/10/27

Doc's numbers keep going up. Is it what he *eats*?

Days without incident, 131

30/10/27

Doc stayed with me for one night.

We watched *Team America: World Police*.

I've never seen anyone laugh so much throughout a movie.

At the end of it, he said that was not very *politically correct*.

I cooked him a roast. He loved it.

He said the army base was not for him. It didn't feel like home and he wished to be back with his family.

He still talks as if they are alive.

Days without incident, 136.

1/11/27

Doc's gone again. I wish he'd tell me if he's going somewhere.

Days without incident, 137.

30/11/27

Doc's been gone for almost a month. Hasn't sent me an email, postcard or a text.

I'm getting his sense of humour.

Days without incident, 167.

25/12/27

Merry Christmas, to mum and dad. I miss you.

Merry Christmas, Mr Lee and Mrs Chamberlain.

Merry Christmas Doc, hope you're enjoying Spain.

To all those who are gone, *Merry Christmas*.

Days without incident, 182.

31/12/27

Happy New Year.

I'm *drunk*. HA hA.

Days without incident, WHO CARES!

1/01/28

Press ups, 30, Sit ups, 100, Pull ups, 30.

Run 4k 20.13mins

New Year's resolution done.

Days without incident, 189.

2/01/28

Met four new people! Sue, Tony, Matt and Luke.

Ran into them in Lower Hutt. They've come down from Auckland.

Really nice people. Numbers look good.

Days without incident, 190.

3/01/28

Good to have people around. Have set up bunks for them.

Am a little worried about Sue's numbers. They went straight down when she walked into the blast room.

She's really nice. I think her and Tony have something going on.

Matt and Luke are good blokes. Cooked them a good meal.

Days without incident, 191.

4/01/28

So good to have company. I'm feeling sane again.

Almost forgot how to have a conversation.

Sue's numbers have dropped to 10. WTF? The boys are all in the high 70's.

Days without incident, 192.

5/01/28

Getting bad vibes from Tony.

Seems like he wants me *gone*. Matt and Luke seem to be on my side.

Keeping my gun on me at all times.

Days without incident, 193.

6/01/28

Sue is down to 5. Can't seem to change the number. No matter what I do.

Had a huge argument with Tony. Told him he needs to change his attitude or he'll be gone.

Matt took Tony's side. Don't know what to do. Everything changed so quickly and it looks like they want the complex for themselves.

Days without incident, 194.

7/01/28

Wanted to check my number so badly. Am I at *risk*?

Days without incident, 195.

8/01/28

The boys asked me to go hunting with them.

I declined. Stayed back with Sue. She's down to 3.

Told them there's enough food. They said they like to do it for *fun*.

They came back late at night. They wouldn't talk about the hunt.

Days without incident, 196.

9/01/28

Tony *threatened* me with Sue's life. Either I go or she *dies*.

I watched her numbers change right in front of me to 0.

I pulled the gun on them. I couldn't stop it.

They shot her and they all had guns on me.

I felt like Clint Eastwood in *Unforgiven*.

I knelt and shot at them. They missed me.

They ran for it. Scared of me. I showed those assholes.

They're all spineless cowards. I'm pretty sure I hit one of them.

I've padlocked the gate now. They can't get in.

They've scared me more than any monster.

Days without incident, 0.

20/01/28

Have stayed in most of the month.

Can't believe what happened. *Buried* Sue out the back by the cross.

Feel like I'm going crazy, but trying to keep it together.

Have started training again. Haven't seen any sign of the boys.
I think they know better than to try and take me on again. Searched
for Doc. Still away.
Days without incident, 11.

22/01/28
1 year since everybody disappeared.
It's gone so fast. Everything has changed so much.
Been noticing more signs of movement on the hills.
Those huge insectoids must be using it like an anthill.
Days without incident, 13.

25/01/28
Noticed a huge monster walking around town.
It's like something from the ice age. Huge tusks on its jaw.
It pushed in one of the fences. Rubbing itself on the barbed wire.
Spent most of the day fixing it.
Days without incident, 16.

27/01/28
Saved a group of travellers who were being chased by the monster.
They were reversing away from it. I don't know where I got the
idea from but I threw some grenades into the hills.
The insectoids were everywhere. Chased me up the road and I lost
them down an alley.
They took on the monster. They seem like nice people, not like the
last.
Only problem, their numbers are really *low*.

Days without incident, 18.

28/01/28

I was invited to lunch. They is Shelby (cheeky), Lucy (nice), Max (bit of a *dick*), Pete (young kid, adorable), and Charlie (older kid, just as adorable). I like them.

When I'm around, their numbers are going *up*.

Days without incident, 19.

30/01/28

Went for dinner yesterday with the gang. Told Shelby, who seems to be the most sensible about the number thing.

Didn't want to tell her about Lucy, Max, her or the boys as it's too much.

It would drive them all crazy I'm sure. Brought them home today.

If I keep them with me they may have more of a chance. Just having them in the blast room made a huge difference.

Have offered my house as theirs. I think they'll move in. They are looking for Lucy's mum and dad.

I think they're dead; it's been over two weeks. Shelby wants to give the boys a birthday.

It's a good idea. I'll stay by them just in case. Feels good to be looking after people again. Especially good people.

Days without incident, 21.

Shelby woke up just before 6 am. The large blast room was still dark due to the lack of windows. Sitting up on her lower bunk, she noticed Tim was already up and his bed was perfectly made. She made her bed also and reached up to check if the boys were still sleeping. They were both gone, the beds unmade. Lucy and Max were both fast asleep. Shelby quickly got dressed and ran into the hallway. She wasn't panicking as the boys were always up early. She checked the barracks bathrooms but no one was there.

Walking upstairs, the sun was streaming in through the windows. She could see Tim outside. It looked like he was doing jumping jacks as he kept bouncing in and out of view. She pushed the main entrance door open and smiled upon seeing Pete trying to do a push up and Charlie doing sit ups.

"That's it boys," Tim encouraged, smiling at Shelby. "*Pain* is your friend."

"Is he?" asked Pete, still struggling to finish his push up.

"Don't know him…" replied Charlie. "…This hurts."

"No pain, no gain." Tim responded as he started doing air squats. Pete finished his push up and noticed Shelby smiling at him.

"Oh, hi Shelby! We're exercising! Want to feel my *muscles*?" Pete got up gracelessly and ran to Shelby flexing his right muscle, Charlie followed doing the same.

"So big!" said Shelby, laughing. "…And you too Charlie! You're both getting so fit."

"Tim says, if we keep doing this every morning we'll get big muscles like his," boasted Pete.

"Oh, will you?"

"Yep." Pete answered confidently.

"I can't wait," said Charlie.

"Talking doesn't grow your muscles boys." Tim reminded them as he was doing pull ups on a bar. Pete and Charlie immediately went back to doing their push ups.

"Shelby, you're getting *fat*, you should do some exercises too." Pete suggested, blowing out breath while going down in the movement. Charlie started to laugh.

"Well I never," Shelby sighed out, putting her hands on her waist and pinching hardly any fat. I suppose it has been a while. She immediately started doing air squats.

"Good girl!" Pete said, smiling.

"How am I doing, Pete?" Charlie asked, not really going up or down on his push up. The only thing moving was his head.

"So good, Charlie," Pete assured him.

"How come no one told me we were exercising?" Lucy asked, rubbing the sleep out of her eyes, she immediately was trying to take Shelby on.

Max came out also, looked at the sun, put his sunglasses on, scratched his tummy, and looked at everyone exercising. He stretched his arms, yawned, turned around and went back inside.

"Okay everyone, we need to follow my lead. Quick sprint around the block and the last one back makes breakfast." Tim took off with Lucy in hot pursuit. Arriving back at the finish line, Tim was well ahead with Lucy just behind, who showed a clean pair of heels. Pete and Charlie came in next, walking, with Shelby last trying to tickle them. They all sat down laughing while Tim went back to his pull ups.

"Michael and I used to do this most mornings." Shelby said to Lucy.

"Yeah, he was a good influence when it came to exercise."

"Most of the time, sometimes, he'd just eat crap, drink and sleep," Shelby smiled.

"I'm so tired," said Pete, in an exhausted voice. "Are you tired Charlie...?" Charlie was lying on the ground, panting. "...Can't talk?" added Pete, Charlie shook his head. "No pain, no gain." Pete smiled, as Tim came over and ruffled their hair.

"Well done boys, I can already see the difference." Pete raised both his arms and flexed. "Strong," said Tim, in a low register. "Don't forget, the only way to feed the muscles so they grow is to have...?" Pete's face wrinkled up in thought, he had one eye closed. He was waiting for the answer to pop up into his head.

"Muscle food?" Pete answered, smiling.

"Yes, so you need a good healthy breakfast."

"Okay!" said Pete as he ran back inside, in search of food. Charlie quickly followed.

"Just ask Max!" Shouted Shelby.

"They're such good boys," said Tim, sitting down next to Shelby.

"You're a good *influence*." Smiled Shelby.

"On *all* of us." Added Lucy, panting.

"They're really *close* those two," Tim said, watching Charlie chasing Pete.

"Thick as thieves," said Shelby.

"You know the offer still stands. You all are more than welcome to stay. The place is far too big for me," said Tim, wiping his sweat with a towel. Lucy turned away.

"Thank you, Tim. What do you think, Lucy?" Shelby asked.

"I feel safe here. Just..."

"...I know, it's like we're giving up on Michael and Teresa," said Shelby.

"We could always go back, every day if you want," suggested Tim. Shelby looked at Lucy who didn't seem convinced.

"How about we do *one* more night Lucy, one more firework. Then, we come here we're it's *safe*. We're it's safe for the boys," Shelby suggested, smiling. Lucy wiped a small tear. It felt like she was giving up.

"...And of course we'll keep *searching*," said Tim.

Lucy turned to Tim. "Thank you Tim, and thank you for the offer, you've been so kind."

"You're welcome, ma'am." Lucy smiled.

"Okay, one more night, one more sky rocket, then *we come here*, if the boys agree, of course," said Shelby.

"Agree about what?" asked Max as he came out of the main entrance.

"About staying here, Maximillian."

"Yeah, yeah, I could *put up* with this place. Tim needs me, I get it." Max said, still wearing his sunglasses, his hands resting on his waist. Shelby smiled as she high-fived Max.

"So, all agreed? One more night to light a sky rocket then it's back to the army base?" She put her hand in the middle of all of them. They all put their hands on top.

"But, first, *shopping*, right?" said Lucy, smiling.

"Of course, we've got to celebrate the boy's birthdays!" said Shelby. They all threw their hands into the air in agreement.

CHAPTER THIRTEEN

The Mall

AISLE I

After a late breakfast the Bushmaster was back on the road making its way to North City Plaza. Lucy and Tim as per usual were in the front. Centre seats were taken by Pete and Charlie and in the back were Shelby and Max. Charlie and Pete were excitedly talking about their favourite toys. "I would like a *Lightsaber*," said Pete, smiling.

"I'd like a green one," Charlie added, grinning.

"Yeah, green would be cool, nice pick Charlie."

Shelby smiled in the back. "Those boys are just to die for," she whispered to Max.

"I know, it's like they're..."

"...sent from heaven?"

"...you read my thoughts." Max replied, smiling. Tim put on some music at the front. A New Zealand band, Dragon's track,

Rain, started powering out of the speakers. Both Charlie and Pete started bouncing up and down to the beat.

"It's hard to believe..." Max started.

"...What's that then?" Asked Shelby, looking out at the landscape passing.

"It's hard to believe that a week ago we were walking with nothing, just trying to survive, you know, and these boys have been..."

"...Juggernauts?" interrupted Shelby.

"...so *brave*, you know? They've lived a lifetime in such a short space of time." Max was starting to break down. "...and you guys have been..."

"Wonderful?"

"...so good to us. I mean we had nothing a week ago, nothing, and now we've got more food than we could ask for, a *safe place* to stay..."

"We're going shopping on *me*."

"We're going shopping on *you*," Max started to laugh and sniff at the same time. "I... I, it means a lot, Shelby. I was so *stressed* before."

"I know." Shelby answered, patting Max on the back.

"It's just so good to see them so..."

"Fruitful?"

"...happy." Max was laughing. "You're a *shit*, Shelby... Um, what is your last name?"

"O'Leary." Shelby offered, smiling. "Middle name, Francis."

"Shelby Francis O'Leary, you're a shit."

"The biggest." Shelby replied.

"Just the pressure is off a little."

"I get it."

"I can let my guard down," said Max. Shelby started nodding.

"Enjoy yourself today," said Shelby, smiling. "You deserve it." She hugged Max, and he broke down.

"Such a shit." He said, as he looked out the window wiping his cheeks dry.

"How long we got to go?" asked Lucy as she was tapping her foot to the music, impatiently.

"About twenty minutes, ma'am."

"You know you can call me, Lucy."

Tim said nothing. He skipped the next song and on came *Sierra Leone*, a song by Coconut Rough.

"This is catchy," Lucy said,

"I like it," said Tim. They drove through the winding hills. The streets are quiet and empty. The lyrics,

"If you want me, I'll come running, come running, come running to you,"

carried through the open windows, echoing over the Paremata mountains. By the time they had made it to North City Plaza it was just before twelve noon. Tim parked up top in the empty car park.

Aisle 2

Tim turned off the car and the music stopped. He looked serious and the mood changed quickly, he turned to Max. "Max, how about you and I do a quick run through the mall? Make sure everything is okay?"

"Sure Tim. He called me Max." Max whispered to Shelby. She smiled.

"I'll lock the car doors, Shelby. Could you sit in the driver's seat in case anything happens? I'll leave the keys with you," said Tim.

"Sure, *Rambo*, you got it." Shelby sat behind the driver's wheel as Tim and Max opened the boot.

"I've got a few rifles here Max and a couple 9mm guns. Take one of each. I'll hold on to the grenades, you don't want those going off in your hand." Tim placed the rifle around Max's shoulder. Max put the gun in the back of his pants.

"I'm getting *nervous*," said Max, looking concerned.

"Don't be. The mall was locked up when everyone vanished. No one will be inside. I'm just taking *precautions*."

"Okay, that makes me feel better," said Max, his hands fidgeting as he stood on his tippy toes.

"Alright, I've got two walkie talkies here. One for me, one for you. I'm on channel ten. If you want to talk, just push this button. *Got it?*"

"Push this button. Got it."

"Good, easy right?" Somehow Max got the feeling that Tim was loving this. "We'll see you in half an hour!" Shouted Tim.

Shelby and Lucy waved back. Pete and Charlie were wondering what was going on. Shelby watched as Tim strutted off looking super professional in his camouflaged army uniform and boots, *hut, hut, hut.* She laughed a little, watching Max in his sneakers, white t-shirt and jeans running behind him, holding a rifle upside down in his hands.

"You never know what the next day will bring." Shelby smiled.

"That's for sure," Lucy replied.

"Where are they going?" asked Pete.

"To make sure the place is... um, *empty*." Answered Lucy.

"Isn't every place empty, Lucy?"

"Yeah, we just got to make sure there's no... um, ah... you know... that the toy shop is open."

"Oh," replied Pete, he turned to Charlie. "They're checking for *monsters*." Shelby laughed. Charlie nodded.

"Pays to be *safe*," said Charlie. Pete nodded back in agreement. Half an hour later, Pete and Charlie were playing slaps with Shelby and Lucy. Shelby and Lucy's hands were especially red.

"It's Tim!" shouted Pete.

"Yay!" Charlie shouted. Tim was running back to the vehicle looking professional. Max was trying to keep up behind him. Max's cheeks were flushed. He was blowing hard and looked exhausted. His rifle was still upside down. Lucy brought down her window.

"All clear team. We are ready to *enter* the mall!" Tim said in his most officious voice.

"Yay!" shouted Pete and Charlie.

Aisle 3

"Hold hands now." Advised Max as they all walked to the mall holding each other's hands. Shelby was at the end of the line holding Max's hand.

"Such a big strong man, checking the mall for me."

"Shut up," Max said, smiling.

"We had to break the lock to get in," Tim shouted. He stood out front, covering everyone as they all shuffled in one by one. It felt like they were in a war zone. "Keep moving, keep moving." Tim said as they passed him. Once inside, Tim and Max pushed a rather large rubbish bin in front of the door.

"That's not going to keep out bigfoot," said Shelby, not looking happy. Tim and Max pushed a three seater couch chair against the door.

"As long as we're out of here before dark, *we'll be fine.*" Tim assured.

"Party, party, *party!*" shouted Lucy as she ran off.

"We meet at the food court in a couple hours, sound good?" Shelby shouted. Lucy was already out of hearing range.

"Don't worry, she'll be waiting for us," said Tim.

Aisle 4

Walking up the main escalator, the group found Lucy waiting outside Glassons. She was standing against the shop front security grill. Her hands gripped the cage like an animal trying to get out. She shook it violently. "Won't open."

Tim smiled. He pulled some bolt cutters from behind his back, broke the cylinder lock and pulled the grill up.

"Madam." He said as he bowed and put his arm out. She ran in like a bird released.

"It's been a long time," said Shelby, smiling at Max.

"Looks like it." Max replied.

"Sir Tim, can we find a shop that sells bags? We need to get some rather large suitcases," asked Shelby.

"Warehouse." Answered Tim. "They have toys as well." The boys' faces lit up. Tim walked ahead leading the way.

"Lucy... see you in a couple," Shelby shouted. Lucy's head poked out from behind the storefront.

"Tim!" Tim stopped and looked back. "Would you be a darling and open all the shoe stores, women's clothing stores, jewellery and chemists...uh, that's it for now," Lucy said, in a musical tone. She stood with her hands entwined. She slightly leaned forward with her eyelids blinking.

"Of course, ma'am."

Lucy disappeared back into the store. Tim had his gun still in the ready position as they walked further into the empty mall. Every now and then he'd stop, break a lock and lift a shop grate.

"Does he ever switch off?" Max whispered to Shelby.

"He's *The Terminator*," said Shelby, ripping off Arnold Schwarzenegger's accent but coming across as sounding more Indian.

"Shall we take the boys first to The Warehouse, get them set up and then do some shopping of our own?" Max asked.

"Sounds like a plan, Stan!" said Shelby as she skipped happily. Tim led the way with the boys eagerly talking about what two toys they would take home. They were all so involved in what they were doing, that they did not notice Shelby and Max, behind them, still holding hands.

Aisle 5

The boys ran into The Warehouse. Tim was keeping up with his rifle out front, his finger poised behind the trigger. "Left boys." He said. "Now right." They followed his directions. "Straight ahead now."

"Oh, *boy!*" shouted Pete, his excitement building.

"Are we almost there, Tim?" asked Charlie.

"This is it, boys!" said Tim as they came to four aisles worth of toys. Each aisle was at least twenty metres long.

"No way!" shouted Pete, his arms up in the air in celebration.

"I didn't know there could be so many toys in one place!" said Charlie, his eyes pooling with emotion.

"Well boys... they're all yours," said Tim, smiling back, his hands resting on his rifle.

"I don't know where to start, I don't know where to start," repeated Pete, with his hand on his forehead, questioning.

"Well, you've got four to five hours to work that out," said Tim.

"Four to five hours? That's not *enough* time," replied Charlie, both hands on his head. Pete started laughing. "Why didn't we leave earlier?" asked Charlie as he started running to the toys. Pete ran towards the Star Wars section. Charlie started at the Marvel section.

"Good luck, Charlie!" said Pete as he opened his first toy, a double-sided lightsaber.

"Thanks Pete!" answered Charlie as he stared at two packets. One containing a Captain America figure. The other a figure from the Spider-verse universe. "I can't decide, I can't decide." Said Charlie, shaking his head.

"You don't have to," responded Shelby, catching up. "You can play with them *all*."

Charlie's face beamed. He ripped both packets open. Max, Shelby and Tim sat down, watching the boys laughing and smiling as they let their imaginations go wild.

"Where are *you* going to shop?" Shelby asked Tim.

"Don't know, I don't really need anything."

"Nothing?" asked Shelby, unbelieving.

"I might pop over to the chemist and grab some smells. Maybe some undies."

"That's it?" asked Max, also not believing him.

"I like what I've got," said Tim, showing off his army uniform.

"Fair enough. What about you, Maximillian?" asked Shelby.

"You had to ask," said Max, smiling.

Shelby smiled also. "A man who likes to *fucking shop*."

"Yes I do, madam. Where should we start?"

Shelby looked around, "The Warehouse, luggage first, then we attack?"

"I like it... I like it a lot," replied Max, laughing. Max walked over to the boys before leaving. "Pete, Charlie..." The boys looked up, Pete holding a figurine of Thanos and Charlie, one of Iron Man. "...Be good for Tim, okay?" Max whispered as he held the back of both their heads.

"Yes sir," said Pete.

"Affirmative," said Charlie, with an army helmet on, complete with left eye scanner.

"Are you both having fun?" he asked.

"So much!" said Pete, Charlie smiled.

"You both deserve it." He hugged them and kissed their foreheads, as he turned and walked away.

Pete called out. "Max?"

"Yeah?" replied Max.

"Love you."

Max turned and smiled, Pete was already talking to Charlie about vanishing everybody out of existence with his Thanos doll.

"Let's go, tiger!" said Shelby as she grabbed Max's hand and ran off with him, both laughing with joy. "See you at the food court in a couple of hours," shouted Shelby as they disappeared down the men's aisle.

Aisle 6

Tim decided to lay back on a three seater, outdoor furniture sofa. He was watching Pete play with a large Batman car and Charlie trying to put together a Harry Potter Lego Castle. Within five minutes, he was fast asleep.

Tim woke up feeling uncomfortable. His body ached. The three seater was definitely not made for sleeping on. He checked to see what the boys were up to. The aisle where they had previously been, was now full of opened plastic boxes. Half-finished projects littered the floor. Tim smiled, the boys were having fun.

He stretched and checked the time, 3.45pm. He'd overslept and was supposed to meet everybody over an hour ago. The fact, no one had come back, told him they were all busy. He walked over to the second aisle of toys and found the same desolation of toys and packets opened. He made his way to the third aisle and found a huge set of army toys and boxes that had been made to be hills and forts. Different toys were pretending to be fortresses and castles. On one side was Pete calling out battle tactics. On the other side, his head hidden behind Ken and G.I. Joes was Charlie. "Hey, birthday boys!" shouted Tim.

"Oh! you scared me, Tim!" replied Pete, his hands on his chest.

"We've got to head back and see the others."

"Aw, can we stay for a little bit longer?" asked Pete.

"Yeah, I'm almost going to win," said Charlie as he released a nerf bullet from a nerf gun. It flew over the fake hills and hit Buzz Lightyear who tumbled down the hill backwards, repeating the same thing. *"To infinity and beyond. To infinity and beyond."*

"Hey, no fair, I wasn't watching!" Shouted Pete.

"Wouldn't have made a difference." Whispered Charlie to himself.

"Just one more minute? Tim, please?" pleaded Pete, his hands pulled together like he was praying.

Tim huffed and smiled. "Okay, I'll go and check the others. I'll close the grill at the front so you're both nice and safe though, okay?"

"Okay Tim, thanks," said Pete, he put out his arms as if to say hug. Tim hugged him and then walked over to Charlie and hugged him too.

"Thanks Tim," Charlie smiled. "Now I can win."

"Good luck," said Tim as he walked away.

"Love you, Tim," Pete said.

"Love you Tim," said Charlie.

Tim smiled back. *"Love* you guys." Tim walked to the front of the huge store. He pulled down the grate, just in case and walked to the food court.

Aisle 7

"Finally!" Said Shelby, her feet rested up on a table, she was writing on a piece of paper.

"Shut up," said Max, sarcastically to Shelby as he sat next to her. "We just got here, Tim." Shelby and Max had two large suitcases beside them. They both had new clothes on and shoes. Shelby, though, still looked like she'd just come from a rock concert. They both looked really happy. Tim sat down in the cubicle next to Shelby.

"How'd you go, Tim? Where's the boys?" asked Shelby.

"They wanted an extra minute, playing their war games. We can pick them up on the way back. I couldn't break them up, they were having the time of their lives."

"Aren't we all?!" agreed Shelby, smiling at Max. Max smiled back. Shelby looked around the food court. "I don't know why we met here. Can't buy any food."

"Mm-hmm," mumbled Max, his head rested on his forearms.

"Wonder where Lucy is?" asked Shelby.

"Probably looking like a *princess*," replied Max.

"*Yo!* Peeps!" said a voice from afar. Lucy came striding into the food court. She was pulling two large suitcases behind her. "What a day!" she shouted, smiling.

"Not what I expected," said Shelby, smiling. "Now, we've got *two* Rambo's." Lucy was wearing a pair of camo overalls. A green t-shirt and a green hat turned backwards. Her hair was pulled tight into a braid at the back. She had large black boots on and completed the look with aviator sunglasses. She looked ready for action.

"Like the look," said Tim.

"Thank you, Tim. Seemed appropriate. Inspired by *yourself* of course." Tim smiled.

Lucy sat down. "I'm tired and I'm hungry."

"What do you feel like, Lucy? Chinese? Indian?" asked Shelby, smiling.

"Something healthy, please. Salmon on rice? Protein drink?" replied Lucy, her eyes glancing at Shelby. "What are you writing?"

Max jumped in, "It's a birthday poem for Pete and Charlie."

"Really?" asked Lucy, smiling.

"Really." Shelby answered as she did a big grandiose full stop. "And it's... almost finished." Shelby smiled at them all.

"Going to read it tonight?" asked Max.

"I don't read poetry out loud."

"But, they'd *love it!*" said Lucy, enthusiastically.

"Well, maybe." Shelby started folding up the poem and placed it in her side pocket.

"I think it's time to go anyway," said Tim. "It's getting late, we'll be driving home in the dark. *Not good.*"

Checkout

"Time to move," said Shelby as she kicked Max, who woke up from his pretend sleep. Tim led the way as per usual. His rifle in front, *hut, hut, hut.* Behind was Lucy pulling her luggage and Max and Shelby, chatting while pulling theirs. Max had his rifle hung behind his back. The light in the mall was starting to darken as they made their way back to The Warehouse.

Tim was pulling down grates. "Closing time," he said.

"My feet hurt," exclaimed Lucy, talking to herself. "Oh shit, *make up!* One more stop, Tim." Seeing the chemist had reminded Lucy. She left her bags in the centre of the corridor and ran into the store.

Max and Shelby noticed a shoe store opposite. "We'll pop in here, Tim."

"Okay, five minutes, people," said Tim, sternly. He walked into the chemist, following Lucy.

"So sorry, Tim," Lucy apologised. "I'll just grab a few things. Could you be a honey and grab a bag?" Tim walked over to one of the counters and found a red shopping bag, that read, 'The Chemist Warehouse', stencilled in white. "Hold it out, sweetie." She asked as she was picking items and throwing them in. After half an hour, Lucy had filled three bags worth.

"Okay, that's it, *I'm calling it*," Tim said, sounding frustrated. "*Hey!* Are you guys ready?" Tim shouted towards the shoe store.

"Yes sir!" came a distant reply from Shelby.

"I'm so sorry," Lucy apologised again.

"No problem, ma'am, it's just after five."

They walked to the front of the shop. Lucy inspected her bags. That's when Tim saw it... The head of the huge insectoid as it walked slowly into view. Black goo was dripping from its open jaw.

Chapter Fourteen

Chaos

"IF IT BE NOW, 'TIS NOT TO COME: IF IT BE NOT
TO COME, IT WILL BE NOW: IF IT BE NOT NOW,
YET IT WILL COME: THE READINESS IS ALL."
WILLIAM SHAKESPEARE.

PART ONE

Tim was stunned into silence. His mouth was wide open.
His fingers paralyzed over the trigger. Lucy lifted her head from the
bags and let out a small shriek. It pierced the air and quickly left.
The insectoid moved its head instantaneously towards the sound.
"Shhh." Tim whispered as he placed his hand on Lucy's shoulders.
The insectoid was still, its large spiked head lowered. Tim thought
it was listening. Listening for noise from its next victim.

The creature took a step forward and Tim gasped. It was massive
and stinking. Liquid fell from its body as it moved. He had seen
these things before, but never so close. He wondered, *Why here,
why now?* It made a noise as its large neck swayed from side to

side. It came from the back of its mouth, back in the throat. A noise made by something grating. Six low clicks. The noise echoed through the mall, like it was using sonar. "Don't move." Tim said quietly, his voice commanding and serious.

A shrill, high pitched, human shriek came from across the other side of the mall. He'd forgotten about Shelby and Max. The insectoid moved towards the sound as six steps were taken at an alarming speed. Tim moved. He turned the safety off the rifle and aimed. A sudden movement came from the right. He turned but it was too late. Another insectoid. It screeched a horrible sound and came bounding towards him. It's hard spikes hitting him hard in the ribs. He lost the wind in his chest as he slid across the ground, his rifle hurtling from his hands due to the impact and spinning across the courtyard before hitting a Thomas the Tank Engine kid's ride. The creature threw what Tim thought was its arms into his body. He tried to avoid it. The spikes hitting the ground like a jackhammer, puncturing tile. He felt it's heat on his face. Slime fell around him like a fountain spraying water. Suddenly, he was pulled back as what would have been a fatal blow broke a square tile in half. The creature screamed and moved rapidly after its prey. Lucy pulled down the shop's grill in front of it as the insectoids huge body hit the grill and punctured it inward. Tim had been saved. "Shelby..."

Part Two

Shelby and Max were facing the other creature, paralyzed with fear. Max was clicking the trigger on his rifle but nothing was happening, the safety was still on. The insectoid was listening for movement. The last thing it heard was Max's loud scream which Max regretted making. They could see the other insectoid on the other side punching the closed grill.

"Shoot it. *Fucking* shoot it," Shelby pleaded. Max was working the gun. He was feverishly trying to find the reason why it was not working. He aimed and fired. Nothing. He shook it. The insectoid went low, its large head moving from side to side as again the clicks came from the back of its throat. Max was moving his arm, frantically trying to work the gun. The creature heard him and moved. Shelby jumped forward. Finding the nerve to act. She pulled the shop's grill. It was stuck. "Fucking hell!" she screamed.

Max's gun came to life as he discovered the safety switch and the gun threw a rapid fire of bullets the monster's way. The gun was so powerful Max lost control of it as it fell out of his hands. The creature stopped and lurched to the side as a bullet hit its armour. It shrieked and the sound hurt both their ears.

"*Close* the grill!" shouted Lucy from the other side of the mall. Max ran to the grill and together, he and Shelby pulled it down halfway. The insectoid heard the movement and sensing its prey, hurtled at the grill pushing it out of shape.

"Pull it!" shouted Max as Shelby gave it her all.

"You can do it!" yelled Lucy.

"Fuck!" screamed Shelby as tears started running down her face from fear. The creature moved one of its large arms under the grill and swiped it from left to right. Max was dancing on tippy toes trying to avoid it. The creature swiped the fallen rifle, sending it spiralling as it bumped into the other rifle by the children's ride. The creature's head was ramming into the grill. If it realises it just needs to go lower then the game would be over.

"Fucking *push it down!*" shouted Shelby at Max as they both pushed the grill in time. The grill shifted and groaned before hitting the ground with full force, the insectoid diving into it at the same time. The grill shook from its huge weight. The creature screamed again as Max and Shelby covered their ears. They both crawled back on their hands. Sweat pouring from Max's forehead. "Fuck, fuck, fuck," swore Shelby, her body still shaking. The creature pounded its body against the grill again. The grill stood fast. On the other side, the other creature was doing the same. Hitting it with force, again and again.

Part Three

"How the *fuck* did this happen?" whispered Tim to Lucy, he finally had his breath back. He was sitting on the floor. His back resting against a '*We Are Open*' billboard sign.

"It's *my* fault," Lucy was crying. Her breath was shaking as she spoke. "I took too long. Makeup. What the hell, *I'm so sorry.*"

"No, no," whispered Tim. "We still had time. It's only now getting dark. They shouldn't be here. We checked. Everything was closed. They shouldn't be here. It doesn't make sense." The creature smashed into the grill again. "Stay quiet and don't move. I think they're blind, they use some sort of radar. I think it's why they come out at night. It gives them some sort of advantage." Lucy nodded and then regretted doing it as the creature smashed into the grill.

"How long?" asked Lucy.

"How long what?" replied Tim, looking worried.

"How long till they discover they just have to pull the grill *up?*" Tim shook his head as if to answer, *I don't know.* "Tim...?" said Lucy, her face looking scared.

"What?" asked Tim, wondering what could be even worse.

"Pete... Charlie..."

Part Four

The sound of the creatures consistently hitting the grill with their gruesome bodies was making Shelby feel ill. It had been over twenty minutes. The shopping mall was now dark. The moon must have been bright outside as blue shadows now covered the corridor. Max and Shelby had moved to the back of the store and were now in the stock area. Boxes of shoes of different sizes worked their way along the walls.

"We've got to get to Pete and Charlie," whispered Max. A clicking sound came from behind them.

"I know, but *how?*" murmured Shelby. A huge bang rang out in the mall as the creature hit the grill, hard.

"We pull up the grill? We go for the guns?" suggested Max.

"We *die?*" answered Shelby.

"Pete, Charlie, we've got to do something. They're all *alone.*" A bang hit the grill again.

"Fuckers," said Shelby. "Fucking insects." Another bang. Shelby was thinking. The mall went silent. Max was listening, waiting for the usual noise of the creature hurling itself at the grill. It never came. Instead, a different noise punctured the air. The sound of something rattling. Like a chain on a bike being turned. "The grill!" shouted Shelby. "It's *lifting* the fucking grill!" They both came running out to the shop as they could see a long tendon sticking out from the creature's spikes. It was lifting the grill. It made it look easy. Max grabbed a broom. "What are you going to do, *sweep it?*" asked Shelby, wryly.

Max was jumping up and down. Willing himself to be ready for battle. Shelby grabbed a pair of scissors. They both stood by the grill, ready for war. The creature stopped. Clicks started to sound from the back of its throat. Suddenly the other creature by Tim and Lucy started to lift its grill. Lucy screamed.

"Get ready to *run!*" Shouted Max, his broom swinging in his hands. Both Lucy and Tim were now standing to the side of the creature.

"Max...?" A distant voice was heard coming from the lower levels. "...Shelby? Lucy? Tim? Where are you?" The small voice asked. The creatures lowered their heads and shook them. They were listening.

Max, looked terrified. Shelby's mouth fell open. She looked sick. The creatures moved. Their speed was incredible as they disappeared to the sound of the trembling scared voice from afar.

The voice that belonged to little Pete.

Part Five

Pete and Charlie were having the time of their lives. Charlie was now dressed in a Darth Vader suit, Pete in an Obi-Wan brown gown. His hood was pulled up. Pete had the green lightsaber, Charlie the red. "You were supposed to be the *chosen one!*" shouted

Pete, sounding very much like a young Obi-Wan Kenobi. His hand out, grasping air.

"Was I?" asked Charlie, not knowing the story.

"Yes!" yelled Pete, still in character.

"Shall we *fight* then?" replied Charlie, politely.

"You were my best friend, Anakin!" hollered Pete, aching pain in his voice.

"I still am?" questioned Charlie, falling for Pete's convincing acting.

"Charlie, oh, Charlie, say..." Pete had an idea, he waved his finger at Charlie enthusiastically. "...You didn't kill Anakin Skywalker."

Charlie looked confused. "I didn't kill... Anakin Skywalker?"

"*No*, oh... let's fight," said Pete. They both laughed and started making ddsshh and vwoom-woom sounds as they pretended to have the greatest duel ever. Finally, after ending up in the kitchen section, the battle was nearing its end. "Now... cut my legs off, Charl... I, I mean, Darth, you've got the higher ground!"

"Why would I do that?" asked Charlie, innocently.

"Go on, Darth, do it, *just do it!*" Shouted Pete, giving an Oscar-winning performance. Charlie pretended to cut Pete's legs, running his lightsaber gently against Pete's thighs. Pete screamed and pretended he was on fire.

"I've had enough," said Charlie as he sat down and laid his lightsaber in front of him. Pete was still writhing in agony. "What time is it?" asked Charlie, looking up at the sky lights which were now starting to darken. Pete stopped his dramatic acting and comically sat up like nothing had happened.

"Don't know, Charlie. It is getting late though."

"I'm really tired and *hungry*," said Charlie, holding his belly.

"Yeah, me too. I wonder where everybody is?"

"Should we go to the front and see if we can see them?" asked Charlie as he swung his lightsaber.

"Yeah, good idea, Charlie. But maybe we should clean up first." Charlie went quiet as they both looked at the huge mess they had created. Open packets and boxes littered each toy aisle. The battleground they had created was a massive hill of boxes, sheets and blankets, with fallen toys showing the huge battle that must have taken place. Pete started to smile. "Just kidding, Charlie, we don't have to clean up!" Charlie didn't look amused, he was too tired to take in Pete's sense of humour.

"Come on, Charlie," said Pete, ever positive as he walked off to the front of the store. Charlie followed, his head down after a big day. Pete pulled back his hood as Charlie caught up to him. "Did you have a good birthday Charlie?" He asked, smiling.

"Yeah, I did Pete, it was the *best*."

"The best *ever?*" asked Pete.

"Yes," said Charlie, still trying to find the energy to talk.

"Do you know what would finish our day off perfectly?"

Charlie looked up at Pete, his mouth barely open. "What?" he asked.

"Fireworks."

"Yeah," said Charlie, suddenly coming to life.

"I reckon we ask Lucy if we can watch."

"Okay, Pete."

"That would be the *best*, wouldn't it Charlie?"

"The *best*." Charlie agreed. They came to the front of the store. The shop grill had been pulled down by Tim. They both stood holding the grill, the other hand holding a lightsaber each. "I can't see anyone, Pete," said Charlie as he sat on his bottom.

"Me neither," replied Pete as he sat down too. The shop was now getting dark. The colours that were once many and bright were now becoming different shades of a dark blue.

"Pete, do you think they forgot about us?" asked Charlie, as he started hitting his lightsaber against the grill. It echoed down the corridor.

"What? No, Charlie, they would never forget about us." Pete and Charlie sat at the grill. Charlie continued hitting it. The night quickly settled and Charlie was beginning to get nervous.

"Pete...?"

"Yeah, Charlie."

"Do you ever see *ghosts*?" Charlie was looking around the large store. He had stopped hitting the grill. It was so dark now, the noise was starting to scare him. *Be brave.* He heard in his head. It was his mum's voice. Pete didn't know how to answer the question. He could tell Charlie was looking nervous.

"I, I once saw Mum, Charlie, remember that time? When we were being chased by that ten-legged huge thing."

"I remember."

"That's when I saw Mum. She was watching me run."

"But, she's a nice ghost, have you ever seen *scary ones?*" Charlie was looking at the different shapes around the store. His imagination was starting to work overtime.

"No, no scary ones, Charlie."

Charlie could see him. The monster that had chased him back when the vanishing happened. His worst nightmare. It was in the far distance. It wasn't moving but stood hunched between two

aisles. Its eyes, staring at him. Its arms were long and dispropor-
tionate. Charlie closed his eyes. *Be brave. I'm trying.* He answered
himself. He opened his eyes and it was closer. At least ten feet
closer. He flew back against the grill. It rattled and echoed down
the corridor. "Pete, Pete..." said Charlie, shaking.

"What? What is it, Charlie? You're scaring me." Pete was following Charlie's scared eyes. He couldn't see anything. He automatically raised his lightsaber and turned it on. Its light did
nothing to the surrounding area. "What is it, Charlie?" Pete asked
again. Charlie was paralysed. He hadn't seen this nightmare in so
long. He thought he had beaten it. But, here in this dark, huge
warehouse, it had found its way back. It moved again. As awkward
as he remembered it before. It's body moving left, right, left, right.
Charlie screamed as it moved quickly.

Be brave. "I can't, I can't, *I can't!*" shouted Charlie, repeatedly
as he started crying.

"What is it, Charlie?" Pete was now holding his lightsaber out
like a weapon. Charlie had his head turned toward the shop grill.
He opened his tear-filled eyes and the thing was now on the other
side of the grill. Staring straight at him. Its demonic elongated face
grinning at him.

"No!" he shouted as he fell backwards onto the floor.

"I've got you, Charlie!" said Pete, not knowing what was going
on. "I've got you!" Pete jumped in front of Charlie. His lightsaber
ready to go. "I can't see anything, Charlie? There's nothing here?"
Charlie sat up and started pulling Pete's brown gown.

"I think it's gone, Pete. I think you scared it." Charlie was looking around but couldn't see the figure. Pete's bravery had helped
him conquer it.

"Oh, that's good, Charlie. I'm glad I could help. I was starting to get scared there."

"Thanks Pete," said Charlie.

"You're welcome," replied Pete, smiling as he gave Charlie a hug. Charlie wiped his tears. They sat together, in the dark, by the shop grill. Charlie still didn't feel very good. His heart was still beating fast.

"I thought it was *real*, Pete."

"I am *real!*" said a voice, loud and to the right of Charlie's ear. He screamed, Pete screamed with him.

"What? What, Charlie?" Charlie was pushing himself into Pete for comfort. "Charlie, there's nothing there. It's your mind playing tricks." Charlie was crying in Pete's arms. Suddenly, they heard noises from a long way, away. It sounded like gunshots.

"Charlie, did you hear that?"

"I heard it, Pete."

"It could be Tim."

"Yeah," Answered Charlie, sounding a little more optimistic. "Why would he be shooting?"

"I don't know, Charlie," answered Pete, they were both trying to look down the long hallway. It was full of shadows and ended in darkness.

"Pete?"

"Yeah, Charlie?"

"I've got to go to the toilet."

"Really, *now?*"

"Yeah, I've been trying to hold it, but I can't anymore." Pete was trying to think. *What should they do? There were gunshots up the hallway.*

"There might be a toilet up the corridor Charlie, would you be okay if we go and have a look?"

"If you come with me, Pete, I might be okay."

"Okay, can you help me pull up the grill, Charlie?"

"Sure." Pete and Charlie both made grunting noises as they heaved and pulled the grill. It moved a little.

"Come on, you can do it!" said Pete, encouraging his friend. They pulled and the grill finally gave in, moving enough for them to crawl under. "Okay, let's go, Charlie," said Pete, as he rolled under the grill. Charlie followed.

"Hold my hand, Pete?" asked Charlie as he held out his hand. He looked behind him. Behind the grill was the demon. Its eyes staring back at him. Its grin smiling at him, taunting him. Its long tongue moving in and out of its mouth. Charlie gripped Pete's hand tightly. *I'm brave, he doesn't exist, he doesn't exist.* Pete was walking in front apprehensively. He was looking for signs on the walls. Something that looked like a toilet. Looking ahead he remembered the gunshots.

"Max...?" He called out. "...Shelby? Lucy...Tim?" Charlie gave Pete's hand a squeeze. He looked behind him. The gorilla demon with the long arms was shuffling towards him. *You're a big boy, there's no such thing as a ghost.* "Toilet!" Shouted Pete, pointing as he pulled Charlie towards it. Charlie closed his eyes, he didn't want to look back.

Had he opened his eyes though, rather than a demon, he would have seen two insectoids clinging onto the ceiling speeding horribly towards them.

Part Six

Pete and Charlie walked into the large, tiled toilet. It was almost pitch black in there. There were no windows. Pete could barely see Charlie. On the left, there were cubicles for peeing in. To the right were large doors that hid the toilets behind. "Number one or number two?" asked Pete, smiling.

"Number two," answered Charlie, his legs pushed together.

"Well, you best hop in behind these doors, Charlie." He opened the door for Charlie.

"Thanks Pete, thanks for looking after me." Charlie said, pulling down his pants. "I couldn't do this without you."

"You're welcome," answered Pete, feeling good about himself.

"Fireworks *tonight!*" Charlie reminded Pete, his smiling face disappearing behind the door as Pete closed it.

"That's right, Charlie, can't wait!" Pete closed the door and turned to look at the dark empty room. For the first time he felt a little scared. Without Charlie to worry about he hadn't really noticed how dark It was, and quiet.

He went and sat on the floor against the back wall, his lightsaber raised. He turned the lightsaber on. The insignificant green light, illuminating a radiant green atmosphere to the room.

"Are you still there, Pete?" Asked Charlie, with a worried voice.

"I'm here, Charlie. I'm waiting for you." Pete replied, nervously, as he kept his lightsaber raised. Pete was scared. He hadn't said it to Charlie but he was worried about where everyone was and why they hadn't come to find them. He knew it couldn't be good. They would never leave them by themselves, at night, in the dark.

Then he heard it. The low clicks. Six in a row. Low and scary. Pete started to shake. His heart started to pound. It was so dark he could hardly see where the door was.

"What was that?" asked Charlie, sounding frightened.

"Nothing, Charlie, it's *nothing*," answered Pete, he was looking around the room. Searching for a way out. There was none. The noise came again, followed by a shadow that was slowly growing larger. Brave Pete, who never cried suddenly started to cry. His body went numb. He couldn't move. Pete held his lightsaber forward ready for battle, it shook terribly in his sweaty, shaking, tiny hands. "Charlie," said Pete, his voice trembling.

"Yeah, Pete?" There was a pause as Pete thought about what to say next. The clicks again. The shadow was now covering the room. "*Stay* in there, don't come out."

"What? Why?" asked Charlie, his voice trembling.

"...And stay quiet, no matter what you hear... *stay quiet*."

"Pete, I'm scared."

"Don't be, I'll always be with *you*," said Pete, the insectoid was now inches from Pete's face. He bravely readied his lightsaber. "I *love* you, Charlie."

Charlie was quiet. He sat on the toilet with his hands over his mouth. He was listening. Pete had told him to be quiet and he would do what Pete said. *Be brave.* A noise rang out that sounded horrible, a scream followed. Charlie's eyes opened wide in response. *You're a big boy.* He heard another scream. A loud horrible scream. *Be brave.* Noises like a boxing bag being punched. Something gurgled. *You're a big boy.* Gunshots punctured the silence. Something large fell in the distance. Voices were screaming. Charlie looked at the toilet door. Wishing he could see behind it. See Pete. See his friend, talk to him. But, he had told him to be quiet.

The voices grew louder. A loud scream followed. Gunshots rattled the doors in the bathroom. Charlie put his hands on his ears. It was so loud. He heard an unearthly squelch. Screaming that sounded like a dying creature. More gunshots.

"Fucking *die*! You fuck, *you fuck*, fucking die!" It sounded like Max. "*Pete!* Oh, my God, Pete!" Max was screaming. Charlie could hear Max's tortured voice. He sounded in pain. "No, no, *no*, Pete, oh, my *God!* Oh, my God! *My Pete!*" Max was bellowing. Charlie was crying too, but Pete had told him to be quiet. He would do what Pete had told him to do. *Be brave.* It was Pete's voice talking to him now, not his mum. *I am Pete, I so am, just like you, Pete.*

Another voice, it was Lucy. "No, not Pete! Not our *little* Pete!" He could hear them both, in tandem, crying together. The door flew open. It was Shelby.

"Charlie!" Charlie held up his arms. His eyes, engulfed in tears. "You *good* little man," said Shelby, hugging him. "You *good* little man." She said again as she kissed his cheek repeatedly, not wanting to stop. Behind her he could see Lucy and Max both smiling. Their eyes, heavy with emotion.

"Charlie!" said Max. "Oh, my God, Charlie." Max's voice was breaking. Shelby pulled Charlie's pants up and lifted him to Max. Lucy kissed Charlie on the cheek. Charlie could see Tim standing at the entrance. His gun resting on his lap. He smiled at Tim and Tim smiled back. Charlie hugged Max hard as he noticed the huge horrible grotesque creature lying on the floor, dead. Charlie looked at Max, a worried look on his face.

"Where's Pete?"

Part Seven

They were running through the dark shopping mall. Charlie could hear them crying, Lucy, Max, even Shelby. Tim was too far ahead to hear. Every now and then there would be a flash of light as Tim shot his rifle at something in front. "Keep up!" Tim shouted. Charlie was bouncing up and down in Max's arms. Behind them, he could see the gorilla demon. It was standing hunched over, watching him. Its eyes were piercing the dark. *Pete,* he thought. It didn't move. It just stayed put, watching. Watching him leave.

"I'm brave!" he shouted out loud. Max held him tighter. Something moved on the ceiling above. Something came down in the dark and hovered above Charlie.

"Max!" Shouted Shelby as Max turned, lifted his rifle and shot it. It screamed and flew into the shadows. It's blood steaming on the ground. "Fucking hell!" yelled Shelby as they carried on making their way from where they had come in.

"Pete," said Charlie. "We can't leave Pete behind?"

Max ignored Charlie as they made their way down a last corridor. The end of the hallway seemed to be bathed in light. The entrance door was pushed open. The three seater lounge sofa and rubbish bin pushed to the side. Near the entrance was a large metal bin. The contents inside were on fire. It gave off a huge light to those who wanted a free dinner. Shelby immediately remembered what Tim had said. *A candle light for dinner.*

"We've been set up!" shouted Tim. "Careful, there could be anything outside!" Tim walked out with his gun at the ready. Some huge creatures were flying above the flame. Looking like a cross between bats and moths. But the size of a dog.

"Like moths to a flame," Lucy said. Tim shot them down and ushered everybody forward.

"Get to the Bushmaster! Keep your heads down!" he led the way. At the back, Max held Charlie's head down as he ran.

"Pete?" Said Charlie. "We can't *leave* Pete."

Part Eight

Tim was driving the Bushmaster as Michael had driven his car many weeks before. When a large shadow appeared on the horizon he'd flick the lights on and drive round whatever it was. He would then turn the lights off and drive by the natural light of the moon. Lucy sat next to him. She was quiet and had only just stopped crying. Her breathing was becoming more natural. Behind them was Max and Shelby. Charlie had fallen asleep on Max. His head resting on Max's shoulder. Max never did answer Charlie's Pete question. Not a word was said as they drove home. Not one word. Max took Charlie inside. Lucy followed.

"Tim, can I have a word?" asked Shelby as she sat in the front seat and closed the car door.

"Sure," said Tim as he closed his open door. He was just about to go inside also. They sat looking out the front windscreen. The moon was full in front of them. The road was silent and empty. The light inside the car stayed on for a second before automatically switching off, leaving them in darkness. Tim could hardly see Shelby's face.

"Did you *know?*" Tim was startled by Shelby's tone.

"Know?"

"Know that Pete's number was *fucking up!*" Shelby sounded pissed off. Tim said nothing. He looked ahead. His mind racing. "Well?" shouted Shelby, she was crying. Her heart was pounding. "*You knew*, didn't you? You *fucking* knew and you took us anyway. His number was fucking *zero* and you took us anyway!" Tim said nothing. He didn't know what to say. "How could you?! He's a kid. We had to look after him!" Shelby started hitting the dashboard. "We put him in danger, no, *no*, you fucking put him in danger! You fuck! *You fuck!*" She hit him hard in the shoulder, she was now crying and out of control. "You *go!* Okay? You just fucking go and *don't come back*. I don't want to hear about your fucking numbers! What use are they when you don't care?! *You don't fucking care!*" She opened the door. "His number was fucking *zero*! And you let him go to the mall! You *killed* him, you fuck!" She slammed the door, gave Tim the finger and stormed inside the house, slamming the door behind her. Tim heard the locks being used.

Tim breathed out a long sigh. His hands held the steering wheel tight. He waited there, staring at the road for at least ten minutes, saying and doing nothing. "His number was always zero... it was just... *a matter of time*." He whispered to himself angrily, as he hit the steering wheel. He looked at the house with sadness. *It's why I don't get attached.* Tears dropped from his eyes as he turned the key. He looked back at the house one last time and then drove off slowly into the quiet, dark night.

CHAPTER FIFTEEN

The World Between

S HELBY FINISHED SETTING THE deadlock when she turned
and was hugged by Lucy. "Oh, Shelby, Shelby, *poor* Pete."
Shelby hugged Lucy back, a tear coming from her eye for Pete and
also because of the argument she'd just had with Tim. She now felt
horrible for how she'd spoken to him. *If only I could text, sorry.* She
spoke in the heat of the moment and now regretted it. "Where's
Tim?" asked Lucy.

"He's gone home. He was a mess. Couldn't handle."

Lucy's head went down. "Poor Tim, he was so *brave*, it must be
cutting him up."

Shelby walked into the dark kitchen. Moonlight was streaming
between the boarded windows. Max was sitting at the table. Charlie was on his lap, fast asleep. Max was patting his forehead, his eyes
were swollen from crying.

"I'm so... so *sorry*, Max," said Shelby, her voice breaking as she hugged him.

"We shouldn't have gone," Max said, quietly. "What were we thinking?" He hugged Charlie closer. "They were my *responsibility*." He moved his head against the back of Charlie's head. "Mine," Max said as he cried again. Shelby had nothing to say. She felt he was right. Hadn't she just said the same thing to Tim?

"Tim said we were *set up*. The door was pushed open, the bin on fire, we were set up by someone," said Shelby as she looked at Max and Lucy. Lucy nodded.

"Yeah, someone Tim knows, I think. We'll find them, *the fucks*, we'll find them." Max said, angrily, a fresh set of tears running down his face. He was now swaying holding Charlie, like a mother and her child.

"We would have been safe otherwise." Said Lucy, trying to be positive.

Max shook his head. "*No*, I should have kept them with me."

"You can't..." Shelby thought better of what she was about to say. She'd already had one argument she regretted. "We *all* should've kept them with us," she corrected. "We were *lost* in just having a normal day."

"A normal day," agreed Lucy.

"Oh, *Pete*!" said Max, breaking down. "Charlie, poor Charlie. *Alone now*."

"He has you," said Lucy.

"Yeah, but him and Pete, that was different. They had a world between them. They *loved* each other," he looked at Charlie. A slight snore came from him. Max smiled. "I'll take him to bed.

I'll stay with him tonight." Max stood and started walking up the stairs.

"Goodnight Max," said Lucy. Max turned and said nothing. Lucy and Shelby sat at the table quietly for a long time. The only sound was something moving around outside.

"I'm going to go to sleep, Lucy."

"What about our rocket?"

"What?"

"Our sky rocket, tonight's our last night here. We have to light it. To say goodbye..." Lucy paused. It hurt to say goodbye to her parents.

"Oh, right, we're going to Tim's tomorrow." *I hope he comes to pick us up, I hope I didn't stuff it.* Shelby thinks. *I'll apologise tomorrow.* "Haven't we had enough *drama* today, Lucy?" said Shelby. "It hasn't been a good day."

"But, we can't *forget* about Mum and Dad. It means a lot."

"Lucy... I love you, but we haven't had much luck today. A firework being shot into the sky?"

"What if they see it? *What if* tonight's the night?" Lucy was starting to cry again. "We can't *forget* about them, we can't."

Shelby gave Lucy a hug. "We haven't seen them for weeks, Lucy, we can still shoot a firework at Tim's."

"It's too *far away*, they'd never see it. Pete would've loved us shooting a sky rocket for him."

Shelby shook her head as if to say no. "I don't want to lose anyone else, not just tonight, but *ever* again. We have to learn from our mistakes Lucy." She put her hand on Lucy's shoulder. Shelby got up, kissed her on the cheek and went up the stairs, leaving Lucy to ponder her thoughts.

Shelby opened the door where everyone slept and saw Max cuddling Charlie. They were both fast asleep. She closed the door and picked a different room. Tonight, she wanted to be alone. She walked into what must have been the master bedroom. The bed was still unmade from whomever had vanished out of it. It made her feel a bit icky getting under the blankets but she was so tired that she didn't care. She took off her t-shirt and started rolling down her new jeans when she noticed a piece of paper sticking out of its top pocket. Her poem. She started to cry. She didn't think she had any tears left. She still had a few passages to go. It was Charlie and Pete's birthday. She was going to surprise everybody and read it out loud when they got back. Now, there was no Pete. She decided to finish it. Even though she was tired, she would do it for him. For Charlie and Pete, and if no one ever read it, that was okay. This was to help her come to peace with an unimaginable event.

She sat in the desk chair writing. The moonlight giving her just enough light to see. She sat there for at least twenty minutes, till she felt she had completed something that might be worthy of the friendship Pete and Charlie had. Once she had finished it, she laid her head on the desk, exhausted, and fell into a deep sleep.

Lucy was still downstairs. Her feet were up on the table. Her mind had been going over scenarios of what had happened in the mall. Running to Pete and Charlie. Killing the beast outside the toilets. Running in and finding the insectoid... Finding it and killing it. Seeing Pete. She would cry and stop, cry and stop. Her memories bring on fresh waves of sadness. She was now thinking of her dad and mum. She'd heard what Shelby had said, but it was *Lucy's* mum and dad. Wouldn't Shelby light a sky rocket if it was her mum? *I'm sure she would.* Dad saved us. Can I not do the same for him? She cried knowing it was probably wrong, but also feeling like she had to do it. She had no choice. If this was the last time, the last chance, then she would do it. Because she had to.

She went through this process of convincing herself many times before she finally got up and walked to where the fireworks were below the stairs. Even there, she paused. *Is this the right thing to do?* She knelt by the box. She grabbed a rocket out. Held it in her hands. *For Mum and Dad.* Lucy walked to the main door, undid the deadlock and opened the door. There was an eerie feeling as a slight breeze met her and blew her hair to one side. Outside the night was quiet and still. She decided to let the firework off further down the street, away from the house so hopefully they wouldn't hear it. Leaving the door slightly ajar so she could rush back in if she needed to, she still didn't feel at all safe. Lucy walked out into the cold night. She walked about fifty metres down the road to where she thought she was out of ear reach. She placed the sky rocket in the jar.

"For you Mum and Dad," whispered Lucy, smiling. She heard something. Something moving quickly back by the house. Her mind started to fill with images of monsters she had seen. She held the lighter by the wick and waited. The night was quiet again. *Should I light it?*

She remembered Shelby's words: "I don't want to lose anyone else, not just tonight, but ever again. We have to learn from our mistakes Lucy."

She looked at the wick. The thought of whatever was out there coming at her was terrifying. Her thumb was shaking on the lighter. She changed her mind. She grabbed the jar, put the lighter back in her pocket and briskly started to walk back to the house.

Looking over her shoulder both ways, the walk suddenly became a run. She felt like something was following her. Her mind making the shadows into all sorts of creatures. She was finally sprinting as she got to the door, slamming it shut and deadlocking it.

"Oh, shit," she whispered as her head fell onto the door. "I'm *sorry* Dad, I'm *sorry* Mum, I...I couldn't do it."

She broke down. Lucy finally gathered herself and went back to place the sky rocket in the box under the stairs. She stood staring at the empty space as she realised, the box was gone. "What?" she said to herself. *Did I move it?* She looked around the kitchen, nothing. The lounge, nothing. *No, I was never in here.* She went back to the door, said a little prayer and opened it. There was no box outside. Nothing down the street. *What the hell, I didn't move it, I couldn't have.* She closed the door, deadlocked it and ran back to the place under the stairs, hoping it had mysteriously reappeared. It was still empty. She scratched her head. She places the jar holding the sky rocket back under the stairs. *Maybe I put it somewhere?* She scratched her head again, *I'll look again tomorrow.*

She walked up the stairs, her head still shaking, thinking she had lost her mind, and obviously it was a reaction to everything that had happened. She opened the bedroom door and saw Max turned over on the side of his bed fast asleep. Strange, no Shelby and no Charlie. *Maybe they are together in another room.* She walked out and checked the toilet. No one there. She opened the master bedroom door, Shelby was asleep at the desk. There was no one else in the room. Lucy started to panic.

She ran through the house, trying to find Charlie. "Shit, shit, shit," she whispered as she searched everywhere. Charlie was nowhere to be found. She placed her hand on her head she remembered the door was ajar. She looked under the stairs, the fireworks gone, the sound outside. "No!" she said as her mind started to click over. She ran up the stairs and threw open Shelby's door. "Shelby! Charlie's *gone*!"

Outside in the far, far distance, a sound like a sky rocket went off, followed by a brilliance of soft light.

CHAPTER SIXTEEN

A Poem for Charlie and Pete

P ART ONE

Charlie had woken up and couldn't go back to sleep. His mind was full of Pete's last words.

"I'll always be with you." He couldn't see him but he could hear him clear as day. *Pete, oh, Pete.* He was crying as he felt an emptiness in the bed. Max, who had been cuddling Charlie, had now turned over. Charlie's body heat had overheated Max and he had turned and thrown off the blankets to get some relief. Charlie sat up and inspected the bed. Looking for his little friend. *Pete, oh, Pete, Where are you?* he thought.

"I'm here," he could hear Pete's voice but couldn't see him.

"You're *not*," he whispered back. Max stirred but stayed asleep, slightly snoring. Charlie looked around the dark room. Dark shadows were everywhere, but he no longer saw his demon, no longer did he feel afraid.

"You're so brave," said Pete. *I am Pete, I am, because of you.* He got up and looked around the room.

"Pete, you're not here, Pete?" he whispered again. *I can't see you?* There was no answer. "I miss you." Nothing. *It was your birthday Pete, our birthday.* "I want you back," he whispered. "I'll bring you *back*, Pete." No answer. Charlie slipped on his shoes and walked to the door and pushed it slightly. Max did not move. He walked past the bathroom and the master bedroom. He was as quiet as a mouse. He knew he had to be. No one would approve of what he was going to do. What he felt he had to do. He missed his friend. *I want you back, Pete.*

"The *fireworks* will bring you back."

He walked down the stairs and found the box in the cubby hole. He turned and saw the door was slightly ajar. *Thank you, Pete.* He thought as he made his way quietly to the door and pushed his way through it. The box squeezing through the door frame as he walked out into the cold night. He shivered but did not in any way feel scared. He was determined to find Pete, to bring him back. His friend. He looked both ways, left and right down the long street. He turned left and ran towards the bank, towards the forest. He failed to see Lucy far down the street to the right, she was trying to decide whether to light a sky rocket or not. She would look his way though, upon hearing him running. But, would not see him, he was already lost in shadow.

Part Two

Charlie ran across the street, where the broken car lay. The broken car that was wheelless, squashed and had now freshly had its roof ripped off. It watched him run past under the pale moonlight. A boy in pyjamas. Holding a box of fireworks he was struggling to carry. If it could think, this broken car, it would probably think he was brave. He made it to the bank. The only sound was his slight breath as he ran.

"You're so brave."

"I am, Pete, I'm doing this for you, *my friend*," Charlie whispered. He walked on an angle down the bank. The bright light from the moon lighting his way. The only time he stopped was when he reached the dense forest. It was only for a moment. But, he did stop. He looked back, back up the bank. He saw the brightly lit lawn. The beautiful stars above. When he looked into the forest it was dark and full of dark shadows. There were noises that made him jump. *I can do it,* he thought, *for Pete.* He knew he had to be far away. Far away from Max, Lucy and Shelby, for they would stop him. He needed to be hidden. *It's our birthday. Pete wanted to see the fireworks.*

He ran. The branches of the thick bush hitting his face. He held the box tightly. He would not drop it. Could not drop it. *I'm coming, Pete.* He felt something tug on his leg. He fought it and kept on going. He felt sticks and twigs cut into his hands. He felt the blood dripping off the back of his hands. But, he kept on going.

He couldn't see anything in front of him. His eyes were closed most of the time. He started to hum. A tune to calm himself. A tune his mum would sing to him. It was all that was in his young brain. A calming tune... and

"Pete." *Pete.*

He ran faster. He had never been this quick before. Maybe it was the cool night air. Maybe, it was the branches and twigs hitting his body as he ran that made him feel so... so swift. He opened his eyes. He saw a shadow. A shadow to the right. He may have screamed. He couldn't hear it. The noise of the forest was so loud. He looked behind him. The gorilla arms of the demon, his stretched, elongated body. His enormous grin. His flaming red eyes. It was behind him. Almost as tall as the trees. It was trying to get through the growth. Trying to get to him. *You're brave.* Charlie was starting to question his bravery. *I don't know if I can do it, Pete?* Thought Charlie.

"You can," replied Pete. For the first time, Charlie started to cry. His tears falling off his face in streams. He screamed out loud as he saw the demon getting closer. It's forked tongue tasting his back. *You're not real.* He thought as he felt something hit his arm. It burned. He turned to see what it was, but it was already gone. A shadow among many. His shoulder started to go numb.

"Hold the box, Charlie," said Pete. *I'm trying, Pete.* His arm started to tingle. *Faster, must run faster.* Something hit him on his back. He screamed again. He felt the burning sensation. Like a river meeting the ocean, it filled his body. His back started to ache like his left arm.

"Run, Charlie."

"I'm running Pete. For *you.*" Finally the forest started to open. A small divide, turned into a circle. From above, it was shaped like a light bulb and in the circle were three small trees. "I'm *here*, Pete," he whispered. "Are *you* here?" There was no answer. "Oh, Pete, *where* are you?" Nothing. He placed the large box down. His left arm almost totally useless. His back was screaming in pain. *I'm hurting, Pete,* thought Charlie.

"You can do it," encouraged Pete.

"I will, Pete. I still can't see you."

"Light a firework," said Pete. Charlie did as he was told. He placed a jar in the middle of the three trees. He put a large sky rocket in the centre of it. He grabbed the lighter from the box and hovered it by the wick.

"For *you*, Pete," he whispered. He lit the wick. It burned a circle of sparks that ran towards the sky rocket. A noise broke the sound of the forest as the fire rocket burst into the sky. From above looking down, Charlie's face looked up in wonder. His surprised face, open eyes and mouth turned into different colours, from red, to green, to blue, to white. Tears fell from his eyes.

"*There* you are, Pete! There you are!" Charlie started to break down as in front of him, barely four metres away from him, was Pete, looking up in the sky. He was clapping and cheering. "You *like* that, Pete? You want some more?" Pete kept clapping and Charlie started to joyously dance as well. He grabbed the next sky rocket.

Part Three

"Max! Charlie's *gone!*" screamed Shelby. Max immediately shot up. He jumped into action.

"What? How? *Where* is he?"

"He's not here. We've checked everywhere!" Shelby said, her voice almost shrieking.

"The fireworks are gone also!" added Lucy. Outside the large bedroom window, a large light lit the sky from a distance.

"No! Charlie! *No!*" shouted Max as he threw on his shoes and sprinted past Shelby and Lucy.

"Wait, Max, your *gun!*" Warned Shelby. It was too late. He was already gone. Shelby mumbled a swear word as she grabbed her gun and passed it to lucy. She then grabbed Max's gun and they sprinted down the steps trying to keep up with Max. As Shelby ran the poem in her pocket fell to the floor. Opening out to an empty audience.

Pete and Charlie, Charlie and Pete.
A poem by Shelby O'Leary.

For Pete.

Pete and Charlie, Charlie and Pete,
No closer friends, would you ever meet.
They came into my life, like a passionate flame,
All smiles and laughter, I'd never be the same.

"You *liked* that one?" asked Charlie, smiling. Pete was cheering and jumping up and down. Charlie's left arm was now totally useless.

"You're so brave."

"Thank you, Pete, *Happy Birthday!*" Charlie lit the next sky rocket. This one spun in circles as it flew into the sky. It then blew into a large umbrella shape that filled the sky with red. The noise was immense. Pete pointed at the sky and clapped. Charlie smiled at Pete and cried with tears of joy. His back now ached. The noise of the jungle was getting louder. The shadows around him were starting to move. Charlie did not notice, as he placed the next firework in the jar.

"There!" shouted Max as he sprinted past the broken car. (which had a six legged, four winged bug on it, eating its left mirror). The car watched as Max flew past, panic written on his face. Shelby followed, running like a track athlete, her gun in her left hand. Lucy came last, running as fast as she could, at the same time watching the fireworks going off in the sky. "Keep up!" shouted Max as he sprinted down the bank. "Charlie!" he screamed. "Charlie!" He flew into the dense forest without a second thought. Shelby followed closely. Lucy was angling down the bank, trying not to fall.

I never had a family to speak of,
It took a world to be erased before I found a friend.
He lost me, and I lost him,
But that is not where my tale ends.

Max was sprinting through the dense forest growth. The branches slapping his face and scratching his skin. He did not care as he was searching the sky. Looking for a sign of which way to go. An explosion of light blew out behind the dark silhouette of trees.

"This *way!*"he shouted. Shelby was trying to keep up. She could hear Max's noise in front of her.

We made it back, a family of four,
Before the world took back, that which it could not ignore
The four became two, and Shelby found a sister,
As we searched for our missing, Michael and Teresa.

Lucy was trying to keep up. She had lost both Max and Shelby. She couldn't hear them or see them. Her sprinting became a slow jog as she started to think she was going nowhere. She was pushing small trees and branches out of the way. She saw a light up in the sky. She paused to look at it. That's when she felt the pain on the back of her head. Like something had hit her, she felt her eyes start to blur over. Another pain. She saw stars. Again something hitting her in the same spot. Before she could turn around, she fell to the ground, unconscious.

Part Four

We came across three. Our world has changed,
Max was so handsome, Pete and Charlie, so brave.
Our family became five and in this, the day after,
Our lives were filled with wonder, Our days with so much laughter.

Charlie was now having trouble standing. Pete was sitting watching him. His hands entwined. His face filled with joy. Charlie lit the wick. A fire burst out and filled the surrounding area with light. Charlie did not look. He only saw Pete. Pete smiled and laughed.

Max was powering through the forest. The light in front of him was just going out. He felt a sting. Something had hit him on the side of his left ribs. He looked to see what it was. A large shadow was following him.

"Fuck!" he swore as he felt his left side start to go numb. He felt something slice his leg. "What the *fuck!*" Straight away his right leg was dragging behind him. Something hit his right chest. Another sting, his right hand grabbed it instinctively. It felt like flesh but it was shaped like a dagger. He ripped it out and threw it to the ground. "Charlie," he said as his voice started to lose strength. Shelby could hear Max in front. He had slowed down. She caught up to him as a creature was getting close to him. It was the size of a lion, its outline, horrible. Its large tail was up in the air like it was about to sting him. She shot it. The light of the gun lighting up the surrounding forest that was full of creatures. She screamed as something whistled past her face, narrowly missing her. She suddenly felt her body lift as something grabbed her by her shoulders. She was violently lifted up into the undergrowth. Up into the trees and just as suddenly was let go. She fell to the ground, the wind taken out of her.

Part Five

Charlie could hardly move. His whole body was numb. He had lit the last firework. He was now lying on the soil, between the three trees.

"Father, Son and... Holy Ghost," he whispered. His Sunday school days calling back to him at his end. *Max, Charlie and Pete.* His mind replied. He smiled. Pete was still smiling at him, looking like a peaceful angel.

"One more, Charlie," Charlie's eyes were closed. His right hand searched the box and felt a sky rocket. He fumbled and only just placed it in the jar. His eyes barely open, he lit the wick and watched the firework burst into the sky. His face lit up and he smiled, tears filled his eyes.

"This was the *best* night ever," he whispered to Pete, who smiled back at him. "You're my *best friend*. You always *helped* me. I'll never forget you," said Charlie, as his heart started to slow. "I love you..." His breathing shallow. "And... *I'll see you soon*." He smiled as he looked over at his best friend who smiled back at him, warming his slowing heart and for the last time, brave little Charlie, closed his eyes.

Pete and Charlie, Charlie and Pete,
The world through your eyes,
So simple and sweet.
Pete and Charlie, Charlie and Pete,
Our family is now complete, with our brave,
Charlie and Pete.

Part Six

Max could not go any further. His right leg would not let him.

"Charlie!" he screamed. His voice was hoarse. "Charlie!" Shelby caught up to him and caught Max before he fell over. She pulled him up and held him under her shoulder. "*No*, Charlie, poor Charlie," he said, his voice cut down to a whisper. A light filled the sky. A large bang followed before the only noise was that of the forest. Loud and angry. Two stings that sounded like arrows flew in front of Shelby. She heard one hit something. Max grunted.

"Max, we got to go!"

"*No*... Charlie," he said. His body angled like he was about to fall.

"If we keep going, we'll *die*," said Shelby, into his ear. He turned to her.

"Then we die."

"No, Max, no, you're not dying on me, there's too many *lost*." She pulled him and started to walk back.

"Charlie," he whispered as tears hit his eyes. "No..." The forest was dark and loud. Shelby was pushing branches and bushes out of their way.

"The fireworks have stopped, Max," she said as she pulled him along. "*Walk* Max. You can do it. I can't carry you. One step, *two steps!*" His body was numb. He couldn't feel anything. It was just her will that was keeping him going.

"Charlie... he might still *be...?*"

"He's not, Max. Now *fucking walk!*" She held him up. He was getting heavier.

"I... I can't," He whispered as his head fell forward, seemingly having no weight. Something ran at them from behind, it was small and vicious. It made a noise like a threatening rattlesnake.

Shelby lifted her gun and shot it. The forest again lit up. Creatures of all sizes were following them.

"Come on, Max!"

"I'm trying."

"Well, fucking *try harder!*" Shelby pulled him out of the dense bush and finally saw the steep bank ahead. She looked back, *goodbye Charlie, goodbye Pete.* She thought as she struggled up the bank practically holding Max up by herself. "I need you to work *hard* here, Max!"

"Okay," he said as his legs moved like a doll pulled by string. They made it to the top of the bank. Shelby shot two small lizard-type creatures that had braved the open bank and had slithered towards them. She pulled him onto the road as she braced him. The broken car (which had a creature pulling at its exhaust) watched them, a different picture to the one it had seen only a few minutes ago. Max was in total agony. His head was lolling up and down. His tongue hanging out of his mouth. His feet scraped across the road. Shelby holding him up. Her left hand throws the gun up every now and then. Her head turning left and right looking for danger. She made it across the road, *just a few more metres.*

"Almost there, Max, you're doing so well."

"Charlie..." He muttered, quietly. "...Pete."

"I know," said Shelby as she dragged him into the open door. She shut it quickly behind her and closed the deadlock.

Part Seven

Shelby lifted Max as he leaned on her and took him to the sofa
in the lounge. She lay him down and then searched the house.
Making sure it was clear and safe from danger. When she got to
the main bedroom she hoped she would see Charlie, and Pete both
asleep. Like this was some bad dream she had woken up from.
The house was empty. She came back to Max. He was delirious.
Screaming in pain.

"Charlie," he breathed out. His forehead was now covered in
sweat. She searched his body. She found two stingers still impaled.
One in his right ribs. The other just below his neck.

"You poor man," she said, a third one he had already pulled out.
It left a bloody round mark about the size of a fifty cent coin. The
two stingers left in his body were pulsating. *Still releasing their
venom,* she thought. She pulled them out and threw them across
the floor. Almost immediately they turned a grey colour and de-
generated, a slight mist rising above them. Blood was pouring out
of his wounds. Too much blood. She ran to the kitchen. Finding a
first aid kit she grabbed some rolls of bandages. She found a bottle
of disinfectant and dabbed the areas with cotton wool. Trying
to get them as clean as possible. She then wrapped the bandages
around his body so they were snug. He grimaced in pain.

"Harden up," she said, a small laugh came from Max's mouth.
She then grabbed a blanket and covered him to keep him warm.
"*Fight it!*" she said as she held his hand. "*Fucking* fight it!" She
wiped his forehead with a towel. He was shaking. His body, fighting the poisons. "Don't die on me boy, you're *all* I've got." She
spent the night, wetting his lips with water and keeping him warm.
He shook violently at times. His face, a pale light green. But, he
fought. Just like she asked, he fought.

Finally after a long night, he quietened and seemed to almost fall asleep. She was about to fall asleep with him when she thought for the first time.

Where the fuck is Lucy?

CHAPTER SEVENTEEN

The Forest of Lost Souls

S HELBY WOKE UP NEXT to Max. He was still sweating but his fever had died a little. She wiped his brow as his head moved her way. He murmured something, but his eyes remained shut.

"It's okay Max, it's okay." She kissed his cheek and walked into the kitchen. Through the boarded window she could see a red sunrise. Little streams of light lay across her body and face. The warmth felt good.

So much had happened yesterday. The two boys lost. Tim, gone. Lucy missing. *Lucy.* She swallowed a heavy gulp. *This world will not let me grieve, Lucy... I will have to look for Lucy.* Her hands rested on the bench as she turned to Max. He was shaking a little. His head moved left and right in spasms. *Nightmare.* Shelby walked back to him. "Shhh, Max, we're safe, we're *home.*"

"Charlie," he whispered.

"This fucking world," she remembered the words the being had said.

"You will probably not survive, Michael Stevenson."

"I'm alive, you fuck," she whispered to herself. "Max..." Max's eyes remained shut. "Max, if you can hear me, I'm going to have to check the forest, I have to see if Lucy is in there, *somewhere*... Jesus." She lowered her head in thought. She knew it was crazy, crazy to go back. "...She may have fallen, she might still be alive." Max's head shook, almost like he was saying, no. "I have to, she's, she went in with us." She patted his forehead. "She would do the same. Also... Charlie, we never *saw* him. If... by some *miracle*." She started to brush his forehead with the back of her hand. "I have to go now, while the sun is up." She grabbed his hand and squeezed it. There was no squeeze back. She kissed his cheek. "I won't be long, an hour at the most. *In and out*." It felt like she was telling herself that it would be okay.

She placed his hand on his stomach and took one last long look. She then walked over to the kitchen bench and loaded the guns. Tim had left a sizable amount of ammunition. *Tim, he hadn't come back.* She placed two guns in her satchel and carried Max's rifle. She chose her clothes carefully. A green U2 Popmart tour vintage t-shirt. Brown cargo pants. Green retro Adidas shoes and to finish off the camouflaged look. A green Radiohead cap turned backward. On the front of the hat, facing backward was the word, *Creep*, written in yellow.

Her red hair was tied back. She opened the door. Turning back and looking at Max she said. "Keep fighting." She turned and looked outside.

"You know I *fucking* will."

She closed the door and strode off like a soldier on the warpath.

Walking up the same street as last night, the difference was amazing. The sun made everything so much more normal. She passed a house where the lawn now was higher than the fence. *Not so normal.* She stopped at the broken car. She stood looking at it for a long while. It looked different. It had no wheels. It was squashed almost flat. Its roof had been ripped off and now, the seats had been eaten from the top. Stuffing was spilling out everywhere. "Good morning." The car did not reply. "Rude," she said as she ran down the steep bank. She stood outside the forest once again. This time, she was prepared. Releasing the safety she thought, *should I say a prayer?* "Fuck that."

She walked into the forest. She walked roughly the same path as Max had taken yesterday. She noticed branches that were broken, small trees that were pushed out of the way. Her gun led the way, her finger itching on the trigger. The further she walked in, the higher the tree rooftop became. The darker it also became. She felt like she was being watched, but she ignored this and walked with purpose. She wouldn't let her mind imagine what the noises could be. *Find Lucy.* She kept looking at the ground. Looking for footprints. Looking for anything that might give away Lucy's presence.

"Lucy." She half heartedly called out. Something moved. She froze. Her hands started to shake. Her mind was remembering the stingers that flew through the air. She had only come across a silhouette of what they were attached to. The movement darted ahead of her and then flew into the sky. "Fuck," she whispered.

"Fuck, fuck, come on Shelby, start *walking*." She moved, quieter than before.

"Lucy?" she murmured again. She tried to stay on the same path but she had no idea if it was the right one. The forest was too big. It was dark last night and nothing looked familiar. She felt frustrated. She knelt and looked around her. Her hand touched the ground. "Fuck... I'm no *hunter tracker*, I'm just a teenager from fucking *Newtown*." She whispered to herself. Suddenly, the ground started to shake. She regretted talking. *Earthquake?* she thought. A large snout started to come out of the ground ahead of her. Rows of teeth appeared as its mouth opened. She stayed completely still. Its snout was vibrating as its eyes opened. Its eyes were totally silver. It blinked when it saw the light and disappeared back into the ground. "Okay...?" she whispered. *So some of them sleep in the ground. Nice.* The forest was so alive last night it must be where a lot of them hide during the day. *I must be quiet and be careful where I stand.* She thought as she started to notice round mounds of soil in places where creatures had dug. She hadn't taken notice of it before. Now, it made sense.

She moved, quickly. Her gun angled around her from side to side. "Lucy?" she whispered again. She still had that feeling like someone or something was following her. Every now and then she'd hear a twig break or see something move.

All of a sudden the forest started to open. A large clearing grew in front of her and she saw three trees standing by themselves in a circle. Above her the light was streaming in. She felt safe here. Moving towards the trees she noticed in the centre was a box, by the box was a jar. Her hand curled and touched her mouth in shock. "Charlie," she said quietly. She knelt down by the jar, the bottom of it blackened from the sky rockets. She grabbed it and studied it. Hoping it might give away some of its secrets. It didn't. She saw the small, grey lighter, lying by itself. She started to cry.

"Poor, brave Charlie." *Did you see Pete?* she thought, remembering the story Michael had told, of seeing his wife and what the blue angel had said, that they would appear as a form of comfort before you die. She had never seen anything or anyone, no ghosts. *Is this why you did it Charlie? to see Pete?* "I hope you *saw* him," She said as she placed the jar back and wiped her cheeks. She checked the box, it was empty. He had used all the fireworks. Some of the burnt remains still littered the area. She searched the clearing but found no sign of Charlie. Nothing. There was no trace left behind. No material or clothing. No blood. She hoped, however it had happened. It was quick and painless.

She got up. "Lucy!" she shouted. Here in the clearing she felt she was safe enough to call out loud. Her voice echoed through the forest. The forest was too big and dangerous for her to search it all. She would go back the same way and call out her name again. She had a feeling that, like Charlie, Lucy may have met her fate last night.

Walking back out of the clearing she felt the warmth quickly change to a slight chill. She was moving quicker now. Walking over logs and between bushes. She knew which way to go. "Lucy?" she whispered, over and over. She noticed a brown and red coloured snake slithering across the ground in S shapes in front of her. She had her gun pointed at it as it stopped by her. Suddenly its tail end rose into the air and started spinning. "*Fuck* that," she said as she shot it before it could reveal what it was going to do. In response to her rifle shot a movement came from the trees above. Something was swinging swiftly down towards her.

She ran. *I'm out,* she thought as she sprinted through the forest. More sounds were coming from above as other creatures were joining in the hunt. She shot her rifle into the air as she ran. Something brushed her cap and she shrieked, shooting wildly behind her. "Fuck off!" she screamed. She blindly shot her rifle behind her again, as she jumped a fallen tree. Something howled and fell hitting the ground. "I'm *sorry,* Lucy! I fucking *tried!"* she shouted as she burst out of the forest and sprinted up the bank, not wanting to look back.

She stopped by the broken car trying to catch her breath. "What the fuck are you looking at?" she yelled at the car. "At least I *tried* to do something. Not like you who just *sit* here, fucking looking *sadder* every day!" *I'm talking to a car,* she thought as she shook herself and walked back to the house.

She opened the door and sighed, happy to see Max was still alive and breathing. She closed the door and deadlocked it. She sat beside him grabbing his hand. She squeezed it. He didn't squeeze back. "No sign, Max. *Nothing.* I tried." She squeezed his hand again. "How goes the battle?" She spoke gently in his ear. She kissed him. "Keep *fighting* buddy, it's just you and me." She brushed his forehead. "Just *you and me.*"

CHAPTER EIGHTEEN

In The Dark

MAX HAD BEEN FIGHTING the poisons running through his body. By the fourth day it seemed like he was winning the fight. His body had calmed. His breathing was constant. He wasn't sweating anymore. Shelby felt like he was finally going to wake up. She'd been wetting his lips with water, trying to keep him hydrated and changing his bandages daily. The wounds looked like they were getting better.

On the fifth day he deteriorated. He started convulsing. The colour had disappeared from his cheeks and whatever liquid he had left in him was coming up every half hour. Shelby was kneeling next to him. His blankets off of him as his body temperature was going through the roof.

"Max, *Max* can you *hear me*?" Max was shivering, he didn't answer. "Max, you're getting *weak*, Max. I'm going... I'm going to find Tim." Her head went down. She hadn't seen Tim in over five days. She remembered how she'd talked to him, rude and angry.

She felt like it was her fault he hadn't come back . "Tim said he knew a *doctor*. I'll try to find Tim and bring the doctor *here*, okay?" She feathered his brow with her hand. She wiped it with the hand towel. He was sweating profusely. She kissed him. "I'll be as quick as possible. *Fucking fast.*" She kissed him again, turning him on his side. She placed a bowl under his face. Feeling helpless, she turned and ran to grab her satchel and rifle and rushed out the door.

The Honda wouldn't start, she swore. The next two cars were the same. Flat batteries. She found a nice Tesla that started but hadn't been charged. She was starting to run out of options. She finally found a bus, the last job it had on its sign was, *Number 11, Newtown Park, Zoo*. It was massive. It started first time and was full of fuel. She had no choice. Luckily, it was an automatic and after driving a few bends she got the hang of it. *I've just got to keep to the main roads.* She thought, as the bus was so big. After a while she could see the humour in it. *I'm fucking driving a bus!* She quite liked driving it as it gave her a sense of power and it didn't drive that different to a car. She just had to be careful when turning a bend or when she came close to a parked car.

After an hour she arrived at Tim's army base. She slowed to a crawl as she arrived. The large gate that Tim had always locked was open. It was around 11 am, so he should have definitely locked it the previous night and he would have if he'd just left. Not only was the gate open, but it was hanging off its rails, like it had been rammed. She drove in slowly over the speed humps as she bounced up and down in her seat. The seat's air pumps noisily working underneath her. The bus was loud and made a cacophony of commotion. She was trying to arrive in stealth mode but it's extremely difficult in this quiet world.

She got closer to Tim's main entrance where he had parked previously. She noticed the main doors were open. Then she saw the Bushmaster. Or, the skeleton of the bush machine. It had been burnt out. Almost like a bomb had gone off from the inside. The top of it was just a husk of black metal. The bottom starts black and then slowly fades into rusted steel, no remnants of its camouflaged green remain. "Oh, Tim." She said, worriedly. "What happened?" The bus came to a loud stop. She pulled the handbrake up and opened the door. Rifle at the ready.

Shelby walked straight into the building. She had no time to waste as she knew Max was on his deathbed. She was almost running down the hallway. The lights were out. The power that was working before seemed to be off. She tried some lights but nothing worked. There was a sinister feeling to the place, like a ghost house that had been empty for too long. She slowed as she got to the lower levels. With no light the large corridors were dark and terrifying. She went back up the stairs and managed to find a torch in one of the many offices. It gave off a little light. Just enough to make you feel like you were playing a blood curdling video game we're a monster would run at you when you least expected it. It didn't help much with her feeling of discomfort.

She made her way back down to the lower levels. The light, giving her a couple metres of vision. "Tim?" she called meekly. No answer. She didn't expect him to be here. She knew if Tim was here, everything would be working. The fact that the place was out of action meant he was hurt, unconscious or worse. It's why she kept going. "Tim, you *here*?" she whispered. No answer, the only sound, a distant dripping faucet. She carried on. The corridor she was in led to his large room. It was not long ago she was here with Max, Lucy, Pete and Charlie. What a time they had. How different the place looked then. It was full of life and colour. Now, everything felt spine-chillingly dead. "Tim?" she whispered again as she made her way to the main door. It was ajar. She pushed it and it squeaked. Her eyes closed as she made a face like she was trying to push the door quietly. It squeaked even more. The massive room remained silent.

She walked in. The large space that had housed them was now completely blanketed in darkness. She would have to be almost touching something to see it. The torch worked pathetically as she saw the fridges. The bunks that were all made. Tim's main bed unmade? *Unusual.* She then saw rows of video machines. Vintage ones, like *Donkey Kong, Ski, Pac Man, Space Invaders, Elevator and Hyper Olympics.* Also, Pinball Machines like, *Monster Bash, Indiana Jones, The Addams Family and Terminator Two.* He had great taste, he also had all the high scores. Though, if she remembered right, Pete was getting close on *Pac Man.* She smiled, remembering the fun they had all had that night.

"Tim? Fucking hell man, just *answer,*" she whispered as the torch revealed the large sofa and two large TVs. Coming back to the main door she saw the air hockey game. A pool table, dart board, and finally, the fridge filled with fizzy drinks. "*Fuck it,* why not?" Shelby said as she opened the fridge and pulled out a coke. She opened the can and the noise echoed in the empty room and hall.

Something moved. Not in the room but outside in the corridor. "Oh, *fuck me.*" She whispered as she sculled the can and walked quietly to the door. Her rifle in front. The torch hanging off it in her left hand. She felt very professional. "Tim?" She whispered again knowing it wasn't him, but probably something she couldn't dream up. The corridor was silent. She stood by the door. Her torch in front shining into the room. The corridor is jet black. "Fuck," She muttered. She stood there for a good five minutes. The only sound was her heart beating frantically against her rib cage. She turned off the torch. Whatever was in the corridor didn't need to know she was coming.

She walked out of the door and placed her palms against the wall behind her. She then slowly walked along. Her hands guiding her. Her face turned towards the direction she was going. Her eyes closed. She was trying not to breathe, trying not to make a noise. She had gone a good ten metres without feeling or hearing anything. She was nearing the steps. The steps that would lead up to safety. *Why the fuck do I do this to myself? For Max, for Tim.* She answered herself. She felt something. Her right foot nudged something on the ground and it moved. She froze. *What do I do, what do I do?* Something snorted. "Fuck!" she ran. She turned on the torch and ran as fast as she could. She didn't look behind. She made it to the steps and sprinted up them. The light started to mix with the dark. Finally she made it to the main hallway. Light was flooding in from the main entrance way and surrounding windows. She started to slow her pace and quickly turned. Her rifle pointing at her would be assassin.

She waited and knelt. Ready to send a barrage of bullets. Another snort, followed by a soft whine. A nostril appeared. A blow of smoke. A head. She aimed her rifle. The eyes. Kind eyes. It walked into view. A creature, like one from a story of fables. It was bigger than a small lizard. Larger than a Komodo Dragon. It was more like the size of a small donkey. It blew out more smoke from its nose and licked its large paw. It then turned in a circle and fell lazily to the ground in front of Shelby. It rested its head on its paws and looked up at her. In fact it looked like it was almost inviting her to come forward. Shelby was wiser than that. "Not in this fucking *world*." She said to herself. As she backed up, the rifle was still pointing at it. The creature got up and started slowly walking towards her. Every now and then it would let out a little whine. As it came into the light she could see it better. It had grey reptile-type skin. On top of its body was a ridge line of scales. Scales that were coloured like the inside of a polished oyster shell. It was beautiful and out of this world. Its legs were short and stubby. The front legs had an excess of skin. But, it's eyes. They were kind eyes. Like the eyes of a kind labrador that wants you to pat it.

"Okay handsome, not too fucking *close*," she said as she kept walking back. The creature blew air from its nostrils, a strong gusterly blew into Shelby's face, sweeping her hair from her brow. She smiled. "Yeah okay, you're a good one, I guess." She passed large closed doors that she remembered Max telling her was the pantry. Inside were shelves and shelves of food. "Hungry boy?" she asked as it got close to her. "Don't *eat* me okay?" Shelby said as she opened the doors. The large creature smelt the air. Made a noise like it approved and walked into the pantry. Its tail brushed Shelby as it walked in.

"Gunther, I don't know why, but you look like a Gunther." Gunther was busy sticking its nose into a large bag of rice. It snorted as some got stuck up its nose. "Got to go, Gunther. Enjoy your lunch." Shelby rushed back into the kitchen. She found a medical kit, some bottles of antibiotics, creams and fresh bandages. "Score." She said as she ran back to the pantry. Gunther was now munching on a box of cereal, box and all. He was lying down on all fours. When he saw her his back tail lifted and started spinning. "Have fun, Gunther. I'll see you down the road." Shelby smiled, turned and hurried back to her bus. She drove out of the base upset that she couldn't find Tim, but feeling positive that she had medicine that could possibly improve Max's condition. She thought of Gunther all the way back to the house.

Max could feel himself shake. His fever was at breaking point. He was delirious and dreaming of a past life. He was back at the orphanage. Where he had spent thirteen years of his life, he'd been told his mother had dropped him off when he was just two. She was a single mum. He had no story for his dad. His dad probably had no idea he existed. Steven or Stevie, his best friend was a blurred image lying in the bed next to him.

"I'm so *excited* Maxy, *tomorrow's* the big day!" Max looked over smiling. Stevie was his best friend. He'd had many best friends over the years. They came and went like the wind.

"I'm so *happy* for you, Stevie." Max was always positive, incredibly earnest. He just wanted the best for his friends.

"Oh, Max, I'll *miss* you mate, I'll miss you so much."

"Me too," Max replied as Stevie looked back up to the ceiling grinning.

"How big do you think the house will be?"

"I'm sure it's *gigantic*."

"How big will my room be?" asked Stevie as he turned Max's way.

"Huge!" answered Max, spreading out his arms.

"...And I bet the fridge will be *full* to the brim."

"Of course."

"I'll get you around as soon as I'm there."

"I can't wait," replied Max, knowing this would never happen. Once they started schooling and had new friends Max would be a distant memory.

"What about you, Maxy? *When* are you leaving?" Max looked confused. Before he could answer, Stevie looked like his mouth was painted with lipstick. Lipstick that was smeared up on both sides. He looked like a cross between Stevie and a woman, with a smidge of Shelby. "Never, right Maxy? *Never*, because *we don't want you!*" His voice had changed to the voice of a crazed woman. "*I* don't want you!" It was what he thought his mum looked like. "I don't *need* you, Maxy. You're a *waste of space* and my space is precious to me!" her voice was evil and sadistic.

Suddenly, he was in the boys toilets, in a cubical crying. *No one wants me,* he thought. He'd been passed over so many times. For boys that were younger, cuter, smarter, the right colour. He was too happy or not happy enough. He never met the criteria. Once he was placed in a house for a day. For *one* day. They never spoke to him. He never said a word. He just sat there, wondering what to do. And they returned him. *What was I supposed to do?*

A knock came at the door.

"Are you okay? Maxy?" It was Stevie. "I've got to *go* now, Maxy." He knocked again. "Come out Maxy and you can *come with me?*" He raised his hand to the door. "*Come on,* Maxy." Footsteps could be heard running away. Max got up and tried to push the door. It wouldn't budge. "Come on, Maxy, before you *lose* us forever," said Stevie, now in the far distance. He tried to push the door but it wouldn't move. Hands grabbed him around his neck and pulled him back onto the seat. They were strong and gripped him tightly. He was losing his breath in his mind and in reality.

"They don't want you," A voice whispered in his ear. "Like I don't want you." It was his mum and her flesh was rotten. Skin was falling off her arms. He screamed. He grabbed the hands and pulled them away from his neck.

Rushing to the door he shoved it and it flew open. He was in a different place. He ran into a large area. Behind him he heard voices.

"What have you got *planned* for us, Max?" It was Pete.

"Can't wait," said Charlie. Max turned and picked them up. They hugged him and kissed him.

"Boys!" he said. He was so happy to see them he was crying with tears of inebriated joy. They pulled away from his arms and ran into the dream. Ahead he saw bouncy castles, car rides, and a large castle with cross bridges, nets and walkways; a kid's perfect dream.

"Yay!" said Pete, running. "Lollipops Land!"

Charlie turned to Max. "Thanks Max! You're the *best*." It was a time that Max remembered. He had broken into the local Lollipops Land arena. They had spent the day there safely inside. The kids loved it. He loved it.

"Don't get *lost!*" he shouted as he followed them into the large castle.

"Try and catch me!" shouted Pete as he ran into the distance.

"*No*, me. Try and catch me, Max!" called Charlie as he climbed up a net. Showing incredible strength and grace.

"I can't keep up!" yelled Max.

"Catch us!" shouted Pete.

"You're too quick!"

"No, you're too slow," replied Charlie, laughing. Max found himself bouncing into soft round logs that were stacked, hanging vertically in front of him. He was trying to push them out of the way.

"*Wait* boys!" They were falling back into him. Hurting him. He fell. He got up and now the soft logs were hard and rough, they felt like trees. He was running between them. "Wait boys, I'm *coming!*" he shouted.

"You've *lost* us, Max!" cried Pete, sounding like he was miles away.

"Where are you, Max? I can't see you, don't you *want* us?" shrieked Charlie.

"Hurry up!" shouted a voice behind him. It was Shelby, she was running powerfully behind him. Easily running between trees and branches. "Don't *lose* them!" she yelled, "Whatever you do, *don't lose them!*"

Max tried to run but the branches were entangling him. "I can't *move!*" He screamed.

"You're *losing* them!" shouted Shelby. Suddenly the branches that were around his neck morphed into his mum's hands. They were squeezing the life out of him, Shelby had become his mum. She whispered in his ear, low and evil,

"...Or they won't want you! *Like I don't want you.*"

Shelby slammed the brakes on the large bus as it shook in retaliation. She pulled up the park brake. Her parking was not the neatest, she was parked on a thirty degree angle and as a result took up the whole narrow street. *There's no fucking traffic anyway.* She grabbed her satchel full of first aid gear and opened the doors. She had discovered a switch on the outside that closed the bus doors shut and was happy that the bus was safe. It still had a mountain of diesel, it ran on the smell of an oily rag. She thrust the gate open and closed it and ran towards the door. Her heart rate always started to elevate as she returned home. In this case it was for a good reason. *Is Max okay? Is he still alive?* But, in general her anxiety would increase as even locked homes were not considered safe in this world.

Shelby opened the door and rushed in. She stood looking at the sofa for a long time before registering what she was seeing. The lounge suite was empty. Just a blanket lay messily on the sofa. She rushed into the kitchen,

"Max!" she shouted. "Max, *where* are you?" Running into the lounge, there was no sign of him. She ran out to the back, past the washhouse. There was no one. She opened the door and rushed out searching the backyard. "Max?" A creature shaped like a spider the size of a large dog. Backed its way sideways like a crab, up the fence and over it. It reminded her of the creature she had encountered in the other house. It had too many eyes and was dripping liquid from its open jaw. It seemed to be as scared of her as she was of it as it disappeared quickly. Just as the last of its eyes was almost out of view a liquid spewed from its mouth, it shot like a pump action water pistol and just missed her. "Fucking hell... *Ew*," said Shelby, disgusted.

She closed the door and hurried back into the house. "Max!" she screamed loudly as she came to the stairs. Taking two steps at a time, she flew up the stairs like an Olympic level athlete, pulling on the bannister as she ran. She sprinted past the master bedroom, past the bathroom and rushed into the bedroom where they had all slept. The room was darkening as it was getting late now. Shadows were creeping into the large room. Shelby had cleared the excess bedding and now there were just the two kids beds she had neatly made.

She saw a rifle to the left of the bed closest to the window. It was lying on its side, the light from the window shining on it, like a glow around a saint on a stained glass window.

"Max?" she questioned, her voice slightly scared. She ran forward past the rifle and saw him. His back leaning against the side of the bed. His tear strewn face illuminated by the light from the window, his mouth open. *Is he alive?* She rushed to him and knelt by him.

"Shelby." He managed emotionally, turning his head towards her as he cried. "I thought... I thought you were *dead*." He could hardly get his words out, he was both sad and happy. "Shelby," he said.

"Call me *Shell*."

"I do." They smiled at each other. He grabbed the back of her head and they pressed foreheads together. They were laughing and crying together. He kissed her, and she kissed him back.

"Shelby... I... I thought you were dead, I thought... Lucy was dead, Pete and Charlie..." He bowed his head and broke down. "I wanted to see them... *I'm sorry*... I wanted to see them." He lost control and broke down even more.

"Max," she said as she hugged him. "You can't *leave* me, *you shit*. You're *all* I have."

"I'm sorry Shelby. I'm so sorry. Pete and Charlie, they didn't appear. *I never saw them*." He looked up at her, his eyes streaming with tears.

"It's because, you... you didn't *mean it*, you fuck! Don't ever give up! Ever. You hear me? *Ever!*"

"I won't..." he said, smiling at her. "Not with *you*, here, *with me*. I won't." They kissed again and Shelby hugged him like she would never hug him again.

Shelby and Max sat together, watching the sky turn to night. "How are you feeling?" she asked, breaking the silence.

"Sick."

"You've been in a coma for a *few days*."

"How?"

"You don't *remember*?"

"*Nothing*, just running, running through the forest. It was dark."

"You were stung."

"Stingers?"

"Yeah, *three times*. They release a poison. Real gross. You could hardly walk."

"Still can't."

"How...?"

"I crawled up the stairs. Luckily, I have a *strong* upper body."

"Yeah, but you obviously *skip* leg day." Max looked at Shelby and smiled. She smiled back. They held hands.

"I can't feel much in my legs. *Tingles* is all."

"Well, that's something. It'll come back."

"Better... or I'll end up like Professor X from The X-men."

"Who's that?"

Max had a surprised look on his face, his mouth open. "Bald guy, handsome? In a wheelchair?"

"Can't use a wheelchair in this world. You'd be like a *snack* on wheels." Max smiled, his face suddenly changed to serious.

"Lucy?"

"...Missing. I went back into the forest the next day just in case."

"So *brave*."

"I know. I went along the track we made, as much as possible. But, she could be anywhere in that forest... *or not*." Max squeezed her hand. "I found the spot where Charlie..." Shelby looked up at Max. Her eyes were big. Max noticed the bottom of her eyes started to slightly pool. "He picked a clearing. He must have been *so courageous*. He used all the fireworks."

"For Pete?"

"For Pete."

They both turned and looked at the window. The stars were shimmering. "I let them down," said Max, his voice breaking.

"How could you know?"

"*Both*, in one day."

"Tim said, we were set up in the mall. *Someone* is to blame," said Shelby.

"Yeah," replied Max, nodding his head.

"...And Charlie, following, was the *beautiful love* he had for his friend."

"I should've guessed."

"Max... we had no idea." She placed her hand on his shoulder and squeezed. They both started to cry.

"My *boys*," said Max, breaking down. Shelby said nothing. She just hugged him. After a long period of time they sat, quietly looking outside. The wind whistling a tune, made Shelby feel a slight chill. "Tim?" Max asked.

"He didn't come back."

"What?"

"Yeah, I went to his place, just this morning, his vehicle was burnt out, the security gates, broken. The powers out... it's like someone destroyed the place."

"...Jeez and no sign of Tim?"

"No sign." Max shook his head not believing. *Tim as well.*

"I did discover a funny-looking creature."

"Yeah?"

"Yeah, not like the other predators out there, this one seemed almost friendly."

"Didn't think that was possible."

"This is the second one I've come across. The first one was a little dog-like creature that flies and breathes fire, Michael called him, *Pup*."

"Breathes fire?"

"Yeah, and flies, this new creature reminds me a little of Pup, just bigger. I called him *Gunther*."

"Gunther?"

"I thought he looked like a Gunther, I might see how he's going tomorrow. We better rest. You need to *recuperate*."

"I am feeling...tired."

"We'll talk more in the morning."

"Sure."

Max sat looking out the window. His mind filled with images of Charlie lighting fireworks, with monsters closing in around him. "Shelby, *Shell*, you awake?" She didn't answer. "We've *lost everyone*," he whispered to himself. After an hour or so he finally closed his eyes.

They slept together facing the window sitting on the charcoal coloured carpet. Their backs rested against the side of the bed. Shelby slept soundly. Her head leaning on Max's shoulder.

In the morning, Shelby helped Max down to the lounge. She made him a breakfast of baked beans that he barely touched.

"You must be hungry," asked Shelby.

"My stomach feels like it's been through a *mincer*," replied Max, rubbing his stomach. He ate a few spoonfuls then sat looking at a picture of the previous family. They all looked happy. Shelby sat eating her food. She was talking about her plans for the day, how she would visit Gunther. How she was driving a large bus now that she thought kicked ass. She would also stop by a shop or dairy and grab some more supplies. Max hadn't heard or registered anything Shelby had said.

"Max, did you want anything from the shop?" Max was still looking at the picture. "Max?"

"Huh?" Max replied, turning to Shelby.

"Did you want anything from the shop? *Are you okay?* Did you want me to stay? I'm sorry, I like to keep busy, I didn't think, did you want me to *stay?*" she repeated, looking worried.

"No, no, of course not. I'm feeling better, don't worry. You go. I... I don't need anything." Shelby sat at the table busy checking her guns and rifle.

"I can go tomorrow."

"No... I... I would come with you but, if I needed to run, or *walk even...*"

"I know, you can't, but you will. *Baby steps*, eh, Max? Little bit each day."

"Little bit each day," he repeated, smiling.

"They've got a bookshelf upstairs with some goodies." Max gave her a funny look. "Oh, right, I'll get them for you before I go."

Shelby set Max up with books and snacks and kissed his forehead. She almost felt like saying, *'Love you'* as she left but just said it in her head. He felt it through her actions. She opened the door and turned smiling at Max as he sat eating a cracker. "You never know who I might bump into! *Hope is alive!*" she said, with her fist raised. Max gave her a beaming smile as he started looking through the novels Shelby had given him.

CHAPTER NINETEEN

Days of Recovery

DAY ONE

Shelby drove her bus back to Tim's army base. On the way, she drove past the area where she and Lucy had encountered the bird. She looked at the time on the dashboard. 9:56 am. She decided to stop and walk down to where the bridge was. She remembered the bells she had heard in the far distance. It was 10 am the last time the bells had rung. She stood watching the waves of water build and fall, build and fall. She made sure to stand a good distance away from the water remembering Tim's advice and also her own encounter in the water which seemed like a lifetime ago. She had no memory of it. Just the feeling of weightlessness. Her starfish body floating in the warm water and then nothing. Her mind had blacked it out like an unwelcome memory that should never be experienced again. It had been locked up and put away in the deepest recesses of her brain.

She noticed something she hadn't seen before. Resting on the pebbled shore was an old fishing boat. Shelby couldn't remember if it was there before or not. As she was trying to remember she heard a bell ring out in the distance. She looked at her watch. Sure enough, it was 10 am. Nine more bells rang out. Someone was telling everyone the time, or something was still on timer. Either way, she could sort of make out where the sound was coming from. Tomorrow, she would get closer to it and find out who was making the noise. Happy to be making plans, she set out for Tim's base.

On the way, she had a large beast walk out and stand in front of the bus. It was part-lion and part-bear and all the worst parts put together. She stayed put hoping it would get bored and leave. Instead it saw the colours of the bus, the red and yellow as an invitation to charge it. Shelby held her wheel tightly as it hit the bus, and the creature came off second best. It walked away wounded, its pride slightly shaken. "*Good* bus," said Shelby as she patted the steering wheel. She felt like she had made a good choice driving the huge, monstrous vehicle. Things were looking brighter and she whistled as she set off again.

Arriving at Tim's base the place looked exactly the same. She walked into the entrance hallway. It still felt like a ghost house that had been left abandoned. She made her way to the large pantry. The door was still open. The pantry was a mess. Half of the food had been turned upside down and inside out. She smiled, knowing Gunther had been busy. She walked to the end of the hall and stepped quietly down the stairs. Everything suddenly turned dark and she only made it halfway when her fear told her to stop.

"Gunther?" she whispered. From far at the back of the hall came a snort and a sound that sounded like a helicopter taking off. She smiled, knowing his tail was spinning.

She backed up the stairs and into the light, hearing heavy footsteps coming her way. She had grabbed a box of Weetbix cereal food and sat by the back wall waiting. A large snout came first, as a blow of air blew her hair back. He was bigger. Almost twice as big as before. He came forward with his intelligent eyes smiling at her. "*Hi* Gunther!" Shelby said, taken aback by his size. He walked over to her and the floor felt like it was shaking. She put out her hand and he nudged his large head against it. "Want some food, *big fella*?" she asked as she opened the box and held out a biscuit size Weetbix at him. He smelt it, sniffed and munched it. His mouth made smacking noises as he struggled with the Weetbix texture.

"Probably not the best choice, eh, boy? You need some milk with these." Shelby smiled as she patted him. Gunther stuck his nose into the box and munched some more, before eating the whole box in one mouthful. "Nice *one* Gunther," said Shelby as she laughed.

Shelby sat back down as Gunther laid down next to her like a large rhino kneeling on its knees. It then stretched out its long neck and placed its head on Shelby's lap. "Awe, Gunther, you're just a big, cuddly *softy*." She patted his head and Gunther made a noise like a helium balloon letting out air. After a good ten minutes, Shelby decided she'd better go, she had business to attend to. "I've got things to do, Gunther! Max needs some food and books buddy." She kissed its snout and rubbed its leg. Gunther let out another high pitched noise. "You're pretty smart aren't you boy?" He again whistled back.

She got up and walked back to the pantry. Gunther followed. "You've still got some food in there, but, after that you'll have to find your own." She rubbed Gunther under his chin. "Got to go boy!" she said as she made her way back to the entrance. Gunther followed. "*No*, you stay, I'll come back." Gunther's head went down like he'd just been told off. "Stay," said Shelby, firmly. She put her hand up like a sign. Gunther's back legs fell back like a dog sitting at attention. "*Good boy*, Gunther." Gunther's tail spun as Shelby turned and walked away. She looked back seeing Gunther turn and gloomily walk back into the shadows. She felt a little sad but he was too big to put in the bus. Plus, how could she look after him?

She drove off and made her way to the nearest supermarket. She found a countdown. The windows had been smashed in. The food inside had been pretty much emptied out and what was left had been rummaged through by other creatures. It was a bit of a worry, she thought. A year or so on and food was now starting to be scarce in some stores. She may have to start growing stuff like what she had been doing with Michael. *Michael,* she thought. She missed him. He had made such an impression in the short time they had been together. She found a dairy on the way home. It still had an abundance of cans. She filled the front of the bus and made her way back, feeling satisfied that she had accomplished everything she had set out to do. She arrived back just shy of three in the afternoon. Opening the door her heart started to skip. What would she find today?

Max was sitting up reading *The Hunger Games*. He seemed to be lost in the page he was reading. Shelby smiled and was relieved to find him busy reading.

"*Good* book?" Max put up his finger, trying to finish the last few lines of something that was obviously epic. He finished.

"*Really good,* Shell, how was your day?" he asked, smiling at her.

"Oh, you know, *usual,*" she answered, smiling back as she went back and forth bringing in the cans of food. Finally she had brought everything in and locked the door shut. She then told Max everything that had happened.

Day Two

Max and Shelby slept downstairs. It was easier as everything they needed was on the bottom level, apart from the bathroom. Shelby was in charge of the bucket which was equally disgusting for her and horribly demeaning for Max. Shelby didn't mind and if anything it made her feel even closer to him. Nothing could get in the way of how she was starting to feel.

"How's the legs today, Maximillion?" she asked as she slopped out some spaghetti on a plate.

"I can wiggle my toes, look!" replied Max, excitedly as his toes wiggled.

"Awe, look at those piggies going to the *fucking market!*" said Shelby, smiling. Max laughed out loud at Shelby's remark. "What do you want for breakfast?" Asked Shelby as she stirred Max's spaghetti.

Max grabbed his novel. "Spaghetti." He answered as he licked his finger and opened the book. He started reading. "Busy day planned?"

"Very…" Answered Shelby as she placed the bowl of spaghetti on a tray and placed it over Max's lap. He put the book down, smiling at her. "I want to check out those bells. I need to check some of the diesel pumps, hopefully find one that works. I don't think I'll have time to visit Gunther today. Do you want anything? I can add it to my list." Shelby offered, loving being organised.

"No, I'm okay, thank you." After breakfast, Shelby cleaned up everything, walked over to Max and kissed him on his forehead. *Love you,* she said in her head as she walked to the door. Turning back she said,

"You never know who I might bump into! *Hope is alive!*" She raised her fist as Max did the same.

"Yes, it is!" he replied as he went back to his novel.

The first petrol station Shelby came to was a truck stop. It was easy for her to drive the bus into. The pumps didn't work and while swearing, she tried another two stations before finding one where the diesel flowed like a river on a stormy day.

"Drink it up, *Stu.*" She had named the bus Stu, she thought the name suited it. She checked the time: 9 am. She had wasted way too much time trying to find diesel. She quickly drove off in the direction she thought the sound had come from.

Arriving at her destination, she parked the bus at a roundabout. There wasn't much in the way of houses around here or shops. It was more of a rural area. Farms, hills and wild, overgrown green pastures in all directions. She opened the bus door and walked out, breathing in the gorgeous air. She must admit, in this new world the air tasted fresh and clean. Without humans polluting it, the earth was thriving. *Apart from Stu here.* She patted the bus. *Diesel dumper.* She checked her watch. 9:59 am. *Perfect,* she walked further away from Stu and raised her head to the sky. The first chime rang out. Loud, but still in the distance. *Fuck where?* She thought. It seemed to be coming from the hills, maybe a kilometre or so further up the road. She hopped back on the bus and drove.

Stu was pushing a hundred kilometres an hour when she stopped it, ran out and listened. No bells. She'd missed it. She drove up and down the road, searching the hills. She couldn't see anything that looked like a house or building. The time had flown by and it was now 11:30 am. She drove back home, promising to come back the next day and start where she'd finished, outside a large, vintage milking shed.

Driving back, she stopped off at an electrical appliance store. She found a Blu-ray player and grabbed a bag chocka full of horror, action and comedy movies. She then stopped off at a hardware store and picked up a generator. It would be loud, but she would place it outside and run a lead in to fire up the TV and Blu-ray player. Michael had taught her well and Max was in for a treat.

Day Three

Max was heavily into his novel when Shelby left for the day. "I didn't realise *The Hunger Games* was a movie?" questioned Max, looking through the titles Shelby had picked for him.

"Five movies in fact," answered Shelby.

"*Really?* I wasn't even born when the first one came out."

"Well, finish your novel, and we can watch the first one when I get back. Legs?" she asked. He wiggled his toes and moved his feet. "Wow, the piggies have a *car!*" Max smiled. She kissed his forehead. *Love you,* she thought and went towards the door. "You never know who I might bump into! *Hope is alive!"* They raised their fists together at the same time and Shelby left smiling.

Shelby arrived back at the same spot she had left the day before. The wind was blowing hard and outside, the clouds had turned to a dark, ominous grey, threatening hard rain and maybe worse. She'd dressed for the weather and had on a large yellow raincoat. She stood outside Stu with her coat zipped up over her mouth, the coat's drawstring tied tightly. Just her nose and eyes appeared out of her hood as she looked to the heavens, waiting for the sound of the bell.

At 10 am just as it had done the previous days, the bell rang. It was closer and louder than it had been before. In front of her was a large green hill. Old wire electric fences that used to house cows and goats still worked their way across wildly, fertile grass paddocks. She ran back inside Stu and drove around the corner of the ridge. A road disappeared up the left of the hillside. She followed it, trying to keep the bus on the narrow road as it bent and turned. Her anxiety did not appreciate the steep view below.

As she got to the top, the road opened up into an oval car park that was trophied by a grand old chapel. At the top of the chapel was a magnificent bell. She looked at the time, 10:10 am. She'd missed the last chimes. In the car park were two cars. One, an old, baby blue, Toyota Corolla hatchback. The other was a massive, dark green Jeep. It was unusual to see cars in car parks as the vanishing had happened at night. Outside, the rain that had been threatening unleashed itself. A distant thunder rumbled out in the distance.

"*Fuck,* fuck, fuck," she swore to herself as she stood just inside Stu's door frame. *Why do I do this to myself?* She pushed a button and the door opened. Its sounds and workings were buried in the rain as it pelted into the gravel. She ran and swore as she managed to hit puddle after puddle. She could feel her socks getting wet and her saturated feet started to sound like waterlogged sponges. She stood outside the chapel doors. They were large and towering. They were made of polished wood with iron bracing. They ascended above her and met together in a large grand peak. She put her hand against the door and pushed it. It opened with the sound of brass hinges under strain.

She walked in and closed the massive doors behind her. As soon as it closed the noise of the rain disappeared and was replaced by a loud echo of noise coming from the door shutting. The rain now sounded like it was off in the far distance. Ahead of her was a circular room that led to more doors. Behind those large glass doors, she could see many rows of chairs. The church looked bigger inside than it did outside.

She pushed the glass door open and was surprised to see two people looking back at her. A rather large man who was bald, was standing at the front right, and a lady who looked Italian on the front left. She wore a red veil on her head. She made a sign of the cross and kissed the crucifix on her rosary beads when she saw Shelby entering. At the front of the altar standing behind a speaking lectern was a man dressed in coloured robes. His mouth was smiling but open. He was brushing his hair to the right with his hand and he had a kind face.

Shelby walked in and sat in the very last row at the back. The priest smiled at Shelby, acknowledging her presence and then checked where he was up to in his reading. The two parishioners who glanced at Shelby, turned back to look at the priest. He carried on with his sermon,

"...As it was in the beginning and world without end. *Amen*." The man on the right shouted out a loud amen before the priest had. The women on the left said a quiet amen after the priest.

Shelby sat enthralled by what was happening. She had never been to a church, or participated in a mass. She listened to every word and tried to understand what they were talking about. But, to her it all sounded like science fiction and made up stories about worship, life and death. At one stage the priest moved away from his readings and came down to the front and talked to the parishioners. All two of them and Shelby. He had his hands clasped together and kept moving them up and down as he spoke. His beard, eyebrows and ears were bushy and he reminded her of Michael. He kept smiling and was always forgetting what he was about to say next. His eyes would close when he was thinking of his next word. But, she couldn't help but feel calmed by his voice.

"We welcome all new visitors." He said, with his eyes closed and his mouth smiling. Shelby smiled back. He made a speech about the end of days and how we were being tested. Also, how we must trust in God for help in this trying time. How, if there was belief in him then a way would present itself. Shelby couldn't help but think that the priest was talking to her. At the end of his talk, he smiled and said: "His door is always open for those who are lost, or... in need of help." You could almost hear the smile in his voice. Shelby almost replied with thanks, as he turned and went back to the large altar and raised his hands and said, "let us pray."

The two people and the priest started saying words they all knew. Shelby felt guilty for not knowing the prayer as well. Everything seemed to be timed. When they knelt, when they stood, the prayers that were said. She joined in as she felt a sense of calm in this church. As the turmoil outside took place. The thunder and rain. The storm that was outside. Everything seemed to be quiet and tranquil in this church with this friendly priest leading.

Near the end of the service, the priest she now knew as Father Roberts, had brought down bread, which he said was the body of Christ and wine, which he said was the blood of Christ. Shelby didn't want any part of that. She stayed put while the other two walked up to receive the bread and wine. Father Roberts made his way down to Shelby. He said a blessing, made a sign of the cross and smiled at the end, quietly saying, "Nice to meet you." He then walked back to the altar. At the end of the service, he said, "You are always welcome every day to join in the service and I will be here as always leading a mass for those who wish to participate."

Shelby quite enjoyed the experience, but it was a lot to take in. Once the mass was finished they all quickly rushed to the back of the church.

"So nice to see you," said the lady, grabbing Shelby's hands. "My name is Maria." Maria was almost in tears while talking to Shelby. She didn't let go of her hand through the whole conversation.

"Philip," said the large bald man, in a strong manly voice.

"Father Roberts," said Father, smiling at her with his eyes closed and his body bobbing up and down.

"Shelby," replied Shelby, smiling politely.

"So nice to meet you, Shelby. Our little parish has grown, so unusual in this day *and before*," said Father, his face glowing with a smile.

"I... followed the bells, Father." Father Roberts started laughing, a roaring laughter that caught Shelby by surprise.

"They work! The bells work!" He smacked Philip on the back, who must have been in charge of ringing them. Philip raised his eyebrows in agreement. Maria was smiling, Father Roberts' positive manner was infectious. Maria sat beside Shelby, still holding her hand. Philip was seated on her right. Father Roberts was leaning against the row of chairs in front of Shelby.

"So... Shelby, you have survived all this time by *yourself?*" asked Father, still smiling broadly, his eyes shut. They all seemed to lean forward, eager to hear what she had to say.

"To start with... I've met a few people along the way." She looked down. "Most have... *gone.*"

"Ah, alas, *the same for us.* We were once a parish of seven. Now just three... plus you," he smiled as he placed his hand on Shelby's and Maria's.

"Thank you, but I'm not *practising*," replied Shelby, shaking her head politely.

"No, of course not but, we are still here. As friends we must all *help* each other," said Father, still smiling. "Do you have a roof to sleep under? Food to eat?" His words sounded like his sermon.

"Yeah, I'm good. Um, it... it's nice to meet more people."

"Good. Well... do you need help of any kind?" Father asked. "Philip is extremely handy, he was a builder back before..."

"I was." Philip interrupted, loudly. His face, was deadly serious.

"And I was a cook. A *very* good cook," said Maria, smiling.

"No, I don't need any help. But, if it's okay I will come back and *listen.*"

"Of course, Shelby, of course. Whatever we can do to *help*. If you need a place to stay..." Father suggested.

"...or food to eat," added Maria.

"...or help of any kind." Philip joined in. "Can we give you a lift?"

"No, I'm fine, thank you. I'd better go."

"Tomorrow then," said Father, still smiling.

"Maybe," Shelby replied as she looked at Maria who was still holding her hand.

"I *once* had a daughter," she said to Shelby. A tear dropped from her eye. "She was much like you, *just...*" she cried and kissed Shelby on the cheek. "If you need somewhere to stay we can help, Shelby. You don't even have to ask."

"Thank you," Shelby replied, as she got up and smiled at them all. She then walked back to the back of the church, which was quiet and inviting. They all sat watching her. Like their new favourite thing was about to leave.

She opened the door and all hell broke loose. Trees were being blown from left to right. Rain was belting down on a hard angle. A silent blast of lightning cut through the blackened clouds. She pulled her hood down and ran to Stu. Opening the door she sat looking at the church. "That was *nice*, Stu. I feel like I'm all clean. There's still some nice people left in the world. But, I tell you Stu, I've never had to hold a swear word back for so long. Fuuuck!" she shouted, long and loud. She felt better as she drove back to Max eager to tell him the day's news.

Day Four

"How was the novel?" Shelby asked as she was preparing herself for the day.

"Pretty *damn* good," Max replied, smiling.

"Ready for the movie?"

"You're not *busy* today?"

"Not really, not when I can spend my day with you."

"You say all the *right* things," said Max. Shelby grabbed a duvet cover and threw it over Max. She then grabbed bags of treats and popcorn.

"Don't know how old these are but, I'm sure they taste good." Max smiled as they settled in for *The Hunger Games*. Shelby and Max loved the movie, and Max was particularly impressed with Jennifer Lawrence's version of Katniss Everdeen. "Tell me, Maxy boy, have you seen The *Shining*?"

"No."

"*The Conjuring*?"

"No."

"*Conan the Barbarian*?"

"What's that then? A Saturday morning cartoon?"

"Just don't, don't say anything more, Max, please. Tell me you've seen The *Thing*?" Max shook his head sideways.

"My God man. I'm not going anywhere. Maximillian, get prepared for some movie schooling!"

Max and Shelby watched each movie one after the other. They took a break at night to keep the noise down. Shelby loved it as it reminded her of the times she used to spend with her mum watching movies and eating treats. She would also give Max run downs on the directors, actors and history of the production. A lot of it was straight from the mouth of Michael. Some were from

Mum. But she loved it. It made things feel like the world inside the room, was almost normal.

Day Five

Shelby and Max had spent two days straight watching movies. It had got to the stage where Shelby felt moved out. Her vision was also going blurry. She got up early and had everything prepared for her day of adventure.

"Plans?" asked Max, now reading, *The Hunger Games: Catching Fire.*

"Church, then Gunther."

"Nice. You're making *friends*."

"Feels like it."

"Don't forget me."

"Never," said Shelby as she ran over and kissed him. *Love you*, she thought. He thought it too. She ran to the door and opened it. Turning to Max. Max said it first.

"You never know who you might bump into! Now *fuck off!*" He gave her the finger. She laughed, and returned the gesture right back at him.

Shelby arrived at the church at 10:15 am. She tried not to make too much noise as she took her usual seat at the back. She noticed straight away that Maria was not there. Philip was, as she could hear his loud amens coming a few seconds before Father Roberts. Father Roberts had his hands outstretched when he saw Shelby. Straight away a huge smile took over his face. He closed his eyes smiling while praying, his feet rocking back and forth on his toes and heels.

The sermon today was of old friends and memories. Take on the lessons of old and don't forget them. Shelby thought it was quite apt considering she had been thinking of Michael and Mum. He then ended the sermon with a joke.

"I really hope coronavirus can't spread through sex. It would be so lonely being *the last man on earth*," he roared with laughter after that one. Philip coughed. Shelby started laughing with Father, more so because of Father's reaction rather than the joke itself as she didn't quite get it.

After giving Shelby a blessing, Father and Philip made their way to Shelby. "So *nice* to see you again Shelby!" said Father Roberts enthusiastically, as he smiled rocking back and forward. Shelby noticed his eyebrows were as bushy as his beard. He also had gardens of hair straws growing out of his ears. He reminded her of a muppet, albeit, a very friendly, humorous one. It all added to his character.

"Nice to see you too, Father! *Loved your joke*."

"Yes, yes, that was a good one. *Joy is the enemy of fear*, you know," he laughed again to himself.

"No... *Maria*?" asked Shelby, sheepishly.

"I'm afraid not, we have not seen her... for a couple of days now. But, it's so good to see you, right, Philip?"

"Yes," said Philip, without emotion. Shelby got the feeling that they knew she was dead.

"I like coming here Father. It feels peaceful and calm, compared to the world outside."

"Yes, *yes* of course, well... you are always welcome," Father replied as he bowed. His eyes closed with his mouth still smiling.

"Thank you, I might bring Max next time."

"*Excellent*, we'd love to meet him wouldn't we, Philip?" Father was trying to bring Philip into the conversation but was failing miserably. Philip nodded. There was a pause where no one knew what to say next. Shelby could tell Father was hoping she would say something cause Philip wouldn't.

"...And ah, um, what have you both been up to?" asked Shelby, smiling politely.

"Thank you for asking Shelby, I've been painting and I... love to *exercise*."

"*Exercise*, really?" said Shelby, not noticing any strong physical form under Father Roberts' clothing.

"Oh, yes, I go to the local gym, I love to *box* you see." Father Roberts started shadow boxing. "Gets rid of the cobwebs and keeps me off the street." Father roared again with laughter. Shelby joined in. Philip was as straight as an arrow.

"...And you, Philip, get up too *much?*" Shelby asked, tentatively.

"Not really," said Philip, killing the conversation dead.

"...Well, on that note, *I better go*," said Shelby, standing. "Loved the mass, thank you, Father. You were very *funny*."

"I aim to please," said Father, smiling proudly.

"I look forward to seeing you both... *again*," said Shelby as she turned and walked back to the foyer. She twirled and waved back. Father Roberts gave her a large friendly wave. He was practically beaming. Philip sat still, watching.

Shelby made her way to Tim's army base. She sat at her usual place at the top of the stairs and called out for Gunther. "Gunther? Here boy, It's *Shelby*." She whispered. There was no familiar snort. No whirling of the tail. She turned on her torch. It gave her a few metres of straight light. She thought about going down into the darkness but then thought. *Fuck that.* She didn't much feel like risking her life. She felt she was getting wiser. "Gunther?" She called again. *He must be out.* She turned and opened a packet of Pineapple Lumps and sprayed them all over the floor. *A treat for you, Gunther.* Taking one for herself, she then made her way back home.

Walking in the doorway she was amazed to find Max standing. His hands outstretched. He was smiling broadly and looking for a hug.

"Look at *me*," he said cheerfully. "I can *stand*."

"Oh, *Max!*" Shelby shouted as she ran to him.

"Careful!" he said. "I'm not that good." They fell back onto the lounge suite laughing.

"Maxy, you're so good at *standing!*" Shelby said proudly, smiling at him, she kissed his cheek.

"Funny girl, watch *this!*" Max got up and started shuffling across the room. He stopped by the kitchen table and leaned against it. "What do you think? Pretty cool right?"

"You look like a duck, walking with a stick up its *ass*." They both were in riots.

"I reckon, give me a day or two and I can come out with you."

"You reckon?" Shelby was still smiling, but there was a touch of worry in her voice.

"I reckon. I can't stay in here... things just keep turning around in my brain. And the noises I hear, outside." Suddenly Max was serious as he looked at the table.

"*I get it*, a day or two and you can come out with me," Shelby said, smiling. Max smiled back. "Now act like a duck with a stick up its ass and *get over here*!" Max stuck his tongue out the side of his mouth, like he was concentrating and waddled over to Shelby. He fell on her laughing.

Day Six

Shelby sat at the table checking her guns. Max was staring at the family picture.

"Do your exercises, Max, then tomorrow you come with me. *Got it?*"

"Yeah, I get it. I was just thinking."

"I can see," said Shelby.

"Sorry, um, I don't mean to be a *wet blanket*," said Max, looking a little despondent.

"You're not, Max, we're going through tough times." She walked over and kissed him on the cheek. He hugged her.

"Thanks Shelby, for being here for me. If it wasn't for *you*..." He started to tear up. She was about to say it but Max beat her to it.

"Love you."

She sat looking into Max's eyes, stunned by what he had just said. It meant so much to her. Especially in this dark age.

"I love you too." She answered back, smiling as they kissed, but it was a kiss that was a mixture of smiles, laughter and tears. "So much," she finished, as they hugged. "I look forward to seeing you, *every day*." She acknowledged, her voice breaking. They smiled. "I better go, this is too much fucking *romance* for one day!" Max laughed.

She ran and picked up her bag. Running to the door she opened it and twirled. "Piss off!" he interrupted, as they both gave each other the finger and laughed.

Shelby ran out into the street. "He *loves* me!" she shouted, as she started dancing in circles with her arms spread out wide. She hopped on the bus. "Stu! Max *loves me!*" She started beeping the horn. "That's right Stu, he is a bit of a *dish*!" She turned the bus on. She beeped the horn again. "A present you say, what a good idea! You're so full of fucking *happiness* today, Stu!" She beeped the horn all the way down the narrow street.

Shelby arrived late again at the church. She quietly walked in not wanting to make a scene. She opened the glass door and peered out towards the altar. Father Roberts was mumbling a prayer to himself. His head was lowered. He didn't seem to be himself. She noticed Philip was absent or dead. Instead of sitting at the back, Shelby made her way to the front cubical. She sat smiling at Father. She felt a little sad for him. This charming man is doing his bit for humanity in this large, old, empty church with no one to witness his selfless bravery.

He lifted his head and opened his eyes to see Shelby smiling and waving at him. His fingers at the end of his outstretched arms started to move like he was waving back. Shelby smiled. He responded with a wink as an even larger smile enveloped his face. His mumbling suddenly became loud confident words as he found his way back into his prayer. Shelby gave him a little clap and Father Roberts reacted by standing up straight.

The mass went quickly with Father giving Shelby his full attention. His sermon was about friends. How it's necessary to look after the good ones and help those in need. She thought it was very moving and that it was all about them. Father came down near the end and gave Shelby a blessing. She could feel the warmth settling around her heart as he said it. At the end of the mass he came down and sat beside her smiling. They said nothing as they both looked at the crucifix hanging over the altar with Jesus laid on it. Shelby thought Jesus looked a lot like Michael.

"Father?"

"Yes Shelby." He turned towards her his hands grasping together. He had a large, warm smile on his face. Shelby could tell he liked her a lot.

"Do you still... *believe*?"

"...In *God?*"

"*Yes*, after... the vanishing, the creatures, do you still *believe* in God?"

"Oh, *yes*, even more so."

"Why?" asked Shelby, still looking at Jesus.

"Well, I think he made... his *decision*, I think he cleansed the earth and we are chosen to *rebuild* it."

Shelby looked at Father Roberts inquisitively. She wanted to tell him about the being and what it had said. To explain how they were all supposed to be vanished. How we had wrecked the Earth as others had done and had been selected for extinction. But, she remembered what Michael had said. *Don't mention it or they will think you're nuts. Would Father think I'm crazy? I saw the being, his belief is blind faith. How different is what he believes from what I saw?*

"You're probably *right*, Father." Father Roberts smiled.

"You don't have to believe it, Shelby. We both know what happened. It's what we *do* from *now on* that matters." Shelby hugged Father Roberts and kissed his cheek.

"Father, did you want to stay with *us?* You're all by yourself out here."

"Oh, Shelby, I can see why God *saved you*," he smiled his biggest smile. "You have a *beautiful soul* and yes, you probably want me to stay because of my *boxing skills!*" He roared with laughter. Shelby laughed with him. His laughter was joyous for the soul. "...Thank you Shelby, but it is my responsibility to take care of the parish and to be here *like a beacon*, for those who are *lost* or need *refuge*. Never fear my Shelby, I will always be here, you can count on that... And if you ever need a place to stay, then... I will have a bed ready for you and Max."

"I hope to bring him *tomorrow.*"

"*Good,* good, I look forward to meeting him."

Shelby hugged Father Roberts again, smiled and ran down the aisle. She turned and waved back at him. *There is still hope.* He thought, as she walked out the door and the door shut closed. As she left, he swore he heard a distant voice shout, 'fuck'. Loudly and for a long time. But, he thought it was probably his imagination.

Shelby sat at the top of the stairs staring into darkness. "Gunther?" she whispered. Straight away there was a snort and swirling sound. Shelby smiled, Gunther was back. She backed up out of the stairwell and walked back into the light. She placed a trail of Pineapple Lumps that ended up by her against the wall. Gunther came out of the shadows. He looked more regal, he was slightly larger and the jewels on his back were shining brightly. "You look so *handsome* Gunther!" Shelby said, smiling. He came over and pushed his nostrils against Shelby, he snorted. She rubbed the bottom of his chin. "Have you been on a *trip*, boy? Did you have a *good* time?" Gunther rubbed his head against Shelby and then licked his tongue up her face, It felt like wet, rough sandpaper. "Who's been a good boy then? Who's a good boy then?" She roughed his head with her hand. He whined a soft noise and pawed his hoof on the ground.

Shelby sat with Gunther and read him a novel she had just started. This time she sat engulfed in his belly, neck and back legs as he hugged her. He was like a huge, soft sofa. She fell asleep with him for a time and woke up startled checking her watch. *Not too late.* "I've got to go Gunther, *sorry* boy, I've got an important *present* to get for Max. *Love you*," she said as she kissed his snout. He snorted back and turned and walked back down into the shadows, knowing not to argue. "Such a good boy," she praised as she sprinted back to Stu.

Shelby made her way back to the mall. Standing outside the open door where they had been only a week ago, the place didn't seem as fearful as when she was here last. The bright sunlight only revealed graffiti and old paint. The barrel that was lit was still sitting outside the open door. She knew there was a jewellery shop inside but upon looking in the doorway decided it wasn't worth the trouble. She had only so many lives left. She visited a hardware store down the road and grabbed some spray cans. She then came back and closed the door, spraying the words. *"Monsters inside. Don't be fucking stupid."* *I'm learning,* she thought as she hopped back on Stu and headed back onto the main road.

She came across a Pandora Jewellery store a few blocks down. *Perfect*, she thought. She smashed the main front window with a wheel tightener she had found inside the bus. A small alarm rang for an instant but quickly dissipated to nothing. The battery must have still had a little life. She walked in and found what she was looking for. A silver friendship bracelet. One for her and one for Max. She then found two halves of a heart. One for her and one for Max. She smiled as she checked what other charms she could get for Max and herself. *Fuck it,* she thought, *I can afford it. Why not take the whole box.* She put everything in a Pandora Jewellery bag and went to the cash register. Pushing the enter button the cash register flew open. She took out fifty dollars, and said "thank you." She then put fifty dollars back in. "Keep the change." She checked the time. *Perfect,* she thought. She rushed back onto Stu. "Stu my *friend,* it's been a wonderful day." Shelby whistled as she drove Stu back to the house. She couldn't wait to see Max.

Driving up the same narrow street to home, Shelby stopped about twenty metres before arriving. She wrapped the present up she had for Max. *He's my first boyfriend.* She thought. *Who would have thought that Shelby Frances O'Leary would have a boyfriend.* She smiled as she sellotaped the wrapping paper. She wrote him a little note and stuck it on the top.

Max.
I saved your life when we first met,
no need to thank me, it's what I do.
You make me smile, I make you laugh,
I bring you books and take out your poo.
But, most important, above all else,
I fucking... love you!
Shelby (Shell) "I do!"

She smiled and laughed as she sat back in the driver's seat. It had been a perfect day and would be a perfect night. "You're still my *number one,* Stu, don't get jealous now," she said as Stu started up and they drove the twenty metres to the house. Shelby stopped the bus and pulled up the parking brake. She sat looking at the door. It was open. She didn't move for a good two minutes. She just stared at the door. *Why is it open? Did he go for a walk and forget to close it?*

She walked slowly to the bus door. She looked at the present sitting on the front seat. She looked out the glass. The door to the house was wide open. She raised her hand to open the bus door. She noticed her hand was shaking. She held it steady with her left hand and pushed the button. The pumps worked loudly as air was released and the bus door opened. She grabbed her satchel and pulled out a rifle. She tried to release the safety. Her hand wouldn't let her. *Fucking hand, start working.* She placed the strap around her shoulder and held the rifle ready. She then grabbed a handgun and placed it behind her, tucked in her jeans.

She took a step down and looked left and right. The streets were empty. A slight breeze blowing the long, flowered weeds in front of her. She stood looking at the door. *Come on, Max, come to the door. Tell me you opened it for me,* she thought. She walked slowly up the pathway. Still moving her rifle left and right. Hoping danger was just in her imagination. She heard something. A growl. *Where did it come from?* It growled again, louder this time. Like a wolf or wild animal was fighting something or tearing at flesh. She ran quickly towards the door. "*No,* fuck no," she whispered to herself as she ran, her heart beating out of her chest. "Max, *no.*"

Running into the entrance way she lost her stomach. A wild animal the size of a large dog was biting into Max's back. Pulling at his flesh. Trying to tear his flesh from his body. It had spikes and fur on its shoulders only, it had no tail and it had skin that resembled a humans. Its snout though was very much like that of a wolf. It was a scavenger of this world. She heard Max cry out in pain. His hand trying to swipe the wolf-type creature away. *He's alive.*

"Fuck off!" Shelby screamed as she let the rifle loose. A barrage of bullets hit the wolf-type creature and it howled. It turned and looked at her, its fangs open and bloody. She never stopped. The bullets hitting it and sending it sprawling backwards. It kept trying to come at Shelby. But it was in pain. Its rear legs collapsed first. Followed by its front and finally its head, which ended up being a mass of unrecognisable flesh once Shelby had finished.

She slammed the door shut, dead locked it and ran to Max. "Max! *Max...*" He was moving only slightly. His fingers wanted to grasp something, like a newborn baby's first movement. She knelt beside him and turned him over slowly. Trying not to hurt him and his wounded back. He had blood coming from the side of his mouth. His face was written with pain. His breathing was rushed. Like he was trying to find breath but no air was coming. "Max, oh, *Max...*" Her voice, aching. She brushed his cheek. "What the *fuck?*" She looked up and down his body. His chest had blood coming from two wounds. His t-shirt was covered in blood. "M ax... talk to me... what *happened?*" He was looking at her but his eyes, while open, seemed to be looking through her. Like the pain was too much and he couldn't register her face. "Max..."

He coughed and blood dripped from the side of his mouth.

"Shell?" he said, quietly. His eyes were not looking at hers.

"Yeah, Max, it's *me*..."

"Shell? *Two* guys... they broke in," his voice, barely audible.

"Who? What?" He coughed again.

"Shell, I can't *feel*..." Shelby started to cry. She kissed his cheek.

"Max... *who*?"

"I... I don't know... they were looking for *you*."

"Me?"

Max grimaced in pain. His stomach hurt. His arms held in front of him, pushing down on his t-shirt. "Shell, I'm *sorry*. I don't want to leave you... *alone*." Tears fell from his eyes. "D...d...don't give up... Shell." She couldn't speak. Her mouth wouldn't open. His breathing started to slow.

"Max... Max, no... *Max!*" His hands started pulling harder on his shirt. She looked down at his bleeding torso and up at his hurt face. "Max..."

"They sh... *shot* me." Max said as he looked up at Shelby, his head shaking slowly. "Lo... love you." He said as he coughed again.

"Max, no! you fuck! *no*! Don't you fucking *leave* me, Max!" Shelby screamed as tears poured from her eyes.

"It's not safe... Sh... Shell... leave." He said as his eyes left hers and he looked straight ahead. He was barely breathing now.

"Max... *no!*"

"Sh... Shelby, I... I can *see* them," he said, his mouth was almost smiling.

"Wha... *who*?" Shelby asked, cradling Max in her arms.

"It... It's *Pete*... and... *Charlie*, Shell!" He looked up at her and smiled and then looked straight ahead again. Shelby followed his eyes but the room was empty. "I know... what you were... mean...

meaning now, *ghosts*." He smiled. "I know why... Charlie *did*..." His voice was shaking.

"Don't you go to them, you fuck! *Stay with me.* It's not fair. Stay with me!" Her head lowered as she kissed Max's forehead tenderly. She then raised her head angrily, ferociously, staring at the empty wall. "You can't fucking *take him*!" Shelby wailed at the mocking walls. She was pulling Max towards her, shielding him from Charlie and Pete.

"Y... you s... *swear*... t... too much," he said, smiling as he tried to touch her face. She was cuddling him hard. "They're bea... *beautiful*, Shell..."

"Max, please... *no*." She whispered, in his ear. "*I love you*." She said,

"Shell...?"

"Yes... Max?" Max was barely breathing.

"Hope... is alive." She broke down. Shelby didn't answer. The last thing this world was giving her, was hope. But she hugged him and loved him even more for saying the words she had spoken to him. Especially words of hope while he was slipping away. She wiped his brow and kissed him tenderly. "Sh... Shelby, Frances...O-O'Leary?" said Max, his voice barely a whisper. She couldn't bring herself to answer. He was looking Shelby's way but she didn't know if he could see her. "I... I meant to... ask." Shelby was sobbing. "Will... you... be my...?" Max stopped breathing and Shelby felt his body go limp.

"No!" Shelby screamed. "*No!* Max..." She hugged him, rocking him back and forth. Feathering his forehead with her hand. "I love you, Max." She carried on rocking his lifeless body, back and forth as she raised her head and looked at the ceiling and screamed.

Finally, her eyes fell on his hurt, sleeping face. "And... *yes*, I will... be your *girlfriend*." She said, in between sobbing, as she hugged him tightly and cried.

CHAPTER TWENTY

Descent Into Madness

"SADNESS, SADNESS, SADNESS, I GAVE MY VERY BEST." THE EXPONENTS.

Part 1

Shelby lay beside Max looking at his face for an hour. She hardly stopped crying the whole time. She was angry. Angry at the two strangers who had shot him. Angry at the wolf-type creature that came in and tried to devour him. Angry at Pete and Charlie for taking him. Angry at the world for taking everyone she loves. She was just angry.

She kissed Max again on his cheek. This poor man. He was just getting better. *Tomorrow he was going to come out with me. Out to see the world, Gunther and Father Roberts.* Now, he lies here dead. "*Fuck* you!" she screamed at the ceiling. She felt like the world was against her. It was payback for her coming back and getting a second chance. Karma had bitten her and she had paid in full. Another wave of tears fell upon her. She felt like just lying here and letting everything engulf her. There was no one left on this earth. Why not just let it all slip away. Her heart was broken and sad. She had finally had enough. She screamed. A long, sad broken scream. She felt like she was having a nervous breakdown.

"It's not safe, Shell, leave." She heard Max talking to her. "They were looking for you." She brushed his forehead. "Don't give up, Shell."

"I won't, I won't my *love*," she said as she got up. She went to the lounge suite and grabbed the blanket Max had been using. She placed it in front of Max.

"Good girl," he said. She then rolled him into it and covered him in the blanket. "Now pull me, Shell." She pulled him towards the door, opened it and dragged him towards the bus. She opened the door. "Push me up, Shell. You can do it." She went behind Max and shoved him forward, her right shoulder doing most of the work. She then hauled him up the rest of the way. "You did it, Shell!"

"It was fucking *hard*, you're so fucking *fat!*" Shelby said, talking to Max's body inside the blanket. It lay sat up, leaning against the front seat.

"I'm not fat, you've felt the six pack."

"More like a one pack," she said, smiling as she ran back into the house.

"Hurry Shell, I don't like being here by myself."

"You're not by yourself, you've got fucking *Stu* to *talk to*." Shelby started packing her satchel with the guns.

"What, the bus?"

"Yes the fucking bus, he's *Stu!*"

"Shelby, have you been seeing Stu behind my back and are you going crazy?" Shelby grabbed a canvas bag and started throwing all her new clothes and shoes into it.

"Are you *jealous*?" she asked, smiling.

"Jealous? What, of a bus? Please."

"He is strong, long and handsome. Plus, he hardly ever runs out of fuel."

"That's what she said."

"I was just going to say that." She zipped up the heavy bag and ran down the stairs. The large bag, bumping up and down behind her.

"Grab some food."

"Good *idea,* Max."

"I'm not just a handsome face."

"Not *anymore*." Shelby laughed out loud. Max was silent. "Too *soon*?" She smiled, as she emptied out a box and shoved cans into it.

"I did just die, you know."

"I know... I was *there*." She carried the cumbersome box filled with cans out to the bus. She pulled up the canvas bag and sat it by Max. It hit his body and he fell over.

"Ow, be careful, I might bruise." Shelby ran back into the house, placed her satchel around her shoulder and grabbed her other packed backpack. She stood at the door looking back at the kitchen and lounge. The dead wolf-type creature was lying in the centre. "Memories," said Max.

Shelby started to cry. "So many... Pete, Charlie, Lucy, Tim."

"You forgot me."

"I didn't *forget*," she said as she ran out. She left the door open so the two guys would think everything was the same. She placed her satchel and backpack in the front seat and shut the bus door. "Max, you *fell* over!" Shelby pulled him back up and placed the large bag behind him so he wouldn't fall again.

"I tried to stay up but then I thought of your face." Shelby started laughing to the point her stomach started to hurt.

"I can't *fucking* breathe!" she said, howling.

"Time to go, Shelby."

"Where?" she asked.

"How about, where you're buried?" she started to nod. "That way, I can chat with you forever."

"Awe, you're such a *sweetie*!" she said as she turned the key. Stu powered into life.

"Here we *go*, Stu!" she shouted.

"Warp factor 11, Stu!" added Max.

Shelby drove the bus back towards the broken car. She indicated to her left. She sat looking at the broken car for a long time. Not because it was looking back at her. Not because it might be the last time they'd see each other and not because it had lost another mechanical part. She sat looking at where the broken car used to be. Her heart sank. The broken car that was a last memory of Michael, Teresa, sweet Lucy, and Pup. The broken car that had slowly been deteriorating, as she had been deteriorating, was now completely gone. If she had any tears left, she would cry again. *This fucking world*, she thought.

Part 2

Shelby was travelling late in the evening. The day had now turned to night. There was no moon and the road was especially dark. She was using the Michael light switch trick. Though she was starting to know this road especially well.

"Stay awake, Shell," advised Max. Shelby looked back at the body-filled blanket.

"I fucking am. *Stop* saying that," she griped as she swerved past a car.

"Nice driving."

"Thank you." She'd been on the road for a couple of hours. "Max, did you see their faces?"

"If I did I couldn't tell you."

"*Why* not?"

"Because I'm me, in your brain."

"Mmm," said Shelby, processing her own thoughts. "Max?"

"Yes, Shelby."

"What did they say?"

"...That they were looking for you and I didn't cut the cake."

"So they *shot* you?"

"I wouldn't tell them anything. Zilch."

"Good man."

"Thank you."

"You're doing *well*, *Stu*." Said Shelby as she stroked the dashboard.

"Does Stu ever answer back, Shelby?"

"No," said Shelby, "I'm not fucking *crazy*."

"Hi!"

"Oh, my God, Stu, is that *you*?" asked Shelby, in disbelief.

"Yep! In the flesh. Though, I'm more wires, plastic and metal, when you think about it."

"Stu, why do you sound like Taika Waititi?" asked Shelby.

"Ah... It's your choice Shelby, lucky me, shame I don't look like him, eh?" answered Stu.

"Hello Stu," said Max.

"Nice to meet you, dead guy," replied Stu.

"I can't believe we are having a three way conversation," said Shelby.

"Word," responded Stu.

"I have so many questions." Max pondered.

"Ask away," Replied Stu, his wheels swerving as he passed a car.

"What's it like being a bus, Stu?"

"Thanks for asking Max. It's pretty cool, really, I get to take people from place to place, sometimes I get a good driver, like Shelby."

"Word," said Shelby, nodding.

"...And you know, I'm providing a service, taking people where they need to go. It makes me feel good!"

"Nice one, Stu," said Shelby, smiling and nodding as she switched on the lights, swerved past a large truck and switched them off again.

"You know, you're in drive two, it would be a lot smoother if you just put it in drive," advised Stu, as his air conditioning was turned to five.

"Again, nice one, Stu," added Shelby, nodding more. She was trying not to laugh at the hilarity that was surrounding her.

"Stu?"

"Yes, dead guy," replied Stu.

"Do you ever feel like you're stuck?"

"What, like you, sitting on the floor?"

"Exactly."

"No, I get to travel. Sometimes I get stuck on the same route but that doesn't happen for too long. I was stuck for a long time before beautiful here, picked me up." Water flew out on Stu's windscreen and the window wipers wiped his front windscreen clean.

"You're too kind," said Shelby.

"Well, it's true." Stu responded.

"You do know you're talking to yourself," Max noted, dryly.

"Keep going Stu," said Shelby, smiling.

"I'm not a show pony, sorry, Shelby. I don't work on demand."

"Rough," said Max.

"We're here!" shouted Shelby, smiling as she stopped Stu and pulled up the parking brake.

"I like it when you do that," said Stu. "You've got such a firm, masculine grip."

"That's gross," said Max.

"That's enough you two!" Shelby smiled playfully. "We're back at the burnt out *holiday home!*"

Part 3

Shelby turned Stu off. The bus went totally dark. She got off her seat, which bounced up and down once her weight left it, and walked towards the left windows. Looking out she could see the burnt out husk of the old holiday home. To the right was the large home they had originally met and stayed in. She remembered meeting Pete, Charlie and Max for the first time there. It felt like so long ago. She sat on the front seat looking at Max, sitting up in his blood stained duvet cover.

"Tired, Shelby?" asked Max.

"A little."

"The adrenaline must be still pumping through your veins, Shelby," said Stu.

"It is," she admitted as she moved the bag that was supporting Max's body and gently laid him down. She lay down next to him and delicately put her arm over his chest. Her leg lay on his leg. She was crying.

"I'm hard," said Max.

"Don't confuse rigour mortis with being sexually aroused, Max," warned Stu.

"Give it a rest you two, let me *grieve,*" said Shelby, still crying but now also laughing.

"Shame, I thought I was about to have my first threesome," quipped Stu.

"How does that work, you're a bus?" asked Max.

"Well, you are inside me," Said Stu cheekily, as his motor finally cooled and a piston could be heard letting out air. Shelby made a sound like she was about to vomit.

"So *gross,*" said Shelby, patting Max. "I think, tomorrow, I'll have to bury you." Her bottom lip was wavering.

"Why would you bury a bus? For God's sake, I'm not just metal, I'm a living thing."

"Not you Stu, Max."

"He knows," said Max. "It's okay, Shell, I'll still be with you," Max reassured her. Shelby hugged him tighter. The bus went quiet. Shelby lay on her back, looking at the bus's ceiling. Outside she could hear a series of low clicks. Something with many legs scampered up the bus and then walked along the ceiling. It started tapping on it, like it was checking if it could somehow get in. It then scampered off to the right and down the other side. *This world is fucked.* Shelby thought as she closed her eyes, and fell asleep.

Part 4

Shelby woke uncomfortable and cramped. Sleeping on the bus floor was not a good idea. But, she wanted to spend one last night with Max before she had to bury him.

"Morning guys," she said as she stretched out her arms.

"Morning Shell," greeted Max.

"Morning Shelby, did you sleep well?" asked Stu.

"Not really, your floor is extremely uncomfortable."

"Sorry about that. It's not meant for sleeping on."

"You're okay, Stu." Said Shelby. "I'm just going to pop inside and check if there's a shovel next door." She raised her hand to her mouth when she realised what she was saying. Tears again started to flow as she looked at Max wrapped in his blue, bloodstained duvet cover.

"Then we'll finally be rid of him," said Stu, sarcastically.

"I'm really stiff, I feel like a statue," Max expressed.

"That would be the stiffening of the body muscles due to chemical changes in their myofibrils," said Stu. Shelby smiled again as she opened the bus.

"I'll leave you guys to chat." She said as she opened the bus door and walked outside.

"We can come with you, Shelby," said Stu.

"Really?" she asked.

"We are just figments of your imagination, why not bring us along?" suggested Stu.

"We'd love to help, if we can," added Max.

"Okay then," she smiled as she skipped up to the house. She pushed the gate open that they had previously closed, and ran to the entrance of the large house. Memories of another time came flooding back. *All gone now.* She thought.

"Still here," said Stu.

"Me too," added Max.

She opened the door. The house seemed massive compared to where they had been staying. She ran past the kitchen with all the dishes still sitting in the sink and on the bench.

"You guys were messy as," Stu commented. She ran through the lounge and saw the 1000 piece Wasgij puzzle still sitting on the table unfinished. She started to tear up again as she ran out the back and found the shed. She found a shovel and some work gloves.

"That will do it," said Max.

"I don't want to *do* it. It's like saying goodbye again."

"I'll still be with you, Shell. I'm part of you." She grabbed a bucket hat from upstairs and some sunglasses that made her look like Dame Edna.

"They suit you," said Stu.

"No they don't," replied Shelby, smiling. She then went outside and stood by the crosses of Lucy and Shelby, buried by Michael Stevenson.

"How the hell did you two get here, and why are you standing in front of us when you are in the ground? Are my bus lights going cross eyed?" asked Stu.

"Buy the book," answered Shelby as she started digging. The day started out relatively cool. But it took Shelby two to three hours to dig a hole large enough. By the time she was finished she was dehydrated, hot and sweaty. She sat by the hole. *It's so final,* she thought.

"Not for you obviously," said Stu. Max laughed.

"You've got to do it," said Max.

Shelby went back in the house and found two pieces of wood. She nailed them together and wrote something on the front. She placed it by the hole outside. Walking back on Stu, reality set in as she saw the body, in the same place as before.

"You can do it, Shell," said Max. She bent down and started pulling the duvet cover. Max felt heavier.

"Make sure you bend your knees, Shelby, don't use your back like a crane," advised Stu.

"Thanks Stu."

"Welcome," answered Stu.

Shelby pulled Max towards the stairs and tried to carefully pull him down while saving his head. She failed miserably as his head knocked on each step, hard. "Oh, that's got to hurt," said Stu.

"Can't feel a thing," responded Max.

Shelby felt a little better as she slowly pulled Max to the hole. She'd take a break every few steps. At one stage he got stuck on something sharp and she tried to pull him past it. The tug caused the duvet to come away and Max's head popped out. Shelby sat and cried when she saw it. His skin, already a pale grey.

"Such a looker," Stu jabbed.

"I try," replied Max. Shelby laughed, as she wiped her nose and carefully placed Max's head back under the cover.

"Almost there," said Max. She stopped and sat when he said it.

"I don't want you to leave me."

"I'm not."

"Will I still hear your voice?"

"Probably best you don't hear his voice, he talks a lot of rubbish if you ask me," said Stu.

Shelby hushed him. "Will I, Max?" she asked again.

"Don't know, that's up to you, Shell." She got up and pulled Max towards the grave. She placed him by the hole.

"Just push him, he won't feel a thing," said Stu.

"I won't." Agreed Max. She did as she was told and pushed the body. It fell with a thump and Max was left lying on his front.

"I'm so sorry, Max," Shelby said as she started to fill up the hole.

"It's okay, Shell, you're doing me a favour."

"...And me," added Stu.

"Stop making me laugh, this is serious," said Shelby.

She kept steadily filling the hole. After an hour or so, the hole was filled. "Max?"

"Still here," he replied.

"Thank God," she said as she grabbed the cross.

"Love you," said Max.

"I love you too, so much," she said.

"I'll always be with you," Max promised, his voice breaking. She cried as she placed the cross into the dirt.

"Max?" There was no reply. "Max? Answer me, Max...?" Nothing.

"Stu?"

"Still here."

"Max, no..." Shelby fell on the soil. "Max..." She sobbed, while hitting the soil. After a long period of time she sat by the grave and looked at the cross, her writing displayed back at her.

Max.
My perfect boyfriend.
Father of Pete and Charlie.
Love you.
Shelby.

"I'm glad you didn't swear on that," said Stu.

"Didn't seem appropriate." She sat and watched the sun move through the sky. She didn't move once. As the sun was setting, she finally stood up.

"That Max was a really nice guy," said Stu.

"He really was Stu...he was the *best*."

CHAPTER TWENTY-ONE

Companion?

DAY ONE

Shelby lay on the bed in the master bedroom upstairs. She loved this room. It was where they had all slept together. Shelby took the mattresses that were on the floor and threw them into the hallway. She hated mess and now the room was immaculate. Just her, the bed, the massive cupboards. The soft linen. The large glass windows and doors that showed the magnificent beach and water.

The stars were out tonight and she lay watching them. Her thoughts were of Max. So much had happened over the last week she was drained, tired and upset. Her eyelids started to grow heavy. Her body relaxed. A snore woke her up for a second. Realising it was her own she let her eyes close again.

She was finally in a deep sleep. Dreaming of Stu and Max. Max was kissing the bus. Stu's horn started to honk. Beeps, consistent and loud. Max was now hugging the bus. A car was racing towards

Stu. "Get out of the way!" she screamed. "Max move!" Max was now busy kissing Stu. His waist started to gyrate. "The car, Max, move out of the way!" The car's headlights turned on. It was going to hit him. A loud bang woke Shelby up.

She sprung up, her arms bracing the bed. She stared at the window. Something small ran past the doors and sped off around the side of the outside deck. She sat and wiped her eyes. Yawning, she remembered her dream. Lying back down she wanted to get back to it. She wanted to know what happened to Max. She couldn't get back to sleep for hours. *Fucking thing, woke me up.* She thought as she finally fell asleep dreaming of shovels dancing around Mickey Mouse.

Day Two

Shelby had spent all day in the house. She'd eaten a few cans of fruit. Finished the puzzle that Pete, Charlie and Lucy had started. Read a little. She was feeling less than enthusiastic about anything. She didn't feel like conversating with Stu. His humour could get quickly grating over time. She needed a break from the world altogether. Not even Father Roberts' optimism or Gunther's friendship could break her feelings of being forlorn. Before she knew it, she was in bed again, staring at the stars and listening to the waves breaking. *There are worse ways to waste time feeling sad.* She thought.

She was lying on her back. Her fingers were crossed together on her tummy. She felt the water blisters in her soft hands. They had littered her palms and the inside of her fingers. Not used to heavy labour the shovel had certainly done its damage. She was still tired from the effort of burying Max, so Shelby quickly fell asleep.

Her dream this time consisted of Max, Pete and Charlie sitting on a roller coaster. They were racing around corners when Pete realised he wasn't seat belted in. Charlie was the same. They were screaming and crying. Somehow over the noise of the roller coaster Shelby could hear Pete and Charlie loud and clear. "Shelby! Help! Our seatbelts don't work!"

"Max!" she screamed. Max looked at her and smiled.

"Don't worry, Shell, I'll always be with you," he said. As he showed her his seatbelt which also wasn't connected. She looked down and saw she wasn't connected either. She screamed. Suddenly, the roller coaster jerked to the right and dived and they were all floating weightlessly. She felt the air disappear out of her stomach. A loud bang rang out under them as Shelby woke up.

"What the *fuck?!*" She heard it again and was annoyed. Something was moving on the deck. It had woken her up for the second night in a row. It moved from the left of the deck and settled right in front of the glass doors. "*Fuck* this," she said as she looked in her satchel bag. She grabbed something out of it and walked firmly and quickly towards the windows. She then pushed the window open. She peered out. One eye winking to see what it was lying on the deck. It was a small shadow of something. She couldn't make it out. She squeezed her hand through the window and released the safety on the gun. She then shot whatever it was three times.

It let out a small whine and slowly fell on its side, dead. Shelby closed the window. "Fucking, *fucker* woke me up!" she said, firmly. She then walked back to her bed eager to jump back into her roller coaster dream. She couldn't sleep for hours. Finally her brain stopped working and she fell asleep dreaming of Michael and Pup both dressed up like goldilocks doing the cha-cha.

CHAPTER TWENTY-TWO

Road to Ruin

ROAD FIVE

Shelby had spent the last six days doing nothing. She felt depressed and unhappy. She'd never felt this way before. She was always the one that was courageous. She was always the one who pushed, who planned, who made things happen. When she was with her mum, she held the household together. When she was with Michael, she kept him ordered and busy. When she was with Lucy, she helped her look for Michael, Teresa and Pup. When she was with Max, Pete and Charlie, she got up and organised their days.

Birthdays, whoops, she thought. *I fucked that.* And Tim, *whoops,* she thought. *I fucked that too. I'm just a waste of fucking space now. A ticking time bomb waiting to go off.*

She was spending the days sleeping upstairs and downstairs. She didn't have the will to do anything, not even shower. "Shelby?" said a voice in her head. She didn't answer. "Shelby, you there? It's

Stu." She said nothing and turned over. She was lying on the sofa. "Shelby, I know you're unhappy." Stu took a pause. "I'm unhappy too, you know a bus can get sad. It's tough sitting out here, alone, in the worst conditions, creatures chewing on my tires, and what they try to do to my exhaust..."

"What do you want, Stu?" Shelby asked, impatiently.

"Shelby... I think... you just need a little bit of structure to your day, you know, we thrive on repetition. Got to get to the next bus stop by 1 pm, got to get to the one after by 1:30 pm. It keeps us pushing to the next thing. You know, set some goals, Shelby."

"Oh, my God, my bus is now trying to be my life coach."

"I'm not just a bus... I'm your friend," Shelby huffed and pulled the blanket up further.

"Are you a loser?" he asked.

"Fuck off!" Shelby shouted towards the bus outside.

"Sorry, that wasn't... Look, I appreciate you have some problems at the moment, and I don't want to force you into anything, but, maybe you can start by having a shower, as you do have to sit on me. Sorry, that sounded rude..." Shelby tried not to laugh. "Baby steps, Shelby?" Shelby looked up at the ceiling. "What if Michael, Teresa, Lucy, Tim and Pup are still out there, somewhere? And you're lying here, in your filth feeling sorry for yourself? They may need your help, Shelby."

Shelby turned towards the door. "Alright, *fuck face*, I'll have a shower."

"Nice start..." Stu said, "And if you want to take me through one of those large truck washes, I wouldn't say no."

"Fuck off."

"Okay, maybe a wipe of the dashboard with a cloth?" Shelby got up and started walking upstairs.

"One of those nice smelling pine things for the inside?"

"How about my *presence*?" suggested Shelby, smiling.

"Perfect," answered Stu.

Road Four

"Okay I'm *showered*," said Shelby as she came downstairs. Her hair was wrapped in a white towel. She had on a gown that said, his.

"Feel better?"

"Much, thank you." Shelby sat at the kitchen bench. "So, Stu, where should I start on this *road to recovery*?"

"I find writing always helps, a little schedule of yesterday or a list for today."

"Hmm, some creative writing."

"Sure, whatever gets you in the flow."

"What should I write about?"

Stu paused, as his left tyre let out a little air. It had been slowly going down, but he didn't want to say anything just in case Shelby chose another vehicle. "The past? How about what happened to you when the being showed up?"

"You just want me to tell you *what happened?!*" Shelby said, looking at the door.

"Me, and everyone else in the world, you could pin it up somewhere as the truth and nothing but the truth."

"Michael said people will just think we're nuts."

"Or not," added Stu.

"*No*, I like that. My days are *numbered*, someone needs to say something. These fuckers are *killing* us?"

"Who?"

"The architects, the engineers, blue angels, whatever they are."

"Okay, so write about it."

"I'm on it."

Shelby's truth and nothing but the truth.

Over a year ago I died. I was eaten. I was staying with a friend called Michael Stevenson. He fought for his family. He wanted them back. One night, he lit fireworks. Lots of creatures and monsters came out because of the fireworks and tried to eat him.

He had done it because he was always seeing the vision of his wife, when he was in danger. He thought by bringing out the monsters, he would then see his wife and finally have her back. His wife never came. Until, he managed to avoid the monsters thanks to Pup and get into the garage. That's when his wife turned up. But, it wasn't his wife. It was an alien, engineer, architect, blue angel, God. It spoke to him. Said that humans were chosen to be extinct. We had fucked up the earth, just like the beings before us and our time was over. Some of us survived the vanishing, and the visions that appear when we die are sent to us as a form of comfort. The new creatures appearing on the earth are the new species that have inherited it.

"This sounds like so much *bullshit*," said Shelby, placing her hand on her forehead in frustration.

"It's the truth."

"Still sounds like *shit*. It sounds like some shit sci-fi novel from the fifties."

"Hey, hey, hey, there was some good stuff from the fifties. Those comics and novels led to some of the best movies ever."

"Yeah, yeah, okay," Shelby carried on writing.

So, the blue angel was impressed with Michael and his bravery and gave him a second chance. She brought everybody back from the dead. Teresa, his wife, Lucy, his daughter and me.

"So that's what happened," said Stu.

"Uh-huh."

"Sounds like a shit sci-fi movie from the fifties."

"Maybe, but throw *Tim Burton* into the mix with a dash of *Guillermo del Toro* and a hint of *Stephen Spielberg* for the emotion, humour, and finish it off with *The Duffer Brothers* and you'll get a feeling for what it was like."

"What about Peter Jackson?" asked Stu. "I reckon he'd do a great job!"

"Nah, he's busy doing docos."

"Probably dead anyway," said Stu, his windscreen and windscreen wipers showing absolutely no emotion. Shelby carried on writing.

But, the being said we would probably not survive. Not in this world meant to kill us all. The being then left and we managed to escape before the monsters got us.

The End.

Signed,

Shelby Frances O'Leary.

"Heavy," said Stu.

"I know, I was *there*."

"Wish I could have been there."

"No you don't, It was *mayhem*." Shelby started to study her story. She was taking it in. "Hang on..." said Shelby, like a light bulb had just turned on above her head. She took off her towel and shook her hair free. "Why the *fuck* should Michael be the only one that gets a *second chance*?"

"I don't know."

"Why can't someone *else* get a chance? I've fucking fought hard for *everyone* in my life."

"Yes, you have, though you haven't taken me through a truck wash yet."

"If anything, I *deserve* it more than him."

"Point taken."

"I'm going to *do* it, Stu."

"Do what, Shelby?"

"Fight!"

"Fight what?"

"I'm going to *fight* to bring everybody back, just like Michael did!" Shelby got up and started pacing around the room. "*Fuck yeah*, that's it."

"You're not serious."

"Never been more serious in my life!"

"You're going to invite creatures to your death party so you can talk to a being and tell them to bring everybody back?"

"Word."

"Maybe you should go back to being depressed, safer that way."

"No, I have you to thank for this Stu. You've opened up my eyes!"

"I'm sorry, close them."

"No, no, no, this is *fantastic*, thank you Stu. Thank you so much." She opened the door and looked at Stu parked on the street. He was giving her the side eye. "I'm going to make that blue angel bring them back, or... I'm going to *fucking kill it!*" She shouted, hysterically. Shelby raised her arms up like she'd just been given the power. She could hear violins and trumpets triumphantly crescendoing in her ears as her arms slowly rose. Stu felt like he had just created a monster.

Road Three

Shelby sat checking the bullets of her guns and rifles. The sun had barely risen. She'd already had two cans of baked beans that she'd have to apologise to Stu for later and was almost ready for action. "Morning Shelby."

"Morning Stu, fucking *great morning* isn't it?" replied Shelby, brimming with enthusiasm.

"So, you're still going to do it then, Shelby?"

"*Hell*, yeah," answered Shelby as she punched the air. "I finally feel like something makes sense Stu!"

"Nothing makes sense, Shelby. You're going to die."

Shelby stopped putting bullets into her handgun and looked at the door. "Little *positivity* please?" she asked.

"I'm just the voice of reason. There are so many factors against you."

Shelby again looked at the door. "I'd rather lay down my life trying, then die by some monster while stealing a can of *pickled onions*."

"I can't argue with that."

"Makes sense, doesn't it?"

"I'm feeling you, so, where are we going to do this?" asked Stu.

"I've been thinking," said Shelby as she placed the guns in her satchel. "First, we visit Father Roberts for a *blessing*."

"Didn't know you were religious."

"I'm not, but a blessing couldn't hurt, plus, I'd like to say good-bye to the *big guy*, just in case."

"I'm going to cry."

"Please don't... *Second*, we'll visit *Gunther*."

"Nice," said Stu.

"Third, we get some flares for tonight's show. Probably visit a boat house, or some shop that sells boating supplies, they're bound to sell flares."

"Makes sense."

"...And lastly *alcohol*."

"You're under age!" said Stu, sounding annoyed.

"I've never been drunk, but I'd like to have a few. Give me some liquid fuel!"

"Liquid stupidity, more like. What if you have too much?"

"My *funeral*."

"Certainly will be if you can't see or walk."

"Stu, *trust me*, I know what I'm doing."

"I don't trust you and you don't know what you're doing."

Shelby put her satchel over her shoulder. She carried two rifles as she opened the door. She turned back looking at the holiday house for what she thought might be her last time. "Thanks." She said, as she smiled and thought of her friends all sitting around the table. *Time to get you back.* She thought as she ran to the bus, opened the door and started Stu up.

Road Two

Arriving at the church, Shelby noticed no cars parked in the car park. "That's *not* good," she said to Stu. She looked at her watch. 9:59 am. Perfect timing. She sat and waited for the bells. The clock turned to 10 am. There was no sound of bells. Just the sound of alien birds and flying insects that didn't look like insects. "I'm going in," said Shell.

"Do you want me to come with you?" asked Stu.

"No, I'll be okay, but thanks for asking."

"Of course."

Shelby hopped off the bus and looked back at Stu laughing at his suggestion. She was picturing sitting in the front cubicle with Stu taking up the whole of the foyer. She pushed the large wooden doors open and walked into the church. The doors closed behind her and an echo rang throughout the church. She stood inside the entrance way examining the open space. The place seemed deserted. She then walked to the large glass doors and pushed them inwards. She walked into the church. There was no Father Roberts to welcome her. There was no voice bellowing through the heavenly space. Shelby walked to the front of the church and sat in the front cubical. She knelt down and did something she had never done before. She said a prayer for Father Roberts.

"*Father,* I don't normally pray. I don't have a God to pray to. I don't believe in such things. I just wanted to say. You were always *kind* to me. I hope you're well and safe. I wish you could be here so you could advise me. But you're not. So, if you're listening, throw me a blessing and if you're not..." Shelby thought about saying, *then to hell with you.* "If not, I *understand.*"

Shelby shed a little tear for Father Roberts. The church felt so empty without his larger than life personality. She did a sign of the cross that was totally wrong and kissed her finger just like Maria did, except Maria had actually kissed the crucifix on her rosary beads. She then walked out from the cubical and knelt before the cross of Jesus. "Lend me a hand, will you buddy?" she asked as she turned, and walked down the aisle.

Pushing the large doors open she stepped out into the glorious sunshine. "Was Father there?" asked Stu.

"You know he wasn't."

"Oh, no," said Stu.

"It's okay," replied Shelby. "I expected it. This world has it in for *me.*"

"Next stop?"

"Yep, but first we stop and get some Pineapple Lumps."

"You got it, boss," said Stu.

Road One

Stu drove into Tim's army base. Everything looked the same as previous. The gate was still hanging off its hinges. The Bushmaster was still sitting burnt out. Shelby stopped the bus and grabbed her rifle, walking into the main entrance. "If anything happens, just call for me," said Stu.

"I will!" replied Shelby, as she walked in looking like a special agent. She walked with stealth, the rifle leading the way. She passed the pantry door. Inside, the food was almost completely gone. *That's good, Gunther's been busy*, she thought. She walked to the stairwell. She'd left the torch at the top of the stairs. She made her way down the stairs and stopped just where the light started to disappear.

"Gunther?" She whispered. No sound. "Gunther boy, are you *there*?" No response. She sat on the stairs and waited.

"Doesn't look like he's around," said Stu. His thought voice surprised Shelby. She jumped a little.

"*Jesus* Stu! Give me a warning before you thought talk, will ya?" Shelby had her torch shining in front of her.

"Sorry, just thought I'd mention the obvious."

"I was hoping he would be here," said Shelby, sounding disappointed.

"Well, you have been away for almost seven days. You can't expect him to be here waiting for you 24/7."

"Yeah, you're right. I just wanted to say *goodbye*." Shelby again started to tear up. The thought of saying goodbye to Gunther cut

her up. "*Well*, no point hanging around. He could be *anywhere.*"
Shelby walked back up the stairs. She emptied a packet of Pineapple Lumps on the floor. "He'll know it's me," she said.

"Or a creature that happens to shit incredibly tasty chocolate," replied Stu. Shelby laughed, then opened another packet. She started leaving a trail of Pineapple Lumps back to the bus. "Are you going to do that all the way to wherever we're going?"

"Maybe, I've got enough packets."

"Are they the original?"

"Damn right."

"He'll find them irresistible then."

"You know it. You never know. He might follow them and meet me before I die. Then I can give him a *big cuddle.*"

"A big drunken cuddle," added Stu. Shelby smiled as she got back on the bus.

Driving back onto the motorway Shelby did as she said. Every kilometre or so, she threw out a few Pineapple Lumps. *You never know*, she thought. "You're reaching," replied Stu.

Arriving in Wellington, Shelby stopped off at a boating shop which sure enough, had boxes of flares. She stocked the bus with a few boxes worth and a few guns. She then stopped Stu outside a liquor store and stocked up on berry vodka cans and a dozen Heineken. It's what Michael used to drink the most, she thought it would do for her too. She then drove the bus down Vivian St and parked it right outside the adjoining Street, Cuba Street.

CHAPTER TWENTY-THREE

End of the Road

"CUBA STREET, EH?" SAID Stu.

"Yep, Cuba Street," answered Shelby. She had a berry vodka can in her hand and was sipping it slowly. Her other arm was raised holding a hand hold in the corner of the bus while she was looking down Cuba Street going South. Down the end of her view was the famous bucket fountain.

"Why Cuba Street?" asked Stu, his engine cooled down and air was released.

"My mum and I used to shop down here, Stu."

"Good memories, eh?"

"*Hardly*, it was once or twice and she basically bought for herself. But, she had spent time with me. That was nice."

"Mum's eh? I never had a Mum." said Stu, sadly.

"Oh, my God," said Shelby as she sculled the rest of her drink. "Want to go for a walk?" asked Shelby, she grabbed her rifle and placed the strap over her shoulder.

"Love too," answered Stu.

In both hands, Shelby carried the two boxes of flares, the flare guns and the other five cans of berry vodka. The door of the bus opened with a noise that rang out down Cuba Street. A few strange birds flew out of neighbouring trees, surprised by the sound. It was around 5:30 pm and the sun was just going down. A beautiful orange sky sat above the wonderful architecture on both sides of Cuba Street. Shops ran down either side. The road had been paved years ago and now was a pedestrian way for shoppers to walk. Shops were on the bottom level. The top levels were either bars or places where students could live with easy access to the popular Wellington nightlife. Now, it was empty and lifeless.

"Where are we going, Shelby?" asked Stu.

"Bucket fountain."

"Why there?"

"Well, Stu, Mum and I used to sit beside it and watch the water flow from each bucket down to the bottom. Seems like the right place to make my *last stand*. And, It's only the greatest form of *sculpture* in the whole fucking world." Shelby smiled as she got closer to it. A little snake-like creature moved across her path. She stood still as it disappeared down an alley.

"Are you sure you want to do this?" asked Stu.

"*Don't* ask me again Stu... My mind is made up."

Shelby reached the bucket fountain and placed her boxes down. She loaded the flare guns and cracked open her third can. She sat down looking at the bucket fountain. The buckets weren't working, but she sat remembering her mum and her sitting watching it. She drank a large amount of the berry vodka can. "You know, Stu, Elijah Wood once *pissed* in this bucket fountain."

"Really?" asked Stu, sounding interested.

"Really, on a drunken night out. I might *join* him."

"No."

"Yes."

"No."

"He did it when there were lots of people around. I'm doing it with *no one* around."

"I'm here."

"Well, look the other way then." Once Shelby had finished she sculled the rest of her drink.

"Well, in some ways, you just mimicked Frodo's brave actions before he went to Mordor and destroyed the ring, so your paths are now interlinked and parallel."

"Exactly," said Shelby, smiling as she opened the next can. She sculled the whole can.

"Feeling courageous?" Stu asked.

"Very," replied Shelby, "my stomach is in knots though." She stood up and let out a loud burp. "Ah, much better." She opened the last can. "Back to the bus, Stu?"

"Sure." answered Stu. Shelby was starting to feel merry. She had a constant smile on her face. Walking back, she started singing a tune.

"I could spend my lifetime holding on to you, my lover,
I could spend forever holding on to you, my lover,

spend my every night time holding on to you, my lover,
till the end of never holding on to, Max, yeah..."

It was *Sweet Lover*, by The Holiday Makers, Shelby sang it tune-lessly as she started dancing while taking sips from her can. "What do you think of the drink, Shtu?" asked Shelby, starting to slur her words. "If I'm drinking it, then you're drinking it too."

"It's nice, do we have more?"

"No, just the beers now. I've never had a beer."

"Me neither," answered Stu as Shelby opened the door and hopped back on the bus. She kept singing as she grabbed a bottle opener and tried her first beer. "It's getting dark," Stu noticed.

"*Gross*, that is gross," said Shelby as she put the beer down on one of the seats and looked at it like it had just done a very bad, bad thing. "How do people drink *that?*"

"It is your first sip, Shelby," said Stu.

"You're right," she drank again. "It's *growing* on me."

Shelby sat down on the right side of the bus. She sat in a side double seat that looked directly down Cuba Street. "It is getting dark," she agreed as she drank her beer heavily.

"Are you scared?" asked Stu.

"Very..." She drank again.

"You can still drive off. Start me up and leave."

Shelby drank her beer till it was finished. "I'm no *coward*, Stu," she said as she opened the next one. She felt something in her pocket. "Hey," she said like she had just found something special. "My paper of truth."

"Your words of wisdom,"

"The bible, according to Shelby."

"Amen," said Stu and they laughed together.

"I think I need to put this up somewhere," Shelby said as she stood up, looking a little drunk. "People need to *know*." Her hand pointed, shaking, at the steering wheel.

"You're totally right." Consented Stu. "Where?"

Shelby thought for a little bit. "Your bus *door!* People might want to use you Stu, they will look at the bush door, I mean Shtu's door, I mean the bus door."

"I concur."

"Outstanding," Shelby started searching in her satchel, "Here it is! Sello vape... tape!"

"Wow, you're like Hermione," said Stu, impressed with how Shelby found what she needed in her bag.

"I am, and you will see some fucking *magic* tonight! Yes shir!" replied Shelby as she took another sip. She opened the doors to the bus and stuck the piece of paper as best she could to the outside of the bus door. "There's some fucking, *holy truth* right there!" said Shelby as she stood back, looking at it with blurry vision. She drank her beer and smiled.

A gust of wind blew the bottom of the paper up. It started flapping. Shelby tried to get there to push it down again, but another gust of wind swept under the paper and ripped it away from the door.

The bible, according to Shelby, flew effortlessly away with the wind, disappearing down Cuba Street. Shelby watched it looking deflated. Her mouth was open and her shoulders were slightly pronounced forward. "Figures," she said as she took another long gulp. "Fucking figures. Story of my life in this world, Stu. *Story of my life.*"

Shelby walked back into the bus, knowing it was almost time. She was feeling very drunk and if she had any more she would probably fall flat on her face. "Stu!" Shelby shouted.

"You don't need to scream, Shelby."

"Sorry Stu, Stu! Look! Slowboat records!"

Shelby ran to the music store and stood with her hands pressed against the glass. Her mouth kissed the window and smudged it. "Music..." she whispered. She put her hand on the door handle. She closed her eyes and made a wish. The door opened. "Yes! *Motherfucker!*"

"Shelby, what are we doing here?"

"Stu, my man, If I'm to die, it will be with *music in my ears.*"

"Very well." Answered Stu. Shelby ran into the store. She picked a CD. "Perfect." And a second hand Walkman as no iPhone or network had been working for over a year. "Very retro." She ran to the cash register, slipping a little.

"Be careful, you're drunk."

"Sho are you," she answered. She opened the cash register.

"Ah, shit, empty." She looked for a paper and pen. Wrote out a message and placed it in the till.

I O U $50.
Keep the change,
Shelby Frances O'Leary.

She then closed the cash register and ran out of the store and back to the bus. "I'm *ready* now, big Stu." Said Shelby as she drank another bottle empty.

"Shelby...?" said Stu.

"Yes, my dear friend," replied Shelby as she placed the empty on the ground and opened another one. She was smiling happily. Her fear and worry drowned in the drink.

"I think it's time for me to go."

Shelby paused as she sat on the bus seat holding her drink by her lips, thinking about what Stu had just said. Stu's voice had never sounded so serious.

"What? No, you can't go Stu. It'll just be *me*." Shelby was shaking her head vigorously, her lips were pouting.

"Shelby, I'm not really here."

"Yes... yes, you fucking are, I can hear you plain as day." She drank half the bottle empty.

"Shelby, you need to concentrate. Your life is in your own hands now. I can't help you." Shelby looked down Cuba Street. It was now completely pitch black. The sky above was sprinkled with stars.

"Don't leave me, Stu... *please*." Pleaded Shelby, suddenly deadly serious. "Stu...?"

Shelby ran to the dashboard and looked at the steering wheel. "Stu!" She sat in the driver's seat as it bounced up and down with the pressure of her weight. "Stu?" She grabbed the steering wheel in a big hug. "Don't *leave* me, Stu! Not fucking *you too!*"

She screamed as she wailed over the steering wheel, her head collapsed on the centre of it. "Don't leave me... *alone*," she whispered and suddenly, she felt like she was very alone. Just the sound of her crying was all she could hear as her eyes peered to her left. Looking down the long narrow street. That led to the bucket fountain.

Shelby sat up, holding the steering wheel in both hands. "I won't *forget* you, Stu." She whispered as she feathered her hand over the wheel lovingly. "You're the *best*," she said as tears came like waves to her eyes. "I'll come *back*. I promise." She rose and took a deep breath. The bus felt dark and ominous. She didn't feel like drinking anymore. She knew now was the time. The time to meet her destiny. To bring everybody back, or... die. She tried to straighten herself up and take another deep breath. She placed the two handguns behind her in her jeans. She had one rifle swung behind her back and another ready in her hands. She turned the safety off.

She was ready. She took one more swig of her beer and finished it. "I'm fucking *ready*," she whispered. "I can *do* this." She grabbed the satchel and pulled out a black cap. She tied her hair back tight, placing the hat on her head turned backwards. She positioned the headphones over her ears, and put the CD into the Walkman. She then slid the Walkman into the top pocket of her jeans. The wire to the headphones was threaded under her t-shirt and kept neatly out of the way. She took a deep breath and pushed play. The music started playing. "Fucking *Motocade*, Bombsquad... Fuck yeah," she said to herself as she opened the bus doors.

The pumps working echoed down Cuba Street. She walked out quickly and with purpose. She tried to walk as straight as possible but was swerving a little. She smiled as she felt the buzz from the drink and the fresh air mixing, it hit her head hard and she was dancing enthusiastically to the music. *"So cut the red wire, cut the blue wire, and see if she blows!"*

She sang, wildly dancing up Cuba Street. The Slow Boat Records store watched her as she danced past.

She was dancing like a lunatic. Her voice singing tunelessly to a song that the record store could not hear. All it could hear was the scraping of her retro, Adidas shoes on the pavement and her unmelodious voice singing to the heavens. It did, however, really appreciate her enthusiasm. If it was capable of smiling, then indeed the Slow Boat Record store was beaming. Out of the corner of her eye, Shelby winked at the store, knowing it was watching her. She slowed as she got closer to the bucket fountain. The vibrant music had stopped abruptly and seriousness fell upon her. Almost instantly, she felt sober.

Her mind went straight to thoughts of Max. *For you, Max. For you, Pete and Charlie,* as she walked past a pub, the Hotel Bristol. *Michael,* she wondered, who she would see. Which person would be her vision of comfort? *Max? Michael? Her mum? Please no, not mum. I'd just shoot her.*

She reached the bucket fountain. The boxes were still sitting where she had left them. The flare guns, waiting to be set off. She placed the rifle on the ground. Her hands were shaking. She could feel her heart pumping rapidly in her chest. She was more frightened than she had ever been in her life, and she felt so alone.

She held the flare gun in her hands and pointed it to the sky. She closed her eyes and for some reason, Father Roberts' smiling, hairy face came to mind. She felt a sense of comfort as she pulled the trigger. The gun gave a loud bang and a red stream of gas and vapour jetted into the sky. Her mouth widened with astonishment as her face turned from red, to orange and then finally to grey. She sat down on the side of the bucket fountain. Her hands were shaking out of control. Her teeth even started chattering though it was not cold. She grabbed the second gun, stood and aimed it at the sky.

She closed her eyes hard and no one's face entered her mind's eye. Slightly disappointed, she pulled the trigger. The flare burst into life, louder than any firework. It burst through the dark night shattering the twinkling stars with red light. She glanced down the street. Something came hurtling towards her. There were so many rows of shadows that it kept disappearing in darkness and reappearing metres closer to her. She pulled out her hand gun from behind her. Aimed and shot it straight between the eyes. The creature fell and tumbled towards her, dead. "*Fuck* yeah," she said, confidently as she filled the next flare gun. Aimed it and shot it into the sky.

She was now starting to believe in herself. The nervous shakes were gone. Adrenaline was now pumping through her. Something leapt at her from a second level railing. It was large and had huge enormous arms. Its claws were protruding from its fingers and she could see a large mouth, open with jagged teeth ready to bite her. She grabbed both handguns this time. She shot it twice in the face and rolled out of the way of the screaming banshee. It fell to the side of her and was trying to get back up and attack her again. Shelby lay on her back, both guns were up and pointed as she shot it straight through what she hoped would have been its brain and killed it. "I'm on *fucking* fire," she whispered, self-assuredly, as she grabbed another flare and loaded it.

This time she aimed and shot it down Cuba Street. It made a loud whistling sound as it spiralled in circles, illuminating Slow Boat Records display window as it flew by and then whizzed, just over Stu. It revealed what she was afraid of. A multitude of small spider-type creatures. Crawling over Stu, and now, coming towards her. Behind them was a large creature. It seemed to have a head at the front and rear. A larger version of a lizard she had once tried to kill. It was attacking the spiders as they were spraying liquid back at it. It ate a few as it lumbered up the street towards her. Following behind it was an even larger monster. It had tusks protruding from its jaw and brow. It smashed into Stu and sent the bus moving a few feet to the right as it charged onto Cuba Street. It was feeding time for all the monsters and she was the main course. There was still no sign of the being.

She loaded one more flare knowing this might be the last one and sent it flying magnificently into the sky. In her eyes the shimmering stars could be seen that were then replaced by the bursting flare. The pools of tears swelling at the bottom of her eyes gave a doubling effect. *I'm about to die.* She thought as her eyes moved from the sky and came down to meet the monsters.

For an instant, time stood still as it was not the monsters she saw in front of her. But, the smiling, comforting face of Michael Stevenson. He was seated on an outside chair. His hair and beard were exactly the same as when she had last seen him. He had on his Hawaiian aloha shirt and his denim shorts. His heavy tracking boots completed the almost perfect replica. "There you are, *you fucker!*" She shouted with anger as she instantly raised her guns at the being.

The sounds of the creatures rushing towards her could be heard behind Michael. It was horrible and piercing. "Give me a fucking *chance!*" she screamed at the being. Her face was ferocious. Her stance was every bit the action hero. "You gave Michael a chance, now, give me a *fucking chance!*" The ghostly image just sat, smiling at her pathetically. "I've done everything that he did and *more!*" She took three steps forward and had the guns aimed at Michael's head. "Why doe's he get fucking *redemption* and all I get is *death!* Bring them *fucking back, now,* damn you!" Tears were now streaming down Shelby's cheeks.

The being kept smiling its callous face at her. The monsters were getting closer, the noise growing ever louder. She was running out of time. "Bring them back or you *die!*" she threatened, she aimed right between his eyes. He smiled back at her and then his head started to sluggishly, tauntingly move from side to side. He was saying, no. It was too late, the monsters were right behind Michael. She swapped to her rifle and sent a bombardment of bullets directed at all the creatures. The night came a light with heavy firing. The monsters hesitated and parted like the red sea for Moses. "Give me a Goddamn *chance!*" She pleaded, her voice frenzied with passion. as she looked out of the corner of her eye at Michael. He stood up, pivoted and started to walk away. "No..." She whispered. "...No! come back you *fucker!*"

She was spraying bullets everywhere. The rifle ran out of bullets, so she grabbed the other rifle. She did the same but this time shooting Michael as well. He just kept walking away. The monsters dispersed from the beings' soft light. He walked slowly and didn't look back. It was like Jesus walking on water. The bullets she shot at it went straight through it. Whispers of gas followed the bullets out of its body, like it was nothing more than vaporous mist. She screamed.

She was pouring bullets everywhere. The monsters, feeling the pain of her anger. She screamed again as the rifle gave up its last. She dropped it. There was nothing more to do. There was no way to stop the wall of creatures. They would come now and kill her. She closed her eyes. Standing in front of the bucket fountain. She had given it her all, and it had failed. She started to cry heavy buckets of tears. They streamed down both cheeks. She grabbed the two guns from behind her and raised her arms and held out her guns facing away from her. Taking the shape of the cross in front of the bucket fountain. She was a portrait of conquered heroism. She then placed the guns to both temples of her head. "Fuck *this* new world," she whispered. The monster's noises had silenced in her head as she finally said.

"I'm not going to let you *take* me."

She pulled the triggers and the world fell noiseless. Nothing happened. The guns were empty. "I'm sorry," she said, thinking of Max, Pete and Charlie. "I failed you."

She felt a tug on her left leg. Then her right. *Here we go.* She thought, her eyes still closed not wanting to see her killer. Then a tug from behind and she found herself hurtling through the air. She skidded across the pavement and ended up at the entrance of the Aroy Thai restaurant.

"What the...?" She said as she looked up. There in front of her was Gunther! "Gunther *Baby!*" She screamed. Gunther looked her way and blew a few puffs of smoke. "Gunther *Baby!*" She started dancing a jig on the spot. Gunther looked bigger. His jewels on his back were catching the moon lit night. Sparkling, heroically. "You're so *fucking handsome!*" she shouted, gleefully. Gunther went into action mode. His tail swung from left to right. Spraying creatures everywhere. His tail moved so powerfully that the instant the monsters were hit, they were either injured or dead. He then lowered his front legs and Shelby knew what was coming next.

"*Fuck yeah,* Gunther! Blow those fucking Pineapple Lumps!"

She shouted, joyfully, her fists punching the air as Gunther let out a massive streaming flame. It was bigger and hotter than Pup's. Shelby could feel the heat hitting her face as she tried to shield herself with her arms raised. The monsters were all running away, trying to survive. Most of the monsters were melted in an instant. Gunther's tail then spun quickly as his back legs and bottom lifted into the air. He was still belting out the flames. The tail then changed direction. So that he shot forwards. He then opened his front legs and the extra skin became large bat-like wings. He glided through the creatures, streaming waves and waves of flames on their monstrous hides. "Fucking A!" shouted Shelby, jumping up and down with her fingers clicking, celebrating.

Suddenly, a hand crawled up to her from the right. It looked like a hand but had eight digits, four on each side. It stopped, pulsing up and down. "Ew..." said Shelby, her hand on her mouth, holding in the puke that was building in her stomach. A tail came up from behind it and what looked like a small stinger was aimed at Shelby. It shot its stinger. She dodged to the right and the stinger breezed passed her face. The hand then stood on its back two digits as it raised its palm. A split in the middle divided revealing large teeth and a tongue. "Oh, no, that's so *wrong*." She instinctively put out her right foot and stepped on it. It combusted into liquid under the weight of her foot.

Shelby felt like puking as another four hands came quickly into view. "No, sorry, *no*." She ran between them, the hands turning and chasing after her. She ran down an alley trying to lose them. Some of them scampered down the other way, one followed her. She turned as it jumped at her aiming straight for her face. It's slit wide open with teeth showing. Shelby's eyes closed and her hands moved up to her face trying to protect herself, when something hit the creature. It sounded like a plank of wood hitting a baseball in the sweet spot.

She felt something hit the back of her head. She opened her eyes as stars started to fill her sight. Her vision got blurry and she felt a pain in her head. Something hit her again and she lost consciousness. She slowly fell forward and hit the ground hard.

CHAPTER TWENTY-FOUR

Prisoner

S HELBY WOKE WITH A splitting headache. It was the sort of headache that would follow your head's movements, she just couldn't escape it. She had piercing pains right in the middle of her head. *Is this what it's like being hungover?* Her eyes remained closed as she stirred. Her shoulder hurt. Her ribs felt like they'd been punched in. The grazes on her elbows and legs were burning. She felt like she had well and truly been through the ringer. Like she'd been in a washing machine, dryer and then thumped with a broom for good measure. Everything hurt, but she was still breathing.

She spat out some straw from her mouth. She wanted to bring her hands forward to wipe her face but found her hands were tied tightly behind her back to a wooden pole. She pulled her arms forward a few times before feeling the pain in her joints.

"*Alright*, alright, alright," said a familiar voice. Shelby's face was half in straw and half not. Her left eye slightly opened. She looked ahead and saw she was in a barn. Stalls that once held animals were in front of her. Her eyes adjusted to the light and she could see a figure lying on his side. He also seemed to be tied up. "You said we'd *meet* down the road and here we are. We just can't stop bumping into each other."

"Uh, *fuck* no," said Shelby as she laid her head back down in the straw.

"Oh, come on now, lovely lady, you wanted to *kiss me* last night when you came in. Someone was liquored up to the max."

"*No...* fucking... way," said Shelby as she spat out more straw and tried to sit up. Her body was fighting every little movement. She made noises like it hurt. She rested her back against the wooden pole. Her head was in agony. She tried to open both eyes. "*Where* the fuck am I?" She asked as she searched the rest of her surroundings.

It was a large barn. At least ten stalls, five on each side. She was in one of them. The Barn was high stud at least four metres high and had a mezzanine floor near the entrance. She noticed chains hanging around the doors. She also noticed in one stall down the end was a body. She could see large black boots hanging out from the stall. They were indeed prisoners. Daylight was trying to get in the barn and she felt like it was around midday.

"Hell." Answered Steven, he started smiling a large handsome grin. He looked pale and dreadfully thin.

"How *long* have you been here?"

"Feels like a long time and thanks for caring."

"I *don't* care," replied Shelby, shaking her head, which hurt. She moved her butt trying to get comfortable. A new pain rose in her lower back.

"Rough night?" asked Steven. Shelby didn't answer. The way she was acting told the story. She studied Steven more. His hair was matted, straw was mixed throughout it. His hands were tied like hers. He had a flannel striped shirt on that was ripped and his body was extremely dirty. *He always seemed like the type to be an asshole, why was he a prisoner?*

"Okay, *Stevo*, I'll bite, *why* is this hell?" Her head was screaming in focused pain, she was finding it hard to concentrate. She lay down on her side again, trying to escape the feelings of discomfort, her head rested on the ground. Some of the pain subsided.

"It's a long story, Miss Shelby, that was your name, right? Shelby," Steven said Shelby's name like it was two separated syllables. Steven sat up. Shelby started to feel her eyes close. She could barely keep them open. Her body, not quite ready to listen. "Well missy..." before Steven could finish his sentence. Shelby passed out.

Shelby heard growls coming from outside. It blended in with her dream. She was running down Cuba Street. Behind her was a wall of monsters chasing her. She was getting slower and slower and they were getting closer and closer. She could hear a growl right beside her left ear. She woke up, startled. "*Bad* dream?" asked Steven. He was staring at her, the barn was now dark. It must have been early evening.

"What's that... *outside*?" She turned and saw she was close to the barn's wall. There were knots in the wood. The hole of one of the knots was large enough for her to see outside.

"The *beast*, you mean?"

"The *beast*?"

"Yeah, it's something Tony brought into camp. Supposed to protect us, *scary thing*. It's caged up outside. He brought it in for protection. He'll release it whenever something, uninvited, wanders into camp."

"Shit," responded Shelby, sitting up again. Her body felt a little better but now her stomach felt empty. She hadn't eaten since yesterday's baked beans.

"If it's as vicious as it is ugly I think it could kill anything."

"How do you get it back in its cage?"

"Meat and lots of it. Pretty simple really. Not the smartest creature in the world." Shelby shifted herself trying to get comfortable, she spat out another piece of straw. She noticed the black boots from yesterday, down the end of the barn. They'd moved slightly.

"Who's *that* down the end?" Steven looked towards the boots.

"Him? Don't worry about him, I think he's already dead. Poor guy's number was up as soon as he was brought in. Tony knew him from way back. Wanted him *dead*. He hasn't spoken a word in days and I don't think he's eaten. I'd be surprised if he's still breathing." Shelby was starting to hate Tony. She felt her ribs aching, she was in so much pain and was finding it hard to breathe.

"Why the fuck are we here, Steven?"

"Ha, I told you the whole story yesterday, Miss Shelby. Didn't realise I was boring you. Put you straight to sleep." *You're putting me straight to sleep now.* Footsteps could be heard walking by the barn door. "I ain't got much time, Shelby, head honcho has already called me up for *execution*."

"What?"

"Yeah, it was supposed to be a few days ago, then yesterday, I'm guessing it will be *today*."

"Why?"

"It's Lord of the Flies out there, Miss Shelby, started out okay, there were only a few of us. Matt, Tony and Luke. We all set this up. But, then we started adding others. Someone wanted to be in charge. You know the story, *shit* happens."

"Why do they want to execute you?"

"I've been accused of doing something I didn't, Miss Shelby. They want me to pay, I'm an example... I did nothing wrong..." Steven looked over at Shelby and smiled. His teeth looked grey. "Tonight, I'll be burned at the stake and what's left will be meat for that thing out there." Steven tried to lie on his back. His tied hands were making him look uncomfortable.

"*The fuck*, is there anybody else that can help us in the camp? Anyone that trusts you? Against this, *Tony* fuck?" Steven looked over Shelby's way.

"*Tony*? It ain't Tony in charge, Shelby. It's *Teresa*."

Shelby looked visibly shocked. She tried to move forward but her tied hands pulled her back. "Teresa?"

"Teresa."

"We were looking for her."

"Lucy's mum."

"Yeah."

"Lucy's *here* too." Said Steven, matter of factly.

"Lucy? *What*? How?" Shelby looked shocked. *Lucy's alive.*

"I brought Lucy in a while back. Teresa wanted to find her and you." Thoughts were racing through Shelby's mind. *Lucy's here? And Teresa?*

"Is Michael *here*?"

"Lucy's dad?"

"You remember."

"I do…we were looking, just, a lots happened." *Teresa's in charge, why the fuck am I locked up?*

"I see you want some answers."

"Yeah, why the fuck am I a prisoner? Why are you a prisoner? Lucy *liked* you."

"As I say Miss Shelby, Lord of the Flies. This world will change you as sure as a *caterpillar* becomes a *butterfly*. Just, she ain't no butterfly. She's a *war machine*."

"Teresa…?" Shelby questioned, not believing.

"Oh yeah, she started out all prissy and nice, you know she's a proper honey, but don't let that fool you, if she doesn't like something, *you're done*. She's already had three people *executed*. I'm *next*."

"Why?"

"It's complicated. Just know I'm a friend. Lucy's a peach."

"I know she is." Shelby noticed Steven had a look on his face. A look that she had once seen on Max's face. A look of love.

"But Teresa, she's accused me of things that I'd never do. My friends…" Steven looked extremely upset. "…She's lost it. She's ruthless." Shelby was visibly shocked. *Teresa was so nice. Such a motherly figure. She loved her family. She loved Lucy. She knew me? What the fuck?* Suddenly, the chains on the barn door started to rattle. Someone was unlocking a padlock. "Looks like my time's up, Miss Shelby. It's been nice chatting to you." Steven sat up and leaned against the wooden pole facing the barn doors. While looking at the doors he whispered to Shelby. "Listen… I've got a few left on my side. We have a plan. We're going to bring this place down. *You with me?*" Shelby sat with legs angled to the side.

Her bum slightly raised off the ground. Her mind was racing at a hundred miles an hour.

What the fuck? Do I believe this fucker? Teresa killing people? Is Steven lying? What if he isn't. What if she is a war machine? I've seen how this world has fucked me up. I've been talking to a bus for the last few days. Why wouldn't it do the same to Teresa? "Shelby, you with *me...?*"

Shelby didn't know what to say. She didn't want to agree with Steven. She just couldn't believe Teresa was this warlord dictator.

"Get me out of here." She whispered back. He smiled a handsome, toothy, wide grin back at her.

"*Be ready*, as soon as I'm free, I'll come and get you." He winked at her. One of the barn doors swung open. A torch light shone Shelby's way. Two large shadows walked in. It was hard to make out their faces. As they got closer to Steven she could see one of them. He was a balding man, huge and rough looking. It was Philip from church. *Fuck it's Philip. Do I talk to him?* She felt like calling out his name but didn't know what was going on. *Whose side is he on? Probably not Steven's.* Philip didn't look Shelby's way. As usual, he said nothing. He went behind Steven and untied his wrists.

The man in front of Steven had dark features. He was thin like Steven. Steven raised his eyebrows to him. He did the same back to Steven. *His helper?* she thought. "Hey boys," said Steven, sounding friendly. "It's been a while, you're both *looking good*." They didn't answer. Philip held Steven's hands with one powerful hand. The other, holding Steven's shoulder leading him out. "Where are we going boys? I ain't even had my last meal yet?" Philip shoved him forward. Steven looked back at Shelby and winked again. "I was looking forward to a large steak, eggs and chips *boys*! The service in this place is just *terrible!*" Steven said as his voice trailed away in the distance and he was led out of the barn. The doors were closed again as she heard the chains and padlock being put back in place.

Shelby sat leaning against the wall. She was placing her eye to the large hole in the knot. Outside she could see the dry paddock. To the right was a massive caged area. She couldn't see inside but guessed it was where the beast was housed. Every now and then a low ominous growl would come from that direction. She heard voices and shouts coming from the way of the barn doors. It sounded like a large group of people agreeing with something. Someone shouted something. Nothing was happening on her side and she couldn't see anything as it was pretty dark out. *How the fuck did this happen to me?* she thought.

For the first time it was just her and her thoughts and the guy with the black boots. She remembered the huge battle from the night before. It had gone so wrong. The being not even acknowledging her. It didn't answer any of her questions. She hated it. She shook her head in disbelief. She'd never hated Michael Stevenson, but that smiling, sadistic, all knowing being had made her hate him with a passion. She remembered Gunther. Saving her life. Brave, Gunther. *The Pineapple Lumps had worked!* She smiled. Her grazes reminded her of falling and the hands, *oh, yuck, the hands.* She remembered holding the guns to her temples. *Fuck no,* she was not proud of that moment. But, at the time there was no choice. It was either that, or a painful death being ripped apart. The last image she had in her mind was of the being, walking silently away as the monsters parted. "You *fuck,*" she whispered.

Suddenly, she heard a large bang outside that sounded like a gun going off. It startled her and she looked the way of the noise.

Steven?! she thought. *Oh, fuck. What's happening? Who will come and save me? Will I see Lucy? Teresa? Will anyone come?* Voices started shouting. Her mind had visions of Teresa shooting Steven and then Lucy. *Poor Lucy,* she thought. *Finding her Mum and then this.* An argument was taking place outside. Someone was wailing in pain.

"Oh, God *no!*" she heard.

More voices screaming. She heard more guns going off. Suddenly the barn had light streaming from outside. It was a moving light. A red and yellow light. A flickering light. The noise that followed confirmed her suspicions. The camp was on fire.

Shelby moved her body back to the knot in the wood. She placed her eye close to the hole. She couldn't see anyone. Another scream came from the barn doors. On the far right by the cage she could see the flames burning. The radiant moving light started to give her sight. She could see the paddock, and its dead grass. She turned back to the barn doors listening. No voices were heard? *Shit, is anyone alive?* She could now feel the heat from the fire. Crackling and hissing noises were coming from outside. The barn was starting to burn.

"No, please, no," she whispered as she put her eye back to the hole. "Hello?!" she shouted. Her voice was drowned out by the fire. "Anyone out *there?!*" If there was, no one would hear her. Her mouth fell open. She pressed her eye closer to the hole. She couldn't believe what she was seeing. She was stunned into silence. Teresa was standing with her hands holding the handle of a knife. Her face was a range of emotions. Shocked, surprised, angry, tearful. She looked different. The flames to the right were lighting up her body with glowing orange light. Her hair was wild, blonded with streaks from the sun. Her skin looked dark and tanned. She was skinnier than she remembered. Any fat had been replaced with sinewy muscle. She looked like she had aged at least ten years. Shelby pushed her eye toward the hole as close as she could get to it. Tears had started to fall from her eyes.

Teresa was holding the handle of a knife and the knife had been placed into *Lucy's* stomach!

Lucy held her hands up to Teresa's shoulders. If Teresa looked shocked, nothing could compare to the shock that was on Lucy's face and now, Shelby's. Lucy was still wearing the same clothes she had worn at the mall. Her camouflaged gear still giving her the look of a soldier.

"*No*...Lucy." Shelby said, tears flowing down her cheeks. "Lucy!" she screamed. Teresa looked Shelby's way, barely hearing the voice and wondering if it was her imagination. All she could see was the outside of the barn's wall. She looked back at Lucy. Her hand was still holding the handle as she laid her on the ground. "You *bitch!*" screamed Shelby as she tried to bang her head against the wall. "It's *your* daughter! Fuck you!" Shelby's hands were pulling on the rope around her wrists. The tears on her face, a mixture of tears and ash. "It's your *fucking* daughter!" She looked once more through the hole. Lucy's eyes were now closed. Teresa was still holding the handle. She touched Lucy's face with her right hand. *Lucy doesn't deserve this*, thought Shelby, anger and pain written in her stare.

Suddenly, Teresa had fear in her face as she was backing away from something. "You *fuck!*" Shelby screamed as Teresa again looked at the barn. She looked back at what was coming. Shelby was breathing in smoke. She coughed. Teresa turned and ran. Something ran past the barn. Right in front of the hole. Then two scavenger wolfhounds pounced on Lucy. They were the same species as the one she had encountered with Max. Lucy's lifeless body shook as the wolf-type creatures started to tear at Lucy's body. Their heavily muscled hairless bodies working. The spikes above their shoulders standing at attention.

Shelby was now distraught. "You fuck! Not Lucy, not my *sweet* Lucy!" She pulled her face away from the hole not wanting to see her friend get torn apart. The smoke was now engulfing her. She couldn't see anything and her throat felt like it was on fire. There was no clean air getting in. She felt herself start to lose consciousness as each breath intake was just more smoke filled air. She finally collapsed unconscious, as the flames danced outside to the sound of the wolf-type creatures tearing at poor Lucy's flesh.

Shelby's eyes opened. She could breathe a little. She looked down towards the entrance and saw that the large barn doors had been opened. Behind the door was waist high flames. Some of the smoke had poured out through the doors and thankfully, she could now breathe, just. She coughed. Her throat felt horrible. Like she'd just eaten smokey ash for dinner. Down the end of the barn the flame had highlighted the black boots. They were still there, with the guy lying in the same position. *He must be dead.* Shelby put her hands underneath herself and pushed herself up.

Wait, I can move my hands. Her hands were indeed loose from her restraints. The rope lying on the ground, it had been cut and she was now free. To her side she saw a small handgun. *Steven?* she questioned. *Where is he?* She grabbed the gun and stood up.

The smoke engulfed her. She couldn't see anything and straight away got a mouthful of disgusting ash. She started to make her way to the barn doors. Her walk was clumsy and aimless. She was constantly coughing and was struggling to take in good air. She knew she needed to get out quickly or she would be dead. She hit a wooden pole. "Fuck," she whispered. "Where the *fuck* is it?" She put her hands out trying to find her way. All she could feel was the horrible heat. She was sweating and her eyes were blinded by the smoke. She walked a few steps when the smoke parted a little.

There, standing at the entrance, was the being. "Fucking *Michael*, fucking *Stevenson!*" she shouted. He was smiling at her. His usual pathetic cheesy smile. *Like he gave a shit*, she thought. She raised the gun. "You *fuck!* You fucking *fuck!*" He smiled even more. He had the usual beard and untidy long hair. But, it was full of even more white strands. His face looked thinner. He wasn't dressed in his usual Hawaiian aloha shirt and denim shorts. Instead he had a black sweat top on and black jeans. But, she still hated him. "Not *today* you fuck!" She stumbled, almost collapsing. She raised the gun again. "Not today, or *any* day!" She shot the gun at the being. This time, it ducked. She shot again.

"Hey!" Screamed the being back at her. She shot again and she swore she hit it. "You *hit* me, Shell!" She paused and looked hard at the being. Her body was almost falling over. Her face, a mess of sweat and ash. Her brain, not working or comprehending. She shot again and missed. "Shell! It's *me*! It's *Michael!*" Michael was holding his right arm in pain. Shelby looked up, her mind trying to work out what was happening. She was half unconscious. Her eyes blinked. She was thinking this was insane.

"...Fuckhead?"

She said, quietly. Michael rushed towards her. He grabbed the back of her head. Their foreheads were touching. They were both in tears. "...*Fuckhead* is that you? Is it really *you*?" She was now shedding voluminous tears. Michael was laughing and crying. He was so happy to see her. Shelby was wearing a fatigued smile. "I *missed* you." Shelby said as Michael kissed her hard on the cheek.

She then gave into exhaustion and collapsed into Michael's arms.

CHAPTER TWENTY-FIVE

Harvest Home

PART ONE: REAPING

"Good morning, sleepyhead!" Said a voice as Shelby's eyes opened, she blinked slowly as her eyes adjusted to the room's light. The blurry image started to come into focus. It was Michael.

"Fuckhead," she whispered in a gravelly voice. She felt like she'd smoked two packets of cigarettes, eaten a vaping stick and followed that with a mouth full of ash.

"Shell." Michael said, affectionately as he leaned down and kissed her cheek. "I'd give you a hug but, Doc's orders are to be careful around you. Apparently, you're made of glass and might shatter." He smiled. Shelby couldn't help but smile back. She started to cry. So much emotion. So much had happened. She felt it welling inside into a tearful climax.

"Michael..." Shelby whispered as she burst into tears.

"It's *okay* Shell, it's *okay*. I'm here now. It's...so good to have you back." She tried to calm herself but the emotion was making her breathe deeply. Her burning lungs did not appreciate it.

"Michael," she said again as she looked at the ceiling, a tear ran down the side of her face. Her heart was hurting as it pounded. *Lucy, Teresa. Was it all a dream?* She felt a weight by her feet. She looked down. "Pup!" She said in a raspy voice. Pup instantly looked up and his mouth opened. She noticed he hadn't grown much. He was still the size of a bulldog puppy. Still cute as pie. But, like everything in this world, Pup was built to last. His tongue popped out and he started breathing quickly. He looked like he was smiling. His three tails stood straight up. A light from the bottom of the tail started to pulsate and gently rise to the top of each tail, they were three different colours. His tails started to spin and his bum started to lift. Shelby laughed and coughed. "His tails all *lit* up," Shelby said.

"Yes, that's one of his new tricks. The other one is, if he lies on the end of your bed, it means you're going to *die*." Shelby smiled at Michael. He smiled back winking.

"It's so *fucking* good to see you," said Shelby, her eyes sparkling at Michael. Michael laughed, he loved hearing her swear. He gave her another kiss as an answer. "You look like you need to eat... *a pie*." Shelby advised, coughing.

"I'm going through my Tom Hanks, Castaway skinny scenes at the moment. Took me a few months to do it, but I mentally set goals and achieved it."

"You're a *dick*."

"No, *you* are." They laughed.

"You're *arm*?" said Shelby, noticing Michael's right arm was bandaged.

"You *shot* me," he said, smiling.

"*Sorry*, I thought you were, the being."

"Really? I'm your vision of comfort?"

"Apparently, ugly choice, right? I was hoping for Brad Pitt."

"I'm *flattered* it was me."

"Don't be, I wanted to *kick your ass*! That's why I shot you. I'm so sorry, is it bad?"

"No, just a graze, you're a really *bad shot*." Shelby smiled, as she felt Pup put his head down and snuggle into her leg.

"I was *looking* for you."

"You were?" asked Michael, suddenly serious.

"I never stopped." It was Michael now who leaked a tear.

"*Where* were you?" asked Shelby.

"Good morning, Shelby!" said a confident voice as in walked a rather cheerful man. He reminded her of one of the actors from an Indian movie called *RRR*, she had watched with her mum. His hair was perfect and he wore a moustache that said, I am the man. It was all caped off with teeth that were as white as snow. He was permanently smiling, which automatically made you smile back. "How is my patient? I hope you're *behaving* yourself?"

"Yes," answered Shelby, not sure how to reply.

"I believe you've had a few *adventures*, Shelby, judging by what your body has been through."

He grabbed her hand and was checking her pulse, he looked at his watch and smiled. For the first time she noticed she was in a comfortable single bed with clean, crisp white sheets. She also noticed the pain in her body. Her ribs hurt. The grazing on her elbows and back seemed to be worse and her throat was stinging.

"You have extensive bruising, your cuts I have cleaned up, you've inhaled a mountain of smoke and your face is still as *beautiful* as ever. But your hand, I'm afraid, is very *hairy*." She laughed, coughed and blushed all at the same time. Michael smiled. "I'm Doctor Stanley and you can call me *Sir* or Doc." He said smiling.

"I'll just call you *cock*." Replied Shelby, smiling. Both Michael and Doc looked at each other shocked. They burst out laughing.

"I like you Shelby, Michael said you were *full of life*." Shelby smiled at Michael. "Now, I'd advise you to get some *rest* and we need to keep these visits very short. You need to recuperate if you want to grow big muscles." Shelby looked incredulously at Doc, he was still smiling. "You luckily have not broken anything, but your body needs to heal." He smiled. "I'll leave you to it. It was lovely to meet you, Miss Shelby." He turned and walked out whistling.

"*Nice* guy," said Shelby.

"The best."

"Where'd you meet him?"

"He *saved* me."

"Really?"

"Yeah, he found me after our big night." He raised his eyebrows and Shelby answered by raising hers. "I was unconscious and badly beaten up." He lifted his shirt to show burns on half his body. Pup looked over with a caring look. "I've been in a coma up to *last week*."

"Excuses," Shelby said. Micheal smiled.

"As soon as I was able to, I came looking for you all."

"That's the man *I know*." Michael smiled again and leaned down and kissed her forehead.

"I'll leave you to rest, *doctor's orders*."

"Are you going to listen to *cock?*" Michael laughed out loud.

"You're going to call him that from now on, aren't you?"

"He asked for it, he wanted me to call him *sir*."

"He was *joking*."

"So am *I*."

"Don't *ever* stop." Said Michael as he squeezed her hand.

"Ow, fuck!" said Shelby.

"Oh, shit, sorry."

"Just *kidding...*" Said Shelby, smiling, "...and don't call me shit."

"I'm out." He said as he got up. "Get *better*...we'll talk later." He kissed her forehead. "My Shell," he said, affectionately, she smiled as he turned and walked out. Within a minute or two, she was fast asleep.

Part Two: Cleaning

It was late afternoon and Shelby was getting restless. The nutrients flowing into her body from the drip were doing their job and she was feeling stronger. Whatever drugs Doc Stanley had been pumping into her body were also working and the pain was minimal. She turned over to her right side and looked out the window. It was overcast. She lay watching the clouds move slowly from right to left. Her thoughts drifted to Lucy and Teresa. She would have to tell Michael soon. How would he take it? She had trouble believing it, but she'd seen it with her own eyes.

Poor Lucy. She'd had such a hard time of it. She was struggling with the whole thing. She seemed to be just working her way out of it and then this. Lucy didn't even know what happened to Pete, Charlie, Max or Tim. Whatever happened to Tim. *Enough thinking,* she thought as she slowly raised herself. Her body rejected the movements, aching in all the wrong places. The grazes felt worse. She was wearing a hospital gown but thankfully had been dressed in undergarments.

She grabbed the IV pole and started walking awkwardly to the door. This room did not feel like a hospital room. In fact the style of the house did not give hospital vibes at all. The room was medium sized but felt like a motel more than anything. It had an eighties feeling that had been modernised. Each movement of her legs brought out new pains in her body. She really had put her body through the works. She coughed as she started to breathe a little faster. It reminded her that her throat had been used like an ashtray.

She pulled the door inward and stared down the hallway. Both ways were empty and quiet. She pushed her IV pole and it broke the quietness as an unevenness in the wheels gave off a large squeaking sound while she hobbled down the hallway. She came to the first door on the right. She gently knocked. It had a number seven on it. This was indeed some sort of motel. No answer. She pushed the door open and squeaked into the lounge. It was relatively tidy apart from a few mugs sitting on a table. She poked her head around a corner and found a bedroom. The door was ajar and she could see a thin man sitting cross legged on the floor. From the back it looked like he was meditating. She tried her best to walk quietly but it sounded like she was pushing the loudest shopping cart in an empty shopping mall. The man's head rose and slightly turned her way. His eyes remained closed.

"Good *afternoon,* Shelby," he said.

"Hello." She answered as she squeezed past him and took a seat beside him. She sat and immediately took notice of the patient lying on the bed. It was Tim. He was fast asleep. She smiled at the man seated who had opened his eyes. "It's *Tim!*" she whispered, excitedly.

"You *know* him?" He asked, smiling back. He had a wise, intelligent face.

"He's *my* friend."

"*Mine* too," said the man, still smiling warmly. He had his hands resting on each leg and indeed seemed to have been meditating. Beside him on the ground was a book called *Ikebana: the art of arranging flowers.* He looked Asian. The man closed his eyes again, smiling. She turned to Tim and studied him. He was thin. Thinner than Michael. His face looked sickly and pale. His hair, like it was ironed to his head. It looked like he had been through the wars. She scanned the room and saw two large black boots. *It was Tim that was the other body in the barn.* She thought. She looked back at the meditating man and he was looking straight at her. It startled her.

"You have wonderful *colours*." He said, smiling. She looked at her gown expecting to see a colourful dress, it was a hospital green.

"Ma'am?" whispered a voice. She smiled looking over at Tim. The man also got up. She got up slowly, and looking like she had been freshly wounded, limped over to Tim.

"You and your *fucking* ma'am, call me Shell will ya!" Asked Shelby, as she just made it to him and gave him a huge hug, she kissed his forehead. Tim was smiling. The man behind her sat in

Shelby's seat and watched with interest. "I'm so sorry, Tim! I'm so sorry for what I said, how we left it." She raised her head from the hug and placed a hand on his cheek. He didn't move. "It was my fault you left...and *this*." She looked at him in the bed.

"I'm okay," he replied, smiling. "...And it wasn't *all* your fault, *I* was just as much to blame. This world will eat you up and spit you out."

Shelby nodded. "Still, I'm so sorry."

"Apology accepted, I'm sorry too, Shelby." She hugged him again.

"It's so good to see you Tim, so good to see someone from...*before*." Shelby could feel Tim move a little with apprehension.

"Max? Charlie? Lucy?" he questioned, quietly, looking into her eyes. She shook her head.

"*You* probably knew already," Shelby said as she heard a creak in the chair behind her. "There's a lot to tell."

"I've got nowhere to go," answered Tim.

Shelby told the whole story to Tim and the man behind her. They both said nothing as she went through the night with Charlie and Max and Lucy's disappearance. She told the story of Max and then what had happened to her in Cuba Street. Tim looked over at the man behind Shelby. "And I thought we had it bad, *Mr Lee*." Shelby turned to Mr Lee.

"Mr Lee?" She turned back to Tim. "Mr Lee?... I thought you said Mr Lee was *dead*?" She turned back to Mr Lee who was smiling.

"Not quite, Shelby. Tim would have told you about the last time he saw me?"

"Yeah, he said you were on the ground outside your apartment. Said he thought you were... *mince meat.*"

"Ha, yes, not quite. That wasn't me, Shelby. I had a visit from something that resembled a human that night. A couple of *human-type creatures* that wanted me for dinner. I was in a different place back then Shelby. I had seen my wife and was...wishing to be back with her. I had left the apartment open. You see, I didn't really care. But, these creatures came in and I decided at that moment that I wanted to *live.*"

"Human-type creatures?" Asked Shelby, interested as she had never come across anything like them before.

"Mostly," he said. "No eyes... teeth, as sharp as daggers, and strong."

"Not as strong as *you* though, Mr Lee," said Tim. Mr Lee smiled at Tim.

"As you know, it's not just about strength, Tim." He said as he thought on his next sentence. "I left the apartment that night. In *search of answers.*"

"Did you *find* them, Mr Lee?" asked Shelby. She was on her best behaviour with Mr Lee. She thought he deserved respect somehow.

"I am here and I am alive, Shelby. That is the *best* answer." He smiled at her and she smiled back. *It is,* she thought. She turned back to Tim.

"...And you Tim, what happened to *you?*"

"I went back to the base." She had her hand on Tim's arm comforting him. "I got home that night and locked everything up as usual. They got me when I was asleep. When I couldn't defend myself. I know it was Tony and Luke. They'd been hunting me, ma'am. They were the ones who *opened* the shopping mall door. I suspect they were the ones who were looking for you and *shot* Max."

Shelby's hands started gripping Tim's arm. Hatred started filling her body. *Who the fuck is this Tony?* Steven had already mentioned him before.

"It was payback. Payback for how I treated them when they stayed with me." Tim looked like he was apologising to Shelby. "They deserved it, I just didn't think, so much *devastation* would come because of it."

"How *long* did they have you as a prisoner, Tim?" Shelby asked, remembering his lying body in the barn.

"A few weeks, a month? I lost track of time. I was working for them to begin with. Doing all the shit jobs under guard. I caused a little trouble and they threw me in the barn as punishment. They didn't execute me straight away. They wanted me to feel pain over a long stretch of time, and I did, *I still am*."

"Did you see Teresa? Or Lucy?"

Tim shook his head. "Never met Teresa, or saw Lucy. I had no idea they were there? But, I was in the barn a long time. They probably thought I was *dead*. Hell, I thought I was dead. Did you see them?" Shelby was about to answer when a smiling Michael came in.

"Shelby! I see you've met Tim and *Malaki*." She looked over at Mr Lee now knowing his name. "You shouldn't be out of bed, you *naughty girl!*" he said, smiling.

"I'm feeling much better. I was growing cobwebs next door," answered Shelby, smiling back.

"Is that *so*? Well, why not put some clothes on if you're feeling so good and come out by the pool. I've got *someone* who wants to see you."

Shelby put on the clothes that had been laid out for her. They definitely were not her style. She wore a green polo shirt. Grey sweatpants and to complete the look, she wore a pair of white sandals. It felt completely wrong but they felt clean and new, so she was happy. Her body was healing quickly. Just the throat was still stinging.

She walked still with a slight limp down to the reception area. The sign behind the reception desk said, Raumati Spa and Resort. *Fancy,* she thought and a good place to stay for lots of people. *Shame I'd never thought of it myself.* She opened the rear entrance doors that had, *Pools* written on them. Walking out it looked like a holiday resort. There was a massive pool shaped like a bean in the centre. It was surrounded by many spa pools and cubicles with seats and outdoor lighting. The whole area was fenced. Down the end she could see a large gate. Behind it the hill seemed to drop to nowhere. The view behind the fence was breath taking. Full of hills and valleys.

She walked out slowly, spotting Michael and Doctor Stanley in deep conversation in one of the cubicles. Pup was curled up sleeping by Michael. Each cubicle had its own pergola. They had empty bottles littered everywhere. In true Michael fashion they seemed to be in good spirits. "Shelby!" Michael shouted. "Over here! Come on *speedy!*" Shelby smiled as she shuffled over to them. Ever so slowly. She reached the cubicle and slid in next to Michael. He put his arm around her and she immediately leaned her head on his shoulder.

"So *good* to see you are up and about!" said Doctor Stanley. Shelby was staring at his moustache which was truly something amazing.

"Cock," she said as both Michael and Doctor Stanley laughed. They were both extremely drunk.

"You always make me *laugh!*" said Michael, giving her a kiss. "Do you *like* your clothes?"

"*Hate* them."

"Thought as much, it was all I could find on such short notice." She looked up at Michael wanting to find out as much as possible.

"How did you *find* me?" asked Shelby. Michael took a sip of his beer, Doctor Stanley joined him.

"We've been searching every day for the last week or so, Doc, Malaki and I. Just got back a half hour ago, truth be told, from looking for Lucy and Teresa." Shelby said nothing. She was waiting for the right time. She knew it would have to be soon. "Yesterday, we were out searching by Newlands and were just about to turn back for home when we saw the fire lit up on the hill. There were quite a few houses at the end of a roundabout. We searched them all but most of them were empty," said Michael, taking another sip of his beer.

"Luckily, Michael wanted to check the barns, even though they all looked well and truly burnt out. He is one, *crazy guy*," said Doctor Stanley, taking a sip of his beer. "That's when he saw you and you *shot* him. Thankfully, it was just a graze."

"I was delirious," said Shelby, looking guilty.

"...And then of course, we found Tim," said Michael.

"Yes, he was in quite a state," added Doctor Stanley, drinking his beer back and realising it was empty. He opened another, took a sip and carried on. "Did you know Tim?... Malaki knew him."

"Yes, I met him when I was with Lucy." answered Shelby.

"*You* were with Lucy?" asked Michael, his beer stopping before it could reach his lips.

Shelby began to tell the story of Lucy, Max, Tim, Pete and Charlie. Not one sip of beer was taken by Michael or Doctor Stanley as they listened. Michael kept raising his hand to his forehead in worry as each predicament was learnt of and ended. Doctor Stanley would bring his beer close to his lips and then put it back on the table without drinking. Shelby got to the end of the Cuba Street walk, with both Michael and Doctor Stanley completely forgetting about their drinks all together. By the time she had been knocked out before waking up in the barn, they both felt the need to drink and both skulled their drinks empty.

"Shit," said Michael, shaking his head in disbelief. He felt emotionally spent.

"You have been *very brave*, my child," said Doctor Stanley. He opened his next beer and gave it to Michael. He then opened a beer for himself and they both drank it at the same time.

"I'm *sorry,* Shelby. You went through *so* much, and I was... *unconscious.*"

"And I, stuck here having to nurse him," added Doctor Stanley.

"That was amazing that you *replicated* what I did," said Michael. Shelby had left out the part about the being, just saying that she went out for a walk, but Michael knew exactly what she had done. She'd also purposely ended the story before the Lucy, Teresa encounter.

Shelby looked around the pool yard. "Who was this person you wanted me to *meet*?"

"Right," said Michael, still thinking about poor Shelby's last few months. "He was just here, but he went to the toilet. He must be lost or something." Suddenly a booming voice came from far in the distance.

"Shelby!" She knew who it was straight away. She got up slowly, her body still in pain.

"Father Roberts!" she called out. He came running over from the rear entrance and pretended to throw some shadow punches before giving Shelby the biggest hug ever.

"I came to see you yesterday, but you were still fast asleep. You look *great!*" He said, his face lit up with smiles. "Doesn't she look great, Michael!" asked Father Roberts as he slapped Michael on the shoulder. He slid into the cubicle by Michael.

"Father! *How*? I came to visit you!" asked Shelby, excitedly, "...a few days ago but you weren't there. I thought something had *happened* to you."

"Alas, forgive an old man, his lack of faith, Shelby. Had I known I would have stayed." He grabbed his beer, opened it. All three of them drank their beers at the same time. Shelby felt very much at home amongst friends. "I was preaching to *ghosts of old,* Shelby. Even *I*, was starting to lose faith in my sermons." He burst out laughing in his usual loud way. They all joined in. Shelby loved hearing his laughter. "I was boxing at the gym when Michael here walked in with Malaki and Doctor Stanley. They'd all come in for a work out. I didn't expect the gym to be so *busy!*" He burst out laughing again as Michael and Doctor Stanley high-fived Father Roberts on his joke. "...And it was a *Sunday* as well!" He laughed even louder and they all started hugging each other, enjoying his joke. They all drank again at the same time. "And then they talked me into joining them on their travels."

"Yes, and when I mentioned *Shelby*," added Michael.

"Yes, it turned out we shared a *common interest*." They all put up their drinks together and said cheers before sculling their drink back. Shelby looked at Michael and Father Roberts. They were arm in arm.

"I've never seen so much *hair* on two people." Shelby noted, smiling.

"Too our *beards!*" said Michael as they crashed their beers together.

"...And *moustache!*" added Doctor Stanley.

"Let us not forget that thing, *it's alive!*" laughed Michael. They smashed their beers together once more. Shelby heard the rear doors open behind her. It was Malaki.

"You *alcoholics* still drinking out here? I thought you had drunk enough *yesterday*," said Malaki, walking like a wise Sharman. His hands put together as if in prayer.

"It is *the end of the world*, Mr Lee!" said Father Roberts, as he raised his beer. He roared with laughter. They all clinked their glasses and sculled.

"I'm so sorry, Shelby, would you like a drink?" asked Michael.

"I don't drink," answered Shelby. "I'm still trying to get over what I drank a few days ago."

"*Wise*, my child," responded Doctor Stanley.

"Thanks, *Cock*," replied Shelby.

Father Roberts looked shocked, his mouth open wide catching flies. Michael was smiling. Malaki slid in next to Doctor Stanley.

"I'll drink to *that*," Malaki said as they all burst out laughing. He opened a beer and they all said cheers and sculled it back.

"To *Shelby!*" said Michael. They all raised their glasses.

"To Shelby!" They all shouted together. Shelby felt the warmth in her heart. After all that had happened it felt so good to be with good friends again. Her eyes started to tear up and she did cry a little as they sang, *for she's a jolly good fellow.*

The afternoon was full of songs, laughter and piss taking. The best kind of merriment between close friends. She did not have the heart to talk about Lucy and Teresa. This would have to wait for when Michael was sober. Today would be a day of fun and happiness. Something she was not used to and so deserved. Tomorrow, she thought, would take care of itself.

Part Three: Threshing

Shelby woke up early. She'd made herself useful by clearing all the bottles the four friends had drunk. It had become quite rowdy with them all playing a game called, a ship came into the harbour carrying a boat load of: Whatever that person could come up with like shoe brands. Then they'd go through all the shoe brands till someone took too long or couldn't think of anything. The person who lost would have to scull. The game had sped up the process of drinking and as a result they had consumed enough drinks to fill a small pub. They were all merry with the afternoon ending with Malaki showing them all some self defence moves. Being all intelligent men, Shelby ended the evening just as they started philosophising and arguing about God and the current state of the world. It was good timing as it was starting to get loud and they had all had enough to drink. It was also starting to get late. They were asleep by seven and Shelby had gotten her body back into bed and was asleep by nine.

Shelby was making a form of pancakes without milk. It still worked with water and some powdered milk she found. Eggs were absent, but she made do with what she could scrape together. She was hoping Michael would be the first one to get up. As per normal he was up at around six and came down to the kitchen, finding Shelby outside sitting on the outdoor furniture. Pancakes, icing sugar, syrups and fruit were laid out.

"Shelby, you are truly something special," said Michael, smiling.

"*Fuck* off," Shelby snapped, smiling back. "I just wanted to say *thank you* for yesterday and for saving me, again. Nothing I could do would ever be enough."

"Having you *here* is enough," Michael replied. Shelby smiled. "So, you enjoyed our company, Shell?" He looked very hungover and his voice was croaky. He poured himself a glass of water from the tap.

"It was like, spending time with my *dad* and *drunk uncles!*" announced Shelby, laughing.

"We did drink a lot. We were so *happy* to see you!" said Michael.

"Any excuse to celebrate," added Shelby, smiling.

"Guilty." Agreed Michael, drinking the whole glass of water.

"Michael...?" Said Shelby, in a serious tone. Michael had not heard his name come out of Shelby's mouth in a long time, something was up.

"Yeah, Shell?" he replied, as he walked down and sat opposite her.

"I wanted to talk to you, I was waiting for a moment *alone*."

"Uh, huh, sure." He filled another glass of water and wiped sleep from his eyes. He needed to be awake for this one.

"Look, there's *no easy* way to say this." Michael leaned forward, wondering what could be so important. "When I was in the barn, I was a prisoner. There was another man there. He was also a prisoner."

"Right," said Michael, listening intently.

"His name was Steven. He was a bit of a dick to begin with but as time went on, I really think he was trying to *save me*, in fact, I think he cut the ropes off my wrist and left me a gun."

"Okay," said Michael, he took another sip of water, not really knowing where this was going. Shelby was trying to tell everything. To try and cover each part of her story, so Michael might understand where she was coming from.

"Michael, Steven said that Teresa and Lucy were *in* the camp." Michael's face changed. He got up from his seat.

"Why didn't you tell me before? We could've..."

"...Mike, sit down, please, *let me finish*." Shelby interrupted, and Michael sat down. His body language had changed. He was looking aggressive and on edge.

"Steven said the original leader, Tony, had been taken *over*. Has Tim told you about Tony?"

"Not really, no." Michael was now tapping his hand on the table. He didn't like not knowing where this was heading.

"Tony was originally with Tim. They had a run in. Apparently Tony's another dick. He opened the door at the shopping mall. Because of him the creatures *killed* Pete. He also, we believe, is the one responsible for *killing* Max. He was also the one who kidnapped Tim and I and brought us to the barn. I *hate* Tony, Michael." Michael started nodding in response. He also didn't like this, Tony. "Michael, I want *revenge* against Tony." Her voice is filled with malice. She paused and took a deep breath. "Max, Pete and Charlie need *payback*."

Michael thought he knew where this was going. He still remained quiet. Listening to everything Shelby was saying. He was feeling sorry for her and what she had been through. "Michael, Steven told me something about *Teresa*. He said that..." Shelby paused, Michael was waiting for the words. "...He said that she had taken over." Michael smiled, thinking that is incredible for Teresa. He felt proud and hopeful. Shelby carried on. "In his words, he said it was like *Lord of the Flies* over there."

"Right..." said Michael.

"He said that... that..."

"*What?* What did he say?" Michael was getting impatient, knowing that something negative was coming up.

"That... Teresa had gone *crazy*."

"What? Bullshit! *My wife*? No way... no fucking way. She's as straight as they come. He's fucking crazy! Who is this bozo?" Michael was tapping the table really loudly. He was not happy. Shelby was breathing deeply. Hating where this had to go.

"We've *all* gone a bit loopy." Said Shelby, trying to back up Steven.

"Yeah, sure, but *not* Teresa. She's as tough as nails. I've never seen her raise her voice once. Calm as. Voice of reason she is." Michael was shaking his head. Shelby thought, *this is going to be really hard.*

"Michael, there's something else I wanted to tell you." Michael went quiet. He already thought she'd given him the bad news. He didn't ask for it, he just waited for Shelby to say it. "When I was in the barn. Steven was taken out to be executed. This was just before you came to save me." The bottom of Michael's fist was now tapping on the table. *Why is she telling me these things? Where is this going?* "A fight broke out, I heard arguments." He was now staring hard into Shelby's eyes. "Michael, I saw Lucy. Through a hole in the barn wall, *I saw her.*" Shelby's voice was breaking. She was starting to cry. Michael's eyes widened. "Michael, *Teresa...*" Michael sat like he was on the edge of the world waiting to fall off it. "...Teresa had a knife, the knife... *it was in Lucy's stomach.*" Michael looked shocked. He was now spiralling down the abyss. "Michael, I think... I think, Teresa *killed* Lucy."

Michael stopped tapping the table. Tears were falling down his cheeks. "You *saw* it?" he growled.

"*I* saw it." He stared into Shelby's eyes, wanting to work out if there were lies in her pupils. Whether the iris in her eyes had seen the wrong thing. All he could see was pools of water.

"Are you *sure*?" his voice, raising.

"Why would I tell you something that wasn't true? *I saw it.* Teresa had her hand on the blade." Doctor Stanley walked in. *Oh, fuck, the worst timing.*

"Morning everyone. How are we?" asked Doctor Stanley, smiling. There was no answer. He poured himself a water and looked over his glasses, noticing tension in the room. "All set for another day of adventure, Michael? What time are we leaving today?" There was a slight pause and all that could be heard was the running tap water. Michael was holding Shelby's stare. Doctor Stanley started to feel a little uncomfortable.

Finally, Michael answered. "Not *today*, Doc, I'm feeling a little hungover."

Michael got up and walked over to the door. He paused by it and turned back as if he was about to say something. Shelby and Doctor Stanley looked at each other. Michael left the room and the door slammed.

"Pancakes?" asked Shelby.

Shelby spent the day hovering around the motel. The conversation with Michael had left her unhappy and tense. She was going over and over what she had said. How Michael had taken the horrible news and what he was doing and thinking now. She was worried about him but hadn't seen him all day.

In the morning Doctor Stanley and Shelby had a conversation about Tim. He filled her in on their days together. In the late morning she spent time with Mr Lee. They arranged flowers and he took her through a Tai Chi session. He said that both of the things they did would aid in her recovery. She had a nap around noon. She then spent the afternoon with Tim. He slept through all of it. He obviously had suffered so much more than her. In the late afternoon she had a great conversation with Father Roberts about how people needed to look after one another.

"A simple gesture is all that is needed." He continued, "talking is easy. Actions *move* mountains." He then showed her some boxing moves. She couldn't stop laughing. Watching Father Roberts box just reminded her of Animal from The Muppets trying to be Rocky, but he was good... very good.

They came inside just before dark and Doctor Stanley who everyone called Doc, but who she would affectionately call Cock, showed Shelby how to cook a beautiful dish of his home food. He spiced it up and she loved it. In the evening they ate quietly together in the dark. Telling their stories of the vanishing. It was both interesting and sad. She affectionately called them all, *The Uncles of the Apocalypse.* Michael was a no show, the whole day.

Part Four: Hauling

Shelby again, made breakfast and spent the day with her uncles. She was so in love with the penned name she had given to her adopted uncles, (The Uncles of the Apocalypse) that she decided to re-style one of her plain white t-shirts that she hated. Cutting off the bottom half that revealed her abs and cutting the circular neck so that it hung off her left shoulder, she had created, in her words: *A fucking work of art.* For the *piece de resistance* she wrote with a black ink permanent marker, *The Uncles of the Apocalypse,* across the chest. She loved it. As far as she was concerned, The Uncles of the Apocalypse were the alternative rock band of this new world.

Tim again did not wake and slept through the day. They were all worried about Michael, and Shelby had suggested he probably just had a bug and didn't want to spread it. In the late afternoon, Shelby sat outside on one of the deck chairs looking out at the view. Pup had floated onto her lap, his tails spinning as his lights gently moved up and down. He purred from the back of his throat and she patted him. She felt happy. Living with her uncles was a wonderful experience. They were teaching her something every day. It kept them all busy and made them feel like they had something worthwhile to do. As for her, she just enjoyed their company. It took her mind off everything that had and was happening.

"Hi Shell," said Michael, from behind her. "Seat taken?" Shelby looked up smiling. Her face changed to shock as she saw what Michael looked like. His eyes looked sunken and drawn. His face, pale. He looked even more skinny than before. But, what shocked her most, was his hair or lack of it. He had shaved his hair back to a number one and his beard was gone. She didn't recognise the man in front of her.

"It's all yours," she said as he sat by her. "*Cold* head?" she asked, smiling.

"Very."

"It looks *good*."

"You think?"

"Yeah, like Neo, from *The Matrix*."

"Get out," Michael said.

"Well, you know, the hair, the black clothes." She smiled. They sat looking at the view.

"Love the t-shirt by the way," he said, smiling.

"Fan club," said Shelby, pointing at her t-shirt.

"I know." He replied, "I've got good taste in friends." She nodded, smiling. Michael reached over and patted Pup. Pup looked up and licked his hands. His tails started to spin and he floated over to Michael and fell on his lap.

"Still *recognises* you," said Shelby.

"It's the *smell*." Michael replied, smiling. "It's beautiful isn't it?"

"The view?" asked Shelby.

"That and the world. We really *didn't deserve it.*" Shelby nodded
her head in agreement. "All we have left is *each other,*" said Michael.
Shelby nodded again. "We stick *together.*" Added Michael, as he
put out his fist. Shelby connected hers and leaned her head on his
shoulder. They sat together, looking at the view for over half an
hour without saying a word. She loved it.

As the sun was going down, Michael got up and Pup floated over
to Shelby. She patted him.

"I'm going out tomorrow. Out to find Teresa and this Tony
person." She nodded at Michael wanting to let him speak. "Are
you up to coming with?" He asked.

"I'm feeling much better. The body feels good."

"Good," he replied.

"Do you... *believe* what I saw?" asked Shelby.

"What, that Teresa *killed* Lucy?"

"Yeah,"

"You, believe that?"

"She killed my *best friend.*"

"Teresa would *never...*"

"She *killed* Lucy, Michael! She killed your *daughter!*" Pup
sensed unease and floated off Shelby and disappeared to the back
of the motel by the rear doors. "Lucy needs *vengeance!*" Shelby
shouted, angrily. Michael shook his head, he was pacing.

"You don't *understand,* Shelby. I've been married to this woman
for over twenty years. She *loved* her daughter. She would never...
kill her!"

"She was *crazy,* Steven said so...I saw it, with my own eyes, *she
looked crazy!*"

"Fuck, come on! *Who* is this Steven anyway? You called him a *dickhead!*"

"He helped *free me*. He wasn't so crazy then!"

"Shelby, you don't *understand!*" Michael was getting frustrated and angry.

"Why? *Why* don't I understand? I saw it! I saw Teresa *kill* Lucy and that's not right!"

"Shell, you *don't* get it!"

"I do get it! I saw it, and poor Lucy died because of it!"

"*No... You* don't get it!" Michael paused. His breathing was fast. His heart pumping through his chest. He could feel the anger rising in him. "It *wasn't* Teresa!"

"It *was!*" They were both screaming. Shelby was now standing. Her heart, beating faster than ever. She was shaking. She was sticking up for Lucy. Her best friend.

"It wasn't, *she never would!*"

"She *did!*"

"You *don't* get it!"

"Why? Why wouldn't I *get* it? You keep *fucking* saying that!" Michael turned and looked at her, his face red. His temple veins pulsing.

"You don't *get* it... you don't get it cause *you're not...*" Shelby stared at Michael with hard intensity, her eyebrows raised.

"What? What am I *not...?*"

"You're *not fucking family!*"

Michael looked shocked at what had just come out of his mouth. There was a pause as Shelby stood taking in what Michael had said. Her stomach had fallen. Her heart was stung, worse than any creature could sting her. She felt like she had just been beaten. Beaten by her most loved one. She sat down, as tears fell onto her cheeks. Michael turned and looked back at the view. *She doesn't understand,* he thought. The anger still fresh inside of him.

There were two torches at either side of the gate. Two torches that used to burn back before the vanishing. It would have been a great look around the pool area as they were spaced out evenly everywhere. It was now almost night time. Michael reached in his pocket and pulled out a lighter. He then lit both torches. They lit up quickly and both burned a beautiful flame. Smoke whispered and carried up into the crisp air. A slight breeze blew the flames this way and that. Michael grabbed one of the torches and lifted it. He screamed. A loud tortured scream of a man in pain. The scream echoed down the valley. He then placed the torch back in place.

"*Very dramatic,* but it will probably *attract* monsters," said Shelby, sniffing.

He quietly responded. "Bring it on…" He looked back at Shelby, his face ripped and torn, he spoke in a low, slow, menacing tone. "…Bring it on."

Shelby studied Michael's face. He looked like a man she hardly recognised. "Remember when you said this world would *change* us?" He turned away from her. She paused looking at the back of his freshly shaved head. Her eyes filled with tears as she turned and started to walk away.

"Well… it *has.*"

Michael woke up feeling crestfallen and guilty. *What have I done? Why did I say that?* He knew Shelby was sticking up for Lucy. The two of them had spent so much time together. Of course she would be on Lucy's side. But, there was no way in his mind that Teresa, mother of their daughter would ever kill her. No matter the circumstance. *You're not fucking family!* So brutal, he was just, angry, so angry. *You're not fucking family! You idiot, how could you say that? Shelby is more than family. Right now she is all the family I have.*

He moved his legs to the side of the bed. Pup made a noise as he was disturbed. His eyes opened and he looked at Michael above his paws. "Don't give me that look. I know I *fucked* up." Michael said to Pup as he patted him on his head. Pup put his head back down. "Oh, is that how it is? What do you suggest I do?" Pup looked up again, wondering what the hell Michael was on about. "A breakfast, you reckon?" Pups' tails started to spin. "Good idea Pup." He patted Pup's head as Pup's bum lifted in the air.

Michael made Shelby's favourite. Oats and strawberries. He had a fresh cup of brewed coffee on the tray also and knocked on her door. There was no answer. He tried again. No answer. He turned the handle and pushed the door open. What he saw broke his heart in two. The bed was made immaculately. The room was neat and tidy. Shelby's clothes and shoes that Michael had gotten for her were all gone. He walked in and placed the tray down beside the bed and sat on the edge of it looking out the window. For a long while he said and thought nothing. He whispered to himself. "Idiot."

Shelby had gone. He searched the room for a note. Something that may have been left for him. Nothing. *I don't deserve a note.* He sat watching the overcast clouds in the sky slowly start to darken. *You're not fucking family!* Kept turning over and over in his head, like a needle on a record. Stuck in a never ending groove.

Michael sat in his chair by a large table. It was the meeting room of the motel. Set aside for business meetings that were in house. He'd set a meeting for 10:00 am, sharp. Everyone had, had their breakfast and were sitting in their chairs facing Michael who was in front of a large white board. It all seemed very official. The main conversation between, The Uncles of the Apocalypse, seemed to be, where Shelby was. There was talk of an argument that Father Roberts had witnessed the night before.

A knock came at the door. Michael got up and answered it. *Could it be?* No, It was Tim. He was standing by himself. The Uncles clapped. He smiled at them. "Couldn't *miss* this." He said as he slowly walked and sat by Malaki. "What's happening?" Tim asked Malaki. Malaki shrugged his shoulders. Michael got up almost as an answer to the question. He wrote on the board in large letters. Teresa, Tony, Steven and Luke. Underneath it, he wrote Shelby and put a heart around it. He stood bracing the whiteboard with one arm, looking at Shelby's name. He looked pained. He turned toward them.

"What are we doing...?" He said, menacingly.

"We... are going... hunting!"

Epilogue

"LOVE CHANGES EVERYTHING: HANDS AND
FACES EARTH AND SKY, LOVE, LOVE CHANGES
EVERYTHING: HOW YOU LIVE AND HOW YOU
DIE, LOVE, LOVE CHANGES EVERYTHING."
ANDREW LLOYD WEBBER.

MORE THAN A YEAR ago.

The Suzuki Swift turbo's rear tyres spun as smoke poured out behind it. The car took off into the distance as the song *Xanadu* could be heard blaring from its speakers. Through the smoke and noise, spun a little lizard. Its tail, spinning like a helicopter's blades. It gave colours of red, white and blue as it landed softly on the footpath. The lizard licked its tail as a foot came out of nowhere and squashed it flat. "Got you, you *fuck!*" shouted Shelby as she watched the Suzuki speed off.

She quite liked the guy who had just come into the shop. He was a little earnest for her liking and so different from the men her mum had brought into her life. But, she felt like she could already trust him. She smiled and looked up at the blue sky. The sun was blaring. Her pale skin would freckle and burn. She walked back into the dairy. She walked over to where the couple had fought. She didn't know who they were but they had left some peanuts on the floor. She picked them up. Roasted, salted peanuts. She preferred the unsalted variety but opened them anyway. She ate them hungrily. The shop had served as a nice base for her to come and go from. The endless supply of food was now disappearing fast and the amount of people she had seen had pretty much doubled. She didn't like her chances if she hung around here for too much longer. *Probably time for a change.* She thought.

She walked over to the cash register and pushed enter. The cash register sprung into life as the drawer sprung out at her. The familiar twenty dollars sat in the same place. She pulled up the lever and took it out. "Thank you very much," she said, then she placed it back in. "For the peanuts, *keep the change*." She then closed the cash register and looked over the store. She ate her peanuts. "Thanks for your *hospitality*, shop!" she said as she walked into the back room. This is where she had first met him. Where she had hid when he came into the back room. *He left a note.* She smiled. She read it.

If you need help,
Michael Stevenson
13 beach Road,
022342547,
your friend,
fuckhead,

"Yes!" she said, smiling. She liked him and he had a sense of humour. She had also had enough of being by herself. She loved this new world. She loved making her own way in it. She didn't miss her mum much, but she needed company.

She grabbed the note and placed it in her pocket. She then grabbed her backpack and placed what little belongings she had inside it. She was happy and was whistling.

She ran over to the cupboard. She opened it to grab whatever snacks she might need. A mass of insects the size of small kittens scattered everywhere. She screamed as she danced around them. It was like she was playing an arcade game where her feet were the hammers and the insects, the soft alligators. She squashed as many as she could. "Fuck you, fuck you, fuck you," she said. Looking in the cupboard she saw a mass of opened black gooey eggs. "*No* thanks." She closed the cupboard and walked back into the shop.

She grabbed a few bags of chips that were left. She was ready. She looked over the shop once more and bowed to it. "Thanks again, *Kemosabe*," she said, as she walked out of the shop, whistling. She put her headphones on. They were the large maroon ones with the beats symbol on the side. She opened her iPhone that at this stage was still working. She typed in Michael's address into Google Maps. It read, two hours walking distance. "Fuck," she swore, she smiled though, happy to have plans. She searched through her music playlist and chose a song. She then turned up the music. "Here we fucking go, *motherfuckers!*" As she walked off, happily walking to her next adventure, listening to *Don't Dream It's Over*, by Crowded House.

... There is freedom within,

There is freedom without,
Try to catch the deluge in a paper cup.
There's a battle ahead,
Many battles are lost,
But you'll never see the end of the road
While you're travelling with me.

... Hey now, hey now,
Don't dream it's over.
Hey now, hey now,
When the world comes in.
They come, they come,
To build a wall between us.
We know they won't win.

Two hours later, she arrived at the large holiday home. She walked up to the door and knocked on it. Her heart was beating apprehensively. Smiling with her biggest smile, she waited for the door to be opened. A lock was unlocked on the other side. She was met with a smiling, welcoming face. Her heart felt warmed. She was going to give him her best, smiling hello!

"Hello! *Fuckhead!*" She said, smiling broadly.

Thank you for reading *The Day After*.
Please share your feedback on social media using our hashtags and handles:*#Adayinthelifebookseries*

Join the review team family and receive a free advanced copy of the next book in the series.
Join the mailing list, place in subject: Review team. please visit:
www.andrewmasseurs.com

To get the latest news, join the mailing list and for additional resources,
or to book *Andrew Masseurs* to speak at your event please visit:
www.andrewmasseurs.com

If you enjoyed this book, please consider writing a review with your honest impressions on Amazon, Goodreads, Audible
or the platform of your choosing.

Your feedback is incredibly valuable for helping independent authors like us reach a wider audience.